MAJIPOOR
CHRONICLES

Robert Silverberg

BANTAM BOOKS
TORONTO • NEW YORK • LONDON • SYDNEY • AUCKLAND

MAJIPOOR CHRONICLES

*A Bantam Book / published by arrangement with
Arbor House Publishing Company*

PRINTING HISTORY
Arbor House edition published December 1981
A Selection of Science Fiction Book Club
Portions of this book have appeared in somewhat
different form in Omni, Fantasy & Science Fiction, *and*
Isaac Asimov's Science Fiction Magazine.
Bantam edition / February 1983

Bantam Books are published by Bantam Books, Inc. Its
trademark, consisting of the words "Bantam Books" and
the portrayal of a rooster, is Registered in U.S. Patent and
Trademark Office and in other countries. Marca Registrada.
Bantam Books, Inc., 666 Fifth Avenue, New York, New
York 10103.

PRINTED IN THE UNITED STATES CF AMERCA

H   0 9 8 7 6 5 4

Praise for LORD VALENTINE'S CASTLE:

"An imaginative fusion of action, sorcery and science fiction."

—*The New York Times Book Review*

"A grand, picaresque tale . . . by one of the great storytellers of the century."

—Roger Zelazny

"A surefire pageturner . . . The giant planet of Majipoor is a brilliant concept of the imagination."

—*Chicago Sun-Times*

"In *Majipoor*, Silverberg has created a big planet chock-ablock with life and potential stories."

—*Washington Post*

And for MAJIPOOR CHRONICLES

"Well-written . . . thought-provoking."

—*West Coast Review of Books*

"These interlocking . . . stories, with their diversity of viewpoints and sharper focus, give us a better picture than ever of magical Majipoor."

—*Publishers Weekly*

"Setting the book down, there are two things that abide . . . absolute awe at Silverberg's capacity for creating images . . . he makes you see, believe, be there witnessing . . . and overarching compassion [that] colors every word and all the souls in his enormous planet."

—Theodore Sturgeon,
Los Angeles Times

"I was happy to visit Majipoor again, and glad to know there's room on that great and grand world for even more events to be chronicled."

—Baird Searles,
Asimov's Science Fiction Magazine

For Kirby

*Who may not have been driven all the way to despair
by this one, but who certainly got as far as the outlying
suburbs.*

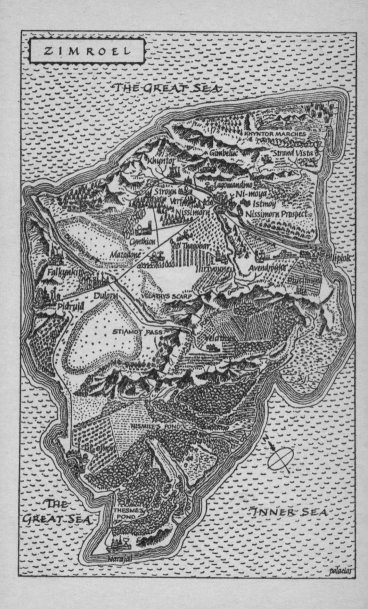

ALHANROEL · THE GREAT SEA

MT. ZYGNOR

Michimang
Bizfern
Kattikawn
Hamifieu
Dangrave
Byelk
Sintalmond
Singaserin
Daniup
Castle Mount
Alaisor Heights
Fualle
Alaisor
RIVER MAVIS
Dundilmir
OLINGAR GARDENS
Morpin
Stipool
Stee
Bailemoona
Chikmoge
Gimbeldorn
Ertsud Grand
Tentag
Minimool
Bombifale
Normork
Mt. Amblemorn
Sisivondal
PIDMY FOREST
Perimor
Bimbak West
Bimbak East
Pendiwane
RIVER GLAYGE
Mazadone
Kikil
Velalisier
LAKE ROGHOIZ
GULF OF STOIEN
RIVER TREY
Treymone
Stee
Stoien
LABYRINTH
HOME OF THE PONTIFEX
STOIENZAR PENINSULA

INNER SEA

palacios

CASTLE MOUNT AND GLAYGE VALLEY

Castle Mount
HOME OF THE CORONAL

MT. ZYGNOR

Halanx

Morpin

KAZKAS PROMONTORY

Stee

Dumdilmir

Stipool

TOLINGAR GARDENS

Chikmoge

MT. HAIMON

Bombifale

Ertsud Grand

Tentag

NORMORK CREST

Normork

Amblemorn

RIVER

Pendiwane

Bimbak East

Gayles

RIVER GLAYGE

Jerrick

Mitripond

Velalisier

N

LAKE ROGHOIZ

TO THE LABYRINTH

TO THE WINE REGION

RIVER STEE

palacias

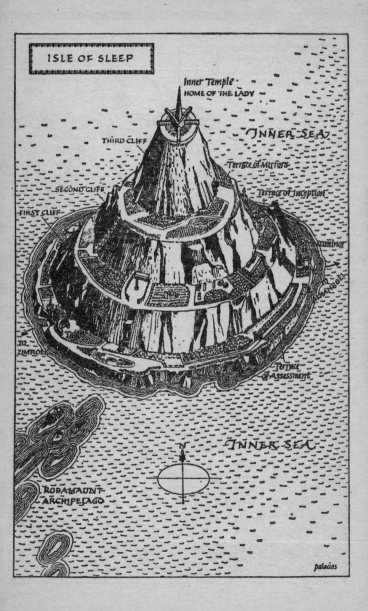

ISLE OF SLEEP

Inner Temple
HOME OF THE LADY

INNER SEA

THIRD CLIFF

Terrace of Mirrors

SECOND CLIFF

Terrace of Inception

FIRST CLIFF

TO NUMINOR

TO ALHANROEL

TO ZIMROEL

Terrace of Assessment

N

INNER SEA

RODAMAUNT ARCHIPELAGO

palacios

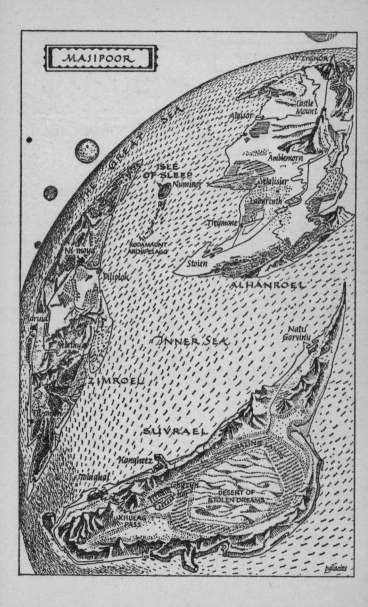

MAJIPOOR

MT. ZYGNOR

Castle
Mount

THE GREAT SEA

Algisor

Amblemorn

ISLE
OF SLEEP

Numinor

Velalisier

Isthmus

Treymone

RODAMAUNT
ARCHIPELAGO

Stoien

Ni-moya

ALHANROEL

Pilipiok

INNER SEA

Natu
Gorvinu

Iarud

 ZIMROEL

Velathys

SUVRAEL

GRANN

Kangheez

DESERT OF
STOLEN DREAMS

Tolaghai

KHULAG
PASS

palacios

MAJIPOOR
CHRONICLES

Prologue

In the fourth year of the restoration of the Coronal Lord Valentine a great mischief has come over the soul of the boy Hissune, a clerk in the House of Records of the Labyrinth of Majipoor. For the past six months it has been Hissune's task to prepare an inventory of the archives of the tax-collectors—an interminable list of documents that no one is ever going to need to consult—and it looks as though the job will keep him occupied for the next year or two or three. To no purpose, so far as Hissune can understand, since who could possibly care about the reports of provincial tax-collectors who lived in the reign of Lord Dekkeret or Lord Calintane or even the ancient Lord Stiamot? These documents had been allowed to fall into disarray, no doubt for good reason, and now some malevolent destiny has chosen Hissune to put them to rights, and so far as he can see it is useless work, except that he will have a fine geography lesson, a vivid experience of the hugeness of Majipoor. So many provinces! So many cities! The three giant continents are divided and subdivided and further divided into thousands of municipal units, each with its millions of people, and as he toils, Hissune's mind overflows with names, the Fifty Cities of Castle Mount, the great urban districts of Zimroel, the mysterious desert settlements of Suvrael, a torrent of metropolises, a lunatic tribute to the fourteen thousand years of Majipoor's unceasing fertility: Pidruid, Narabal, Ni-moya, Alaisor, Stoien, Piliplok, Pendiwane, Amblemorn, Minimool, Tolaghai, Kangheez, Natu Gorvinu—so much, so much, so much! A million names of places! But when one is fourteen years old one can tolerate only a certain amount of geography, and then one begins to grow restless.

Restlessness invades Hissune now. The mischievousness that is never far from the surface in him wells up and overflows.

Close by the dusty little office in the House of Records where Hissune sifts and classifies his mounds of tax reports is a far more interesting place, the Register of Souls, which is closed to all but authorized personnel, and there are said to

be not many authorized personnel. Hissune knows a good
deal about that place. He knows a good deal about every part
of the Labyrinth, even the forbidden places, especially the
forbidden places—for has he not, since the age of eight,
earned his living in the streets of the great underground capital by guiding bewildered tourists through the maze, using his
wits to pick up a crown here and a crown there? "House of
Records," he would tell the tourists. "There's a room in there
where millions of people of Majipoor have left memory-readings. You pick up a capsule and put it in a special slot, and
suddenly it's as if you were the person who made the reading,
and you find yourself living in Lord Confalume's time, or
Lord Siminave's, or out there fighting the Metamorph Wars
with Lord Stiamot—but of course hardly anyone is allowed
to consult the memory-reading room." Of course. But how
hard would it be, Hissune wonders, to insinuate himself into
that room on the pretext of needing data for his research into
the tax archives? And then to live in a million other minds at
a million other times, in all the greatest and most glorious
eras of Majipoor's history—yes!

Yes, it would certainly make this job more tolerable if he
could divert himself with an occasional peek into the Register
of Souls.

From that realization it is but a short journey to the actual
attempting of it. He equips himself with the appropriate
passes—he knows where all the document-stampers are kept
in the House of Records—and makes his way through the
brightly lit curving corridors late one afternoon, dry-throated,
apprehensive, tingling with excitement.

It has been a long time since he has known any excitement. Living by his wits in the streets was exciting, but he no
longer does that; they have civilized him, they have housebro-
ken him, they have given him a job. A job! They! And who
are they? The Coronal himself, that's who! Hissune has not
overcome his amazement over that. During the time when
Lord Valentine was wandering in exile, displaced from his
body and his throne by the usurper Barjazid, the Coronal had
come to the Labyrinth, and Hissune had guided him, recog-
nizing him somehow for what he truly was; and that had
been the beginning of Hissune's downfall. For the next thing
Hissune knew, Lord Valentine was on his way from the Labyrinth to Castle Mount to regain his crown, and then the usurper was overthrown, and then at the time of the second

coronation Hissune found himself summoned, the Divine only knew why, to attend the ceremonies at Lord Valentine's Castle. What a time that was! Never before had he so much as been out of the Labyrinth to see the light of day, and now he was journeying in an official floater, up the valley of the Glayge past cities he had known only in dreams, and there was Castle Mount's thirty-mile-high bulk rising like another planet in the sky, and at last he was at the Castle, a grimy ten-year-old boy standing next to the Coronal and trading jokes with him—yes, that had been splendid, but Hissune was caught by surprise by what followed. The Coronal believed that Hissune had promise. The Coronal wished him to be trained for a government post. The Coronal admired the boy's energy and wit and enterprise. Fine. Hissune would become a protege of the Coronal. Fine. Fine. Back to the Labyrinth, then—and into the House of Records! Not so fine. Hissune has always detested the bureaucrats, those mask-faced idiots who pushed papers about in the bowels of the Labyrinth, and now, by special favor of Lord Valentine, he has become such a person himself. Well, he supposes he has to do something by way of earning a living besides take tourists around—but he never imagined it would be this! *Report of the Collector of Revenue for the Eleventh District of the Province of Chorg, Prefecture of Bibiroon, 11th Pont. Kinniken Cor. Lord Ossier*—oh, no, no, not a lifetime of that! A month, six months, a year of doing his nice little job in the nice little House of Records, Hissune hopes, and then Lord Valentine might send for him and install him in the Castle as an aide-de-camp, and then at last life would have some value! But the Coronal seems to have forgotten him, as one might expect. He has an entire world of twenty or thirty billion people to govern, and what does one little boy of the Labyrinth matter? Hissune suspects that his life has already passed its most glorious peak, in his brief time on Castle Mount, and now by some miserable irony he has been metamorphosed into a clerk of the Pontificate, doomed to shuffle documents forever—

But there is the Register of Souls to explore.

Even though he may never leave the Labyrinth again, he might—if no one caught him—roam the minds of millions of folk long dead, explorers, pioneers, warriors, even Coronals and Pontifexes. That's some consolation, is it not?

He enters a small antechamber and presents his pass to the dull-eyed Hjort on duty.

Hissune is ready with a flow of explanations: special assignment from the Coronal, important historical research, need to correlate demographic details, necessary corroboration of data profile—oh, he's good at such talk, and it lies coiled waiting back of his tongue. But the Hjort says only, "You know how to use the equipment?"

"It's been a while. Perhaps you should show me again."

The ugly warty-faced fellow, many-chinned and flabby, gets slowly to his feet and leads Hissune to a sealed enclosure, which he opens by some deft maneuver of a thumblock. The Hjort indicates a screen and a row of buttons. "Your control console. Send for the capsules you want. They plug in here. Sign for everything. Remember to turn out the lights when you're done."

That's all there is to it. Some security system! Some guardian!

Hissune finds himself alone with the memory-readings of everyone who has ever lived on Majipoor.

Almost everyone, at any rate. Doubtless billions of people have lived and died without bothering to make capsules of their lives. But one is allowed every ten years, beginning at the age of twenty, to contribute to these vaults, and Hissune knows that although the capsules are minute, the merest flecks of data, there are miles and miles of them in the storage levels of the Labyrinth. He puts his hands to the controls. His fingers tremble.

Where to begin?

He wants to know everything. He wants to trek across the forests of Zimroel with the first explorers, he wants to drive back the Metamorphs, to sail the Great Sea, to slaughter seadragons off the Rodamaunt Archipelago, to—to—to—he shakes with the frenzy of yearning. Where to begin? He studies the keys before him. He can specifiy a date, a place, a specific person's identity—but with fourteen thousand years to choose from—no, more like eight or nine thousand, for the records, he knows, go back only to Lord Stiamot's time or a little before—how can he decide on a starting point? For ten minutes he is paralyzed with indecision.

Then he punches at random. Something early, he thinks. The continent of Zimroel; the time of the Coronal Lord Bar-

hold, who had lived even before Stiamot; and the person—
why, anyone! Anyone!

A small gleaming capsule appears in the slot.

Quivering in amazement and delight, Hissune plugs it into
the playback outlet and dons the helmet. There are crackling
sounds in his ears. Vague blurred streaks of blue and green
and scarlet cross his eyes behind his closed lids. Is it working?
Yes! Yes! He feels the presence of another mind! Someone
dead nine thousand years, and that person's mind—*her* mind,
she was a woman, a young woman—flows into Hissune's, until he cannot be sure whether he is Hissune of the Labyrinth
or this other, this Thesme of Narabal—

With a little sobbing sound of joy he releases himself entirely from the self he has lived with for the fourteen years of
his life and lets the soul of the other take possession of him.

ONE

Thesme and the Ghayrog

I

For six months now Thesme had lived alone in a hut that she had built with her own hands, in the dense tropical jungle half a dozen miles or so east of Narabal, in a place where the sea breezes did not reach and the heavy humid air clung to everything like a furry shroud. She had never lived by herself before, and at first she wondered how good she was going to be at it; but she had never built a hut before either, and she had done well enough at that, cutting down slender sijaneel saplings, trimming away the golden bark, pushing their slippery sharpened ends into the soft moist ground, lashing them together with vines, finally tying on five enormous blue vramma leaves to make a roof. It was no masterpiece of architecture, but it kept out the rain, and she had no need to worry about cold. Within a month her sijaneel timbers, trimmed though they were, had all taken root and were sprouting leathery new leaves along their upper ends, just below the roof; and the vines that held them were still alive too, sending down fleshy red tendrils that searched for and found the rich fertile soil. So now the house was a living thing, daily becoming more snug and secure as the vines tightened and the sijaneels put on girth, and Thesme loved it. In Narabal

1

nothing stayed dead for long; the air was too warm, the sunlight too bright, the rainfall too copious, and everything quickly transformed itself into something else with the riotous buoyant ease of the tropics.

Solitude was turning out to be easy too. She had needed very much to get away from Narabal, where her life had somehow gone awry: too much confusion, too much inner noise, friends who became strangers, lovers who turned into foes. She was twenty-five years old and needed to stop, to take a long look at everything, to change the rhythm of her days before it shook her to pieces. The jungle was the ideal place for that. She rose early, bathed in a pond that she shared with a sluggish old gromwark and a school of tiny crystalline chichibors, plucked her breakfast from a thokka vine, hiked, read, sang, wrote poems, checked her traps for captured animals, climbed trees and sunbathed in a hammock of vines high overhead, dozed, swam, talked to herself, and went to sleep when the sun went down. In the beginning she thought there would not be enough to do, that she would soon grow bored, but that did not seem to be the case; her days were full and there were always a few projects to save for tomorrow.

At first she expected that she would go into Narabal once a week or so, to buy staple goods, to pick up new books and cubes, to attend an occasional concert or a play, even to visit her family or those of her friends that she still felt like seeing. For a while she actually did go to town fairly often. But it was a sweaty, sticky trek that took half a day, nearly, and as she grew accustomed to her reclusive life she found Narabal ever more jangling, ever more unsettling, with few rewards to compensate for the drawbacks. People there stared at her. She knew they thought she was eccentric, even crazy, always a wild girl and now a peculiar one, living out there by herself and swinging through the treetops. So her visits became more widely spaced. She went only when it was unavoidable. On the day she found the injured Ghayrog she had not been to Narabal for at least five weeks.

She had been roving that morning through a swampy region a few miles northeast of her hut, gathering the sweet yellow fungi known as calimbots. Her sack was almost full and she was thinking of turning back when she spied something strange a few hundred yards away: a creature of some sort with gleaming, metallic-looking gray skin and thick tubular limbs, sprawled awkwardly on the ground below a great sijaneel tree. It reminded her of a predatory reptile her father and brother once had killed in Narabal Channel, a sleek, elongated, slow-moving thing with curved claws and a vast toothy mouth. But as she drew closer she saw that this life-form was vaguely human in construction, with a massive rounded head, long arms, powerful legs. She thought it might be dead, but it stirred faintly when she approached and said, "I am damaged. I have been stupid and now I am paying for it."

"Can you move your arms and legs?" Thesme asked

"The arms, yes. One leg is broken, and possibly my back. Will you help me?"

She crouched and studied it closely. It did look reptilian, yes, with shining scales and a smooth, hard body. Its eyes were green and chilly and did not blink at all; its hair was a weird mass of thick black coils that moved of their own accord in a slow writhing; its tongue was a serpent-tongue, bright scarlet, forked, flickering constantly back and forth between the narrow fleshless lips.

"What are you?" she asked.

"A Ghayrog. Do you know of my kind?"

"Of course," she said, though she knew very little, really. All sorts of non-human species had been settling on Majipoor in the past hundred years, a whole menagerie of aliens invited here by the Coronal Lord Melikand because there were not enough humans to fill the planet's immensities. Thesme had heard that there were four-armed ones and two-headed ones and tiny ones with tentacles and these scaly snake-tongued snake-haired ones, but none of the alien beings had yet come as far as Narabal, a town on the edge of nowhere, as distant from civilization as one could get. So this was a Ghayrog, then? A strange creature, she thought, almost human in the shape of its body and yet not at all human in any of its details, a monstrosity, really, a nightmare-being, though not especially frightening. She pitied the poor Ghayrog, in fact—a wanderer, doubly lost, far from its home world and far from anything that mattered on Majipoor. And badly hurt, too. What was she going to do with it? Wish it well and abandon it to its fate? Hardly. Go all the way into Narabal and organize a rescue mission? That would take at least two days, assuming anyone cared to help. Bring it back to her hut and nurse it to good health? That seemed the most likely thing to do, but what would happen to her solitude, then, her privacy, and how did one take care of a Ghayrog, anyway, and did she really want the responsibility? And the risk, for that matter: this was an alien being and she had no idea what to expect from it.

It said, "I am Vismaan."

Was that its name, its title, or merely a description of its condition? She did not ask. She said, "I am called Thesme. I live in the jungle an hour's walk from here. How can I help you?"

"Let me brace myself on you while I try to get up. Do you think you are strong enough?"

"Probably."

"You are female, am I right?"

She was wearing only sandals. She smiled and touched her hand lightly to her breasts and loins and said, "Female, yes."

"So I thought. I am male and perhaps too heavy for you."

Male? Between his legs he was as smooth and sexless as a machine. She supposed that Ghayrogs carried their sex somewhere else. And if they were reptiles, her breasts would indicate nothing to him about her sex. Strange, all the same, that he should need to ask.

She knelt beside him, wondering how he was going to rise and walk with a broken back. He put his arm over her shoulders. The touch of his skin against hers startled her: it felt cool, dry, rigid, smooth, as though he wore armor. Yet it was not an unpleasant texture, only odd. A strong odor came from him, swampy and bitter with an undertaste of honey. That she had not noticed it before was hard to understand, for it was pervasive and insistent; she decided she must have been distracted by the unexpectedness of coming upon him. There was no ignoring the odor now that she was aware of it, and at first she found it intensely disagreeable, though within moments it ceased to bother her.

He said, "Try to hold steady. I will push myself up."

Thesme crouched, digging her knees and hands into the soil, and to her amazement he succeeded in drawing himself upward with a peculiar coiling motion, pressing down on her, driving his entire weight for a moment between her shoulder blades in a way that made her gasp. Then he was standing, tottering, clinging to a dangling vine. She made ready to catch him if he fell, but he stayed upright.

"This leg is cracked," he told her. "The back is damaged but not, I think, broken."

"Is the pain very bad?"

"Pain? No, we feel little pain. The problem is functional. The leg will not support me. Can you find me a strong stick?"

She scouted about for something he might use as a crutch and spied, after a moment, the stiff aerial root of a vine dangling out of the forest canopy. The glossy black root was thick but brittle, and she bent it backward and forward until she succeeded in snapping off some two yards of it. Vismaan grasped it firmly, draped his other arm around Thesme, and cautiously put his weight on his uninjured leg. With difficulty he took a step, another, another, dragging the broken leg along. It seemed to Thesme that his body odor had changed: sharper, now, more vinegar, less honey. The strain of walking, no doubt. The pain was probably less trivial than he wanted her to think. But he was managing to keep moving, at any rate.

"How did you hurt yourself?" she asked.

"I climbed this tree to survey the territory just ahead. It did not bear my weight."

He nodded toward the slim shining trunk of the tall sijaneel. The lowest branch, which was at least forty feet above her, was broken and hung down by nothing more than shreds of bark. It amazed her that he had survived a fall from such a height; after a moment she found herself wondering how he had been able to get so high on the slick smooth trunk in the first place.

He said, "My plan is to settle in this area and raise crops. Do you have a farm?"

"In the jungle? No, I just live here."

"With a mate?"

"Alone. I grew up in Narabal, but I needed to get away by myself for a while." They reached the sack of calimbots she had dropped when she first noticed him lying on the ground, and she slung it over her shoulder. "You can stay with me until your leg has healed. But it's going to take all afternoon to get back to my hut this way. Are you sure you're able to walk?"

"I am walking now," he pointed out.

"Tell me when you want to rest."

"In time. Not yet."

Indeed it was nearly half an hour of slow and surely painful hobbling before he asked to halt, and even then he remained standing, leaning against a tree, explaining that he thought it unwise to go through the whole difficult process of lifting himself from the ground a second time. He seemed altogether calm and in relatively little discomfort, although it was impossible to read expression into his unchanging face and unblinking eyes: the constant flickering of his forked tongue was the only indicator of apparent emotion she could see, and she had no idea how to interpret those ceaseless darting movements. After a few minutes they resumed the walk. The slow pace was a burden to her, as was his weight against her shoulder, and she felt her own muscles cramping and protesting as they edged through the jungle. They said little. He seemed preoccupied with the need to exert control over his crippled body, and she concentrated on the route, searching for shortcuts, thinking ahead to avoid streams and dense undergrowth and other obstacles he would not be able to cope with. When they were halfway back to her hut a warm rain began to fall, and after that they were enveloped in hot clammy fog the rest of the way. She was nearly exhausted by the time her little cabin came into view.

"Not quite a palace," she said, "but it's all I need. I built it myself. You can lie down here." She helped him to her zanja-down bed. He sank onto it with a soft hissing sound that was surely relief. "Would you like something to eat?" she asked.

"Not now."

"Or to drink? No? I imagine you just want to get some rest. I'll go outside so you can sleep undisturbed."

"This is not my season of sleep," Vismaan said.

"I don't understand."

"We sleep only one part of the year. Usually in winter."

"And you stay awake all the rest of the time?"

"Yes," he said. "I am finished with this year's sleep. I understand it is different with humans."

"Extremely different," she told him. "I'll leave you to rest by yourself, anyway. You must be terribly tired."

"I would not drive you from your home."

"It's all right," Thesme said, and stepped outside. The rain was beginning again, the familiar, almost comforting rain that fell every few hours all day long. She sprawled out on a bank of dark yielding rubbermoss and let the warm droplets of rain wash the fatigue from her aching back and shoulders.

A houseguest, she thought. And an alien one, no less. Well,

why not? The Ghayrog seemed undemanding: cool, aloof, tranquil even in calamity. He was obviously more seriously hurt than he was willing to admit, and even this relatively short journey through the forest had been a struggle for him. There was no way he could walk all the way into Narabal in this condition. Thesme supposed that she could go into town and arrange for someone to come out in a floater to get him, but the idea displeased her. No one knew where she was living and she did not care to lead anyone here, for one thing. And she realized in some confusion that she did not want to give the Ghayrog up, that she wanted to keep him here and nurse him until he had regained his strength. She doubted that anyone else in Narabal would have given shelter to an alien, and that made her feel pleasantly perverse, set apart in still another way from the citizens of her native town. In the past year or two she had heard plenty of muttering about the offworlders who were coming to settle on Majipoor. People feared and disliked the reptilian Ghayrogs and the giant hulking hairy Skandars and the little tricky ones with the many tentacles—Vroons, were they?—and the rest of that bizarre crew, and even though aliens were still unknown in remote Narabal the hostility toward them was already there. Wild and eccentric Thesme, she thought, was just the kind who *would* take in a Ghayrog and pat his fevered brow and give him medicine and soup, or whatever you gave a Ghayrog with a broken leg. She had no real idea of how to care for him, but she did not intend to let that stop her. It occurred to her that she had never taken care of anyone in her life, for somehow there had been neither opportunity nor occasion; she was the youngest in her family and no one had ever allowed her any sort of responsibility, and she had not married or borne children or even kept pets, and during the stormy period of her innumerable turbulent love affairs she had never seen fit to visit any of her lovers while he was ill. Quite likely, she told herself, that was why she was suddenly so determined to keep this Ghayrog at her hut. One of the reasons she had quitted Narabal for the jungle was to live life in a new way, to break with the uglier traits of the former Thesme.

She decided that in the morning she would go into town, find out if she could what kind of care the Ghayrog needed, and buy such medicines or provisions as seemed appropriate.

2

After a long while she returned to the hut. Vismaan lay as she had left him, flat on his back with arms stiff against his sides, and he did not seem to be moving at all, except for the perpetual serpentine writhing of his hair. Asleep? After all his talk of needing none? She went to him and peered down at the strange massive figure on her bed. His eyes were open, and she saw them tracking her.

"How do you feel?" she asked.

"Not well. Walking through the forest was more difficult than I realized."

She put her hand to his forehead. His hard scaly skin felt cool. But the absurdity of her gesture made her smile. What was a Ghayrog's normal body temperature? Were they susceptible to fever at all, and if so, how could she tell? They were reptiles, weren't they? Did reptiles run high temperatures when they were sick? Suddenly it all seemed preposterous, this notion of nursing a creature of another world.

He said, "Why do you touch my head?"

"It's what we do when a human is sick. To see if you have a fever. I have no medical instruments here. Do you know what I mean by running a fever?"

"Abnormal body temperature. Yes. Mine is high now."

"Are you in pain?"

"Very little. But my systems are disarranged. Can you bring me some water?"

"Of course. And are you hungry? What sort of things do you normally eat?"

"Meat. Cooked. And fruits and vegetables. And a great deal of water."

She fetched a drink for him. He sat up with difficulty—he seemed much weaker than when he had been hobbling through the jungle; most likely he was suffering a delayed reaction to his injuries—and drained the bowl in three greedy gulps. She watched the furious movements of his forked tongue, fascinated. "More," he said, and she poured a second bowl. Her water-jug was nearly empty, and she went outside to fill it at the spring. She plucked a few thokkas from the vine, too, and brought them to him. He held one of the juicy blue-white berries at arm's length, as though that was the only way he could focus his vision properly on it, and rolled it experimentally between two of his fingers. His hands were almost human, Thesme observed, though there were two extra fingers and he had no fingernails, only lateral scaly ridges running along the first two joints.

"What is this fruit called?" he asked.

"Thokka. They grow on a vine all over Narabal. If you like them, I'll bring you as many as you want."

He tasted it cautiously. Then his tongue flickered more rapidly, and he devoured the rest of the berry and held out his hand for another. Now Thesme remembered the reputation of thokkas as aphrodisiacs, but she looked away to hide her grin, and chose not to say anything to him about that. He described himself as a male, so the Ghayrogs evidently had sexes, but did they have sex? She had a sudden fanciful image of male Ghayrogs squirting milt from some concealed orifice into tubs into which female Ghayrogs climbed to fertilize themselves. Efficient but not very romantic, she thought, wondering if that was actually how they did it—fertilization at a distant remove, like fishes, like snakes.

She prepared a meal for him of thokkas and fried calimbots and the little many-legged delicate-flavored hiktigans that she netted in the stream. All her wine was gone, but she had lately made a kind of fermented juice from a fat red fruit whose name she did not know, and she gave him some of that. His appetite seemed healthy. Afterward she asked him if she could examine his leg, and he told her she could.

The break was more than midway up, in the widest part of his thigh. Thick though his scaly skin was, it showed some signs of swelling there. Very lightly she put her fingertips to the place and probed. He made a barely audible hiss but otherwise gave no sign that she might be increasing his discomfort. It seemed to her that something was moving inside his thigh. The broken ends of the bone, was it? Did Ghayrogs *have* bones? She knew so little, she thought dismally—about Ghayrogs, about the healing arts, about anything.

"If you were human," she said, "we would use our machines to see the fracture, and we would bring the broken place together and bind it until it knitted. Is it anything like that with your people?"

"The bone will knit of its own," he replied. "I will draw the break together through muscular contraction and hold it until it heals. But I must remain lying down for a few days, so that the leg's own weight does not pull the break apart when I stand. Do you mind if I stay here that long?"

"Stay as long as you like. As long as you need to stay."

"You are very kind."

"I'm going into town tomorrow to pick up supplies. Is there anything you particularly want?"

"Do you have entertainment cubes? Music, books?"

"I have just a few here. I can get more tomorrow."

"Please. The nights will be very long for me as I lie here without sleeping. My people are great consumers of amusement, you know."

"I'll bring whatever I can find," she promised.

She gave him three cubes—a play, a symphony, a color composition—and went about her after-dinner cleaning. Night had fallen, early as always, this close to the equator. She heard a light rainfall beginning again outside. Ordinarily she would read for a while, until it grew too dark, and then lie down to sleep. But tonight everything was different. A mysterious reptilian creature occupied her bed; she would have to put together a new sleeping-place for herself on the floor; and all this conversation, the first she had had in so many weeks, had left her mind buzzing with unaccustomed alertness. Vismaan seemed content with his cubes. She went outside and collected bubblebush leaves, a double armful of them and then another, and strewed them on the floor near the door of her hut. Then, going to the Ghayrog, she asked if she could do anything for him; he answered by a tiny shake of his head, without taking his attention from the cube. She wished him a good night and lay down on her improvised bed. It was comfortable enough, more so than she had expected. But sleep was impossible. She turned this way and that, feeling cramped and stiff, and the presence of the other a few yards away seemed to announce itself by a tangible pulsation in her soul. And there was the Ghayrog's odor, too, pungent and inescapable. Somehow she had ceased noticing it while they ate, but now, with all her nerve-endings tuned to maximum sensitivity as she lay in the dark, she perceived it almost as she would a trumpet-blast unendingly repeated. From time to time she sat up and stared through the darkness at Vismaan, who lay motionless and silent. Then at some point slumber overtook her, for when the sounds of the new morning came to her, the many familiar piping and screeching melodies, and the early light made its way through the door-opening, she awakened into the kind of disorientation that comes often when one has been sleeping soundly in a place that is not one's usual bed. It took her a few moments to collect herself, to remember where she was and why.

He was watching her. "You spent a restless night. My being here disturbs you."

"I'll get used to it. How do you feel?"

"Stiff. Sore. But I am already beginning to mend, I think. I sense the work going on within."

She brought him water and a bowl of fruit. Then she went out into the mild misty dawn and slipped quickly into the pond to bathe. When she returned to the hut the odor hit her with new impact. The contrast between the fresh air of morning and the acrid Ghayrog-flavored atmosphere indoors was severe; yet soon it passed from her awareness once again.

As she dressed she said, "I won't be back from Narabal until nightfall. Will you be all right here by yourself?"

"If you leave food and water within my reach. And something to read."

"There isn't much. I'll bring more back for you. It'll be a quiet day for you, I'm afraid."

"Perhaps there will be a visitor."

"A visitor?" Thesme cried, dismayed. "Who? What sort of visitor? No one comes here! Or do you mean some Ghayrog who was traveling with you and who'll be out looking for you?"

"Oh, no, no. No one was with me. I thought, possibly friends of yours——"

"I have no friends," said Thesme solemnly.

It sounded foolish to her the instant she said it—self-pitying, melodramatic. But the Ghrayrog offered no comment, leaving her without a way of retracting it, and to hide her embarrassment she busied herself elaborately in the job of strapping on her pack.

He was silent until she was ready to leave. Then he said, "Is Narabal very beautiful?"

"You haven't seen it?"

"I came down the inland route from Til-omon. In Til-omon they told me how beautiful Narabal is."

"Narabal is nothing," Thesme said. "Shacks. Muddy streets. Vines growing over everything, pulling the buildings apart before they're a year old. They told you that in Til-omon? They were joking with you. The Til-omon people

despise Narabal. The towns are rivals, you know—the two
main tropical ports. If anyone in Til-omon told you how
wonderful Narabal is, he was lying, he was playing games
with you."

"But why do that?"

Thesme shrugged. "How would I know? Maybe to get you
out of Til-omon faster. Anyway, don't look forward to Narabal. In a thousand years it'll be something, I suppose, but
right now it's just a dirty frontier town."

"All the same, I hope to visit it. When my leg is stronger,
will you show me Narabal?"

"Of course," she said. "Why not? But you'll be disappointed, I promise you. And now I have to leave. I want to
get the walk to town behind me before the hottest part of the
day."

3

As she made her way briskly toward Narabal she envisioned herself turning up in town one of these days with a
Ghayrog by her side. How they'd love that, in Narabal!
Would she and Vismaan be pelted with rocks and clots of
mud? Would people point and snicker, and snub her when
she tried to greet them? Probably. There's that crazy Thesme,
they would say to each other, bringing aliens to town, running around with snaky Ghayrogs, probably doing all sorts of
unnatural things with them out in the jungle. Yes. Yes.
Thesme smiled. It might be fun to promenade about Narabal
with Vismaan. She would try it as soon as he was capable of
making the long trek through the jungle.

The path was no more than a crudely slashed track,
blaze-marks on the trees and an occasional cairn, and it was
overgrown in many places. But she had grown skilled at
jungle travel and she rarely lost her way for long; by late
morning she reached the outlying plantations, and soon Narabal itself was in view, straggling up one hillside and down another in a wobbly arc along the seashore.

Thesme had no idea why anyone had wanted to put a city
here—halfway around the world from anywhere, the extreme
southwest point of Zimroel. It was some idea of Lord
Melikand's, the same Coronal who had invited all the aliens to
settle on Majipoor, to encourage development on the western

continent. In Lord Melikand's time Zimroel had only two cities, both of them terribly isolated, virtual geographic accidents founded in the earliest days of human settlement on Majipoor, before it became apparent that the other continent was going to be the center of Majipoori life. There was Pidruid up in the northwest, with its wondrous climate and its spectacular natural harbor, and there was Piliplok all the way across on the eastern coast, where the hunters of the migratory sea-dragons had their base. But now also there was a little outpost called Ni-moya on one of the big inland rivers, and Til-omon had sprung up on the western coast at the edge of the tropical belt, and evidently some settlement was being founded in the central mountains, and supposedly the Ghayrogs were building a town a thousand miles or so east of Pidruid, and there was Narabal down here in the steaming rainy south, at the tip of the continent with sea all around. If one stood by the shore of Narabal Channel and looked toward the water one felt the terrible weight of the knowledge that at one's back lay thousands of miles of wilderness, and then thousands of miles of ocean, separating one from the continent of Alhanroel where the real cities were. When she was young Thesme had found it frightening to think that she lived in a place so far from the centers of civilized life that it might as well be on some other planet; and other times Alhanroel and its thriving cities seemed merely mythical to her, and Narabal the true center of the universe. She had never been anywhere else, and had no hope of it. Distances were too great. The only town within reasonable reach was Til-omon, but even that was far away, and those who had been there said it was much like Narabal, anyway, only with less rain and the sun standing constantly in the sky like a great boring inquisitive green eye.

In Narabal she felt inquisitive eyes on her wherever she turned: everyone staring, as though she had come to town naked. They all knew who she was—wild Thesme who had run off to the jungle—and they smiled at her and waved and asked her how everything was going, and behind those trivial pleasantries were the eyes, intent and penetrating and hostile, drilling into her, plumbing her for the hidden truths of her life. *Why do you despise us? Why have you withdrawn from us? Why are you sharing your house with a disgusting snake-man?* And she smiled and waved back, and said, "Nice to see you again," and "Everything's just fine," and replied silently to the probing eyes, *I don't hate anybody, I just needed to get away from myself, I'm helping the Ghayrog because it's time I helped someone and he happened to come along.* But they would never understand.

No one was at home at her mother's house. She went to her old room and stuffed her pack with books and cubes, and ransacked the medicine cabinet for drugs that she thought might do Vismaan some good, one to reduce inflammation, one to promote healing, a specific for high fever, and some others—probably all useless to an alien, but worth trying, she supposed. She wandered through the house, which was becoming strange to her even though she had lived in it nearly all her life. Wooden floors instead of strewn leaves—real transparent windows—doors on hinges—a cleanser, an actual mechanical cleanser with knobs and handles!—all those *civilized* things, the million and one humble little things that humanity had invented so many thousands of years ago on another world, and from which she had blithely walked away to live in her humid little hut with live branches sprouting from its walls—

"Thesme?"

She looked up, taken by surprise. Her sister Mirifaine had come in: her twin, in a manner of speaking, same face, same long thin arms and legs, same straight brown hair, but ten years older, ten years more reconciled to the patterns of her life, a married woman, a mother, a hard worker. Thesme had always found it distressing to look at Mirifaine. It was like looking in a mirror and seeing herself old.

Thesme said, "I needed a few things."

"I was hoping you'd decided to move back home."

"What for?"

Mirifaine began to reply—most likely some standard homily, about resuming normal life, fitting into society and being useful, et cetera, et cetera—but Thesme saw her shift direction while all that was still unspoken, and Mirifaine said finally, "We miss you, love."

"I'm doing what I need to do. It's been good to see you, Mirifaine."

"Won't you at least stay the night? Mother will be back soon—she'd be delighted if you were here for dinner—"

"It's a long walk. I can't spend more time here."

"You look good, you know. Tanned, healthy. I suppose being a hermit agrees with you, Thesme."

"Yes. Very much."

"You don't mind living alone?"

"I adore it," Thesme said. She began to adjust her pack. "How are you, anyway?"

A shrug. "The same. I may go to Til-omon for a while."

"Lucky you."

"I think so. I wouldn't mind getting out of the mildew zone for a little holiday. Holthus has been working up there all month, on some big scheme to build new towns in the mountains—housing for all these aliens that are starting to move in. He wants me to bring the children up, and I think I will."

"Aliens?" Thesme said.

"You don't know about them?"

"Tell me."

"The offworlders that have been living up north are starting to filter this way, now. There's one kind that looks like lizards with human arms and legs that's interested in starting farms in the jungles."

"Ghayrogs."

"Oh, you've heard of them, then? And another kind, all puffy and warty, frog-faced ones with dark gray skins—they do practically all the government jobs now in Pidruid, Holthus says, the customs-inspectors and market clerks and things like that—well, they're being hired down here too, and Holthus and some syndicate of Til-omon people are planning housing for them inland—"

"So that they won't smell up the coastal cities?"

"What? Oh, I suppose that's part of it—nobody knows how they'll fit in here, after all—but really I think it's just that we don't have accommodations for a lot of immigrants in Narabal, and I gather it's the same in Til-omon, and so—"

"Yes, I see," said Thesme. "Well, give everyone my love. I have to begin heading back. I hope you enjoy your holiday in Til-omon."

"Thesme, please—"

"Please what?"

Mirifaine said sadly, "You're so brusque, so distant, so chilly! It's been months since I've seen you, and you barely tolerate my questions, you look at me with such anger—anger for what, Thesme? Have I ever hurt you? Was I ever anything other than loving? Were any of us? You're such a mystery, Thesme."

Thesme knew it was futile to try once more to explain her-

self. No one understood her, no one ever would, least of all
those who said they loved her. Trying to keep her voice
gentle, she said, "Call it an overdue adolescent rebellion,
Miri. You were all very kind to me. But nothing was working
right and I had to run away." She touched her fingertips
lightly to her sister's arm. "Maybe I'll be back one of these
days."

"I hope so."

"Just don't expect it to happen soon. Say hello to everybody for me," said Thesme, and went out.

She hurried through town, uneasy and tense, afraid of running into her mother or any of her old friends and especially
any of her former lovers; and as she carried out her errands
she looked about furtively, like a thief, more than once duck-
ing into an alleyway to avoid someone she needed to avoid.
The encounter with Mirifaine had been disturbing enough.
She had not realized, until Mirifaine had said it, that she had
been showing anger; but Miri was right, yes, Thesme could
still feel the dull throbbing residue of fury within her. These
people, these dreary little people with their little ambitions
and their little fears and their little prejudices, going through
the little rounds of their meaningless days—they infuriated
her. Spilling out over Majipoor like a plague, nibbling at the
unmapped forests, staring at the enormous uncrossable ocean,
founding ugly muddy towns in the midst of astounding
beauty, and never once questioning the purpose of anything—that was the worst of it, their bland unquestioning
natures. Did they never once look up at the stars and ask
what it all meant, this outward surge of humanity from Old
Earth, this replication of the mother world on a thousand
conquered planets? Did they care? This could *be* Old Earth
for all it mattered, except that that was a tired drab plun-
dered forgotten husk of a world and this, even after centuries
and centuries of human occupation, was still beautiful; but
long ago Old Earth had no doubt been as beautiful as
Majipoor was now; and in five thousand more years Majipoor
would be the same way, with hideous cities stretching for
hundreds of miles wherever you looked, and traffic everywhere, and filth in the rivers, and the animals wiped out and
the poor cheated Shapeshifters penned up in reservations
somewhere, all the old mistakes carried out once again on a
virgin world. Thesme boiled with an indignation so fierce it
amazed her. She had never known that her quarrel with the

world was so cosmic. She had thought it was merely a matter
of failed love affairs and raw nerves and muddled personal
goals, not this irate dissatisfaction with the entire human universe that had so suddenly overwhelmed her. But the rage
held its power in her. She wanted to seize Narabal and push
it into the ocean. But she could not do that, she could not
change a thing, she could not halt for a moment the spread
of what they called civilization here; all she could do was
flee, back to her jungle, back to the interlacing vines and the
steamy foggy air and the shy creatures of the marshes, back
to her hut, back to her lame Ghayrog, who was himself part
of the tide that was overwhelming the planet but for whom she
would care, whom she would even cherish, because the others
of her kind disliked or even hated him and so she could use
him as one of her ways of distinguishing herself from *them*,
and because also he needed her just now and no one had ever
needed her before.

Her head was aching and the muscles of her face had gone
rigid, and she realized she was walking with her shoulders
hunched, as if to relax them would be to surrender to the
way of life that she had repudiated. As swiftly as she could,
she escaped once again from Narabal; but it was not until she
had been on the jungle trail for two hours, and the last outskirts of the town were well behind her, that she began to feel
the tensions ebbing. She paused at a little lake she knew and
stripped and soaked herself in its cool depths to rid herself of
the last taint of town, and then, with her going-to-town
clothes slung casually over her shoulder, she marched naked
through the jungle to her hut.

4

Vismaan lay in bed and did not seem to have moved at all
while she was gone. "Are you feeling better?" she asked.
"Were you able to manage by yourself?"

"It was a very quiet day. There is somewhat more of a
swelling in my leg."

"Let me see."

She probed it cautiously. It *did* seem puffier, and he pulled
away slightly as she touched him, which probably meant that
there was real trouble in there, if the Ghayrog sense of pain
was as weak as he claimed. She debated the merit of getting

him into Narabal for treatment. But he seemed unworried, and she doubted that the Narabal doctors knew much about Ghayrog physiology anyway. Besides, she wanted him here. She unpacked the medicines she had brought from town and gave him the ones for fever and inflammation, and then prepared fruits and vegetables for his dinner. Before it grew too dark she checked the traps at the edge of the clearing and found a few small animals in them, a young sigimoin and a couple of mintuns. She wrung their necks with a practiced hand—it had been terribly hard at first, but meat was important to her and no one else was likely to do her killing for her, out here—and dressed them for roasting. Once she had the fire started she went back inside. Vismaan was playing one of the new cubes she had brought him, but he put it aside when she entered.

"You said nothing about your visit to Narabal," he remarked.

"I wasn't there long. Got what I needed, had a little chat with one of my sisters, came away edgy and depressed, felt better as soon as I was in the jungle."

"You have great hatred for that place."

"It's worth hating. Those dismal boring people, those ugly squat little buildings—" She shook her head. "Oh: my sister told me that they're going to found some new towns inland for offworlders, because so many are moving south. Ghayrogs, mainly, but also some other kind with warts and gray skins—"

"Hjorts," said Vismaan.

"Whatever. They like to work as customs-inspectors, she told me. They're going to be settled inland because no one wants them in Til-omon or Narabal, is my guess."

"I have never felt unwanted among humans," the Ghayrog said.

"Really? Maybe you haven't noticed. I think there's a great deal of prejudice on Majipoor."

"It has not been evident to me. Of course, I have never been in Narabal, and perhaps it is stronger there than elsewhere. Certainly in the north there is no difficulty. You have never been in the north?"

"No."

"We find ourselves welcome among humans in Pidruid."

"Is that true? I hear that the Ghayrogs are building a city for themselves somewhere east of Pidruid, quite a way east, on the Great Rift. If everything's so wonderful for you in Pidruid, why settle somewhere else?"

Vismaan said calmly, "It is we who are not altogether comfortable living with humans. The rhythms of our lives are so different from yours—our habits of sleep, for instance. We find it difficult living in a city that goes dormant eight hours every night, when we ourselves remain awake. And there are other differences. So we are building Dulorn. I hope you see it some day. It is quite marvelously beautiful, constructed entirely from a white stone that shines with an inner light. We are very proud of it."

"Why don't you live there, then?"

"Is your meat not burning?" he asked.

She reddened and ran outside, barely in time to snatch dinner from the spits. A little sullenly she sliced it and served it, along with some thokkas and a flask of wine she had bought that afternoon in Narabal. Vismaan sat up, with some awkwardness, to eat.

He said after a while, "I lived in Dulorn for several years. But that is very dry country, and I come from a place on my planet that is warm and wet, like Narabal. So I journeyed down here to find fertile lands. My distant ancestors were farmers, and I thought to return to their ways. When I heard that in the tropics of Majipoor one could raise six harvests a year, and that there was land everywhere for the claiming, I set out to explore the territory."

"Alone?"

"Alone, yes. I have no mate, though I intend to obtain one as soon as I am settled."

"And you'll raise crops and market them in Narabal?"

"So I intend. On my home world there is scarcely any wild land anywhere, and hardly enough remaining for agriculture. We import most of our food, do you know that? And so Majipoor has a powerful appeal for us, this gigantic planet with its sparse population and its great wilderness awaiting development. I am very happy to be here. And I think that you are not right, about our being unwelcome among your fellow citizens. You Majipoori are kind and gentle folk, civil, law-abiding, orderly."

"Even so: if anyone knew I was living with a Ghayrog, they'd be shocked."

"Shocked? Why?"

"Because you're an alien. Because you're a reptile."

Vismaan made an odd snorting sound. Laughter? "We are not reptiles! We are warm-blooded, we nurse our young—"

"Reptilian, then. *Like* reptiles."

"Externally, perhaps. But we are nearly as mammalian as you, I insist."

"Nearly?"

"Only that we are egg-layers. But there are some mammals of that sort, too. You much mistake us if you think—"

"It doesn't really matter. Humans perceive you as reptiles, and we aren't comfortable with reptiles, and there's always going to be akwardness between humans and Ghayrogs because of that. It's a tradition that goes back into prehistoric times on Old Earth. Besides—" She caught herself just as she was about to make a reference to the Ghayrog odor. "Beside," she said clumsily, "you look scary."

"More so than a huge shaggy Skandar? More so than a Su-Suheris with two heads?" Vismaan turned toward her and fixed his unsettling lidless eyes on her. "I think you are telling me that *you* are uncomfortable with Ghayrogs yourself, Thesme."

"No."

"The prejudices of which you speak have never been visible to me. This is the first time I have heard of them. Am I troubling to you, Thesme? Shall I go?"

"No. No. You're completely misunderstanding me. I want you to stay here. I want to help you. I feel no fear of you at all, no dislike, nothing negative whatever. I was only trying to tell you—trying to explain about the people in Narabal, how they feel, or how I think they feel, and—" She took a long gulp of her wine. "I don't know how we got into all this. I'm sorry. I'd like to talk about something else."

"Of course."

But she suspected that she had wounded him, or at least aroused some discomfort in him. In his cool alien way he seemed to have considerable insight, and maybe he was right, maybe it was her own prejudice that was showing, her own uneasiness. She had bungled all of her relationships with humans; quite conceivably she was incapable of getting along with anyone, she thought, human or alien, and had shown Vismaan in a thousand unconscious ways that her hospitality was merely a willed act, artificial and half reluctant, intended to cover an underlying dislike for his presence here. Was that so? She understood less and less of her own motivations, it appeared, as she grew older. But wherever the truth might lie, she did not want him to feel like an intruder here. In the days ahead, she resolved, she would find ways of showing him that her taking him in and caring for him were genuinely founded.

She slept more soundly that night than the one before, although she was still not accustomed to sleeping on the floor in a pile of bubblebush leaves or having someone with her in the hut, and every few hours she awakened. Each time she did, she looked across at the Ghayrog, and saw him each time busy with the entertainment cubes. He took no notice of her. She tried to imagine what it was like to do all of one's sleeping in a single three-month stretch, and to spend the rest of one's time constantly awake; it was, she thought, the most alien thing about him. And to lie there hour after hour, unable to stand, unable to sleep, unable to hide from the discomfort of the injury, making use of whatever diversion was available to consume the time—few torments could be worse. And yet his mood never changed: serene, unruffled, placid, impassive. Were all Ghayrogs like that? Did they never get drunk, lose their tempers, brawl in the streets, bewail their destinies, quarrel with their mates? If Vismaan was a fair sample, they had no human frailties. But, then, she reminded herself, they were not human.

5

In the morning she gave Ghayrog a bath, sponging him until his scales glistened, and changed his bedding. After she had fed him she went off for the day, in her usual fashion; but she felt guilty wandering the jungle by herself while he remained marooned in the hut, and wondered if she should have stayed with him, telling him stories or drawing him into a conversation to ease his boredom. But she was aware that if she were constantly at his side they would quickly run out of things to talk about, and very likely get on each other's nerves; and he had dozens of entertainment cubes to help him ward off boredom, anyway. Perhaps he preferred to be alone most of the time. In any case she needed solitude herself, more than ever now that she was sharing her hut with him, and she made a long reconnaissance that morning, gathering an assortment of berries and roots for dinner. At midday it rained, and she squatted under a vramma tree whose broad leaves sheltered her nicely. She let her eyes go out of focus and emptied her mind of everything, guilts, doubts, fears, memories, the Ghayrog, her family, her former lovers, her unhappiness, her loneliness. The peace that settled over her lasted well into the afternoon.

She grew used to having Vismaan living with her. He continued to be easy and undemanding, amusing himself with his cubes, showing great patience with his immobility. He rarely asked her questions or initiated any sort of talk, but he was friendly enough when she spoke with him, and told her about his home world—shabby and horribly overpopulated, from the sound of things—and about his life there, his dream of settling on Majipoor, his excitement when he first saw the beauty of his adopted planet. Thesme tried to visualize him showing excitement. His snaky hair jumping around, perhaps, instead of just coiling slowly. Or maybe he registered emotion by changes of body odor.

On the fourth day he left the bed for the first time. With her help he hauled himself upward, balancing on his crutch and his good leg and tentatively touching the other one to the ground. She sensed a sudden sharpness of his aroma—a kind of olfactory wince—and decided that her theory must be right, that Ghayrogs did show emotion that way.

"How does it feel?" she asked. "Tender?"

"It will not bear my weight. But the healing is proceeding well. Another few days and I think I will be able to stand. Come, help me walk a little. My body is rusting from so little activity."

He leaned on her and they went outside, to the pond and back at a slow, wary hobble. He seemed refreshed by the little journey. To her surprise she realized that she was saddened by this first show of progress, because it meant that soon—a week, two weeks?—he would be strong enough to leave, and she did not want him to leave. *She did not want him to leave.* That was so odd a perception that it astonished her. She longed for her old reclusive life, the privilege of sleeping in her own bed and going about her forest pleasures without worrying about whether her guest were being sufficiently well amused, and all of that; in some ways she was finding it more and more irritating to have the Ghayrog around. And yet, and yet, and yet, she felt downcast and disturbed at the thought that he would shortly leave her. How strange, she thought, how peculiar, how very Thesme-like.

Now she took him walking several times a day. He still could not use the broken leg, but he grew more agile without it, and he said that the swelling was abating and the bone appeared to be knitting properly. He began to talk of the farm he would establish, the crops, the ways of clearing the jungle.

One afternoon at the end of the first week Thesme, as she returned from a calimbot-gathering expedition in the meadow where she had first found the Ghayrog, stopped to check her traps. Most were empty or contained the usual small animals; but there was a strange violent thrashing in the underbrush beyond the pond, and when she approached the trap she had placed there she discovered she had caught a bilantoon. It was the biggest creature she had ever snared. Bilantoons were found all over western Zimroel—elegant fast-moving little beasts with sharp hooves, fragile legs, a tiny upturned tufted tail—but the Narabal form was a giant, twice the size of the dainty northern one. It stood as high as a man's waist, and was much prized for its tender and fragrant meat. Thesme's first impulse was to let the pretty thing go: it seemed much too beautiful to kill, and much too big, also. She had taught herself to slaughter little things that she could seize in one hand, but this was another matter entirely, a major animal, intelligent-looking and noble, with a life that it surely valued, hopes and needs and yearnings, a mate probably waiting somewhere nearby. Thesme told herself that she was being foolish. Droles and mintuns and sigimoins also very likely were eager to go on living, certainly as eager as this bilantoon was, and she killed them without hesitation. It was a mistake to romanticize animals, she knew—especially when in her more civilized days she had been willing to eat their flesh quite gladly, if slain by other hands. The bilantoon's bereaved mate had not mattered to her then.

As she drew nearer she saw that the bilantoon in its panic had broken one of its delicate legs, and for an instant she thought of splinting it and keeping the creature as a pet. But that was even more absurd. She could not adopt every cripple the jungle brought her. The bilantoon would never calm down long enough for her to examine its leg; and if by some miracle she did manage to repair it, the animal would probably run away the first chance that it got. Taking a deep breath, she came around behind the struggling creature, caught it by its soft muzzle, and snapped its long graceful neck.

The job of butchering it was bloodier and more difficult than Thesme expected. She hacked away grimly for what seemed like hours, until Vismaan called from within the hut to find out what she was doing.

"Getting dinner ready," she answered. "A surprise. A great treat: roast bilantoon!"

She chuckled quietly. She sounded so wifely, she thought, as she crouched here with blood all over her naked body, sawing away at haunches and ribs, while a reptilian alien creature lay in her bed waiting for his dinner.

But eventually the ugly work was done and she had the meat smouldering over a smoky fire, as one was supposed to do, and she cleansed herself in the pond and set about collecting thokkas and boiling some ghumba-root and opening the remaining flasks of her new Narabal wine. Dinner was ready as darkness came, and Thesme felt immense pride in what she had achieved.

She expected Vismaan to gobble it without comment, in his usual phlegmatic way, but no: for the first time she thought she detected a look of animation on his face—a new sparkle in the eyes, maybe, a different pattern of tongue-flicker. She decided she might be getting better at reading his expressions. He gnawed the roast bilantoon enthusiastically, praised its flavor and texture, and asked again and again for more. For each serving she gave him she took one for herself, forcing the meat down until she was glutted and going onward anyway well past satiation, telling herself that whatever was not consumed now would spoil before morning. "The meat goes so well with the thokkas," she said, popping another of the blue-white berries into her mouth.

"Yes. More, please."

He calmly devoured whatever she set before him. Finally she could eat no more, nor could she even watch him. She put what remained within his reach, took a last gulp of the wine, shuddered a little, laughed as a few drops trickled down her chin and over her breasts. She sprawled out on the bubble-bush leaves. Her head was spinning. She lay face down, clutching the floor, listening to the sounds of biting and chewing going on and on and on not far away. Then even the Ghayrog was done feasting, and all was still. Thesme waited for sleep, but sleep would not come. She grew dizzier, until she feared being flung in some terrible centrifugal arc through the side of the hut. Her skin was blazing, her nipples felt hard and sore. I have had much too much to drink, she thought, and I have eaten too many thokkas. Seeds and all, the most potent way, a dozen berries at least, their fiery juice now coursing wildly through her brain.

She did not want to sleep alone, huddled this way on the floor.

With exaggerated care Thesme rose to her knees, steadied herself, and crawled slowly toward the bed. She peered at the Ghayrog, but her eyes were blurred and she could make out only a rough outline of him.

"Are you asleep?" she whispered.

"You know that I would not be sleeping."

"Of course. Of course. Stupid of me."

"Is something wrong, Thesme?"

"Wrong? No, not really. Nothing wrong. Except—it's just that—" She hesitated. "I'm drunk, do you know? Do you understand what being drunk means?"

"Yes."

"I don't like being on the floor. Can I lie beside you?"

"If you wish."

"I have to be very careful. I don't want to bump into your bad leg. Show me which one it is."

"It's almost healed, Thesme. Don't worry. Here: lie down." She felt his hand closing around her wrist and drawing her upward. She let herself float, and drifted easily to his side. She could feel the strange hard shell-like skin of him against her from breast to hip, so cool, so scaly, so smooth. Timidly she rubbed her hand across his body. Like a fine piece of luggage, she thought, digging her fingertips in a little, probing the powerful muscles beneath the rigid surface. His odor changed, becoming spicy, piercing.

"I like the way you smell," she murmured.

She buried her forehead against his chest and held tight to him. She had not been in bed with anyone for months and months, almost a year, and it was good to feel him so close. Even a Ghayrog, she thought. Even a Ghayrog. Just to have the contact, the closeness. It feels so good.

He touched her.

She had not expected that. The entire nature of their relationship was that she cared for him and he passively accepted her services. But suddenly his hand—cool, ridged, scaly,

smooth—was passing over her body. Brushing lightly across
her breasts, trailing down her belly, pausing at her thighs.
What was this? Was Vismaan making *love* to her? She.
thought of his sexless body, like a machine. He went on
stroking her. This is very weird, she thought. Even for
Thesme, she told herself, this is an extremely weird thing. He
is not human. And I—

And I am very lonely—

And I am very drunk—

"Yes, please," she said softly. "Please."

She hoped only that he would continue stroking her. But
then he slipped one arm about her shoulders and lifted her
easily, gently, rolling her over on top of him and lowering
her, and she felt the unmistakable jutting rigidity of maleness
against her thigh. What? Did he carry a concealed penis
somewhere beneath his scales, that he let slide out when it
was needed for use? And was he going to—

Yes.

He seemed to know what to do. Alien he might be, uncer-
tain at their first meeting even whether she was male or female, and nevertheless he plainly understood the theory of
human lovemaking. For an instant, as she felt him entering
her, she was engulfed by terror and shock and revulsion,
wondering if he would hurt her, if he would be painful to receive, and thinking also that this was grotesque and monstrous, this coupling of human and Ghayrog, something that
quite likely had never happened before in the history of the
universe. She wanted to pull herself free and run out into the
night. But she was too dizzy, too drunk, too confused to
move; and then she realized that he was not hurting her at
all, that he was sliding in and out like some calm clockwork
device, and that waves of pleasure were spreading outward
from her loins, making her tremble and sob and gasp and
press herself against that smooth leathery carapace of his—

She let it happen, and cried out sharply at the best moment, and afterward lay curled up against his chest, shivering, whimpering a little, gradually growing calm. She was
sober now. She knew what she had done, and it amazed her,
but more than that it amused her. Take *that*, Narabal! The
Ghayrog is my lover! And the pleasure had been so intense,
so extreme. Had there been any pleasure in it for him? She
did not dare ask. How did one tell if a Ghayrog had an or-
gasm? Did they have them at all? Would the concept mean

anything to him? She wondered if he had made love to human women before. She did not dare ask that, either. He had been so capable—not exactly skilled, but definitely very certain about what needed to be done, and he had done it rather more competently than many men she had known, though whether it was because he had had experience with humans or simply because his clear, cool mind could readily calculate the anatomical necessities she did not know, and she doubted that she would ever know.

He said nothing. She clung to him and drifted into the soundest sleep she had had in weeks.

6

In the morning she felt strange but not repentant. They did not talk about what had passed between them that night. He played his cubes; she went out at dawn for a swim to clear her throbbing head, and tidied some of the debris left from their bilantoon feast, and made breakfast for them, and afterward she took a long walk toward the north, to a little mossy cave, where she sat most of the morning, replaying in her mind the texture of his body against her and the touch of his hand on her thighs and the wild shudder of ecstasy that had run through her body. She could not say that she found him in any way attractive. Forked tongue, hair like live snakes, scales all over his body—no, no, what had happened last night had not had anything whatever to do with physical attraction, she decided. Then why had it happened? The wine and the thokkas, she told herself, and her loneliness, and her readiness to rebel against the conventional values of the citizens of Narabal. Giving herself to a Ghayrog was the finest way she knew of showing her defiance for all that those people believed. But of course such an act of defiance was meaningless unless they found out about it. She resolved to take Vismaan to Narabal with her as soon as he was able to make the trip.

After that they shared her bed every night. It seemed absurd to do otherwise. But they did not make love the second night, or the third, or the fourth; they lay side by side without touching, without speaking. Thesme would have been willing to yield herself if he had reached out for her, but he did not. Nor did she choose to approach him. The silence between them became an embarrassment to her, but she was afraid to break it for fear of hearing things that she did not want to hear—that he had disliked their lovemaking, or that he regarded such acts as obscene and unnatural and had done it that once only because she seemed so insistent, or that he was aware that she felt no true desire for him but was merely using him to make a point in her ongoing warfare against convention. At the end of the week, troubled by the accumulated tensions of so many unspoken uncertainties, Thesme risked rolling against him when she got into the bed, taking trouble to make it seem accidental, and he embraced her easily and willingly, gathering her into his arms without hesitation. After that they made love on some nights and did not on others, and it was always a random and unpremeditated thing, casual, almost trivial, something they occasionally did before she went to sleep, with no more mystery or magic about it than that. It brought her great pleasure every time. The alienness of his body soon became invisible to her.

He was walking unaided now and each day he spent more time taking exercise. First with her, then by himself, he explored the jungle trails, moving cautiously at the beginning but soon striding along with only a slight limp. Swimming seemed to further the healing process, and for hours at a time he paddled around Thesme's little pond, annoying the gromwark that lived in a muddy burrow at its edge; the slow-moving old creature crept from its hiding-place and sprawled out at the pond's rim like some bedraggled bristly sack that had been discarded there. It eyed the Ghayrog glumly and would not return to the water until he was done with his swim. Thesme consoled it with tender green shoots that she plucked upstream, far beyond the reach of the gromwark's little sucker-feet.

"When will you take me to Narabal?" Vismaan asked her one rainy evening.

"Why not tomorrow?" she replied.

That night she felt unusual excitement, and pressed herself insistently against him.

They set out at dawn in light rainshowers that soon gave way to brilliant sunshine. Thesme adopted a careful pace, but soon it was apparent that the Ghayrog was fully healed, and before long she was walking swiftly. Vismaan had no difficulty keeping up. She found herself chattering—telling him the names of every plant or animal they encountered, giving him bits of Narabal's history, talking about her brothers and sisters and people she knew in town. She was desperately eager to be seen by them with him—*look, this is my alien lover, this is the Ghayrog I've been sleeping with*—and when they came to the outskirts she began looking around intently, hoping to find someone familiar; but scarcely anyone seemed visible on the outer farms, and she did not recognize those who were. "Do you see how they're staring at us?" she whispered to Vismaan, as they passed into a more thickly inhabited district. "They're afraid of you. They think you're the vanguard of some sort of alien invasion. And they're wondering what I'm doing with you, why I'm being so civil to you."

"I see none of that," said Vismaan. "They appear curious about me, yes. But I detect no fear, no hostility. Is it because I am unfamiliar with human facial expressions? I thought I had learned to interpret them quite well."

"Wait and see," Thesme told him. But she had to admit to herself that she might be exaggerating things a little, or even more than a little. They were nearly in the heart of Narabal, now, and some people had glanced at the Ghayrog in surprise and curiosity, yes, but they had quickly softened their stares, while others had merely nodded and smiled as though it were the most ordinary thing in the world to have some kind of offworld creature walking through the streets. Of actual hostility she could find none. That angered her. These mild sweet people, these bland amiable people, were not at all reacting as she had expected. Even when she finally met familiar people—Khanidor, her oldest brother's best friend, and Hennimont Sibroy who ran the little inn near the waterfront, and the woman from the flower-shop—they were nothing other than cordial as Thesme said, "This is Vismaan, who has been living with me lately." Khanidor smiled as though he had always known Thesme to be the sort of person who would set up housekeeping with an alien, and spoke of the new towns for Ghayrogs and Hjorts that Mirifaine's husband was planning to build. The innkeeper reached out jovially to shake Vismaan's hand and invited him down for some wine on the house, and the flower-shop woman said over and over, "How interesting, how interesting! We hope you like our little town!" Thesme felt patronized by their cheerfulness. It was as if they were going out of their way not to let her shock them—as if they had already taken all the wildness from Thesme that they were going to take, and now would accept anything,

anything at all from her, without caring, without surprise, without comment. Perhaps they misunderstood the nature of her relationship with the Ghayrog and thought he was merely boarding with her. Would they give her the reaction she wanted if she came right out and said they were lovers, that his body had been inside hers, that they had done that which was unthinkable between human and alien? Probably not. Probably even if she and the Ghayrog lay down and coupled in Pontifex Square it would cause no stir in this town, she thought, scowling.

And did Vismaan like their little town? It was, as always, difficult to detect emotional response in him. They walked up one street and down another, past the haphazardly planned plazas and the flat-faced scruffy shops and the little lopsided houses with their overgrown gardens, and he said very little. She sensed disappointment and disapproval in his silence, and for all her own dislike of Narabal she began to feel defensive about the place. It was, after all, a young settlement, an isolated outpost in an obscure corner of a second-class continent, just a few generations old. "What do you think?" she asked finally. "You aren't very impressed by Narabal, are you?"

"You warned me not to expect much."

"But it's even more dismal than I led you to expect, isn't it?"

"I do find it small and crude," he said. "After one has seen Pidruid, or even—"

"Pidruid's thousands of years old."

"—Dulorn," he went on. "Dulorn is extraordinarily beautiful even now, when it is just being built. But of course the white stone they use there is—"

"Yes," she said. "Narabal ought to be built out of stone too, because this climate is so damp that wooden buildings fall apart, but there hasn't been time yet. Once the population's big enough, we can quarry in the mountains and put together something marvelous here. Fifty years from now, a hundred, when we have a proper labor force. Maybe if we got some of those giant four-armed aliens to work here—"

"Skandars," said Vismaan.

"Skandars, yes. Why doesn't the Coronal send us ten thousand Skandars?"

"Their bodies are covered with thick hair. They will find this climate difficult. But doubtless Skandars will settle here,

and Vroons, and Su-Suheris, and many, many wet-country
Ghayrogs like me. It is a very bold thing your government is
doing, encouraging offworld settlers in such numbers. Other
planets are not so generous with their land."

"Other planets are not so large," Thesme said. "I think I've
heard that even with all the huge oceans we have, Majipoor's
land mass is still three or four times the size of any other
settled planet. Or something like that. We're very lucky, being
such a big world, and yet having such gentle gravity, so that
humans and humanoids can live comfortably here. Of course,
we pay a high price for that, not having anything much in
the way of heavy elements, but still—oh. Hello." The tone of
her voice changed abruptly, dropping off to a startled blurt.
A slim young man, very tall, with pale wavy hair, had nearly
collided with her as he emerged from the bank on the corner,
and now he stood gaping at her, and she at him. He was Ruskelorn Yulvan, Thesme's lover for the four months just prior
to her withdrawal into the jungle, and the person in Narabal
she was least eager to see. But if there had to be a confronta-
tion with him, she intended to make the most of it; and, seiz-
ing the initiative after her first moment of confusion, she said,
"You look well, Ruskelorn."

"And you. Jungle life must agree with you."

"Very much. It's been the happiest seven months of my
life. Ruskelorn, this is my friend Vismaan, who's been living
with me the past few weeks. He had an accident while
scouting for farmland near my place—broke his leg falling
out of a tree—and I've been looking after him."

"Very capably, I imagine," Ruskelorn Yulvan said evenly.
"He seems to be in excellent condition." To the Ghayrog he
said, "Pleased to meet you," in a way that made it seem as
though he might actually mean it.

Thesme said, "He comes from a part of his planet where
the climate is a lot like Narabal's. He tells me that there'll be
plenty of his country-people settling down here in the tropics
in the next few years."

"So I've heard." Ruskelorn Yulvan grinned and said,
"You'll find it amazingly fertile territory. Eat a berry at
breakfast time and toss the seed away, you'll have a vine as
tall as a house by nightfall. That's what everyone says, so it
must be true."

The light and casual manner of his speaking infuriated her.
Did he not realize that this scaly alien creature, this offworld-

er, this Ghayrog, was his replacement in her bed? Was he immune to jealousy, or did he simply not understand the real situation? With a ferocious silent intensity she attempted to convey the truth of things to Ruskelorn Yulvan in the most graphic possible way, thinking fierce images of herself in Vismaan's arms, showing Ruskelorn Yulvan the alien hands of Vismaan caressing her breasts and thighs and flicking his little scarlet two-pronged tongue lightly over her closed eyelids, her nipples, her loins. But it was useless. Ruskelorn was no more of a mind-reader than she. *He is my lover,* she thought, *he enters me, he makes me come again and again, I can't wait to get back to the jungle and tumble into bed with him,* and all the while Ruskelorn Yulvan stood there smiling, chatting politely with the Ghayrog, discussing the potential for raising niyk and glein and stajja in these parts, or perhaps lusavender-seed in the swampier districts, and only after a good deal of that did he turn his glance back toward Thesme and ask, as placidly as though he were asking the day of the week, whether she intended to live in the jungle indefinitely

She glared. "So far I prefer it to life in town. Why?"

"I wondered if you missed the comforts of our splendid metropolis, that's all."

"Not yet, not for a moment. I've never been happier."

"Good. I'm so pleased for you, Thesme." Another serene smile. "How nice to have run into you. How good to have met you," he said to the Ghayrog, and then he was gone.

Thesme smouldered with rage. He had not cared, he had not cared in the slightest, she could be coupling with Ghayrogs or Skandars or the gromwark in the pond for all it mattered to him! She had wanted him to be wounded or at least shocked, and instead he had simply been polite. Polite! It must be that he, like all the others, failed to comprehend the real state of affairs between her and Vismaan—that it was simply inconceivable to them that a woman of human stock would offer her body to a reptilian offworlder, and so they did not consider—they did not even suspect—

"Have you seen enough of Narabal now?" she asked the Ghayrog.

"Enough to realize that there is little to see."

"How does your leg feel? Are you ready to begin the journey back?"

"Have you no errands to perform in town?"

"Nothing important," she said. "I'd like to go."

"Then let us go," he answered.

His leg did seem to be giving him some trouble—the muscles stiffening, probably; that was a taxing hike even for someone in prime condition, and he had traveled only much shorter distances since his recovery—but in his usual uncomplaining way he followed her toward the jungle road. This was the worst time of day to be making the trip, with the sun almost straight overhead and the air moist and heavy from the first gatherings of what would be this afternoon's rainfall. They walked slowly, pausing often, though never once did he say he was tired; it was Thesme herself who was tiring, and she pretended that she wanted to show him some geological formation here, some unusual plant there, in order to manufacture occasions to rest. She did not want to admit fatigue. She had suffered enough mortification today.

The venture into Narabal had been a disaster for her. Proud, defiant, rebellious, scornful of Narabal's conventional ways, she had hauled her Ghayrog lover to town to flaunt him before the tame city-dwellers, and they had not cared. Were they such puddings that they could not guess at the truth? Or had they seen instantly through her pretensions, and were determined to give her no satisfaction? Either way she felt outraged, humiliated, defeated—and very foolish. And what about the bigotry she imagined she had found earlier among the Narabal folk? Were they not threatened by the influx of these aliens? They had all been so charming to Vismaan, so friendly. Perhaps, Thesme thought gloomily, the prejudice was in her mind alone and she had misinterpreted the remarks of others, and in that case it had been stupid to give herself to the Ghayrog, it had accomplished nothing, flouted no Narabal decorum, served no purpose at all in the private war she had been fighting against those people. It had only been a strange and willful and grotesque event.

Neither she nor the Ghayrog spoke during the long slow uncomfortable return to the jungle. When they reached her hut he went inside and she bustled about ineffectually in the clearing, checking traps, pulling berries from vines, setting things down and forgetting what she had done with them.

After a while she entered the hut and said to Vismaan, "I think you may as well leave."

"Very well. It *is* time for me to be on my way."

"You can stay here tonight, of course. But in the morning—"

"Why not leave now?"

"It'll be dark soon. You've already walked so many miles today—"

"I have no wish to trouble you. I will go now, I think."

Even now she found it impossible to read his feelings. Was he surprised? Hurt? Angry? He showed her nothing. He offered no gestures of farewell, either, but simply turned and began walking at a steady pace toward the interior of the jungle. Thesme watched him, throat dry, heart pounding, until he disappeared beyond the low-hanging vines. It was all she could do to keep herself from running after him. But then he was gone, and soon the tropical night descended.

She rummaged together a sort of dinner for herself, but she ate very little, thinking, He is out there sitting in the darkness, waiting for the morning to come. They had not even said goodbye. She could have made some little joke, warning him to stay out of sijaneel trees, or he could have thanked her for all she had done on his behalf, but instead there had been nothing, just her dismissal of him and his calm uncomplaining departure. An alien, she thought, and his ways were alien. And yet, when they had been together in bed, and he had touched her and held her and drawn her body down on top of his—

It was a long bleak night for her. She lay huddled in the crudely sewn zanja-down bed that they had so lately shared, listening to the night rain hammering on the vast blue leaves that were her roof, and for the first time since she had entered the jungle she felt the pain of loneliness. Until this moment she had not realized how much she had valued the bizarre parody of domesticity that she and the Ghayrog had enacted here; but now that was over, and she was alone again, somehow more alone than she had been before, and far more cut off from her old life in Narabal than before, also, and he was out there, unsleeping in the darkness, unsheltered from the rain. I am in love with an alien, she told herself in wonderment, I am in love with a scaly *thing* that speaks no words of endearment and asks hardly any questions and leaves without saying thank you or goodbye. She lay awake for hours, crying now and then. Her body felt tense and clenched from the long walk and the day's frustrations; she drew her knees to her breasts and stayed that way a long

while, and then put her hands between her legs and stroked
herself, and finally there came a moment of release, a gasp
and a little soft moan, and sleep after that.

7

In the morning she bathed and checked her traps and as-
sembled a breakfast and wandered over all the familiar trails
near her hut. There was no sign of the Ghayrog. By midday
her mood seemed to be lifting, and the afternoon was almost
cheerful for her; only as nightfall approached, the time of
solitary dinner, did she begin to feel the bleakness descending
again. But she endured it. She played the cubes she had
brought from home for him, and eventually dropped into
sleep, and the next day was a better day, and the next, and
the one after that.

Gradually Thesme's life returned to normal. She saw nothing of the Ghayrog and he started to slip from her mind. As
the solitary weeks went by she rediscovered the joy of solitude, or so it seemed to her, but then at odd moments she
speared herself on some sharp and painful memory of him—
the sight of a bilantoon in a thicket or the sijaneel tree with
the broken branch or the gromwark sitting sullenly at the
edge of the pond—and she realized that she still missed him.
She roved the jungle in wider and wider circles, not quite
knowing why, until at last she admitted to herself that she
was looking for him.

It took her three more months to find him. She began
seeing indications of settlement off to the southeast—an apparent clearing, visible two or three hilltops away, with what
looked like traces of new trails radiating from it—and in time
she made her way in that direction and across a considerable
river previously unknown to her, to a zone of felled trees, beyond which was a newly established farm. She skulked along
its perimeter and caught sight of a Ghayrog—it was
Vismaan, she was certain of that—tilling a field of rich black
soil. Fear swept her spirit and left her weak and trembling.
Could it be some other Ghayrog? No, no, no, she was sure it
was he, she even imagined she detected a little limp. She
ducked down out of sight, afraid to approach him. What
could she say to him? How could she justify having come this
far to seek him out, after having so coolly dismissed him

from her life? She drew back into the underbrush and came close to turning away altogether. But then she found her courage and called his name.

He stopped short and looked around.

"Vismaan? Over here! It's Thesme!"

Her cheeks were blazing, her heart pounded terrifyingly. For one dismal instant she was convinced that this was a strange Ghayrog, and apologies for her intrusion were already springing to her lips. But as he came toward her she knew that she had not been mistaken.

"I saw the clearing and thought it might be your farm," she said, stepping out of the tangled brush. "How have you been, Vismaan?"

"Quite excellent. And yourself?"

She shrugged. "I get along. You've done wonders here, Vismaan. It's only been a few months, and look at all this!"

"Yes," he said. "We have worked hard."

"We?"

"I have a mate now. Come: let me introduce you to her, and show you what we have accomplished here."

His tranquil words withered her. Perhaps they were meant to do that—instead of showing any sort of resentment or pique over the way she had sent him out of her life, he was taking his revenge in a more diabolical fashion, through utter dispassionate restraint. But more likely, she thought, he felt no resentment and saw no need for revenge. His view of all that had passed between them was probably entirely unlike hers. Never forget that he is an alien, she told herself.

She followed him up a gentle slope and across a drainage ditch and around a small field that was obviously newly planted. At the top of the hill, half hidden by a lush kitchen-garden, was a cottage of sijaneel timbers not very different from her own, but larger and somewhat more angular in design. From up here the whole farm could be seen, occupying three faces of the little hill. Thesme was astounded at how much he had managed to do—it seemed impossible to have cleared all this, to have built a dwelling, to have made ready the soil for planting, even to have begun planting, in just these few months. She remembered that Ghayrogs did not sleep; but had they no need of rest?

"Turnome!" he called. "We have a visitor, Turnome!"

Thesme forced herself to be calm. She understood now that she had come looking for the Ghayrog because she no longer wanted to be alone, and that she had had some half-conscious fantasy of helping him establish his farm, of sharing his life as well as his bed, of building a true relationship with him; she had even, for one flickering instant, seen herself on a holiday in the north with him, visiting wonderful Dulorn, meeting his countrymen. All that was foolish, she knew, but it had had a certain crazy plausibility until the moment when he told her he had a mate. Now she struggled to compose herself, to be cordial and warm, to keep all absurd hints of rivalry from surfacing—

Out of the cottage came a Ghayrog nearly as tall as Vismaan, with the same gleaming pearly armor of scales, the same slowly writhing serpentine hair; there was only one outward difference between them, but it was a strange one indeed, for the Ghayrog woman's chest was festooned with dangling tubular breasts, a dozen or more of them, each tipped with a dark green nipple. Thesme shivered. Vismaan had said Ghayrogs were mammals, and the evidence was impossible to refute, but the reptilian look of the woman was if anything heightened by those eerie breasts, which made her seem not mammalian but weirdly hybrid and incomprehensible. Thesme looked from one to the other of these creatures in deep discomfort.

Vismaan said, "This is the woman I told you about, who found me when I hurt my leg, and nursed me back to health. Thesme: my mate Turnome."

"You are welcome here," said the Ghayrog woman solemnly.

Thesme stammered some further appreciation of the work they had done on the farm. She wanted only to escape, now, but there was no getting away; she had come to call on her jungle neighbors, and they insisted on observing the niceties. Vismaan invited her in. What was next? A cup of tea, a bowl of wine, some thokkas and grilled mintun? There was scarcely anything inside the cottage except a table and a few cushions and, in the far corner, a curious high-walled woven container of large size, standing on a three-legged stool. Thesme glanced toward it and quickly away, thinking without knowing why that it was wrong to display curiosity about it; but Vismaan took her by the elbow and said, "Let us show you. Come: look." She peered in.

It was an incubator. On a nest of moss were eleven or

twelve leathery round eggs, bright green with large red
speckles.

"Our firstborn will hatch in less than a month," Vismaan
said.

Thesme was swept by a wave of dizziness. Somehow this
revelation of the true alienness of these beings stunned her as
nothing else had, not the chilly stare of Vismaan's unblinking
eyes nor the writhing of his hair nor the touch of his skin
against her naked body nor the sudden amazing sensation of
him moving inside her. Eggs! A litter! And Turnome already
puffing up with milk to nurture them! Thesme had a vision of
a dozen tiny lizards clinging to the woman's many breasts,
and horror transfixed her: she stood motionless, not even
breathing, for an endless moment, and then she turned and
bolted, running down the hillside, over the drainage ditch,
right across, she realized too late, the newly planted field, and
off into the steaming humid jungle.

8

She did not know how long it was before Vismaan appeared at her door. Time had gone by in a blurred flow of
eating and sleeping and weeping and trembling, and perhaps
it was a day, perhaps two, perhaps a week, and then there he
was, poking his head and shoulders into the hut and calling
her name.

"What do you want?" she asked, not getting up.

"To talk. There were things I had to tell you. Why did you
leave so suddenly?"

"Does it matter?"

He crouched beside her. His hand rested lightly on her
shoulder.

"Thesme, I owe you apologies."

"For what?"

"When I left here, I failed to thank you for all you had
done for me. My mate and I were discussing why you had
run away, and she said you were angry with me, and I could
not understand why. So she and I explored all the possible
reasons, and when I described how you and I had come to
part, Turnome asked me if I had told you that I was grateful
for your help, and I said no, I had not, I was unaware that

such things were done. So I have come to you. Forgive me for my rudeness, Thesme. For my ignorance."

"I forgive you," she said in a muffled voice. "Will you go away, now?"

"Look at me, Thesme."

"I'd rather not."

"Please. Will you?" He tugged at her shoulder.

Sullenly she turned to him.

"Your eyes are swollen," he said.

"Something I ate must have disagreed with me."

"You are still angry. Why? I have asked you to understand that I meant no discourtesy. Ghayrogs do not express gratitude in quite the same way humans do. But let me do it now. You saved my life, I believe. You were very kind. I will always remember what you did for me when I was injured. It was wrong of me not to have told you that before."

"And it was wrong of me to throw you out like that," she said in a low voice. "Don't ask me to explain why I did, though. It's very complicated. I'll forgive you for not thanking me if you'll forgive me for making you leave like that."

"No forgiveness was required. My leg had healed; it was time for me to go, as you pointed out; I went on my way and found the land I needed for my farm."

"It was that simple, then?"

"Yes. Of course."

She got to her feet and stood facing him. "Vismaan, why did you have sex with me?"

"Because you seemed to want it."

"That's all?"

"You were unhappy and did not seem to wish to sleep alone. I hoped it would comfort you. I was trying to do the friendly thing, the compassionate thing."

"Oh. I see."

"I believe it gave you pleasure," he said.

"Yes. Yes. It did give me pleasure. But you didn't desire me, then?"

His tongue flickered in what she thought might be the equivalent of a puzzled frown.

"No," he said. "You are human. How can I feel desire for a human? You are so different from me, Thesme. On Majipoor my kind are called aliens, but to me *you* are the alien, is that not so?"

"I suppose. Yes."

"But I was very fond of you. I wished your happiness. In that sense I had desire for you. Do you understand? And I will always be your friend. I hope you will come to visit us, and share in the bounty of our farm. Will you do that, Thesme?"

"I—yes, yes, I will."

"Good. I will go now. But first—"

Gravely, with immense dignity, he drew her to him and enfolded her in his powerful arms. Once again she felt the strange smooth rigidity of his alien skin; once again the little scarlet tongue fluttered across her eyelids in a forked kiss. He embraced her for a long moment.

When he released her he said, "I am extremely fond of you, Thesme. I can never forget you."

"Nor I you."

She stood in the doorway, watching until he disappeared from sight beyond the pond. A sense of ease and peace and warmth had come over her spirit. She doubted that she ever would visit Vismaan and Turnome and their litter of little lizards, but that was all right: Vismaan would understand. Everything was all right. Thesme began to gather her possessions and stuff them into her pack. It was still only mid-morning, time enough to make the journey to Narabal.

She reached the city just after the afternoon showers. It was over a year since she had left it, and a good many months since her last visit; and she was surprised by the changes she saw now. There was a boom-town bustle to the place, new buildings going up everywhere, ships in the Channel, the streets full of traffic. And the town seemed to have been invaded by aliens—hundreds of Ghayrogs, and other kinds too, the warty ones that she supposed were Hjorts, and enormous double-shouldered Skandars, a whole circus of strange beings going about their business and taken absolutely for granted by the human citizens. Thesme found her way with some difficulty to her mother's house. Two of her sisters were there, and her brother Dalkhan. They stared at her in amazement and what seemed like fear.

"I'm back," she said. "I know I look like a wild animal, but I just need my hair trimmed and a new tunic and I'll be human again."

She went to live with Ruskelorn Yulvan a few weeks later, and at the end of the year they were married. For a time she thought of confessing to him that she and her Ghayrog guest had been lovers, but she was afraid to do it, and eventually it seemed unimportant to bring it up at all. She did, finally, ten or twelve years later, when they had dined on roast bilantoon at one of the fine new restaurants in the Ghayrog quarter of town, and she had had much too much of the strong golden wine of the north, and the pressure of old associations was too powerful to resist. When she had finished telling him the story she said, "Did you suspect any of that?" And he said, "I knew it right away, when I saw you with him in the street. But why should it have mattered?"

TWO

The Time of the Burning

For weeks after that astounding experience Hissune does not dare return to the Register of Souls. It was too powerful, too raw; he needs time to digest, to absorb. He had lived months of that woman's life in an hour in that cubicle, and the experience blazes in his soul. Strange new images tumble tempestuously through his consciousness now.

The jungle, first of all—Hissune has never known anything but the carefully controlled climate of the subterranean Labyrinth, except for the time he journeyed to the Mount, the climate of which is in a different way just as closely regulated. So he was amazed by the humidity, the denseness of the foliage, the rainshowers, the bird-sounds and insect-sounds, the feel of wet soil beneath bare feet. But that is only a tiny slice of what he has taken in. To be a woman—how astonishing! And then to have an alien for a lover—Hissune has no words for that; it is simply an event that has become part of him, incomprehensible, bewildering. And when he has begun to work his way all through that there is much more for his meditations: the sense of Majipoor as a developing world, parts of it still young, unpaved streets in Narabal, wooden shacks, not at all the neat and thoroughly tamed planet he inhabits, but a turbulent and mysterious land with many dark regions. Hissune mulls these things hour upon hour, while mindlessly arranging his meaningless revenue archives, and

42

*gradually it occurs to him that he has been forever trans-
formed by that illicit interlude in the Register of Souls. He
can never be only Hissune again; he will always be, in some
unfathomable way, not just Hissune but also the woman
Thesme who lived and died nine thousand years ago on another continent, in a hot steamy place that Hissune will never
see.*

*Then, of course, he hungers for a second jolt of the mirac-
ulous Register. A different official is on duty this time, a
scowling little Vroon whose mask is askew, and Hissune has
to wave his documents around very quickly to get inside. But
his glib mind is a match for any of these sluggish civil servants, and soon enough he is in the cubicle, punching out
coordinates with swift fingers. Let it be the time of Lord Stiamot, he decides. The final days of the conquest of the Metamorphs by the armies of the human settlers of Majipoor.
Give me a soldier of Lord Stiamot's army, he tells the hidden
mind of the recording vaults. And perhaps I'll have a glimpse
of Lord Stiamot himself!*

The dry foothills were burning along a curving crest from
Milimorn to Hamifieu, and even up here, in his eyrie fifty
miles east on Zygnor Peak, Group Captain Eremoil could
feel the hot blast of the wind and taste the charred flavor of
the air. A dense crown of murky smoke rose over the entire
range. In an hour or two the fliers would extend the fire-line
from Hamifieu down to that little town at the base of the valley, and tomorrow they'd torch the zone from there south to
Sintalmond. And then this entire province would be ablaze,
and woe betide any Shapeshifters who lingered in it.

"It won't be long now," Viggan said. "The war's almost
over."

Eremoil looked up from his charts of the northwestern corner of the continent and stared at the subaltern. "Do you
think so?" he asked vaguely.

"Thirty years. That's about enough."

"Not thirty. Five thousand years, six thousand, however
long it's been since humans first came to this world. It's been
war all the time, Viggan."

"For a lot of that time we didn't realize we were fighting a
war, though."

"No," Eremoil said. "No, we didn't understand. But we understand now, don't we, Viggan?"

He turned his attention back to the charts, bending low, squinting, peering. The oily smoke in the air was bringing tears to his eyes and blurring his vision, and the charts were very finely drawn. Slowly he drew his pointer down the contour lines of the foothills below Hamifieu, checking off the villages on his report-sheets.

Every village along the arc of flame was marked on the charts, he hoped, and officers had visited each to bring notice of the burning. It would go hard for him and those beneath him if the mappers had left any place out, for Lord Stiamot had issued orders that no human lives were to be lost in this climactic drive: all settlers were to be warned and given time to evacuate. The Metamorphs were being given the same warning. One did not simply roast one's enemies alive, Lord Stiamot had said repeatedly. One aimed only to bring them under one's control, and just now fire seemed to be the best means of doing that. Bringing the fire itself under control afterward might be a harder job, Eremoil thought, but that was not the problem of the moment.

"Kattikawn—Bizfern—Domgrave—Byelk—so many little towns, Viggan. Why do people want to live up here, anyway?"

"They say the land is fertile, sir. And the climate is mild, for such a northerly district."

"Mild? I suppose, if you don't mind half a year without rain." Eremoil coughed. He imagined he could hear the crackling of the distant fire through the tawny knee-high grass. On this side of Alhanroel it rained all winter long and then rained not at all the whole summer: a challenge for farmers, one would think, but evidently they had surmounted it, considering how many agricultural settlements had sprouted along the slopes of these hills and downward into the valleys that ran to the sea. This was the height of the dry season now, and the legion had been baking under summer sun for months—dry, dry, dry, the dark soil cracked and gullied, the winter-growing grasses dormant and parched, the thick-leaved shrubs folded and waiting. What a perfect time to put the place to the torch and force one's stubborn enemies down to the edge of the ocean, or into it! But no lives lost, no lives lost—Eremoil studied his lists. "Chikmoge—Fualle—Daniup—Michimang—" Again he looked up. To the subaltern he said, "Viggan, what will you do after the war?"

"My family owns lands in the Glayge Valley. I'll be a farmer again, I suppose. And you, sir?"

"My home is in Stee. I was a civil engineer—aqueducts, sewage conduits, other such fascinating things. I can be that again. When did you last see the Glayge?"

"Four years ago," said Viggan.

"And five for me, since Stee. You were at the Battle of Treymone, weren't you?"

"Wounded. Slightly."

"Ever kill a Metamorph?"

"Yes, sir."

Eremoil said, "Not I. Never once. Nine years a soldier, never a life taken. Of course, I've been an officer. I'm not a good killer, I suspect."

"None of us are," said Viggan. "But when they're coming at you, changing shape five times a minute, with a knife in one hand and an axe in the other—or when you know they've raided your brother's land and murdered your nephews—"

"Is that what happened, Viggan?"

"Not to me, sir. But to others, plenty of others. The atrocities—I don't need to tell you how—"

"No. No, you don't. What's this town's name, Viggan?"

The subaltern leaned over the charts. "Singaserin, sir. The lettering's a little smudged, but that's what it says. And it's on our list. See, here. We gave them notice day before yesterday."

"I think we've done them all, then."

"I think so, sir," said Viggan.

Eremoil shuffled the charts into a stack, put them away, and looked out again toward the west. There was a distinct line of demarcation between the zone of the burning and the untouched hills south of it, dark green and seemingly lush with foliage. But the leaves of those trees were shriveled and greasy from months without rain, and those hillsides would explode as though they had been bombed when the fire reached them. Now and again he saw little bursts of flame, no more than puffs of sudden brightness as though from the striking of a light. But it was a trick of distance, Eremoil knew; each of those tiny flares was the eruption of a vast new territory as the fire, carrying itself now by airborne embers where the fliers themselves were not spreading it, devoured the forests beyond Hamifieu.

Viggan said, "Messenger here, sir."

Eremoil turned. A tall young man in a sweaty uniform had clambered down from a mount and was staring uncertainly at him.

"Well?" he said.

"Captain Vanayle sent me, sir. Problem down in the valley. Settler won't evacuate."

"He'd better," Eremoil said, shrugging. "What town is it?"

"Between Kattikawn and Bizfern, sir. Substantial tract. The man's name is Kattikawn too, Aibil Kattikawn. He told Captain Vanayle that he holds his land by direct grant of the Pontifex Dvorn, that his people have been here thousands of years, and that he isn't going to——"

Eremoil sighed and said, "I don't care if he holds his land by direct grant of the Divine. We're burning that district tomorrow and he'll fry if he stays there."

"He knows that, sir."

"What does he want us to do? Make the fire go around his farm, eh?" Eremoil waved his arm impatiently. "Evacuate him, regardless of what he is or isn't going to do."

"We've tried that," said the messenger. "He's armed and he offered resistance. He says he'll kill anyone who tries to remove him from his land."

"Kill?" Eremoil said, as though the word had no meaning. "Kill? Who talks of killing other human beings? The man is crazy. Send fifty troops and get him on his way to one of the safe zones."

"I said he offered resistance, sir. There was an exchange of fire. Captain Vanayle believes that he can't be removed without loss of life. Captain Vanayle asks that you go down in person to reason with the man, sir."

"That I——"

Viggan said quietly, "It may be the simplest way. These big landholders can be very difficult."

"Let Vanayle go to him," Eremoil said.

"Captain Vanayle has already attempted to parley with the man, sir," the messenger said. "He was unsuccessful. This Kattikawn demands an audience with Lord Stiamot. Obviously that's impossible, but perhaps if you were to go——"

Eremoil considered it. It was absurd for the commanding officer of the district to undertake such a task. It was Vanayle's direct responsibility to clear the territory before tomorrow's burning; it was Eremoil's to remain up here and direct the action. On the other hand, clearing the territory was ultimately Eremoil's responsibility also, and Vanayle had plainly failed to do it, and sending in a squad to make a forcible removal would probably end in Kattikawn's death and the deaths of a few soldiers too, which was hardly a useful outcome. Why not go? Eremoil nodded slowly. Protocol be damned: he would not stand on ceremony. He had nothing significant left to do this afternoon and Viggan could look after any details that came up. And if he could save one life, one stupid stubborn old man's life, by taking a little ride down the mountainside—

"Get my floater," he said to Viggan.

"Sir?"

"Get it. Now, before I change my mind. I'm going down to see him."

"But Vanayle has already—"

"Stop being troublesome, Viggan. I'll only be gone a short while. You're in command here until I get back, but I don't think you'll have to work very hard. Can you handle it?"

"Yes, sir," the subaltern said glumly.

It was a longer journey than Eremoil expected, nearly two hours down the switchbacked road to the base of Zygnor Peak, then across the uneven sloping plateau to the foothills that ringed the coastal plain. The air was hotter though less smoky down there; shimmering heatwaves spawned mirages, and made the landscape seem to melt and flow. The road was empty of traffic, but he was stopped again and again by panicky migrating beasts, strange animals of species that he could not identify, fleeing wildly from the fire zone ahead. Shadows were beginning to lengthen by the time Eremoil reached the foothill settlements. Here the fire was a tangible presence, like a second sun in the sky; Eremoil felt the heat of it against his cheek, and a fine grit settled on his skin and clothing.

The places he had been checking on his lists now became uncomfortably real to him: Byelk, Domgrave, Bizfern. One was just like the next, a central huddle of shops and public buildings, an outer residential rim, a ring of farms radiating outward beyond that, each town tucked in its little valley where some stream cut down out of the hills and lost itself on the plain. They were all empty now, or nearly so, just a few stragglers left, the others already on the highways leading to the coast. Eremoil supposed that he could walk into any of these houses and find books, carvings, souvenirs of holidays abroad, even pets, perhaps, abandoned in grief; and tomorrow all this would be ashes. But this territory was infested with Shapeshifters. The settlers here had lived for centuries under the menace of an implacable savage foe that flitted in and out of the forests in masquerade, disguised as one's friend, one's lover, one's son, on errands of murder, a secret quiet war between the dispossessed and those who had come after them, a war that had been inevitable since the early outposts on Majipoor had grown into cities and sprawling agricultural territories that consumed more and more of the domain of the natives. Some remedies involve drastic cautery: in this final convulsion of the struggle between humans and Shapeshifters there was no help for it, Byelk and Domgrave and Bizfern must be destroyed so that the agony could end. Yet that did not make it easy to face abandoning one's home, Eremoil thought, nor was it even particularly easy to destroy someone else's home, as he had been doing for days, unless one did it from a distance, from a comfortable distance where all this torching was only a strategic abstraction.

Beyond Bizfern the foothills swung westward a long way, the road following their contour. There were good streams here, almost little rivers, and the land was heavily forested where it had not been cleared for planting. Yet even here the months without rain had left the forests terribly combustible, drifts of dead fallen leaves everywhere, fallen branches, old cracked trunks.

"This is the place, sir," the messenger said.

Eremoil beheld a box canyon, narrow at its mouth and much broader within, with a stream running down its middle. Against the gathering shadows he made out an impressive manor, a great white building with a roof of green tiles, and beyond that what seemed to be an immense acreage of crops. Armed guards were waiting at the mouth of the canyon. This was no simple farmer's spread; this was the domain of one who regarded himself as a duke. Eremoil saw trouble in store.

He dismounted and strode toward the guards, who studied him coldly and held their energy-throwers at the ready. To one that seemed the most imposing he said, "Group Captain Eremoil to see Aibil Kattikawn."

"The Kattikawn is awaiting Lord Stiamot," was the flat chilly reply.

"Lord Stiamot is occupied elsewhere. I represent him today. I am Group Captain Eremoil, commanding officer in this district."

"We are instructed to admit only Lord Stiamot."

"Tell your master," Eremoil said wearily, "that the Coronal sends his regrets and asks him to offer his grievances to Group Captain Eremoil instead."

The guard seemed indifferent to that. But after a moment he spun around and entered the canyon. Eremoil watched him walking unhurriedly along the bank of the stream until he disappeared in the dense shrubbery of the plaza before the manor-house. A long time passed; the wind changed, bringing a hot gust from the fire zone, a layer of dark air that stung the eyes and scorched the throat. Eremoil envisioned a coating of black gritty particles on his lungs. But from here, in this sheltered place, the fire itself was invisible.

Eventually the guard returned, just as unhurriedly.

"The Kattikawn will see you," he announced.

Eremoil beckoned to his driver and his guide, the messenger. But Kattikawn's guard shook his head.

"Only you, captain."

The driver looked disturbed. Eremoil waved her back. "Wait for me here," he said. "I don't think I'll be long."

He followed the guard down the canyon path to the manor-house.

From Aibil Kattikawn he expected the same sort of hard-eyed welcome that the guards had offered; but Eremoil had underestimated the courtesy a provincial aristocrat would feel obliged to provide. Kattikawn greeted him with a warm smile and an intense, searching stare, gave him what seemed to be an unfeigned embrace, and led him into the great house, which was sparsely furnished but elegant in its stark and rugged way. Exposed beams of oiled black wood dominated the vaulted ceilings; hunting trophies loomed high on the walls; the furniture was massive and plainly ancient. The whole place had an archaic air. So too did Aibil Kattikawn. He was a big man, much taller than the lightly built Eremoil and broad through the shoulders, a breadth dramatically enhanced by the heavy steetmoy-fur cloak he wore. His forehead was high, his hair gray but thick, rising in heavy ridges; his eyes were dark, his lips thin. In every aspect he was of the most imposing presence.

When he had poured bowls of some glistening amber wine and they had had the first sips, Kattikawn said, "So you need to burn my lands?"

"We must burn this entire province, I'm afraid."

"A stupid stratagem, perhaps the most foolish thing in the whole history of human warfare. Do you know how valuable the produce of this district is? Do you know how many generations of hard work have gone into building these farms?"

"The entire zone from Milimorn to Sintalmond and beyond is a center of Metamorph guerrilla activity, the last one remaining in Alhanroel. The Coronal is determined to end this ugly war finally, and it can only be done by smoking the Shapeshifters out of their hiding-places in these hills."

"There are other methods."

"We have tried them and they have failed," Eremoil said.

"Have you? Have you tried moving from inch to inch through the forests searching for them? Have you moved every soldier on Majipoor in here to conduct the mopping-up operations? Of course not. It's too much trouble. It's much simpler to send out those fliers and set the whole place on fire."

"This war has consumed an entire generation of our lives."

"And the Coronal grows impatient toward the end," said Kattikawn. "At my expense."

"The Coronal is a master of strategy. The Coronal has defeated a dangerous and almost incomprehensible enemy and has made Majipoor safe for human occupation for the first time—all but this district."

"We have managed well enough with these Metamorphs skulking all around us, captain. I haven't been massacred yet. I've been able to handle them. They haven't been remotely as much of a threat to my welfare as my own government seems to be. Your Coronal, captain, is a fool."

Eremoil controlled himself. "Future generations will hail him as a hero among heroes."

"Very likely," said Kattikawn. "That's the kind that usually gets made into heroes. I tell you that it was not necessary to destroy an entire province in order to round up the few thousand aborigines that remain at large. I tell you that it is a rash and shortsighted move on the part of a tired general who is in a hurry to return to the ease of Castle Mount."

"Be that as it may, the decision has been taken, and everything from Milimorn to Hamifieu is already ablaze."

"So I have noticed."

"The fire is advancing toward Kattikawn village. Perhaps by dawn the outskirts of your own domain will be threatened. During the day we'll continue the incendiary attacks past this region and on south as far as Sintalmond."

"Indeed," said Kattikawn calmly.

"This area will become an inferno. We ask you to abandon it while you still have time."

"I choose to remain, captain."

Eremoil let his breath out slowly. "We cannot be responsible for your safety if you do."

"No one has ever been responsible for my safety except myself."

"What I'm saying is that you'll die, and die horribly. We have no way of laying down the fire-line in such a way as to avoid your domain."

"I understand."

"You ask us to murder you, then."

"I ask nothing of the sort. You and I have no transaction at all. You fight your war; I maintain my home. If the fire that your war requires should intrude on the territory I call my own, so much the worse for me, but no murder is involved. We are bound on independent courses, Captain Eremoil."

"Your reasoning is strange. You will die as a direct result of our incendiary attack. Your life will be on our souls."

"I remain here of free will, after having been duly warned," said Kattikawn. "My life will be on my own soul alone."

"And your people's lives? They'll die too."

"Those who choose to remain, yes. I've given then warning of what is about to happen. Three have set out for the coast. The rest will stay. Of their own will, and not to please me. This is our place. Another bowl of wine, captain?"

Eremoil refused, then instantly changed his mind and proffered the empty bowl. Kattikawn, as he poured, said, "Is there no way I can speak with Lord Stiamot?"

"None."

"I understand the Coronal is in this area."

"Half a day's journey, yes. But he is inaccessible to such petitioners."

"By design, I imagine." Kattikawn smiled. "Do you think he's gone mad, Eremoil?"

"The Coronal? Not at all."

"This burning, though—such a desperate move, such an idiotic move. The reparations he'll have to pay afterward—millions of royals; it'll bankrupt the treasury; it'll cost more than fifty castles as grand as the one he's built on top of the Mount. And for what? Give us two or three more years and we'd have the Shapeshifters tamed."

"Or five or ten or twenty," said Eremoil. "This must be the end of the war, now, this season. This ghastly convulsion, this shame on everyone, this strain, this long nightmare—"

"Oh, you think the war's been a mistake, then?"

Eremoil quickly shook his head. "The fundamental mistake was made long ago, when our ancestors chose to settle on a world that was already inhabited by an intelligent species. By our time we had no choice but to crush the Metamorphs, or else retreat entirely from Majipoor, and how could we do that?"

"Yes," Kattikawn said, "how could we give up the homes that had been ours and our forebears' for so long, eh?"

Eremoil ignored the heavy irony. "We took this planet from an unwilling people. For thousands of years we attempted to live in peace with them, until we admitted that coexistence was impossible. Now we are imposing our will by force, which is not beautiful, but the alternatives are even worse."

"What will Lord Stiamot do with the Shapeshifters he has in his internment camps? Plough them under as fertilizer for the fields he's burned?"

"They'll be given a vast reservation in Zimroel," said Eremoil. "Half a continent to themselves—that's hardly cruelty. Alhanroel will be ours, and an ocean between us. Already the resettlement is under way. Only your area remains unpacified. Lord Stiamot has taken upon himself the terrible burden of responsibility for a harsh but necessary act, and the future will hail him for it."

"I hail him now," said Kattikawn. "O wise and just Coronal! Who in his infinite wisdom destroys this land so that his world need not have the bother of troublesome aborigines lurking about. It would have been better for me, Eremoil, if he had been less noble of spirit, this hero-king of yours. Or more noble, perhaps. He'd seem much more wondrous to me

if he'd chosen some slower method of conquering these last
holdouts. Thirty years of war—what's another two or three?"

"This is the way he has chosen. The fires are approaching
this place as we speak."

"Let them come. I'll be here, defending my house against
them."

"You haven't seen the fire zone," Eremoil said. "Your defense won't last ten seconds. The fire eats everything in its
way."

"Quite likely. I'll take my chances."

"I beg you—"

"You beg? Are you a beggar, then? What if I were to beg?
I beg you, captain, spare my estate!"

"It can't be done. I beg you indeed: retreat, and spare your
life and the lives of your people."

"What would you have me do, go crawling along that highway to the coast, and live in some squalid little cabin in
Alaisor or Bailemoona? Wait on table at an inn, or sweep the
streets, or curry mounts in a stable? This is my place. I would
rather die here in ten seconds tomorrow than live a thousand
years in cowardly exile." Kattikawn walked to the window.
"It grows dark, captain. Will you be my guest for dinner?"

"I am unable to stay, I regret to tell you."

"Does this dispute bore you? We can talk of other things. I
would prefer that."

Eremoil reached for the other man's great paw of a hand.
"I have obligations at my headquarters. It would have been
an unforgettable pleasure to accept your hospitality. I wish it
were possible. Will you forgive me for declining?"

"It pains me to see you leave unfed. Do you hurry off to
Lord Stiamot?"

Eremoil was silent.

"I would ask you to gain me an audience with him," said
Kattikawn.

"It can't be done, and it would do no good. Please: leave
this place tonight. Let us dine together, and then abandon
your domain."

"This is my place, and here I remain," Kattikawn said. "I
wish you well, captain, a long and harmonious life. And I
thank you for this conversation." He closed his eyes a moment and inclined his head: a tiny bow, a delicate dismissal.
Eremoil moved toward the door of the great hall. Kattikawn
said, "The other officer thought he would pull me out of here

by force. You had more sense, and I compliment you. Farewell, Captain Eremoil."

Eremoil searched for appropriate words, found none, and settled for a gesture of salute.

Kattikawn's guards led him back to the mouth of his canyon, where Eremoil's driver and the messenger waited, playing some game with dice by the side of the floater. They snapped to attention when they saw Eremoil, but he signaled them to relax. He looked off to the east, at the great mountains that rose on the far side of the valley. In these northerly latitudes, on this summer night, the sky was still light, even to the east, and the heavy bulk of Zygnor Peak lay across the horizon like a black wall against the pale gray of the sky. South of it was its twin, Mount Haimon, where the Coronal had made his headquarters. Eremoil stood for a time studying the two mighty peaks, and the foothills below them, and the pillar of fire and smoke that ascended on the other side, and the moons just coming into the sky; then he shook his head and turned and looked back toward Aibil Kattikawn's manor, disappearing now in the shadows of the late dusk. In his rise through the army ranks Eremoil had come to know dukes and princes and many other high ones that a mere civil engineer does not often meet in private life, and he had spent more than a little time with the Coronal himself and the intimate circle of advisers around him, and yet he thought he had never encountered anyone quite like this Kattikawn, who was either the most noble or the most misguided man on the planet, and perhaps both.

"Let's go," he said to the driver. "Take the Haimon road."

"The Haimon, sir?"

"To the Coronal, yes. Can you get us there by midnight?"

The road to the southern peak was much like the Zygnor road, but steeper and not as well paved. In darkness its twists and turns would probably be dangerous at the speed Eremoil's driver, a woman of Stoien, was risking; but the red glow of the fire zone lit up the valley and the foothills and much reduced the risks. Eremoil said nothing during the long journey. There was nothing to say: how could the driver or the messenger-lad possibly understand the nature of Aibil Kattikawn? Eremoil himself, on first hearing that one of the local farmers refused to leave his land, had misunderstood that nature, imagining some crazy old fool, some stubborn fanatic blind to the realities of his peril. Kattikawn was stubborn, surely, and possibly he could be called a fanatic, but he was none of the other things, not even crazy, however crazy his philosophy might seem to those, like Eremoil, who lived by different codes.

He wondered what he was going to tell Lord Stiamot.

No use rehearsing: words would come, or they would not. He slipped after a time into a kind of waking sleep, his mind lucid but frozen, contemplating nothing, calculating nothing. The floater, moving lightly and swiftly up the dizzying road, climbed out of the valley and into the jagged country beyond. At midnight it was still in the lower reaches of Mount Haimon, but no matter: the Coronal was known to keep late hours, often not to sleep at all. Eremoil did not doubt he would be available.

Somewhere on the upper slopes of Haimon he dropped without any awareness of it into real sleep, and he was surprised and confused when the messenger shook him gently awake, saying, "This is Lord Stiamot's camp, sir." Blinking, disoriented, Eremoil found himself still sitting erect, his legs cramped, his back stiff. The moons were far across the sky and the night now was black except for the amazing fiery gash that tore across it to the west. Awkwardly Eremoil scrambled from the floater. Even now, in the middle of the night, the Coronal's camp was a busy place, messengers running to and fro, lights burning in many of the buildings. An adjutant appeared, recognized Eremoil, gave him an exceedingly formal salute. "This visit comes as a surprise, Captain Eremoil!"

"To me also, I'd say. Is Lord Stiamot in the camp?"

"The Coronal is holding a staff meeting. Does he expect you, captain?"

"No," said Eremoil. "But I need to speak with him."

The adjutant was undisturbed by that. Staff meetings in the middle of the night, regional commanders turning up unannounced for conferences—well, why not? This was war, and protocols were improvised from day to day. Eremoil followed the man through the camp to an octagonal tent that bore the starburst insignia of the Coronal. A ring of guards surrounded the place, as grim and dedicated-looking as those who had held the mouth of Kattikawn's canyon. There had been four attempts on Lord Stiamot's life in the past eighteen months—all Metamorphs, all thwarted. No Coronal in

Majipoor's history had ever died violently, but none had ever waged war, either, before this one.

The adjutant spoke with the commander of the guard; suddenly Eremoil found himself at the center of a knot of armed men, with lights shining maddeningly in his eyes and fingers digging painfully into his arms. For an instant the onslaught astonished him. But then he regained his poise and said, "What is this? I am Group Captain Eremoil."

"Unless you're a Shapeshifter," one of the men said.

"And you think you'd find that out by squeezing me and blinding me with your glare?"

"There are ways," said another.

Eremoil laughed. "None that ever proved reliable. But go on: test me, and do it fast. I must speak with Lord Stiamot."

They did indeed have tests. Someone gave him a strip of green paper and told him to touch his tongue to it. He did, and the paper turned orange. Someone else asked for a snip of his hair, and set fire to it. Eremoil looked on in amazement. It was a month since he had last been to the Coronal's camp, and none of these practices had been employed then; there must have been another assassination attempt, he decided, or else some quack scientist had come among them with these techniques. So far as Eremoil knew, there was no true way to distinguish a Metamorph from an authentic human when the Metamorph had taken on human form, except through dissection, and he did not propose to submit to that.

"You pass," they said at last. "You can go in."

But they accompanied him. Eremoil's eyes, dazzled already, adjusted with difficulty to the dimness of the Coronal's tent, but after a moment he saw half a dozen figures at the far end, and Lord Stiamot among them. They seemed to be praying. He heard murmured invocations and responses, bits of the old scripture. Was this the sort of staff meetings the Coronal held now? Eremoil went forward and stood a few yards from the group. He knew only one of the Coronal's attendants, Damlang of Bibiroon, who was generally considered second or third in line for the throne; the others did not seem even to be soldiers, for they were older men, in civilian dress, with a soft citified look about them, poets, dream-speakers perhaps, certainly not warriors. But the war was almost over.

The Coronal looked in Eremoil's direction without seeming to notice him.

Eremoil was startled by Lord Stiamot's harried, ragged

look. The Coronal had been growing visibly older all through the past three years of the war, but the process seemed to have accelerated now: he appeared shrunken, colorless, frail, his skin parched, his eyes dull. He might have been a hundred years old, and yet he was no older than Eremoil himself, a man in middle life. Eremoil could remember the day Stiamot had come to the throne, and how Stiamot had vowed that day to end the madness of this constant undeclared warfare with the Metamorphs, to collect the planet's ancient natives and remove them from the territories settled by mankind. Only thirty years, and the Coronal looked the better part of a century older; but he had spent his reign in the field, as no Coronal before him had done and probably none after him ever would do, campaigning in the Glayge Valley, in the hotlands of the south, in the dense forests of the northeast, in the rich plains along the Gulf of Stoien, year after year encircling the Shapeshifters with his twenty armies and penning them in camps. And now he was nearly finished with the job, just the guerrillas of the northwest remaining at liberty—a constant struggle, a long fierce life of war, with scarcely time to return to the tender springtime of Castle Mount for the pleasures of the throne. Eremoil had occasionally wondered, as the war went on and on, how Lord Stiamot would respond if the Pontifex should die, and he be called upward to the other kingship and be forced to take up residence in the Labyrinth: would he decline, and retain the Coronal's crown so that he might remain in the field? But the Pontifex was in fine health, so it was said, and here was Lord Stiamot now a tired little old man, looking to be at the edge of the grave himself. Eremoil understood abruptly what Aibil Kattikawn had failed to comprehend, why it was that Lord Stiamot was so eager to bring the final phase of the war to its conclusion regardless of cost.

The Coronal said, "Who do we have there? Is that Finiwain?"

"Eremoil, my lord. In command of the forces carrying out the burning."

"Eremoil. Yes. Eremoil. I recall. Come, sit with us. We are giving thanks to the Divine for the end of the war, Eremoil. These people have come to me from my mother the Lady of the Isle, who guards us in dreams, and we will spend the night in songs of praise and gratitude, for in the morning the

circle of fire will be complete. Eh, Eremoil? Come, sit, sing
with us. You know the songs to the Lady, don't you?"

Eremoil heard the Coronal's cracked and frayed voice with
shock. That faded thread of dry sound was all that remained
of his once majestic tone. This hero, this demigod, was
withered and ruined by his long campaign; there was nothing
left of him; he was a spectre, a shadow. Seeing him like this,
Eremoil wondered if Lord Stiamot had ever been the mighty
figure of memory, or if perhaps that was only mythmaking
and propaganda, and the Coronal had all along been less
than met the eye.

Lord Stiamot beckoned. Eremoil reluctantly moved closer.

He thought of what he had come here to say. *My lord,
there is a man in the path of the fire who will not move and
will not allow himself to be moved, and who cannot be
moved without the loss of life, and, my lord, he is too fine a
man to be destroyed in this way. So I ask you, my lord, to
halt the burning, perhaps to devise some alternative strategy,
so that we may seize the Metamorphs as they flee the fire
zone but do not need to extend the destruction beyond the
point it already reaches, because—*

No.

He saw the utter impossibility of asking the Coronal to
delay the end of the war a single hour. Not for Kattikawn's
sake, not for Eremoil's sake, not for the sake of the holy Lady
his mother could the burning be halted now, for these were
the last days of the war and the Coronal's need to proceed to
the end was the overriding force that swept all else before it.
Eremoil might try to halt the burning on his own authority,
but he could not ask the Coronal for approval.

Lord Stiamot thrust his head toward Eremoil.

"What is it, captain? What bothers you? Here. Sit by me.
Sing with us, captain. Raise your voice in thanksgiving."

They began a hymn, some tune Eremoil did not know. He
hummed along, improvising a harmony. After that they sang
another, and another, and that one Eremoil did know; he
sang, but in a hollow and tuneless way. Dawn could not be
far off now. Quietly he moved into the shadows and out of
the tent. Yes, there was the sun, beginning to cast the first
greenish light along the eastern face of Mount Haimon,
though it would be an hour or more before its rays climbed
the mountain wall and illuminated the doomed valleys to the
southwest. Eremoil yearned for a week of sleep. He looked

for the adjutant and said, "Will you send a message for me to my subaltern on Zygnor Peak?"

"Of course, sir."

"Tell him to take charge of the next phase of the burning and proceed as scheduled. I'm going to remain here during the day and will return to my headquarters this evening, after I've had some rest."

"Yes, sir."

Eremoil turned away and looked toward the west, still wrapped in night except where the terrible glow of the fire zone illuminated it. Probably Aibil Kattikawn had been busy all this night with pumps and hoses, wetting down his lands. It would do no good, of course; a fire of that magnitude takes all in its path, and burns until no fuel is left. So Katti-kawn would die and the tiled roof of the manor-house would collapse, and there was no helping it. He could be saved on-ly at the risk of the lives of innocent soldiers, and probably not even then; or he could be saved if Eremoil chose to disre-gard the orders of Lord Stiamot, but not for long. So he will die. After nine years in the field, Eremoil thought, I am at last the cause of taking a life, and he is one of our own cit-izens. So be it. So be it.

He remained at the lookout post, weary but unable to move on, another hour or so, until he saw the first explosions of flame in the foothills near Bizfern, or maybe Domgrave, and knew that the morning's incendiary bombing had begun. The war will soon be over, he told himself. The last of our enemies now flee toward the safety of the coast, where they will be interned and transported overseas, and the world will be quiet again. He felt the warmth of the summer sun on his back and the warmth of the spreading fires on his cheeks. The world will be quiet again, he thought, and went to find a place to sleep.

THREE

In the Fifth Year of the Voyage

That one was quite different from the first. Hissune is less amazed by it, less shattered; it is a sad and moving tale, but it does not rock his soul's depths the way the embrace of human and Ghayrog had done. Yet he has learned a great deal from it about the nature of responsibility, about the conflicts that arise between opposing forces neither of which can be said to be in the wrong, and about the meaning of true tranquillity of spirit. Then too he has discovered something about the process of mythmaking: for in all the history of Majipoor there has been no figure more godlike than Lord Stiamot, the shining warrior-king who broke the strength of the sinister aboriginal Shapeshifters, and eight thousand years of idolization have transformed him into an awesome being of great majesty and splendor. That Lord Stiamot of myth still exists in Hissune's mind, but it has been necessary to move him to one side in order to make room for the Stiamot he has seen through Eremoil's eyes—that weary, pallid, withered little man, old before his time, who burned his soul to a husk in a lifetime of battle. A hero? Certainly, except perhaps to the Metamorphs. But a demigod? No, a human being, very human, all frailty and fatigue. It is important never to forget that, Hissune tells himself, and in that moment he realizes that these stolen minutes in the Register of Souls are providing him with his true education, his doctoral degree in life.

It is a long while before he feels ready to return for another course. But in time the dust of the tax archives begins to seep to the depths of his being and he craves a diversion, an adventure. So, too, back to the Register. Another legend needs exploring; for once, long ago, a shipload of madmen set out to sail across the Great Sea—folly if ever folly had been conceived, but glorious folly, and Hissune chooses to take passage aboard that ship and discover what befell its crew. A little research produces the captain's name: Sinnabor Lavon, a native of Castle Mount. Hissune's fingers lightly touch the keys, giving date, place, name, and he sits back, poised, expectant, ready to go to sea.

In the fifth year of the voyage Sinnabor Lavon noticed the first strands of dragon-grass coiling and writhing in the sea alongside the hull of the ship.

He had no idea of what it was, of course, for no one on Majipoor had ever seen dragon-grass before. This distant reach of the Great Sea had never been explored. But he did know that this was the fifth year of the voyage, for every morning Sinnabor Lavon had carefully noted the date and the ship's position in his log, so that the explorers would not lose their psychological bearings on this boundless and monotonous ocean. Thus he was certain that this day lay in the twentieth year of the Pontificate of Dizimaule, Lord Arioc being Coronal, and that this was the fifth year since the *Spurifon* had set out from the port of Til-omon on her journey around the world.

He mistook the dragon-grass for a mass of sea-serpents at first. It seemed to move with an inner force, twisting, wriggling, contracting, relaxing. Against the calm dark water it gleamed with a shimmering richness of color, each strand iridescent, showing glints of emerald and indigo and vermilion. There was a small patch of it off the port side and a somewhat broader streak of it staining the sea to starboard.

Lavon peered over the rail to the lower deck and saw a trio of shaggy four-armed figures below: Skandar crewmen, mending nets, or pretending to. They met his gaze with sour, sullen looks. Like many of the crew, they had long ago grown weary of the voyage. "You, there!" Lavon yelled. "Put out the scoop! Take some samples of those serpents!"

"Serpents, captain? What serpents you mean?"

"There! There! Can't you see?"

The Skandars glanced at the water, and then, with a certain patronizing solemnity, up at Sinnabor Lavon. "You mean that grass in the water?"

Lavon took a closer look. Grass? Already the ship was beyond the first patches, but there was more ahead, larger masses of it, and he squinted, trying to pick individual strands out of the tangled drifts. The stuff moved, as serpents might move. But yet Lavon saw no heads, no eyes. Well, possibly grass, then. He gestured impatiently and the Skandars, in no hurry, began to extend the jointed boom-mounted scoop with which biological specimens were collected.

By the time Lavon reached the lower deck a dripping little mound of the grass was spread on the boards and half a dozen staffers had gathered about it: First Mate Vormecht, Chief Navigator Galimoin, Joachil Noor and a couple of her scientists, and Mikdal Hasz, the chronicler. There was a sharp ammoniac smell in the air. The three Skandars stood back, ostentatiously holding their noses and muttering, but the others, pointing, laughing, poking at the grass, appeared more excited and animated than they had seemed for weeks.

Lavon knelt beside them. No doubt of it, the stuff was seaweed of some sort, each flat fleshy strand about as long as a man, about as wide as a forearm, about as thick as a finger. It twitched and jerked convulsively, as though on strings, but its motions grew perceptibly slower from moment to moment as it dried, and the brilliant colors were fading quickly.

"Scoop up some more," Joachil Noor told the Skandars. "And this time, dump it in a tub of sea-water to keep it alive."

The Skandars did not move. "The stench—such a filthy stench—" one of the hairy beings grunted.

Joachil Noor walked toward them—the short wiry woman looked like a child beside the gigantic creatures—and waved her hand brusquely. The Skandars, shrugging, lumbered to their task.

Sinnabor Lavon said to her, "What do you make of it?"

"Algae. Some unknown species, but everything's unknown this far out at sea. The color changes are interesting. I don't know whether they're caused by pigment fluctuations or simply result from optical tricks, the play of light over the shifting epidermal layers."

"And the movements? Algae don't have muscles."

"Plenty of plants are capable of motion. Minor oscillations of electrical current, causing variances in columns of fluid within the plant's structure—you know the sensitivos of northwestern Zimorel? You shout at them and they cringe. Sea-water's an excellent conductor; these algae must pick up all sorts of electrical impulses. We'll study them carefully." Joachil Noor smiled. "I tell you, they come as a gift from the Divine. Another week of empty sea and I'd have jumped overboard."

Lavon nodded. He had been feeling it too: that hideous killing boredom, that frightful choking feeling of having condemned himself to an endless journey to nowhere. Even he, who had given seven years of his life to organizing this expedition, who was willing to spend all the rest of it carrying it to completion, even he, in this fifth year of the voyage, paralyzed by listlessness, numb with apathy—

"Tonight," he said, "give us a report, eh? Preliminary findings. Unique new species of seaweed."

Joachil Noor signaled and the Skandars hoisted the tub of seaweed to their broad backs and carried it off toward the laboratory. The three biologists followed.

"There'll be plenty of it for them to study," said Vormecht. The first mate pointed. "Look, there! The sea ahead is thick with it!"

"Too thick, perhaps?" Mikdal Hasz said.

Sinnabor Lavon turned to the chronicler, a dry-voiced little man with pale eyes and one shoulder higher than the other. "What do you mean?"

"I mean fouled rotors, captain. If the seaweed gets much thicker. There are tales from Old Earth that I've read, of oceans where the weeds were impenetrable, where ships became hopelessly enmeshed, their crews living on crabs and fishes and eventually dying of thirst, and the vessels drifting on and on for hundreds of years with skeletons aboard—"

Chief Navigator Galimoin snorted. "Fantasy. Fable."

"And if it happens to us?" asked Mikdal Hasz.

Vormecht said, "How likely is that?"

Lavon realized they were all looking at him. He stared at the sea. Yes, the weeds did appear thicker; beyond the bow they gathered in bunched clumps, and their rhythmic writhings made the flat and listless surface of the water seem to throb and swell. But broad channels lay between each clump.

Was it possible that these weeds could engulf so capable a ship as the *Spurifon?* There was silence on the deck. It was almost comic: the dread menace of the seaweed, the tense officers divided and contentious, the captain required to make the decision that might mean life or death—

The true menace, Lavon thought, is not seaweed but boredom. For months the journey had been so uneventful that the days had become voids that had to be filled with the most desperate entertainments. Each dawn the swollen bronze-green sun of the tropics rose out of Zimroel, by noon it blazed overhead out of a cloudless sky, in the afternoon it plunged toward the inconceivably distant horizon, and the next day it was the same. There had been no rain for weeks, no changes of any kind in the weather. The Great Sea filled all the universe. They saw no land, not even a scrap of island this far out, no birds, no creatures of the water. In such an existence an unknown species of seaweed became a delicious novelty. A ferocious restlessness was consuming the spirits of the voyagers, these dedicated and committed explorers who once had shared Lavon's vision of an epic quest and who now were gimly and miserably enduring the torment of knowing that they had thrown away their lives in a moment of romantic folly. No one had expected it to be like this, when they had set out to make the first crossing in history of the Great Sea that occupied nearly half of their giant planet. They had imagined daily adventure, new beasts of fantastic nature, unknown islands, heroic storms, a sky riven by lightning and daubed with clouds of fifty unfamiliar hues. But not this, this grinding sameness, this unvarying repetition of days. Lavon had already begun to calculate the risks of mutiny, for it might be seven or nine or eleven more years before they made landfall on the shores of far-off Alhanroel, and he doubted that there were many on board who had the heart to see it through to the end. There must be dozens who had begun to dream dreams of turning the ship around and heading back to Zimroel; there were times when he dreamed of it himself. Therefore let us seek risks, he thought, and if need be let us manufacture them out of fantasy. Therefore let us brave the peril, real or imagined, of the seaweed. The possibility of danger will awaken us from our deadly lethargy.

"We can cope with seaweed," Lavon said. "Let's move onward."

Within an hour he was beginning to have doubts. From his

pacing-place on the bridge he stared warily at the ever-thickening seaweed. It was forming little islands now, fifty or a hundred yards across, and the channels between were narrower. All the surface of the sea was in motion, quivering, trembling. Under the searing rays of an almost vertical sun the seaweed grew richer in color, sliding in a manic way from tone to tone as if pumped higher by the inrush of solar energy. He saw creatures moving about in the tight-packed strands: enormous crablike things, many-legged, spherical, with knobby green shells, and sinuous serpentine animals something like squid, harvesting other life-forms too small for Lavon to see.

Vormecht said nervously, "Perhaps a change of course—"

"Perhaps," Lavon said. "I'll send a lookout up to tell us how far this mess extends."

Changing course, even by a few degrees, held no appeal for him. His course was set; his mind was fixed; he feared that any deviation would shatter his increasingly frail resolve. And yet he was no monomaniac, pressing ahead without regard to risk. It was only that he saw how easy it would be for the people of the *Spurifon* to lose what was left of their dedication to the immense enterprise on which they had embarked.

This was a golden age for Majipoor, a time of heroic figures and mighty deeds. Explorers were going everywhere, into the desert barrens of Suvrael and the forests and marshes of Zimroel and the virgin outlands of Alhanroel, and into the archipelagoes and island clusters that bordered the three continents. The population was expanding rapidly, towns were turning into cities and cities into improbably great metropolises, non-human settlers were pouring in from the neighboring worlds to seek their fortunes, everything was excitement, change, growth. And Sinnabor Lavon had chosen for himself the craziest feat of all, to cross the Great Sea by ship. No one had ever attempted that. From space one could see that the giant planet was half water, that the continents, huge though they were, were cramped together in a single hemisphere and all the other face of the world was a blankness of ocean. And though it was some thousands of years since the human colonization of Majipoor had begun, there had been work aplenty to do on land, and the Great Sea had been left to itself and to the armadas of sea-dragons that untiringly crossed it from west to east in migrations lasting decades.

But Lavon was in love with Majipoor and yearned to embrace it all. He had traversed it from Amblemorn at the foot of Castle Mount to Til-omon on the other shore of the Great Sea; and now, driven by the need to close the circle, he had poured all his resources and energies into outfitting this awesome vessel, as self-contained and self-sufficient as an island, aboard which he and a crew as crazy as himself intended to spend a decade or more exploring that unknown ocean. He knew, and probably they knew too, that they had sent themselves off on what might be an impossible task. But if they succeeded, and brought their argosy safely into harbor on Alhanroel's eastern coast where no ocean-faring ship had ever landed, their names would live forever.

"Hoy!" cried the lookout suddenly. "Dragons ho! Hoy! Hoy!"

"Weeks of boredom," Vormecht muttered, "and then everything at once!"

Lavon saw the lookout, dark against the dazzling sky, pointing rigidly north-northwest. He shaded his eyes and followed the outstretched arm. Yes! Great humped shapes, gliding serenely toward them, flukes high, wings held close to their bodies or in a few cases magnificently outspread—

"Dragons!" Galimoin called. "Dragons, look!" shouted a dozen other voices at once.

The Spurifon had encountered two herds of sea-dragons earlier in the voyage: six months out, among the islands that they had named the Stiamot Archipelago, and then two years after that, in the part of the ocean that they had dubbed the Arioc Deep. Both times the herds had been large ones, hundreds of the huge creatures, with many pregnant cows, and they had stayed far away from the Spurifon. But these appeared to be only the outliers of their herd, no more than fifteen or twenty of them, a handful of giant males and the others adolescents hardly forty feet in length. The writhing seaweed now looked inconsequential as the dragons neared. Everyone seemed to be on deck at once, almost dancing with excitement.

Lavon gripped the rail tightly. He had wanted risk for the sake of diversion: well, here was risk. An angry adult sea-dragon could cripple a ship, even one so well defended as the Spurifon, with a few mighty blows. Only rarely did they attack vessels that had not attacked them first, but it had been known to happen. Did these creatures imagine that the *Spuri-fon* was a dragon-hunting ship? Each year a new herd of sea-dragons passed through the waters between Piliplok and the Isle of Sleep, where hunting them was permitted, and fleets of dragon-ships greatly thinned their numbers then; these big ones, at least, must be survivors of that gamut, and who knew what resentments they harbored? The *Spurifon's* harpooners moved into readiness at a signal from Lavon.

But no attack came. The dragons seemed to regard the ship as a curiosity, nothing more. They had come here to feed. When they reached the first clumps of seaweed they opened their immense mouths and began to gulp the stuff down by the bale, sucking in along with it the squid-things and the crab-things and all the rest. For several hours they grazed noisily amid the seaweed; and then, as if by common agreement, they slipped below the surface and within minutes were gone.

A great ring of open sea now surrounded the *Spurifon*.

"They must have eaten tons of it," Lavon murmured. "Tons!"

"And now our way is clear," said Galimoin.

Vormecht shook his head. "No. See, captain? The dragon-grass, farther out. Thicker and thicker and thicker!"

Lavon stared into the distance. Wherever he looked there was a thin dark line along the horizon.

"Land," Galimoin suggested. "Islands—atolls—"

"On every side of us?" Vormecht said scornfully. "No, Galimoin. We've sailed into the middle of a continent of this dragon-grass stuff. The opening that the dragons ate for us is just a delusion. We're trapped!"

"It's only seaweed," Galimoin said. "If we have to, we'll cut our way through it."

Lavon eyed the horizon uneasily. He was beginning to share Vormecht's discomfort. A few hours ago the dragongrass had amounted to mere isolated strands, then scattered patches and clumps; but now, although the ship was for the moment in clear water, it did indeed look as if an unbroken ring of the seaweed had come to enclose them fore and aft. And yet could it possibly become thick enough to block their passage?

Twilight was descending. The warm heavy air grew pink, then quickly gray. Darkness rushed down upon the voyagers out of the eastern sky.

"We'll send out boats in the morning and see what there is to see," Lavon announced.

That evening after dinner Joachil Noor reported on the dragon-grass: a giant alga, she said, with an intricate bio-chemistry, well worth detailed investigation. She spoke at length about its complex system of color-nodes, its powerful contractile capacity. Everyone on board, even some who had been lost in fogs of hopeless depresion for weeks, crowded around to peer at the specimens in the tub, to touch them, to speculate and comment. Sinnabor Lavon rejoiced to see such liveliness aboard the *Spurifon* once again after these weeks of doldrums.

He dreamed that night that he was dancing on the water, performing a vigorous solo in some high-spirited ballet. The dragon-grass was firm and resilient beneath his flashing feet.

An hour before dawn he was awakened by urgent knock-ing at his cabin door. A Skandar was there—Skeen, standing third watch. "Come quickly—the dragon-grass, captain—"

The extent of the disaster was evident even by the faint pearly gleams of the new day. All night the *Spurifon* had been on the move and the dragon-grass had been on the move, and now the ship lay in the heart of a tight-woven fabric of seaweed that seemed to stretch to the ends of the universe. The landscape that presented itself as the first green streaks of morning tinted the sky was like something out of a dream: a single unbroken carpet of a trillion trillion knotted strands, its surface pulsing, twitching, throbbing, trembling, and its colors shifting everywhere through a restless spectrum of deep assertive tones. Here and there in this infinitely entangled webwork its inhabitants could be seen variously scuttling, creeping, slithering, crawling, clambering, and scampering. From the densely entwined masses of seaweed rose an odor so piercing it seemed to go straight past the nos-trils to the back of the skull. No clear water was in sight. The *Spurifon* was becalmed, stalled, as motionless as if in the night she had sailed a thousand miles overland into the heart of the Suvrael desert.

Lavon looked toward Vormecht—the first mate, so queru-lous and edgy all yesterday, now bore a calm look of vindication—and toward Chief Navigator Galimoin, whose boisterous confidence had given way to a tense and volatile frame of mind, obvious from his fixed, rigid stare and the grim clamping of his lips.

"I've shut the engines down," Vormecht said. "We were sucking in dragon-grass by the barrel. The rotors were completely clogged almost at once."

"Can they be cleared?" Lavon asked.

"We're clearing them," said Vormecht. "But the moment we start up again, we'll be eating seaweed through every intake."

Scowling, Lavon looked to Galimoin and said, "Have you been able to measure the area of the seaweed mass?"

"We can't see beyond it, captain."

"And have you sounded its depth?"

"It's like a lawn. We can't push our plumbs through it."

Lavon let his breath out slowly. "Get boats out right away. We need to survey what we're up against. Vormecht, send two divers down to find out how deep the seaweed goes, and whether there's some way we can screen our intakes against it. And ask Joachil Noor to come up here."

The little biologist appeared promptly, looking weary but perversely cheerful. Before Lavon could speak she said, "I've been up all night studying the algae. They're metal-fixers, with a heavy concentration of rhenium and vanadium in their—"

"Have you noticed that we're stopped?"

She seemed indifferent to that. "So I see."

"We find ourselves living out an ancient fable, in which ships are caught by impenetrable weeds and become derelicts. We may be here a long while."

"It will give us a chance to study this unique ecological province, captain."

"The rest of our lives, perhaps."

"Do you think so?" asked Joachil Noor, startled at last.

"I have no idea. But I want you to shift the aim of your studies, for the time being. Find out what kills these weeds, aside from exposure to the air. We may have to wage biological warfare against them if we're ever going to get out of here. I want some chemical, some method, some scheme, that'll clear them away from our rotors."

"Trap a pair of sea-dragons," Joachil Noor said at once, "and chain one to each side of the bow, and let them eat us free."

Sinnabor Lavon did not smile. "Think about it more seriously," he said, "and report to me later."

He watched as two boats were lowered, each bearing a

crew of four. Lavon hoped that the outboard motors would
be able to keep clear of the dragon-grass, but there was no
chance of that: almost immediately the blades were snarled,
and it became necessary for the boatmen to unship the oars
and beat a slow, grueling course through the weeds, while
pausing occasionally to drive off with clubs the fearless giant
crustaceans that wandered over the face of the choked sea. In
fifteen minutes the boats were no more than a hundred yards
from the ship. Meanwhile a pair of divers clad in breathing-
masks had gone down, one Hjort, one human, hacking open-
ings in the dragon-grass alongside the ship and vanishing into
the clotted depths. When they failed to return after half an
hour Lavon said to the first mate, "Vormecht, how long can
men stay underwater wearing those masks?"

"About this long, captain. Perhaps a little longer for a
Hjort, but not much."

"So I thought."

"We can hardly send more divers after them, can we?"

"Hardly," said Lavon bleakly. "Do you imagine the submersible would be able to penetrate the weeds?"

"Probably not."

"I doubt it too. But we'll have to try it. Call for volunteers."

The *Spurifon* carried a small underwater vessel that it employed in its scientific research. It had not been used in
months, and by the time it could be readied for descent more
than an hour had passed; the fate of the two divers was certain; and Lavon felt the awareness of their deaths settling
about his spirit like a skin of cold metal. He had never
known anyone to die except from extreme old age, and the
strangeness of accidental mortality was a hard thing for him
to comprehend, nearly as hard as the knowledge that he was
responsible for what had happened.

Three volunteers climbed into the submersible and it was
winched overside. It rested a moment on the surface of the
water; then its operators thrust out the retractible claws with
which it was equipped, and like some fat glossy crab it began
to dig its way under. It was a slow business, for the dragon-
grass clung close to it, reweaving its sundered web almost as
fast as the claws could rip it apart. But gradually the little
vessel slipped from sight.

Galimoin was shouting something over a bullhorn from another deck. Lavon looked up and saw the two boats he had

sent out, struggling through the weeds perhaps half a mile away. By now it was mid-morning and in the glare it was hard to tell which way they were headed, but it seemed they were returning.

Alone and silent Lavon waited on the bridge. No one dared approach him. He stared down at the floating carpet of dragon-grass, heaving here and there with strange and terrible life-forms, and thought of the two drowned men and the others in the submersible and the ones in the boats, and of those still safe aboard the *Spurifon,* all enmeshed in the same grotesque plight. How easy it would have been to avoid this, he thought; and how easy to think such thoughts. And how futile.

He held his post, motionless, well past noon, in the silence and the haze and the heat and the stench. Then he went to his cabin. Later in the day Vormecht came to him with the news that the crew of the submersible had found the divers hanging near the stilled rotors, shrouded in tight windings of dragon-grass, as though the weeds had deliberately set upon and engulfed them. Lavon was skeptical of that; they must merely have become tangled in it, he insisted, but without conviction. The submersible itself had had a hard time of it and had nearly burned out its engines in the effort to sink fifty feet. The weeds, Vormecht said, formed a virtually solid layer for a dozen feet below the surface. "What about the boats?" Lavon asked, and the first mate told him that they had returned safely, their crews exhausted by the work of rowing through the knotted weeds. In the entire morning they had managed to get no more than a mile from the ship, and they had seen no end to the dragon-grass, not even an opening in its unbroken weave. One of the boatmen had been attacked by a crab-creature on the way back, but had escaped with only minor cuts.

During the day there was no change in the situation. No change seemed possible. The dragon-grass had seized the *Spurifon* and there was no reason for it to release the ship, unless the voyagers compelled it to, which Lavon did not at present see how to accomplish.

He asked the chronicler Mikdal Hasz to go among the people of the *Spurifon* and ascertain their mood. "Mainly calm," Hasz reported. "Some are troubled. Most find our predicament strangely refreshing: a challenge, a deviation from the monotony of recent months."

"And you?"

"I have no fears, captain. But I want to believe we will find a way out. And I respond to the beauty of this weird landscape with unexpected pleasure."

Beauty? Lavon had not thought to see beauty in it. Darkly he stared at the miles of dragon-grass, bronze-red under the bloody sunset sky. A red mist was rising from the water, and in that thick vapor the creatures of the algae were moving about in great numbers, so that the enormous raftlike weed-structures were constantly in tremor. Beauty? A sort of beauty indeed, Lavon conceded. He felt as if the *Spurifon* had become stranded in the midst of some painting, a vast scroll of soft fluid shapes, depicting a dreamlike disorienting world without landmarks, on whose liquid surface there was unending change of pattern and color. So long as he could keep himself from regarding the dragon-grass as the enemy and destroyer of all he had worked to achieve, he could to some degree admire the shifting glints and forms all about him.

He lay awake much of the night searching without success for a tactic to use against this vegetable adversary.

Morning brought new colors in the weed, pale greens and streaky yellows under a discouraging sky burdened with thin clouds. Five or six colossal sea-dragons were visible a long way off, slowly eating a path for themselves through the water. How convenient it would be, Lavon reflected, if the *Spurifon* could do as much!

He met with his officers. They too had noticed last night's mood of general tranquillity, even fascination. But they detected tensions beginning to rise this morning. "They were already frustrated and homesick," said Vormecht, "and now they see a new delay here of days or even weeks."

"Or months or years or forever," snapped Galimoin. "What makes you think we'll ever get out?"

The navigator's voice was ragged with strain and cords stood out along the sides of his thick neck. Lavon had long ago sensed an instability somewhere within Galimoin, but even so he was not prepared for the swiftness with which Galimoin had been undone by the onset of the dragon-grass.

Vormecht seemed amazed by it also. The first mate said in surprise, "You told us yourself the day before yesterday, 'It's only seaweed. We'll cut our way through it.' Remember?"

"I didn't know then what we were up against," Galimoin growled.

Lavon looked toward Joachil Noor. "What about the possibility that this stuff is migratory, that the whole formation will sooner or later break up and let us go?"

The biologist shook her head. "It could happen. But I see no reason to count on it. More likely this is a quasi-permanent ecosystem. Currents might carry it to other parts of the Great Sea, but in that case they'd carry us right along with it."

"You see?" Galimoin said glumly. "Hopeless!"

"Not yet," said Lavon. "Vormecht, what can we do about using the submersible to mount screens over the intakes?"

"Possibly. Possibly."

"Try it. Get the fabricators going on some sort of screens right away. Joachil Noor, what are your thoughts on a chemical counterattack against the seaweed?"

"We're running tests," she said. "I can't promise anything."

No one could promise anything. They could only think and work and wait and hope.

Designing screens for the intakes took a couple of days; building them took five more. Meanwhile Joachil Noor experimented with methods of killing the grass around the ship, without apparent result.

In those days not only the *Spurifon* but time itself seemed to stand still. Daily Lavon took his sightings and made his log entries; the ship was actually traveling a few miles a day, moving steadily south-southwest, but it was going nowhere in relation to the entire mass of algae: to provide a reference point they marked the dragon-grass around the ship with dyes, and there was no movement in the great yellow and scarlet stains as the days went by. And in this ocean they could drift forever with the currents and not come within reach of land.

Lavon felt himself fraying. He had difficulty maintaining his usual upright posture; his shoulders now were beginning to curve, his head felt like a dead weight. He felt older; he felt old. Guilt was eroding him. On him was the responsibility for having failed to pull away from the dragon-grass zone the moment the danger was apparent; only a few hours would have made the difference, he told himself, but he had let himself be diverted by the spectacle of the sea-dragons and by his idiotic theory that a bit of peril would add spice to what had become a lethally bland voyage. For that he assailed himself mercilessly, and it was not far from there to blaming himself for having led these unwitting people into this entire absurd and futile journey. A voyage lasting ten or fifteen years, from nowhere to nowhere? Why? Why?

Yet he worked at maintaining morale among the others. The ration of wine—limited, for the ship's cellars had to last out the voyage—was doubled. There were nightly entertainments. Lavon ordered every research group to bring its oceanographic studies up to date, thinking that this was no moment for idleness on anyone's part. Papers that should have been written months or even years before, but which had been put aside in the long slow progress of the cruise, now were to be completed at once. Work was the best medicine for boredom, frustration, and—a new and growing factor—fear.

When the first screens were ready, a volunteer crew went down in the submersible to attempt to weld them to the hull over the intakes. The job, a tricky one at best, was made more complicated by the need to do it entirely with the little vessel's extensor claws. After the loss of the two divers Lavon would not risk letting anyone enter the water except in the submersible. Under the direction of a skilled mechanic named Duroin Klays the work proceeded day after day, but it was a thankless business. The heavy masses of dragon-grass, nudging the hull with every swell of the sea, frequently ripped the fragile mountings loose, and the welders made little progress.

On the sixth day of the work Duroin Klays came to Lavon with a sheaf of glossy photographs. They showed patterns of orange splotches against a dull gray background.

"What is this?" Lavon asked.

"Hull corrosion, sir. I noticed it yesterday and took a series of underwater shots this morning."

"Hull corrosion?" Lavon forced a smile. "That's hardly possible. The hull's completely resistant. What you're showing me here must be barnacles or sponges of some sort, or—"

"No, sir. Perhaps it's not clear from the pictures," said Duroin Klays. "But you can tell very easily when you're down in the submersible. It's like little scars, eaten into the metal. I'm quite sure of it, sir."

Lavon dismissed the mechanic and sent for Joachil Noor. She studied the photographs a long while and said finally, "It's altogether likely."

"That the dragon-grass is eating into the hull?"

"We've suspected the possibility of it for a few days. One

of our first findings was a sharp pH gradient between this part of the ocean and the open sea. We're sitting in an acid bath, captain, and I'm sure it's the algae that are secreting the acids. And we know that they're metal-fixers whose tissues are loaded with heavy elements. Normally they pull their metals from sea-water, of course. But they must regard the *Spurifon* as a gigantic banquet table. I wouldn't be surprised to find that the reason the dragon-grass became so thick so suddenly in our vicinity is that the algae have been flocking from miles around to get in on the feast."

"If that's the case, then it's foolish to expect the algae jam to break up of its own accord."

"Indeed."

Lavon blinked. "And if we remain locked in it long enough, the dragon-grass will eat holes right through us?"

The biologist laughed and said, "That might take hundreds of years. Starvation's a more immediate problem."

"How so?"

"How long can we last eating nothing but what's currently in storage on board?"

"A few months, I suppose. You know we depend on what we can catch as we go along. Are you saying—"

"Yes, captain. Everything in the ecosystem around us right now is probably poisonous to us. The algae absorb oceanic metals. The small crustaceans and fishes eat the algae. The bigger creatures eat the smaller ones. The concentration of metallic salts gets stronger and stronger as we go up the chain. And we—"

"Won't thrive on a diet of rhenium and vanadium."

"And molybdenum and rhodium. No, captain. Have you seen the latest medical reports? An epidemic of nausea, fever, some circulatory problems—how have *you* been feeling, captain? And it's only the beginning. None of us yet has a serious buildup. But in another week, two weeks, three—"

"May the Lady protect us!" Lavon gasped.

"The Lady's blessings don't reach this far west," said Joachil Noor. She smiled coolly. "I recommend that we discontinue all fishing at once and draw on our stores until we're out of this part of the sea. And that we finish the job of screening the rotors as fast as possible."

"Agreed," said Lavon.

When she had left him he stepped to the bridge and looked

gloomily out over the congested, quivering water. The colors today were richer than ever, heavy umbers, sepias, russets, indigos. The dragon-grass was thriving. Lavon imagined the fleshy strands slapping up against the hull, searing the gleaming metal with acid secretions, burning it away molecule by molecule, converting the ship to ion soup and greedily drinking it. He shivered. He could no longer see beauty in the intricate textures of the seaweed. That dense and tightly interwoven mass of algae stretching toward the horizon now meant only stink and decay to him, danger and death, the bubbling gases of rot and the secret teeth of destruction. Hour by hour the flanks of the great ship grew thinner, and here she still sat, immobilized, helpless, in the midst of the foe that consumed her.

Lavon tried to keep these new perils from becoming general knowledge. That was impossible, of course: there could be no secrets for long in a closed universe like the *Spurifon*. His insistence on secrecy did at least serve to minimize open discussion of the problems, which could lead so swiftly to panic. Everyone knew, but everyone pretended that he alone realized how bad things were.

Nevertheless the pressure mounted. Tempers were short; conversations were strained; hands shook, words were slurred, things were dropped. Lavon remained apart from the others as much as his duties would allow. He prayed for deliverance and sought guidance in dreams, but Joachil Noor seemed to be right: the voyagers were beyond the reach of the loving Lady of the Isle whose counsel brought comfort to the suffering and wisdom to the troubled.

The only new glimmer of hope came from the biologists. Joachil Noor suggested that it might be possible to disrupt the electrical system of the dragon-grass by conducting a current through the water. It sounded doubtful to Lavon, but he authorized her to put some of the ship's technicians to work on it.

And finally the last of the intake screens was in place. It was late in the third week of their captivity.

"Start the rotors," Lavon ordered.

The ship throbbed with renewed life as the rotors began to move. On the bridge the officers stood frozen: Lavon, Vormecht, Galimoin, silent, still, barely breathing. Tiny wavelets formed along the bow. The *Spurifon* was beginning to move!

Slowly, stubbornly, the ship began to cut a path through the close-packed masses of writhing dragon-grass—

—and shuddered, and bucked, and fought, and the throb of the rotors ceased—

"The screens aren't holding!" Galimoin cried in anguish.

"Find out what's happening," Lavon told Vormecht. He turned to Galimoin, who was standing as though his feet had been nailed to the deck, trembling, sweating, muscles rippling weirdly about his lips and cheeks. Lavon said gently, "It's probably only a minor hitch. Come, let's have some wine, and in a moment we'll be moving again."

"No!" Galimoin bellowed. "I felt the screens rip loose. The dragon-grass is eating them."

More urgently Lavon said, "The screens will hold. By this time tomorrow we'll be far from here, and you'll have us on course again for Alhanroel—"

"We're lost!" Galimoin shouted, and broke away suddenly, arms flailing as he ran down the steps and out of sight. Lavon hesitated. Vormecht returned, looking grim: the screens had indeed broken free, the rotors were fouled, the ship had halted again. Lavon swayed. He felt infected by Galimoin's despair. His life's dream was ending in failure, an absurd catastrophe, a mocking farce.

Joachil Noor appeared. "Captain, do you know that Galimoin's gone berserk? He's up on the observation deck, wailing and screaming and dancing and calling for a mutiny."

"I'll go to him," said Lavon.

"I felt the rotors start. But then—"

Lavon nodded. "Fouled again. The screens ripped loose." As he moved toward the catwalk he heard Joachil Noor say something about her electrical project, that she was ready to make her first full-scale test, and he replied that she should begin at once, and report to him as soon as there were any encouraging results. But her words were quickly out of his mind. The problem of Galimoin occupied him entirely.

The chief navigator had taken up a position on the high platform to starboard where once he had made his observations and calculations of latitudes and longitudes. Now he capered like a deranged beast, strutting back and forth, flinging out his arms, shouting incoherently, singing raucous snatches of balladry, denouncing Lavon as a fool who had deliberately led them into this trap. A dozen or so members of the crew were gathered below, listening, some jeering, some calling out their agreement, and others were arriving quickly: this was the sport of the moment, the day's divertissement. To Lavon's horror he saw Mikdal Hasz making his way out onto Galimoin's platform from the far side. Hasz was speaking in low tones, beckoning to the navigator, quietly urging him to come down; and several times Galimoin broke off his harangue to look toward Hasz and growl a threat at him. But Hasz kept advancing. Now he was just a yard or two from Galimoin, still speaking, smiling, holding out his open hands as if to show that he carried no weapons.

"Get away!" Galimoin roared. "Keep back!"

Lavon, edging toward the platform himself, signaled to Hasz to keep out of reach. Too late: in a single frenzied moment the infuriated Galimoin lunged at Hasz, scooped the little man up as if he were a doll, and hurled him over the railing into the sea. A cry of astonishment went up from the onlookers. Lavon rushed to the railing in time to see Hasz, limbs flailing, crash against the surface of the water. Instantly there was convulsive activity in the dragon-grass. Like maddened eels the fleshy strands swarmed and twisted and writhed; the sea seemed to boil for a moment; and then Hasz was lost to view.

A terrifying dizziness swept through Lavon. He felt as though his heart filled his entire chest, crushing his lungs, and his brain was spinning in his skull. He had never seen violence before. He had never heard of an instance in his lifetime of the deliberate slaying of one human by another. That it should have happened on his ship, by one of his officers upon another, in the midst of this crisis, was intolerable, a mortal wound. He moved forward like one who walks while dreaming and laid his hands on Galimoin's powerful, muscular shoulders and with a strength he had never had before he shoved the navigator over the rail, easily, unthinkingly. He heard a strangled wail, a splash; he looked down, amazed, appalled, and saw the sea boiling a second time as the dragon-grass closed over Galimoin's thrashing body.

Slowly, numbly, Lavon descended from the platform.

He felt dazed and flushed. Something seemed broken within him. A ring of blurred figures surrounded him. Gradually he discerned eyes, mouths, the patterns of familiar faces.

He started to say something, but no words would come, only
sounds. He toppled and was caught and eased to the desk.
Someone's arm was around his shoulders; someone was giving
him wine. "Look at his eyes," he heard a voice say. "He's
gone into shock!" Lavon began to shiver. Somehow—he was
unaware of being lifted—he found himself in his cabin, with
Vormecht bending over him and others standing behind.

The first mate said quietly, "The ship is moving, captain."

"What? What? Hasz is dead. Galimoin killed Hasz and I
killed Galimoin."

"It was the only possible thing to do. The man was insane."

"I *killed* him, Vormecht."

"We couldn't have kept a madman locked on board for the
next ten years. He was dangerous to us all. His life was for-
feit. You had the power. You acted rightly."

"We do not kill," Lavon said. "Our barbarian ancestors
took each other's lives, on Old Earth long ago, but we do not
kill. *I* do not kill. We were beasts once, but that was in another era, on a different planet. I killed him, Vormecht."

"You are the captain. You had the right. He threatened the
success of the voyage."

"Success? Success?"

"The ship is moving again, captain."

Lavon stared, but could barely see. "What are you saying?"

"Come. Look."

Four massive arms enfolded him and Lavin smelled the
musky tang of Skandar fur. The giant crewman lifted him
and carried him to the deck, and put him carefully down.
Lavon tottered, but Vormecht was at his side, and Joachil
Noor. The first mate pointed toward the sea. A zone of open
water bordered the *Spurifon* along the entire length of her
hull.

Joachil Noor said, "We dropped cables into the water and
gave the dragon-grass a good jolt of current. It shorted out
their contractile systems. The ones closest to us died instantly
and the rest began to pull back. There's a clear channel in
front of us as far as we can see."

"The voyage is saved," said Vormecht. "We can go onward
now, captain!"

"No," Lavon said. He felt the haze and confusion lifting
from his mind. "Who's navigator now? Have him turn the
ship back toward Zimroel."

"But—"

"Turn her around! Back to Zimroel!"

They were gaping at him, bewildered, stunned. "Captain, you're not yourself yet. To give such an order, in the very moment when all is well again—you need to rest, and in a few hours you'll feel—"

"The voyage is ended, Vormecht. We're going back."

"No!"

"No? Is this a mutiny, then?" Their eyes were blank. Their faces were expressionless. Lavon said, "Do you really want to continue? Aboard a doomed ship with a murderer for a captain? You were all sick of the voyage before any of this happened. Don't you think I knew that? You were hungry for home. You didn't dare say it, is all. Well, now I feel as you do."

Vormecht said, "We've been at sea five years. We may be halfway across. It might take us no longer to reach the farther shore than to return."

"Or it might take us forever," said Lavon. "It does not matter. I have no heart for going forward."

"Tomorrow you may think differently, captain."

"Tomorrow I will still have blood on my hands, Vormecht. I was not meant to bring this ship safely across the Great Sea. We bought our freedom at the cost of four lives; but the voyage was broken by it."

"Captain—"

"Turn the ship around," said Lavon.

When they came to him the next day, pleading to be allowed to continue the voyage, arguing that eternal fame and immortality awaited them on the shores of Alhanroel, Lavon calmly and quietly refused to discuss it with them. To continue now, he told them again, was impossible. So they looked at one another, those who had hated the voyage and yearned to be free of it and who in the euphoric moment of victory over the dragon-grass had changed their minds, and they changed their minds again, for without the driving force of Lavon's will there was no way of going on. They set their course to the east and said no more about the crossing of the Great Sea. A year afterward they were assailed by storms and severely thrown about, and in the following year there was a bad encounter with sea-dragons that severely damaged the ship's stern; but yet they continued, and of the hundred and sixty-three voyagers who had left Til-omon long before, more than a hundred were still alive, Captain Lavon among them, when the *Spurifon* came limping back into her home port in the eleventh year of the voyage.

FOUR

Calintane Explains

Hissune is downcast for days after that. He knows, of course, that the voyage failed: no ship has ever crossed the Great Sea, and no ship ever will, for the idea is absurd and realization of it is probably impossible. But to fail in such a way, to go so far and then turn back, not out of cowardice or because of illness or famine but rather from sheer moral despair—Hissune finds that hard to comprehend. He would never turn back. Through the fifteen years of his life he has always gone steadily forward toward whatever he perceived as his goal, and those who faltered along their own routes have always seemed to him idle and weak. But, then, he is not Sinnabor Lavon; and, too, he has never taken life. Such a deed of violence might shake anyone's soul. For Sinnabor Lavon he feels a certain contempt, and a great deal of pity, and then, the more he considers the man, seeing him from within, a kind of admiration replaces the contempt, for he realizes that Sinnabor Lavon was no weakling but in fact a person of enormous moral strength. That is a startling insight, and Hissune's depression lifts the moment he reaches it. My education, he thinks, continues.

All the same he has gone to Sinnabor Lavon's records in search of adventure and diversion, not such sober-minded philosophizing. He has not found quite what he sought. But a few years afterward, he knows, there was an event in this

82

*very Labyrinth that had diverted everyone most extremely,
and that even after more than six thousand years still rever-
berates through history as one of the strangest events
Majipoor has seen. When his duties permit, Hissune takes the
time to do a bit of historical research; and then he returns to
the Register of Souls to enter the mind of a certain young
official at the court of the Pontifex Arioc of bizarre repute.*

On the morning after the day when the crisis had reached its
climax and the final lunacies had occurred, a strange hush
settled over the Labyrinth of Majipoor, as if everyone were
too stunned even to speak. The impact of yesterday's extraordinary events was just beginning to be felt, although even
those who had witnessed what had taken place could not yet
fully believe it. All the ministries were closed that morning,
by order of the new Pontifex. The bureaucrats both major
and minor had been put to extreme strain by the recent
upheavals, and they were set at liberty to sleep it off, while
the new Pontifex and the new Coronal—each amazed by the
unanticipated attainment of kingship that had struck him
with thunderclap force—withdrew to their private chambers
to contemplate their astounding transformations. Which gave
Calintane at last an opportunity to see his beloved Silimoor.
Apprehensively—for he had treated her shabbily all month,
and she was not an easily forgiving sort—he sent her a note
that said, *I know I am guilty of shameful neglect, but perhaps now you begin to understand. Meet me for lunch at the
cafe by the Court of Globes ta midday and I will explain everything.*

She had a quick temper at the best of times. It was virtually her only fault, but it was a severe one, and Calintane
feared her wrath. They had been lovers a year; they were
nearly betrothed to be betrothed; all the senior officials at the
Pontifical court agreed he was making a wise match. Silimoor
was lovely and intelligent and knowledgeable in political matters, and of good family, with three Coronals in her ancestry,
including no less than the fabled Lord Stiamot himself.
Plainly she would be an ideal mate for a young man destined
for high places. Though still some distance short of thirty,
Calintane had already attained the outer rim of the inner
circle about the Pontifex, and had been given responsibilities
well beyond his years. Indeed, it was those very responsibili-

ties that had kept him from seeing or even speaking at any
length to Silimoor lately. For which he expected her to berate
him, and for which he hoped without much conviction that
she would eventually pardon him.

All this past sleepless night he had rehearsed in his weary
mind a long speech of extenuation that began, "As you know,
I've been preoccupied with urgent matters of state these last
weeks, too delicate to discuss in detail with you, and so—"
And as he made his way up the levels of the Labyrinth to the
Court of Globes for his rendezvous with her he continued to
roll the phrases about. The ghostly silence of the Labyrinth
this morning made him feel all the more edgy. The lowest
levels, where the government offices were, seemed wholly
deserted, and higher up just a few people could be seen,
gathering in little knotted groups in the darkest corners, whis-
pering and muttering as though there had been a coup d'etat,
which in a sense was not far wrong. Everyone stared at him.
Some pointed. Calintane wondered how they recognized him
as an official of the Pontificate, until he remembered that he
was still wearing his mask of office. He kept it on anyway, as
a kind of shield against the glaring artificial light, so harsh on
his aching eyes. Today the Labyrinth seemed stifling and oppressive. He longed to escape its somber subterranean depths,
those levels upon levels of great spiralling chambers that
coiled down and down. In a single night the place had become loathsome to him.

On the level of the Court of Globes he emerged from the
lift and cut diagonally across that intricate vastness, decorated with its thousands of mysteriously suspended spheres, to
the little cafe on the far side. The midday hour struck just as
he entered it. Silimoor was already there—he knew she would
be; she used punctuality to express displeasure—at a small
table along the rear wall of polished onyx. She rose and offered him not her lips but her hand, also as he expected. Her
smile was precise and cool. Exhausted as he was, he found
her beauty almost excessive: the short golden hair arrayed
like a crown, the flashing turquoise eyes, the full lips and high
cheekbones, an elegance too painful to bear, just now. "I've
missed you so," he said hoarsely.

"Of course. So long a separation—it must have been a
dreadful burden—"

"As you know, I've been preoccupied with urgent matters

of state these last weeks, too delicate to discuss in detail with
you, and so——"

The words sounded impossibly idiotic in his own ears. It
was a relief when she cut him off, saying smoothly, "There's
time for all that, love. Shall we have some wine?"

"Please. Yes."

She signaled. A liveried waiter, a haughty-looking Hjort,
came to take the order, and stalked away.

Silimoor said, "And won't you even remove your mask?"

"Ah. Sorry. It's been such a scrambled few days——"

He set aside the bright yellow strip that covered his nose
and eyes and marked him as the Pontifex's man. Silimoor's
expression changed as she saw him clearly for the first time;
the look of serenely self-satisfied fury faded and something
close to concern appeared on her face. "Your eyes are so
bloodshot—your cheeks are so pale and drawn——"

"I've had no sleep. It's been a crazy time."

"Poor Calintane."

"Do you think I kept away from you because I *wanted* to?
I've been caught up in this insanity, Silimoor."

"I know. I can see how much of a strain it's been."

He realized suddenly that she was not mocking him, that
she was genuinely sympathetic, that in fact this was possibly
going to be easier than he had been imagining.

He said, "The trouble with being ambitious is that you get
engulfed in affairs far beyond your control, and you have no
choice but to let yourself be swept along. You've heard what
the Pontifex Arioc did yesterday?"

She stifled a laugh. "Yes, of course. I mean, I've heard the
rumors. Everyone has. Are they true? Did it really happen?"

"Unfortunately, it did."

"How marvelous, how perfectly marvelous! But such a
thing turns the world upside down, doesn't it? It affects you
in some dreadful way?"

"It affects you, and me, and everyone in the world," said
Calintane, with a gesture that reached beyond the Court of
Globes, beyond the Labyrinth itself, encompassing the entire
planet beyond these claustrophobic depths, from the awesome
summit of Castle Mount to the far-off cities of the western
continent. "Affects us all to a degree that I hardly understand
yet myself. But let me tell you the story from the beginning——"

Perhaps you were not aware that the Pontifex Arioc has been behaving strangely for months. I suppose there's something about the pressures of high office that eventually drives people crazy, or perhaps you have to be at least partly mad in the first place to aspire to high office. But you know that Arioc was Coronal for thirteen years under Dizimaule, and now he's been Pontifex a dozen years more, and that's a long time to hold that sort of power. Especially living here in the Labyrinth. The Pontifex must yearn for the outside world now and then, I'd imagine—to feel the breezes on Castle Mount or hunt gihornas in Zimroel or just to swim in a real river anywhere—and here he is miles and miles underground in this maze, presiding over his rituals and his bureaucrats until the end of his life.

One day about a year ago Arioc suddenly began talking about making a grand processional of Majipoor. I was in attendance at court that day, along with Duke Guadeloom. The Pontifex called for maps and started laying out a journey down the river to Alaisor, over to the Isle of Sleep for a pilgrimage and a visit to the Lady at Inner Temple, then across to Zimroel, with stops at Piliplok, Ni-moya, Pidruid, Narabal, you know, *everywhere*, a tour that would last at least five years. Guadeloom gave me a funny look and gently pointed out to Arioc that it's the Coronal who makes grand processionals, not the Pontifex, and that Lord Struin had only just come back from one a couple of years ago.

"Then I am forbidden to do so?" the Pontifex asked.

"Not precisely forbidden, your majesty, but custom dictates—"

"That I remain a prisoner in the Labyrinth?"

"Not at all a prisoner, your majesty, but—"

"But I am rarely if ever to venture into the upper world?"

And so on. I must say my sympathies were with Arioc; but remember that I am not, like you, a native of the Labyrinth, only one whose government duties have brought him here, and I do find life underground a little unnatural at times. At any rate Guadeloom did convince his majesty that a grand processional was out of the question. But I could see the restlessness in the Pontifex's eyes.

The next thing that happened was that his majesty started slipping out by night to wander around the Labyrinth by himself. No one knows how often he did it before we found

out what was going on, but we began to hear odd rumors
that a masked figure who looked much like the Pontifex had
been seen in the small hours lurking about in the Court of
Pyramids or the Hall of Winds. We regarded that as so much
nonsense, until the night when some flunky of the bedchamber imagined he had heard the Pontifex ring for service and
went in and found the room empty. I think you will remember that night, Silimoor, because I was spending it with you
and one of Guadeloom's people hunted me down and made
me leave, claiming that an urgent meeting of the high advisers had been convened and my services were needed. You
were quite upset—furious, I'd say. Of course what the meeting was about was the disappearance of the Pontifex, though
later we covered it up by claiming it was a discussion of the
great wave that had devastated so much of Stoienzar.

We found Arioc about four hours past midnight. He was
in the Arena—you know, that stupid empty thing that the
Pontifex Dizimaule built in one of *his* crazier moments—sitting crosslegged at the far side, playing a zootibar and singing
songs to an audience of five or six ragged little boys. We
brought him home. A few weeks later he got out again and
managed to get as far up as the Court of Columns. Guadeloom
discussed it with him: Arioc insisted that it is important for a
monarch to go among his people and hear their grievances,
and he cited precedents as far back as the kings of Old Earth.
Quietly Guadeloom began posting guards in the royal precincts, supposedly to keep assassins out—but who would assassinate a Pontifex? The guards were put there to keep
Arioc in. But though the Pontifex is eccentric he's far from
stupid, and despite the guards he slipped out twice more in
the next couple of months. It was becoming a critical problem. What if he vanished for a week? What if he got out of
the Labyrinth entirely, and went for a stroll in the desert?

"Since we can't seem to prevent him from roaming," I said
to Guadeloom, "why don't we give him a companion, someone who'll go on his adventures with him and at the same
time see to it that no harm comes to him?"

"An excellent idea," the duke replied. "And I appoint you
to the post. The Pontifex is fond of you, Calintane. And you
are young enough and agile enough to be able to extricate
him from any trouble into which he may stumble."

That was six weeks ago, Silimoor. You will surely recall

that I suddenly ceased spending my nights with you at that time, pleading an increase of responsibilities at court, and thus our estrangement began. I could not tell you what duty it was that now occupied my nights, and I could only hope you did not suspect me of having shifted my affections to another. But I can now reveal that I was compelled to take up lodgings close by the bedchamber of the Pontifex and give him attendance every night; that I began to do most of my sleeping at random hours of the day; and that by one strata-gem and another I became companion to Arioc on his noc-turnal jaunts.

It was taxing work. I was in truth the Pontifex's keeper, and we both knew it, but I had to take care not to underscore the fact by unduly imposing my will on him. And yet I had to guard him from rough playmates and risky excursions. There are rogues, there are brawlers, there are hotheads; no one would knowingly harm the Pontifex but he might easily come by accident between two who meant to harm each other. In my rare moments of sleep I sought the guidance of the Lady of the Isle—may she rest in the bosom of the Divine—and she came to me in a blessed sending, and told me that I must make myself the Pontifex's friend if I meant not to be his jailer. How fortunate we are to have the counsel of so kind a mother in our dreams! And so I dared to initiate more than a few of Arioc's adventures myself. "Come, let us go out tonight," I said to him, which would have frozen Guadeloom's blood, had he known. It was my idea to take the Pontifex up into the public levels of the Labyrinth for a night of taverns and marketplaces—masked, of course, be-yond chance of recognition. I led him into mysterious alley-ways where gamblers lived, but gamblers known to me, who posed no threats. And it was I who on the boldest night of all actually guided him beyond the walls of the Labyrinth itself. I knew it was what he most desired, and even he feared to at-tempt it, so I proposed it to him as my secret gift, and he and I took the private royal passageway upward that emerges at the Mouth of Waters. We stood together so close to the River Glayge that we could feel the cool air that blows down from Castle Mount, and we looked up at the blazing stars. "I have not been out here in six years," said the Pontifex. He was trembling and I think he was weeping behind his mask; and I, who had not seen the stars either for much too long, was nearly as deeply moved. He pointed to this one and that, saying it was the star of the world from which the Ghayrog folk came, and this the star of the Hjorts, and that one there, that trifling dot of light, was none other than the sun of Old Earth. Which I doubted, since I had been taught otherwise in school, but he was in such joy that I could not contradict him then. And he turned to me and gripped my arm and said in a low voice, "Calintane, I am the supreme ruler of this whole colossal world, and I am nothing at all, a slave, a prisoner. I would give everything to escape this Labyrinth and spend my last years in freedom under the stars."

"Then why not abdicate?" I suggested, astounded at my audacity.

He smiled. "It would be cowardice. I am the elect of the Divine, and how can I reject that burden? I am destined to be a Power of Majipoor to the end of my days. But there must be some honorable way to free myself from this subterranean misery."

And I saw that the Pontifex was neither mad nor wicked nor capricious, but only lonely for the night and the mountains and the moons and the trees and the streams of the world he had been forced to abandon so that the government might be laid upon him.

Next came word, two weeks ago, that the Lady of the Isle, Lord Struin's mother and the mother of us all, had fallen ill and was not likely to recover. This was an unusual crisis that created major constitutional problems, for of course the Lady is a Power of rank equal to Pontifex and Coronal, and replacing her should hardly be done casually. Lord Struin himself was reported to be on his way from Castle Mount to confer with the Pontifex—foregoing a journey to the Isle of Sleep, for he could not possibly reach it in time to bid his mother farewell. Meanwhile Duke Guadeloom, as high spokesman of the Pontificate and chief officer of the court, had begun to compile a list of candidates for the post, which would be compared with Lord Struin's list to see if any names were on both. The counsel of the Pontifex Arioc was necessary in all of this, and we thought that would be beneficial to him in his present unsettled state by involving him more deeply in imperial matters. In at least a technical sense the dying Lady was his wife, for under the formalities of our succession law he had adopted Lord Struin as his son when choosing him to be Coronal; of course the Lady had a lawful husband of her

own somewhere on Castle Mount, but you understand the le-
galities of the custom, do you not? Guadeloom informed the
Pontifex of the impending death of the Lady and a round of
governmental conferences began. I did not take part in these,
since I am not of that level of authority or responsibility.

I am afraid we assumed that the gravity of the situation
might cause Arioc to become less erratic in his behavior,
and at least unconsciously we must have relaxed our vigi-
lance. On the very night that the news of the death of the
Lady reached the Labyrinth, the Pontifex slipped away alone
for the first time since I had been assigned to keep watch
over him. Past the guards, past me, past his servants—out
into the interminable intricate complexities of the Labyrinth,
and no one could find him. We searched all night and half
the next day. I was beside myself with terror, both for him
and for my career. In the greatest of apprehension I sent officers out each of the seven mouths of the Labyrinth to
search that bleak and torrid desert outside; I myself visited all
the rakish haunts to which I had introduced him; Guadeloom's staff prowled in places unknown to me; and through-
out all this we sought to keep the populace from knowing
that the Pontifex was missing. I think we must have
succeeded in that.

We found him in mid-afternoon of the day after his disappearance. He was in a house in the district known as Stiamot's Teeth in the first ring of the Labyrinth and he was
disguised in women's clothes. We might never have found him
at all but for some quarrel over an unpaid bill, which brought
proctors to the scene, and when the Pontifex was unable to
identify himself satisfactorily and a man's voice was heard
coming from a supposed woman the proctors had the sense to
summon me, and I hurried to take custody of him. He looked
appallingly strange in his robes and his bangles, but he
greeted me calmly by name, acting perfectly composed and
rational, and said he hoped he had not caused me great inconvenience.

I expected Guadeloom to demote me. But the duke was in a
forgiving mood, or else he was too bound up in the larger crisis to care about my lapse, for he said nothing whatever about
the fact that I had let the Pontifex get out of his bedchamber.
"Lord Struin arrived this morning," Guadeloom told me,
looking harried and weary. "Naturally he wanted to meet

with the Pontifex at once, but we told him that Arioc was asleep and it was unwise to disturb him—this while half my people were out searching for him. It pains me to lie to the Coronal, Calintane."

"The Pontifex is genuinely asleep in his chambers now," I said.

"Yes. Yes. And there he will stay, I think."

"I will make every effort to see to that."

"That's not what I mean," said Guadeloom. "The Pontifex Arioc is plainly out of his mind. Crawling through laundry chutes, creeping around the city at night, decking himself out in female finery—it goes beyond mere eccentricity, Calintane. Once we have this business of the new Lady out of the way, I'm going to propose that we confine him permanently to his quarters under strong guard—for his own protection, Calintane, his own protection—and hand the Pontifical duties over to a regency. There's precedent for that. I've been through the records. When Barhold was Pontifex he fell ill of swamp fever and it affected his mind, and—"

"Sir," I said, "I don't believe the Pontifex is insane."

Guadeloom frowned. "How else could you characterize one who does what he's been doing?"

"They are the acts of a man who has been king too long, and whose soul rebels against all that he must continue to bear. But I have come to know him well, and I venture to say that what he expresses by these escapades is a torment of the soul, but not any kind of madness."

It was an eloquent speech and, if I have to say it myself, courageous, for I am a junior counsellor and Guadeloom was at that moment the third most powerful figure in the realm, behind only Arioc and Lord Struin. But there comes a time when one must put diplomacy and ambition and guile aside, and simply speak the plain truth; and the idea of confining the unhappy Pontifex like a common lunatic, when he already suffered great pain from his confinement in the Labyrinth alone, was horrifying to me. Guadeloom was silent a long while and I suppose I should have been frightened, speculating whether I would be dismissed altogether from his service or simply sent down to the record-keeping halls to spend the remainder of my life shuffling papers, but I was calm, totally calm, as I awaited his reply.

Then came a knock at the door: a messenger, bearing a note sealed with the great starburst that was the Coronal's

personal seal. Duke Guadeloom ripped it open and read the
message and read it again, and read it a third time, and I
have never seen such a look of incredulity and horror pass
over a human face as crossed his then. His hands were shaking; his face was without color.

He looked at me and said in a strangled voice, "This is in
the Coronal's own hand, informing me that the Pontifex has
left his quarters and has gone to the Place of Masks, where
he has issued a decree so stupefying that I cannot bring myself to frame the words with my own lips." He handed me
the note. "Come," he said, "I think we should hasten to the
Place of Masks."

He ran out, and I followed, trying desperately to glance at
the note as I went. But Lord Struin's handwriting is jagged
and difficult, and Guadeloom was moving with phenomenal
speed, and the corridors were winding and the way poorly
lit; so I could only get a snatch of the content here and there,
something about a proclamation, a new Lady designated, an
abdication. Whose abdication if not that of the Pontifex
Arioc? Yet he had said to me out of tht depths of his spirit
that it would be cowardice to turn his back on the destiny
that had chosen him to be a Power of the realm.

Breathless I came to the Place of Masks, a zone of the
Labyrinth that I find disturbing at the best of times, for the
great slit-eyed faces that rise on those gleaming marble
plinths seem to me figures out of nightmare. Guadeloom's
footsteps clattered on the stone floor, and mine doubled the
sound of his a good way behind, for though he was more
than twice my age he was moving like a demon. Up ahead I
heard shouts, laughter, applause. And then I saw a gathering
of perhaps a hundred fifty citizens, among whom I recognized several of the chief ministers of the Pontificate. Guadeloom and I barged into the group and halted only when we
saw figures in the green-and-gold uniform of the Coronal's
service, and then the Coronal himself. Lord Struin looked
furious and dazed at the same time, a man in shock.

"There is no stopping him," the Coronal said hoarsely. "He
goes from hall to hall, repeating his proclamation. Listen: he
begins again!"

And I saw the Pontifex Arioc at the head of the group,
riding on the shoulders of a colossal Skandar servant. His
majesty was dressed in flowing white robes of the female

style, with a splendid brocaded border, and on his breast lay a glowing red jewel of wondrous immensity and radiance.

"Whereas a vacancy has developed among the Powers of Majipoor!" cried the Pontifex in a marvelously robust voice. "And whereas it is needful that a new Lady of the Isle of Sleep! Be appointed herewith and swiftly! So that she may minister to the souls of the people! By appearing in their dreams to give aid and comfort! And! Whereas! It is my earnest desire! To yield up the burden of the Pontificate that I have borne these twelve years!

"Therefore—

"I do herewith! Using the supreme powers at my command! Proclaim that I be acclaimed hereafter as a member of the female sex! And as Pontifex I do name as Lady of the Isle the woman Arioc, formerly male!"

"Madness," muttered Duke Guadeloom.

"This is the third time I have heard it, and still I cannot believe it," and the Coronal Lord Struin.

"—and do herewith simultaneously abdicate my Pontifical throne! And call on the dwellers of the Labyrinth! To fetch for the Lady Arioc a chariot! To transport her to the port of Stoien! And thence to the Isle of Sleep so that she may bring her consolations to you all!"

And in that moment the gaze of Arioc turned toward me, and his eyes for an instant held mine. He was flushed with excitement and his forehead gleamed with sweat. He recognized me, and he smiled, and he *winked*, and undeniable wink, a wink of joy, a wink of triumph. Then he was carried away out of my sight.

"This must be stopped," Guadeloom said.

Lord Struin shook his head. "Listen to the cheering! They love it. The crowd grows larger as he goes from level to level. They'll sweep him up to the top and out the Mouth of Blades and off to Stoien before this day is out."

"You are Coronal," said Guadeloom. "Is there nothing you can do?"

"Overrule the Pontifex, whose every command I have sworn to serve? Commit treason before hundreds of witnesses? No, no, no, Guadeloom, what's done is done, preposterous as it may be, and now we must live with it."

"All hail the Lady Arioc!" a booming voice bellowed.

"All hail! The Lady Arioc! All hail! All hail!"

I watched in utter disbelief as the procession moved on through the Place of Masks, heading for the Hall of Winds or the Court of Pyramids beyond. We did not follow, Guadeloom and the Coronal and I. Numb, silent, we stood motionless as the cheering, gesticulating figures disappeared. I was abashed to be among these great men of our realm at so humiliating a moment. It was absurd and fantastic, this abdication and appointment of a Lady, and they were shattered by it.

At length Guadeloom said thoughtfully, "If you accept the abdication as valid, Lord Struin, then you are Coronal no longer, but must make ready to take up residence here in the Labyrinth, for you are now our Pontifex."

Those words fell upon Lord Struin like mighty boulders. In the frenzy of the moment he had evidently not thought Arioc's deed through even to its first consequence.

His mouth opened but no words came forth. He opened and closed his hands as though making the starburst gesture in his own honor, but I knew it was only an expression of bewilderment. I felt shivers of awe, for it is no small thing to witness a transfer of succession, and Struin was wholly unprepared for it. To give up the joys of Castle Mount in the midst of life, to exchange its brilliant cities and splendid forests for the gloom of the Labyrinth, to put aside the starburst crown for the senior diadem—no, he was not ready at all, and as the truth of it came home to him his face turned ashen and his eyelids twitched madly.

After a very long while he said, "So be it, then. I am the Pontifex. And who, I ask you, is to be Coronal in my place?"

I suppose it was a rhetorical question. Certainly I gave no answer, and neither did Duke Guadeloom.

Angrily, roughly, Struin said again, "Who is to be Coronal? I ask you!"

His gaze was on Guadeloom.

I tell you, I was near to destroyed by being witness of these events, that will never be forgotten if our civilization lasts another ten thousand years. But how much more of an impact all this must have had on them! Guadeloom fell back, spluttering. Since Arioc and Lord Struin both were relatively young men, little speculation on the succession to their thrones had taken place; and though Guadeloom was a man of power and majesty, I doubt that he had ever expected himself to reach the heights of Castle Mount, and certainly not in any such way as this. He gaped like a gaffed gromwark and could not speak, and in the end it was I who reacted first, going down on my knee, making the starburst to him, crying out in a choked voice, "Guadeloom! Lord Guadeloom! Hail, Lord Guadeloom! Long life to Lord Guadeloom!"

Never again will I see two men so astonished, so confused, so instantly altered, as were the former Lord Struin now Pontifex and the former Duke Guadeloom now Coronal. Struin was stormy-faced with rage and pain, Lord Guadeloom half broken with amazement.

There was another huge silence.

Then Lord Guadeloom said in an oddly quavering voice, "If I am Coronal, custom demands that my mother be named the Lady of the Isle, is that not so?"

"How old is your mother?" Struin asked.

"Quite old. Ancient, one could say."

"Yes. And neither prepared for the tasks of the Ladyship nor strong enough to bear them."

"True," said Lord Guadeloom.

Struin said, "Besides, we have a new Lady this day, and it would not do to select another so soon. Let us see how well her Ladyship Arioc conducts herself in Inner Temple before we seek to put another in her place, eh?"

"Madness," said Lord Guadeloom.

"Madness indeed," said the Pontifex Struin. "Come, let us go to the Lady, and see her safely off to her Isle."

I went with them to the upper reaches of the Labyrinth, where we found ten thousand people hailing Arioc as he or she, barefoot and in splendid robes, made ready to board the chariot that would conduct her or him to the port of Stoien. It was impossible to get close to Arioc, so close was the press of bodies. "Madness," said Lord Guadeloom over and over. "Madness, madness!"

But I knew otherwise, for I had seen Arioc's wink, and I understood it completely. This was no madness at all. The Pontifex Arioc had found his way out of the Labyrinth, which was his heart's desire. Future generations, I am sure, will think of him as a synonym for folly and absurdity; but I know that he was altogether sane, a man to whom the crown had become an agony and whose honor forbade him simply to retire into private life.

And so it is, after yesterday's strange events, that we have a Pontifex and a Coronal and a Lady, and they are none of them the ones we had last month, and now you understand, beloved Silimoor, all that has befallen our world.

Calintane finished speaking and took a long draught of his wine. Silimoor was staring at him with an expression that seemed to him a mixture of pity and contempt and sympathy.

"You are like small children," she said at last, "with your titles and your royal courts and your bonds of honor. Nevertheless I understand, I think, what you have experienced and how it has unsettled you."

"There is one thing more," said Calintane.

"Yes?"

"The Coronal Lord Guadeloom, before he took to his chambers to begin the task of comprehending these transformtions, appointed me his chancellor. He will leave next week for Castle Mount. And I must be at his side, naturally."

"How splendid for you," said Silimoor coolly.

"I ask you therefore to join me there, to share my life at the Castle," he said as measuredly as he could.

Her dazzling turquoise eyes stared frostily into his.

"I am native to the Labyrinth," she answered. "I love dearly to dwell in its precincts."

"Is that my answer, then?"

"No," said Silimoor. "You will have your answer later. Much like your Pontifex and your Coronal, I require time to accustom myself to great changes."

"Then you *have* answered!"

"Later," she said, and thanked him for the wine and for the tale he had told, and left him at the table. Calintane eventually rose, and wandered like a spectre through the depths of the Labyrinth in an exhaustion beyond all exhaustion, and heard the people buzzing as the news spread—Arioc the Lady now, Struin the Pontifex, Guadeloom the Coronal—and it was to him like the droning of insects in his ears. He went to his chamber and tried to sleep, but no sleep came, and he fell into gloom over the state of his life, fearing that this sour period of separation from Silimoor had done fatal harm to their love, and that despite her oblique hint to the contrary she would reject his suit. But he was wrong. For, a day later, she sent word that she was ready to go with him, and when Calintane took up his new residence at Castle Mount she was at his side, as she still was many years later when he succeeded Lord Guadeloom as Coronal. His reign in that post was short but cheerful, and during his time he accomplished the construction of the great highway at the summit of the Mount that bears his name; and when in old age he returned to the Labyrinth as Pontifex himself it was without the slightest surprise, for he had lost all capacity for surprise that day long ago when the Pontifex Arioc had proclaimed himself to be the Lady of the Isle

FIVE

The Desert of Stolen Dreams

So the legend of Arioc has obscured the truth of him, Hissune sees now, as legend has obscured truth in so many other ways. For in the distortions of time Arioc has come to seem grotesque, whimsical, a clown of sudden instability; and yet if the testimony of Lord Calintane means anything, it was not that way at all. A suffering man sought freedom and chose an outlandish way to attain it: no clown, no madman at all. Hissune, himself trapped in the Labyrinth and longing to taste the fresh air without, finds the Pontifex Arioc an unexpectedly congenial figure—his brother in spirit across the thousands of years.

For a long while thereafter Hissune does not go to the Register of Souls. The impact of those illicit journeys into the past has been too powerful; his head buzzes with stray strands out of the souls of Thesme and Calintane and Sinnabor Lavon and Group Captain Eremoil, so that when all of them set up a clamor at once he has difficulty locating Hissune, and that is dismaying. Besides, he has other things to do. After a year and a half he has finished with the tax documents, and by then he has established himself so thoroughly in the House of Records that another assignment is waiting for him, a survey of the distribution of aboriginal population groups in present-day Majipoor. He knows that Lord Valentine has had some problems with Metamorphs—

that in fact it was a conspiracy of the Shapeshifter folk that tumbled him from his throne in that weird event of a few years back—and he remembers from what he had overheard among the great ones on Castle Mount during his visit there that it is Lord Valentine's plan to integrate them more fully into the life of the planet, if that can be done. So Hissune suspects that these statistics he has been asked to compile have some function in the grand strategy of the Coronal, and that gives him a private pleasure.

It gives him, too, occasion for ironic smiles. For he is shrewd enough to see what is happening to the street-boy Hissune. That agile and cunning urchin who caught the Coronal's eye seven years ago is now an adolescent bureaucrat, transformed, tamed, civil, sedate. So be it, he thinks: one does not remain fourteen years old forever, and a time comes to leave the streets and become a useful member of society. Even so he feels some regret for the loss of the boy he had been. Some of that boy's mischief still bubbles in him; only some, but enough. He finds himself thinking weighty thoughts about the nature of society on Majipoor, the organic interrelationship of the political forces, the concept that power implies responsibility, that all beings are held together in harmonious union by a sense of reciprocal obligation. The four great Powers of the realm—the Pontifex, the Coronal, the Lady of the Isle, the King of Dreams—how, Hissune wonders, have they been able to work so well together? Even in this profoundly conservative society, where over thousands of years so little has changed, the harmony of the Powers seems miraculous, a balance of forces that must be divinely inspired. Hissune has had no formal education; there is no one to whom he can turn for knowledge of such things; but nevertheless, there is the Register of Souls, with all the teeming life of Majipoor's past held in a wondrous suspension, ready to release its passionate vitality at a command. It is folly not to explore that pool of knowledge now that such questions trouble his mind. So once again Hissune forges the documents; once again he slides himself glibly past the slow-witted guardians of the archives; once again he punches the keys, seeking now not only amusement and the joy of the forbidden but also an understanding of the evolution of his planet's political institutions. What a serious young man you are becoming, he tells himself, as the dazzling lights of many *colors throb in his mind and the dark, intense presence of an-other human being, long dead but forever timeless, invades his soul.*

İ

Suvrael lay like a glowing sword across the southern horizon—an iron band of dull red light, sending shimmering heat-pulsations into the air. Dekkeret, standing at the bow of the freighter on which he had made the long dreary sea journey, felt a quickening of the pulse. Suvrael at last! That dreadful place, that abomination of a continent, that useless and miserable land, now just a few days away, and who knew what horrors would befall him there? But he was prepared. Whatever happens, Dekkeret believed, happens for the best, in Suvrael as on Castle Mount. He was in his twentieth year, a big burly man with a short neck and enormously broad shoulders. This was the second summer of Lord Prestimion's glorious reign under the great Pontifex Confalume.

It was as an act of penance that Dekkeret had undertaken the voyage to the burning wastes of barren Suvrael. He had committed a shameful deed—certainly not intending it, at first barely realizing the shame of it—while hunting in the Khyntor Marches of the far northland, and some sort of expiation seemed necessary to him. That was in a way a romantic and flamboyant gesture, he knew, but he could forgive himself that. If he did not make romantic and flamboyant gestures at twenty, then when? Surely not ten or fifteen years from now, when he was bound to the wheel of his destinies and had settled snugly in for the inevitable bland easy career in Lord Prestimion's entourage. This was the moment, if ever. So, then, to Suvrael to purge his soul, no matter the consequences.

His friend and mentor and hunting companion in Khyntor, Akbalik, had not been able to understand. But of course Akbalik was no romantic, and a long way beyond twenty, besides. One night in early spring, over a few flasks of hot golden wine in a rough mountain tavern, Dekkeret had announced his intention and Akbalik's response had been a blunt snorting laugh. "Suvrael?" he had cried. "You judge yourself too harshly. There's no sin so foul that it merits a jaunt in Suvrael."

And Dekkeret, stung, feeling patronized, had slowly shaken his head. "Wrongness lies on me like a stain. I'll burn it from my soul under the hotland sun."

"Make the pilgrimage to the Isle instead, if you think you need to do something. Let the blessed Lady heal your spirit."

"No. Suvrael."

"Why?"

"To suffer," said Dekkeret. "To take myself far from the delights of Castle Mount, to the least pleasant place on Majipoor, to a dismal desert of fiery winds and loathsome dangers. To mortify the flesh, Akbalik, and show my contrition. To lay upon myself the discipline of discomfort and even pain—*pain*, do you know what that is?—until I can forgive myself. All right?"

Akbalik, grinning, dug his fingers into the thick robe of heavy black Khyntor furs that Dekkeret wore. "All right. But if you must mortify, mortify thoroughly. I assume you'll not take this from your body all the while you're under the Suvraelu sun."

Dekkeret chuckled. "There are limits," he said, "to my need for discomfort." He reached for the wine. Akbalik was nearly twice Dekkeret's age, and doubtless found his earnestness funny. So did Dekkeret, to a degree; but that did not swerve him.

"May I try once more to dissuade you?"

"Pointless."

"Consider the waste," said Akbalik anyway. "You have a career to look after. Your name is frequently heard at the Castle now. Lord Prestimion has said high things of you. A promising young man, due to climb far, great strength of character, all that kind of noise. Prestimion's young; he'll rule a long while; those who are young in his early days will rise as he rises. And here you are, deep in the wilds of Khyntor playing when you should be at court, and already planning another and more reckless trip. Forget this Suvrael nonsense, Dekkeret, and return to the Mount with me. Do the Coronal's bidding, impress the great ones with your worth, and build for the future. These are splendid times on Majipoor, and it will be splendid to be among the wielders of power as things unfold. Eh? Eh? Why throw yourself away in Suvrael? No one knows of this—ah—*sin* of yours, this one little lapse from grace—"

"*I know.*"

"Then promise never to do it again, and absolve yourself."

"It's not so simple," Dekkeret said.

"To squander a year or two of your life, or perhaps lose your life entirely, on a meaningless, useless journey to—"

"Not meaningless. Not useless."

"Except on a purely personal level it is."

"Not so, Akbalik. I've been in touch with the people of the Pontificate and I've wangled an official appointment. I'm a mission of inquiry. Doesn't that sound grand? Suvrael isn't exporting its quota of meat and livestock and the Pontifex wants to know why. You see? I continue to further my career even while going off on what seems to you a wholly private adventure."

"So you've already made arrangements."

"I leave on Fourday next." Dekkeret reached his hand toward his friend. "It'll be at least two years. We'll meet again on the Mount. What do you say, Akbalik, the games at High Morpin, two years from Winterday?"

Akbalik's calm gray eyes fastened intently on Dekkeret's. "I will be there," he said slowly. "I pray that you'll be too."

That conversation lay only some months in the past; but to Dekkeret now, feeling the throbbing heat of the southern continent reaching toward him over the pale green water of the Inner Sea, it seemed incredibly long ago, and the voyage infinitely long. The first part of the journey had been pleasing enough—down out of the mountains to the grand metropolis of Ni-moya, and then by riverboat down the Zimr to the port of Piliplok on the eastern coast. There he had boarded a freighter, the cheapest transport he could find, bound for the Suvraelu city of Tolaghai, and then it had been south and south and south all summer long, in a ghastly little cabin just downwind from a hold stuffed with bales of dried baby sea-dragons, and as the ship crossed into the tropics the days presented a heat unlike anything he had ever known, and the nights were little better; and the crew, mostly a bunch of shaggy Skandars, laughed at his discomfort and told him that he had better enjoy the cool weather while he could, for real heat was waiting for him in Suvrael. Well, he had wanted to suffer, and his wish was being amply granted already, and worse to come. He did not complain. He felt no regret. But his comfortable life among the young knights of Castle

Mount had not prepared him for sleepless nights with the reek of sea-dragon in his nostrils like stilettos, nor for the stifling heat that engulfed the ship a few weeks out of Piliplok, nor for the intense boredom of the unchanging seascape. The planet was so impossibly *huge*, that was the trouble. It took forever to get from anywhere to anywhere. Crossing from his native continent of Alhanroel to the western land of Zimroel had been a big enough project, by riverboat to Alaisor from the Mount, then by sea to Piliplok and up the river into the mountain marches, but he had had Akbalik with him to lighten the time, and there had been the excitement of his first major journey, the strangeness of new places, new foods, new accents. And he had had the hunting expedition to look forward to. But this? This imprisonment aboard a dirty creaking ship stuffed with parched meat of evil odor? This interminable round of empty days without friends, without duties, without conversation? If only some monstrous sea-dragon would heave into view, he thought, and enliven the journey with a bit of peril; but no, no, the dragons in their migrations were elsewhere, one great herd said to be in western waters out by Narabal just now and another midway between Piliplok and the Rodamaunt Archipelago, and Dekkeret saw none of the vast beasts, not even a few stragglers. What made the boredom worse was that it did not seem to have any value as catharsis. He was suffering, true, and suffering was what he imagined would heal him of his wound, but yet the awareness of the terrible thing he had done in the mountains did not seem to diminish at all. He was hot and bored and restless, and guilt still clawed at him, and still he tormented himself with the ironic knowledge that he was being praised by no less than the Coronal Lord Prestimion for great strength of character while he could find only weakness and cowardice and foolishness in himself. Perhaps it takes more than humidity and boredom and foul odors to cure one's soul, Dekkeret decided. At any rate he had had more than enough of the process of getting to Suvrael, and he was ready to begin the next phase of his pilgrimage into the unknown.

2

Every journey ends, even an endless one. The hot wind out of the south intensified day after day until the deck was too

hot to walk and the barefoot Skandars had to swab it down
every few hours; and then suddenly the burning mass of sullen darkness on the horizon resolved itself into a shoreline
and the jaws of a harbor. They had reached Tolaghai at last.

All of Suvrael was tropical; most of its interior was desert,
oppressed perpetually by a colossal weight of dry dead air
around the periphery of which searing cyclones whirled; but
the fringes of the continent were more or less habitable, and
there were five major cities along the coasts, of which Tolaghai was the largest and the one most closely linked by commerce to the rest of Majipoor. As the freighter entered the
broad harbor Dekkeret was struck by the strangeness of the
place. In his brief time he had seen a great many of the giant
world's cities—a dozen of the fifty on the flanks of Castle
Mount, and towering windswept Alaisor, and the vast astounding white-walled Ni-moya, and magnificent Piliplok,
and many others—and never had he beheld a city with the
harsh, mysterious, forbidding look of this one. Tolaghai clung
like a crab to a low ridge along the sea. Its buildings were
flat, squat things of sun-dried orange brick, with mere slits
for windows, and there were only sparse plantings around
them, dismaying angular palms, mainly, that were all bare
trunk with tiny feathery crowns far overhead. Here at midday the streets were almost deserted. The hot wind blew
sprays of sand over the cracked paving-stones. To Dekkeret
the city seemed like some sort of prison outpost, brutal and
ugly, or perhaps a city out of time, belonging to some prehistoric folk of a regimented and authoritarian race. Why had
anyone chosen to build a place so hideous? Doubtless it was
out of mere efficiency, ugliness like this being the best way to
cope with the climate of the land, but still, still, Dekkeret
thought, the challenges of heat and drought might surely have
called forth some less repellent architecture.

In his innocence Dekkeret thought he could simply go
ashore at once, but that was not how things worked here. The
ship lay at anchor for more than an hour before the port officials, three glum-looking Hjorts, came aboard. Then followed
a lengthy business with sanitary inspections and cargo
manifests and haggling over docking fees; and finally the
dozen or so passengers were cleared for landing. A porter of
the Ghayrog race seized Dekkeret's luggage and asked the
name of his hotel. He replied that he had not booked one,

and the reptilian-looking creature, tongue flickering and black fleshy hair writhing like a mass of serpents, gave him an icy mocking look and said, "What will you pay? Are you rich?"

"Not very. What can I get for three crowns a night?"

"Little. Bed of straw. Vermin on the walls."

"Take me there," said Dekkeret.

The Ghayrog looked as startled as a Ghayrog is capable of looking. "You will not be happy there, fine sir. You have the bearing of lordship about you."

"Perhaps so, but I have a poor man's purse. I'll take my chances with the vermin."

Actually the inn turned out to be not as bad as he feared: ancient, squalid, and depressing, yes, but so was everything else in sight, and the room he received seemed almost palatial after his lodgings on the ship. Nor was there the reek of sea-dragon flesh here, only the arid piercing flavor of Suvraelu air, like the stuff within a flask that had been sealed a thousand years. He gave the Ghayrog a half-crown piece, for which he had no thanks, and unpacked his few belongings.

In late afternoon Dekkeret went out. The stifling heat had dropped not at all, but the thin cutting wind seemed less fierce now, and there were more people in the streets. All the same the city felt grim. This was the right sort of place for doing a penance. He loathed the blank-faced brick buildings, he hated the withered look of the landscape, and he missed the soft sweet air of his native city of Normork on the lower slopes of Castle Mount. Why, he wondered, would anyone choose to live here, when there was opportunity aplenty on the gentler continents? What starkness of the soul drove some millions of his fellow citizens to scourge themselves in the daily severities of life on Suvrael?

The representatives of the Pontificate had their offices on the great blank plaza fronting the harbor. Dekkeret's instructions called upon him to present himself there, and despite the lateness of the hour he found the place open, for in the searing heat all citizens of Tolaghai observed a midday closing and transacted business well into evening. He was left to wait a while in an antechamber decorated with huge white ceramic portraits of the reigning monarchs, the Pontifex Confalume shown in full face with a look of benign but overwhelming grandeur, and young Lord Prestimion the Coronal in profile, his visage aglitter with intelligence and dynamic

energy, Majipoor was fortunate in her rulers, Dekkeret
thought. When he was a boy he had seen Confalume, then
Coronal, holding court in the wondrous city of Bombifale
high the Mount, and he had wanted to cry out from sheer
joy at the man's calmness and radiant strength. A few years
later Lord Confalume succeeded to the Pontificate and went
to dwell in the subterranean recesses of the Labyrinth, and
Prestimion had been made Coronal—a very different man,
equally impressive but all dash and vigor and impulsive
power. It was while Lord Prestimion was making the grand
processional through the cities of the Mount that he had
spied the young Dekkeret in Normork and had chosen him,
in his random unpredictable way, to join the knights in training in the High Cities. Which seemed an epoch ago, such
great changes having occurred in Dekkeret's life since then.
At eighteen he had allowed himself fantasies of ascending the
Coronal's throne himself one day; but then had come his ill-
starred holiday in the mountains of Zimroel, and now,
scarcely past twenty, fidgeting in a dusty outer office in this
drab city of cheerless Suvrael, he felt he had no future at all,
only a barren stretch of meaningless years to use up.

A pudgy sour-faced Hjort appeared and announced, "The
Archiregimand Golator Lasgia will see you now."

That was a resonant title; but its owner proved to be a
slender dark-skinned woman not greatly older than Dekkeret,
who gave him careful scrutiny out of large glossy solemn
eyes. In a perfunctory way she offered him greeting with the
hand-symbol of the Pontificate and took the document of his
credentials from him. "The Initiate Dekkeret," she murmured. "Mission of inquiry, under commission of the Khyntor provincial superstrate. I don't understand, Initiate
Dekkeret. Do you serve the Coronal or the Pontifex?"

Uncomfortably Dekkeret said, "I am of Lord Prestimion's
staff, a very low echelon. But while I was in Khyntor Province a need arose at the office of the Pontificate for an investigation of certain things in Suvrael, and when the local
officials discovered that I was bound for Suvrael anyway,
they asked me in the interests of economy to take on the job
even though I was not in the employ of the Pontifex. And—"

Tapping Dekkeret's papers thoughtfully against her desk-
top, Golator Lasgia said, "You were bound for Suvrael anyway? May I ask why?"

Dekkeret flushed. "A personal matter, if you please."

She let it pass. "And what affairs of Suvrael can be of such compelling interest to my Pontifical brothers of Khyntor, or is my curiosity on that subject also misplaced?"

Dekkeret's discomfort grew. "It has to do with an imbalance of trade," he answered, barely able to meet her cool penetrating gaze. "Khyntor is a manufacturing center; it exchanges goods for the livestock of Suvrael; for the past two years the export of blaves and mounts out of Suvrael has declined steadily, and now strains are developing in the Khyntor economy. The manufacturers are encountering difficulty in carrying so much Suvraelu credit."

"None of this is news to me."

"I've been asked to inspect the rangelands here," said Dekkeret, "in order to determine whether an upturn in livestock production can soon be expected."

"Will you have some wine?" Golator Lasgia asked unexpectedly.

Dekkeret, adrift, considered the proprieties. While he faltered she produced two flasks of golden, deftly snapped their seals, and passed one to him. He took it with a grateful smile. The wine was cold, sweet, with a faint sparkle.

"Wine of Khyntor," she said. "Thus we contribute to the Suvraelu trade deficit. The answer, Initiate Dekkeret, is that in the final year of the Pontifex Prankipin a terrible drought struck Suvrael—you may ask, Initiate, how we can tell the difference here between a year of drought and a year of normal rainfall, but there is a difference, Initiate, there is a significant difference—and the grazing districts suffered. There was no way of feeding our cattle, so we butchered as many as the market could hold, and sold much of the remaining stock to ranchers in western Zimroel. Not long after Confalume succeeded to the Labyrinth, the rains returned and the grass began to grow in our savannas. But it takes several years to rebuild the herds. Therefore the trade imbalance will continue a time longer, and then will be cured." She smiled without warmth. "There. I have spared you the inconvenience of an uninteresting journey to the interior."

Dekkeret found himself perspiring heavily. "Nevertheless I must make it, Archiregimand Golator Lasgia."

"You'll learn nothing more than I've just told you."

"I mean no disrespect. But my commission specifically requires me to see with my own eyes—"

She closed hers a moment. "To reach the rangelands just now will involve you in great difficulties, extreme physical discomfort, perhaps considerable personal danger. If I were you, I'd remain in Tolaghai, sampling such pleasures as are available here, and dealing with whatever personal business brought you to Suvrael; and after a proper interval, write your report in consultation with my office and take yourself back to Khyntor."

Immediate suspicions blossomed in Dekkeret. The branch of the government she served was not always cooperative with the Coronal's people; she seemed quite transparently trying to conceal something that was going on in Suvrael; and, although his mission of inquiry was only the pretext for his voyage to this place and not his central task, all the same he had his career to consider, and if he allowed a Pontifical Archiregimand to bamboozle him too easily here it would go badly for him later. He wished he had not accepted the wine from her. But to cover his confusion he allowed himself a series of suave sips, and at length said, "My sense of honor would not permit me to follow such an easy course."

"How old are you, Initiate Dekkeret?"

"I was born in the twelfth year of Lord Confalume."

"Yes, your sense of honor would still prick you, then. Come, look at this map with me." She rose briskly. She was taller than he expected, nearly his own height, which gave her a fragile appearance. Her dark, tightly coiled hair emitted a suprising fragrance, even over the aroma of the strong wine. Golator Lasgia touched the wall and a map of Suvrael in brilliant ochre and auburn hues sprang into view. "This is Tolaghai," she said, tapping the northwest corner of the continent. "The grazing lands are here." She indicated a band that began six or seven hundred miles inland and ran in a rough circle surrounding the desert at the heart of Suvrael. "From Tolaghai," she went on, "there are three main routes to the cattle country. This is one. At present it is ravaged by sandstorms and no traffic can safely use it. This is the second route: we are experiencing certain difficulties with Shapeshifter bandits there, and it is also closed to travelers. The third way lies here, by Khulag Pass, but that road has fallen into disuse of late, and an arm of the great desert has begun to encroach on it. Do you see the problems?"

As gently as he could Dekkeret said, "But if it is the

business of Suvrael to raise cattle for export, and all the routes between the grazing lands and the chief port are blocked, is it correct to say that a lack of pasture is the true cause of the recent shortfalls of cattle exports?"

She smiled. "There are other ports from which we ship our produce in this current situation."

"Well, then, if I go to one of those, I should find an open highway to the cattle country."

Again she tapped the map. "Since last winter the port of Natu Gorvinu has been the center of the cattle trade. This is it, in the east, under the coast of Alhanroel, about six thousand miles from here."

"Six thousand—"

"There is little reason for commerce between Tolaghai and Natu Gorvinu. Perhaps once a year a ship goes from one to the other. Overland the situation is worse, for the roads out of Tolaghai are not maintained east of Kangheez—" she indicated a city perhaps a thousand miles away—"and beyond that, who knows? This is not a heavily settled continent."

"Then there's no way to reach Natu Gorvinu?" Dekkeret said, stunned.

"One. By ship from Tolaghai to Stoien on Alhanroel, and from Stoien to Natu Gorvinu. It should take you only a little over a year. By the time you reach Suvrael again and penetrate the interior, of course, the crisis that you've come to investigate will probably be over. Another flask of the golden, Initiate Dekkeret?"

Numbly he accepted the wine. The distances stupefied him. Another horrendous voyage across the Inner Sea, all the way back to his native continent of Alhanroel, only to turn around and cross the water a third time, sailing now to the far side of Suvrael, and then to find, probably, that the ways to the interior had meanwhile been closed out there, and— no. No. There was such a thing as carrying a penance too far. Better to abandon the mission altogether than subject himself to such absurdities.

While he hesitated Golator Lasgia said, "The hour is late and your problems need longer consideration. Have you plans for dinner, Initiate Dekkeret?"

Suddenly, astoundingly, her somber eyes gleamed with mischief of a familiar kind.

3

In the company of the Archiregimand Golator Lasgia,
Dekkeret discovered that life in Tolaghai was not necessarily
as bleak as first superficial inspection had indicated. By
floater she returned him to his hotel—he could see her dis-
taste at the look of the place—and instructed him to rest and
cleanse himself and be ready in an hour. A coppery twilight
had descended, and by the time the hour had elapsed the sky
was utterly black, with only a few alien constellations cutting
jagged tracks across it, and the crescent hint of one or two
moons down near the horizon. She called for him punctually.
In place of her stark official tunic she wore now something of
clinging mesh, almost absurdly seductive. Dekkeret was
puzzled by all this. He had had his share of success with
women, yes, but so far as he knew he had given her no sign
of interest, nothing but the most formal of respect; and yet
she clearly was assuming a night of intimacy. Why? Certainly
not his irresistible sophistication and physical appeal, nor any
political advantage he could confer on her, nor any other rational motive. Except one, that this was a foul backwater outpost where life was stale and uncomfortable, and he was a
youthful stranger who might provide a woman herself still
young with a night's amusement. He felt used by that, but
otherwise he could see no great harm in it. And after months
at sea he was willing to run a little risk in the name of
pleasure.

They dined at a private club on the outskirts of town, in a
garden elegantly decorated with the famous creature-plants of
Stoienzar and other flowering wonders that had Dekkeret calculating how much of Tolaghai's modest water supply was
diverted toward keeping this one spot flourishing. At other
tables, widely separated, were Suvraelinu in handsome costume, and Golator Lasgia nodded to this one and that, but no
one approached her, nor did they stare unduly at Dekkeret.
From within the building blew a cool refreshing breeze, the
first he had felt in weeks, as though some miraculous
machine of the ancients, some cousin to the ones that gener-
ated the delicious atmosphere of Castle Mount, were at work
in there. Dinner was a magnificent affair of lightly fermented

fruits and tender juicy slabs of pale green-fleshed fish, accompanied by a fine dry wine of Amblemorn, no less, the very fringes of Castle Mount. She drank freely, as did he; they grew bright-eyed and animated; the chilly formality of the interview in her office dropped away. He learned that she was nine years his senior, that she was a native of moist lush Narabal on the western continent, that she had entered the service of the Pontifex when still a girl, and had been stationed in Suvrael for the past ten years, rising upon Confalume's accession to the Pontificate to her present high administrative post in Tolaghai.

"Do you *like* it here?" he asked.

She shrugged. "One gets accustomed to it."

"I doubt that I would. To me Suvrael is merely a place of torment, a kind of purgatory."

Golator Lasgia nodded. "Exactly."

There was a flash from her eyes to his. He did not dare ask for amplification; but something told him that they had much in common.

He filled their glasses once again and permitted himself the perils of a calm, knowing smile.

She said, "Is it purgatory you seek here?"

"Yes."

She indicated the lavish gardens, the empty wine-flasks, the costly dishes, the half-eaten delicacies. "You have made a poor start, then."

"Milady, dinner with you was no part of my plan."

"Nor mine. But the Divine provides, and we accept. Yes? Yes?" She leaned close. "What will you do now? The voyage to Natu Gorvinu?"

"It seems to heavy an enterprise."

"Then do as I say. Stay in Tolaghai until you grow weary of it; then return and file your report. No one will be the wiser in Khyntor."

"No. I must go inland."

Her expression grew mocking. "Such dedication! But how will you do it? The roads from here are closed."

"You mentioned the one by Khulag Pass, that had fallen into disuse. Mere disuse doesn't seem as serious as deadly sandstorms, or Shapeshifter bandits. Perhaps I can hire a caravan leader to take me that way."

"Into the desert?"

"If needs be."

"The desert is haunted," said Golator Lasgia casually.
"You should forget that idea. Call the waiter over: we need
more wine."

"I think I've had enough, milady."

"Come, then. We'll go elsewhere."

Stepping from the breeze-cooled garden to the dry hot
night air of the street was a shock; but quickly they were in
her floater, and not long after they were in a second garden,
this one in the courtyard of her official residence, surrounding
a pool. There were no weather-machines here to ease the
heat, but the Archiregimand had another way, dropping her
gown and going to the pool. Her lean, supple body gleamed a
moment in the starlight; then she dived, sliding nearly without a splash beneath the surface. She beckoned to him and
quickly he joined her.

Afterward they embraced on a bed of close-cropped thick-
bladed grass. It was almost as much like wrestling as lovemaking, for she clasped him with her long muscular legs,
tried to pinion his arms, rolled over and over with him,
laughing, and he was amazed at the strength of her, the playful ferocity of her movements. But when they were through
testing one another they moved with more harmony, and it
was a night of little sleep and much exertion.

Dawn was an amazement: without warning, the sun was in
the sky like a trumpet-blast, roasting the surrounding hills
with shafts of hot light.

They lay limp, exhausted. Dekkeret turned to her—by
cruel morning light she looked less girlish than she had under
the stars—and said abruptly, "Tell me about this haunted
desert. What spirits will I meet there?"

"How persistent you are!"

"Tell me."

"There are ghosts there that can enter your dreams and
steal them. They rob your soul of joy and leave fears in its
place. By day they sing in the distance, confusing you, leading you from the path with their clatter and their music."

"Am I supposed to believe this?"

"In recent years many who have entered that desert have
perished there."

"Of dream-stealing ghosts."

"So it is said."

"It will make a good tale to tell when I return to Castle Mount, then."

"*If* you return," she said.

"You say that not everyone who has gone into that desert has died of it. Obviously not, for someone has come out to tell the tale. Then I will hire a guide, and take my chances among the ghosts."

"No one will accompany you."

"Then I'll go alone."

"And certainly die." She stroked his powerful arms and made a little purring sound. "Are you so interested in dying, so soon? Dying has no value. It confers no benefits. Whatever peace you seek, the peace of the grave is not it. Forget the desert journey. Stay here with me."

"We'll go together."

She laughed. "I think not."

It was, Dekkeret realized, madness. He had doubts of her tales of ghosts and dream-stealers, unless what went on in that desert was some trickery of the rebellious Shapeshifter aborigines, and even then he doubted it. Perhaps all her tales of danger were only ruses to keep him longer in Tolaghai. Flattering if true, but of no help in his quest. And she was right about death being a useless form of purgation. If his adventures in Suvrael were to have meaning, he must succeed in surviving them.

Golator Lasgia drew him to his feet. They bathed briefly in the pool; then she led him within, to the most handsomely appointed dwelling he had seen this side of Castle Mount, and gave him a breakfast of fruits and dried fish.

Suddenly in mid-morning she said, "*Must* you go into the interior?"

"An inner need drives me in that direction."

"Very well. We have in Tolaghai a certain scoundrel who often ventures inland by way of Khulag Pass, or so he claims, and seems to survive it. For a purse full of royals he'll no doubt guide you there. His name is Barjazid; and if you insist, I'll summon him and ask him to assist you."

4

"Scoundrel" seemed the proper word for Barjazid. He was a lean and disreputable-looking little man, shabbily dressed in an old brown robe and worn leather sandals, with an ancient necklace of mismatched sea-dragon bones at his throat. His lips were thin, his eyes had a feverish glaze, his skin was burned almost black by the desert sun. He stared at Dekkeret as though weighing the contents of his purse.

"If I take you," said Barjazid in a voice altogether lacking in resonance but yet not weak, "you will first sign a quitclaim absolving me of any responsibility to your heirs, in the event of your death."

"I have no heirs," Dekkeret replied.

"Kinfolk, then. I won't be hauled into the Pontifical courts by your father or your elder sister because you've perished in the desert."

"Have you perished in the desert yet?"

Barjazid looked baffled. "An absurd question."

"You go into that desert," Dekkeret persisted, "and you return alive. Yes? Well ten, if you know your trade, you'll come out alive again this time, and so will I. I'll do what you do and go where you go. If you live, I live. If I perish, you'll have perished too, and my family will have no lien."

"I can withstand the power of the stealers of dreams," said Barjazid. "This I know from ample tests. How do you know you'll prevail over them as readily?"

Dekkeret helped himself to a new serving of Barjazid's tea, a rich infusion brewed from some potent shrub of the sandhills. The two men squatted on mounds of haigus-hide blankets in the musty backroom of a shop belonging to Barjazid's brother's son: it was evidently a large clan. Dekkeret sipped the sharp, bitter tea reflectively and said, after a moment, "Who are these dream-stealers?"

"I cannot say."

"Shapeshifters, perhaps?"

Barjazid shrugged. "They have not bothered to tell me their pedigree. Shapeshifters, Ghayrogs, Vroons, ordinary humans—how would I know? In dreams all voices are alike. Certainly there are tribes of Shapeshifters loose in the desert, and some of them are angry folk given to mischief, and perhaps they have the skill of touching minds along with the skill of altering their bodies. Or perhaps not."

"If the Shapeshifters have closed two of the three routes out of Tolaghai, the Coronal's forces have work to do here."

"This is no affair of mine."

"The Shapeshifters are a subjugated race. They must not be allowed to disrupt the daily flow of life on Majipoor."

"It was you who suggested that the dream-stealers were Shapeshifters," Barjazid pointed out acidly. "I myself have no such theory. And who the dream-stealers are is not important. What is important is that they make the lands beyond Khulag Pass dangerous for travelers."

"Why do you go there, then?"

"I am not likely ever to answer a question that begins with *why*," said Barjazid. "I go there because I have reason to go there. Unlike others, I seem to return alive."

"Does everyone else who crosses the pass die?"

"I doubt it. I have no idea. Beyond question many have perished since the dream-stealers first were heard from. At the best of times that desert has been perilous." Barjazid stirred his tea. He began to appear restless. "If you accompany me, I'll protect you as best I can. But I make no guarantees for your safety. Which is why I demand that you give me legal absolution from responsibility."

Dekkeret said, "If I sign such a paper it would be signing a death warrant. What would keep you from murdering me ten miles beyond the pass, robbing my corpse, and blaming it all on the dream-stealers?"

"By the Lady, I am no murderer! I am not even a thief."

"But to give you a paper saying that if I die on the journey you are not to be blamed—might that not tempt even an honest man beyond all limits?"

Barjazid's eyes blazed with fury. He gestured as though to bring the interview to an end. "What goes beyond limits is your audacity," he said, rising and tossing his cup aside. "Find another guide, if you fear me so much."

Dekkeret, remaining seated, said quietly, "I regret the suggestion. I ask you only to see my position: a stranger and a young man in a remote and difficult land, forced to seek the aid of those he does not know to take him into places where improbable things happen. I must be cautious."

"Be even more cautious, then. Take the next ship for Stoien and return to the easy life of Castle Mount."

"I ask you again to guide me. For a good price, and nothing more about signing a quitclaim to my life. How much is your fee?"

"Thirty royals," Barjazid said.

Dekkeret grunted as though he had been struck below the ribs. It had cost him less than that to sail from Piliplok to Tolaghai. Thirty royals was a year's wage for someone like Barjazid; to pay it would require Dekkeret to draw on an expensive letter of credit. His impulse was to respond with knightly scorn, and offer ten; but he realized that he had forfeited his bargaining strength by objecting to the quitclaim. If he haggled now over the price as well, Barjazid would simply terminate the negotiations.

He said at length, "So be it. But no quitclaim."

Barjazid gave him a sour look. "Very well. Not quitclaim, as you insist."

"How is the money to be paid?"

"Half now, half on the morning of departure."

"Ten now," said Dekkeret, "and ten on the morning of departure, and ten on the day of my return to Tolaghai."

"That makes a third of my fee conditional on your surviving the trip. Remember that I make no guarantee of that."

"Perhaps my survival becomes more likely if I hold back a third of the fee until the end."

"One expects a certain haughtiness from one of the Coronal's knights, and one learns to ignore it as a mere mannerism, up to a point. But I think you have passed the point." Once again Barjazid made a gesture of dismissal. "There is too little trust between us. It would be a poor idea for us to travel together."

"I meant no disrespect," said Dekkeret.

"But you ask me to leave myself to the mercies of your kinfolk if you perish, and you seem to regard me as an ordinary cutthroat or at best a brigand, and you feel it necessary to arrange my fee so that I will have less motivation to murder you." Barjazid spat. "The other face of haughtiness is courtesy, young knight. A Skandar dragon-hunter would have shown me more courtesy. I did not seek your employ, bear in mind. I will not humiliate myself to aid you. If you please—"

"Wait."

"I have other business this morning."

"Fifteen royals now," said Dekkeret, "and fifteen when we set forth, as you say. Yes?"

"Even though you think I'll murder you in the desert?"

"I became too suspicious because I didn't want to appear too innocent," said Dekkeret. "It was tactless for me to have said the things I said. I ask you to hire yourself to me on the terms agreed."

Barjazid was silent.

From his purse Dekkeret drew three five-royal coins. Two were pieces of the old coinage, showing the Pontifex Prankipin with Lord Confalume. The third was a brilliant newly minted one, bearing Confalume as Pontifex and the the image of Lord Prestimion on the reverse. He extended them toward Barjazid, who selected the new coin and examined it with great curiosity.

"I have not seen one of these before," he said. "Shall we call in my brother's son for an opinion of its authenticity?"

It was too much. "Do you take me for a passer of false money?" Dekkeret roared, leaping to his feet and looming ferociously over the small man. Rage throbbed in him; he came close to striking Barjazid.

But he perceived that the other was altogether fearless and unmoving in the face of his wrath. Barjazid actually smiled, and took the other two coins from Dekkeret's trembling hand.

"So you too have little liking for groundless accusations, eh, young knight?" Barjazid laughed. "Let us have a treaty, then. You'll not expect me to assassinate you beyond Khulag Pass, and I'll not send your coins out to the money changer's for an appraisal, eh? Well? Is it agreed?"

Dekkeret nodded wearily.

"Nevertheless this is a risky journey," said Barjazid, "and I would not have you too confident of a safe return. Much depends on your own strength when the time of testing comes."

"So be it. When do we leave?"

"Fiveday, at the sunset hour. We depart the city from Pinitor Gate. Is that place known to you?"

"I'll find it," Dekkeret said. "Till Fiveday, at sunset." He offered the little man his hand.

5

Fiveday was three days hence. Dekkeret did not regret the delay, for that gave him three more nights with the Archiregi-

mand Golator Lasgia; or so he thought, but in fact it happened otherwise. She was not at her office by the waterfront
on the evening of Dekkeret's meeting with Barjazid, nor
would her aides transmit a message to her. He wandered the
torrid city disconsolately until long after dark, finding no
companionship at all, and ultimately ate a drab and gritty
meal at his hotel, still hoping that Golator Lasgia would
miraculously appear and whisk him away. She did not, and
he slept fitfully and uneasily, his mind obsessed by the
memories of her smooth flanks, her small firm breasts, her
hungry, aggressive mouth. Toward dawn came a dream,
vague and unreadable, in which she and Barjazid and some
Hjorts and Vroons performed a complex dance in a roofless
sandswept stone ruin, and afterward he fell into a sound
sleep, not awakening until midday on Seaday. The entire city
appeared to be in hiding then, but when the cooler hours came
he went round to the Archiregimand's office once again, once
again not seeing her, and then spent the evening in the same
purposeless fashion as the night before. As he gave himself
up to sleep he prayed fervently to the Lady of the Isle to
send Golator Lasgia to him. But it was not the function of the
Lady to do such things, and all that did reach him in the
night was a bland and cheering dream, perhaps a gift of the
blessed Lady but probably not, in which he dwelled in a
thatched hut on the shores of the Great Sea by Til-omon and
nibbled on sweet purplish fruits that squirted juice to stain his
cheeks. When he awakened he found a Hjort of the Archiregimand's staff waiting outside his room, to summon him to the
presence of Golator Lasgia.

That evening they dined together late, and went to her villa
again, for a night of lovemaking that made their other one
seem like a month of chastity. Dekkeret did not ask her at
any time why she had refused him these two nights past, but
as they breakfasted on spiced gihornaskin and golden wine,
both he and she vigorous and fresh after having had no sleep
whatever, she said, "I wish I had had more time with you this
week, but at least we were able to share your final night.
Now you'll go to the Desert of Stolen Dreams with my taste
on your lips. Have I made you forget all other women?"

"You know the answer."

"Good. Good. You may never embrace a woman again;
but the last was the best, and few are so lucky as that."

"Were you so certain I'll die in the desert, then?"

"Few travelers return," she said. "The chances of my seeing you again are slight."

Dekkeret shivered faintly—not out of fear, but in recognition of Golator Lasgia's inner motive. Some morbidity in her evidently had led her to snub him those two nights, so that the third would be all the more intense, for she must believe that he would be a dead man shortly after and she wanted the special pleasure of being his last woman. That chilled him. If he were going to die before long, Dekkeret would just as soon have had the other two nights with her as well; but apparently the subtleties of her mind went beyond such crass notions. He bade her a courtly farewell, not knowing if they would meet again or even if he wished it, for all her beauty and voluptuary skills. Too much that was mysterious and dangerously capricious lay coiled within her.

Not long before sunset he presented himself at Pinitor Gate on the city's southeastern flank. It would not have surprised him if Barjazid had reneged on their agreement, but no, a floater was waiting just outside the pitted sandstone arch of the old gate, and the little man stood leaning against the vehicle's side. With him were three companions: a Vroon, a Skandar, and a slender, hard-eyed young man who was obviously Barjazid's son.

At a nod from Barjazid the giant four-armed Skandar took hold of Dekkeret's two sturdy bags and stowed them with a casual flip in the floater's keep. "Her name," said Barjazid, "is Khaymak Gran. She is unable to speak, but far from stupid. She has served me many years, since I found her tongueless and more than half dead in the desert. The Vroon is Serifain Reinaulion, who often speaks too much, but knows the desert tracks better than anyone of this city." Dekkeret exchanged brusque salutes with the small tentacular being. "And my son, Dinitak, will also accompany us," Barjazid said. "Are you well rested, Initiate?"

"Well enough," Dekkeret answered. He had slept most of the day, after his unsleeping night.

"We travel mainly by darkness, and camp in heat of day. My understanding is that I am to take you through Khulag Pass, across the wasteland known as the Desert of Stolen Dreams, and to the edge of the grazing lands around Ghyzyn Kor, where you have certain inquiries to make among the herdsmen. And then back to Tolaghai. Is this so?"

"Exactly," Dekkeret said.

Barjazid made no move to enter the floater. Dekkeret frowned; and then he understood. From his purse he produced three more five-royal pieces, two of them old ones of the Prankipin coinage, the third a shining coin of Lord Prestimion. These he handed to Barjazid, who plucked forth the Prestimion coin and tossed it to his son. The boy eyed the bright coin suspiciously. "The new Coronal," said Barjazid. "Make yourself familiar with his face. We'll be seeing it often."

"He will have a glorious reign," said Dekkeret. "He will surpass even Lord Confalume in grandeur. Already a wave of new prosperity sweeps the northern continents, and they were prosperous enough before. Lord Prestimion is a man of vigor and decisiveness, and his plans are ambitious."

Barjazid said, with a shrug, "Events on the northern continents carry very little weight here, and somehow prosperity on Alhanroel or Zimroel has a way of mattering hardly at all to Suvrael. But we rejoice that the Divine has blessed us with another splendid Coronal. May he remember, occasionally, that there is a southern land also, and citizens of his realm dwelling in it. Come, now: time to be traveling."

6

The Pinitor Gate marked an absolute boundary between city and desert. To one side there was a district of low sprawling villas, walled and faceless; to the other was only barren waste beyond the city's perimeter. Nothing broke the emptiness of the desert but the highway, a broad cobbled track that wound slowly upward toward the crest of the ridge that encircled Tolaghai.

The heat was intolerable. By night the desert was perceptibly cooler than by day, but scorching all the same. Though the great blazing eye of the sun was gone, the orange sands, radiating the stored heat of the day toward the sky, shimmered and sizzled with the intensity of a banked furnace. A strong wind was blowing—with the coming of the darkness, Dekkeret had noticed, the flow of the wind reversed, blowing now from the heart of the continent toward the sea—but it made no difference: shore-wind or sea-wind, both were oppressive streams of dry baking air that offered no mercies.

In the clear arid atmosphere the light of the stars and

moons was unusually bright, and there was an earthly glow as well, a strange ghostly greenish radiance that rose in irregular patches from the slopes flanking the highway. Dekkeret asked about it. "From certain plants," said the Vroon. "They shine with an inner light in the darkness. To touch such a plant is always painful and often fatal."

"How am I to know them by daylight?"

"They look like pieces of old string, weathered and worn, sprouting in bunches from clefts in the rock. Not all the plants of such a form are dangerous, but you would do well to avoid any of them."

"And any other," Barjazid put in. "In this desert the plants are well defended, sometimes in surprising ways. Each year our garden teaches us some ugly new secret."

Dekkeret nodded. He did not plan to stroll about out there, but if he did, he would make it his rule to touch nothing.

The floater was old and slow, the grade of the highway steep. Through the broiling night the car labored unhurriedly onward. There was little conversation within. The Skandar drove, with the Vroon beside her, and occasionally Serifain Reinaulion made some comment on the condition of the road; in the rear compartment the two Barjazids sat silently, leaving Dekkeret alone to stare with growing dismay at the infernal landscape. Under the merciless hammers of the sun the ground had a beaten, broken look. Such moisture as winter had brought this land had long ago been sucked forth, leaving gaunt, angular fissures. The surface of the ground was pockmarked where the unceasing winds had strafed it with sand particles, and the plants, low and sparsely growing things, were of many varieties but all appeared twisted, tortured, gnarled, and knobby. To the heat Dekkeret gradually found himself growing accustomed: it was simply there, like one's skin, and after a time one came to accept it. But the deathly ugliness of all that he beheld, the dry rough spiky uncaring bleakness of everything, numbed his soul. A landscape that was hateful was a new concept to him, almost an inconceivable one. Wherever he had gone on Majipoor he had known only beauty. He thought of his home city of Normork spread along the crags of the Mount, with its winding boulevards and its wondrous stone wall and its gentle midnight rains. He thought of the giant city of Stee higher on the Mount, where once he had walked at dawn in a garden of trees no taller than his ankle, with leaves of a green hue that dazzled his eyes. He thought of High Morpin, that glimmering miracle of a city devoted wholly to pleasure, that lay almost in the shadow of the Coronal's awesome castle atop the Mount. And the rugged forested wilds of Khyntor, and the brilliant white towers of Ni-moya, and the sweet meadows of the Glayge Valley—how beautiful a world this is, Dekkeret thought, and what marvels it holds, and how terrible this place I find myself in now!

He told himself that he must alter his values and strive to discover the beauties of this desert, or else it would paralyze his spirit. Let there be beauty in utter dryness, he thought, and beauty in menacing angularity, and beauty in pockmarks, and beauty in ragged plants that shine with a pale green glow by night. Let spiky be beautiful, let bleak be beautiful, let harsh be beautiful. For what is beauty, Dekkeret asked himself, if not a learned response to things beheld? Why is a meadow intrinsically more beautiful than a pebbled desert? Beauty, they say, is in the eye of the beholder; therefore reeducate your eye, Dekkeret, lest the ugliness of this land kill you.

He tried to make himself love the desert. He pulled such words as "bleak" and "dismal" and "repellent" from his mind as though pulling fangs from a wild beast, and instructed himself to see this landscape as tender and comforting. He made himself admire the contorted strata of the exposed rock faces and the great gouges of the dry washes. He found aspects of delight in the bedraggled beaten shrubs. He discovered things to esteem in the small toothy nocturnal creatures that occasionally scuttered across the road. And as the night wore on, the desert did become less hateful to him, and then neutral, and at last he believed he actually could see some beauty in it; and by the hour before dawn he had ceased to think about it at all.

Morning came suddenly: a shaft of orange flame breaking against the mountain wall to the west, a limb of bright red fire rising over the opposite rim of the range, and then the sun, its yellow face tinged more with bronzy-green than in the northern latitudes, bursting into the sky like an untethered balloon. In this moment of apocalyptic sunrise Dekkeret was startled to find himself thinking in sharp pain of the Archiregimand Golator Lasgia, wondering whether she was watching the dawn, and with whom; he savored the pain a little, and then, banishing the thought, said to Barjazid, "It was a night without phantoms. Is this desert not supposed to be haunted?"

"Beyond the pass is where the real trouble begins," the little man replied.

They rode onward through the early hours of the day. Dinitak served a rough breakfast, dry bread and sour wine. Looking back, Dekkeret saw a mighty view, the land sloping off below him like a great tawny apron, all folds and cracks and wrinkles, and the city of Tolaghai barely visible as a huddled clutter at the bottom end, with the vastness of the sea to the north rolling on to the horizon. The sky was without clouds, and the blue of it was so enhanced by the terracotta hue of the land that it seemed almost to be a second sea above him. Already the heat was rising. By mid-morning it was all but unendurable, and still the Skandar driver moved impassively up the breast of the mountain. Dekkeret dozed occasionally, but in the cramped vehicle sleep was impossible. Were they going to drive all night and then all day too? He asked no questions. But just as weariness and discomfort were reaching intolerable levels in him, Khaymak Gran abruptly swung the floater to the left, down a short spur of the road, and brought it to a halt.

"Our first day's camp," Barjazid announced.

Where the spur ended, a high flange of rock reared out of the desert floor, forming an overarching shelter. In front of it, protected by shadows at this time of day, was a wide sandy area that had obviously been used many times as a campsite. At the base of the rock formation Dekkeret saw a dark spot where water mysteriously seeped from the ground, not exactly a gushing spring but useful and welcome enough to parched travelers in this terrible desert. The place was ideal. And plainly the entire first day's journey had been timed to bring them here before the worst of the heat descended.

The Skandar and young Barjazid pulled straw mats from some compartment of the floater and scattered them on the sand; the midday meal was offered, chunks of dried meat, a bit of tart fruit, and warm Skandar mead; then, without a word, the two Barjazids and the Vroon and the Skandar sprawled out on their mats and dropped instantly into sleep. Dekkeret stood alone, probing between his teeth for a bit of meat caught there. Now that he could sleep, he was not at all sleepy. He wandered the edge of the campsite, staring into the sun-blasted wastes just outside the area in shadow. Not a creature could be seen, and even the plants, poor shabby things, seemed to be trying to pull themselves into the ground. The mountains rose steeply above him to the south; the pass could not be far off. And then? And then?

He tried to sleep. Unwanted images plagued him. Golator Lasgia hovered above his mat, so close that he felt he could seize her and draw her down to him, but she bobbed away and was lost in the heat-haze. For the thousandth time he saw himself in that forest in the Khyntor Marches, pursuing his prey, aiming, suddenly trembling. He shook that off and found himself scrambling along the great wall at Normork, with cool delectable air in his lungs. But these were not dreams, only idle fantasies and fugitive memories; sleep would not come for a long time, and when it did, it was deep and dreamless and brief.

Strange sounds awakened him: humming, singing, musical instruments in the distance, the faint but distinct noises of a caravan of many travelers. He thought he heard the tinkle of bells, the booming of drums. For a time he lay still, listening, trying to understand. Then he sat up, blinked, looked around. Twilight had come. He had slept away the hottest part of the day, and the shadows now encroached from the other side. His four companions were up and packing the mats. Dekkeret cocked an ear, seeking the source of the sounds. But they seemed to come from everywhere, or from nowhere. He remembered Golator Lasgia's tale of the ghosts of the desert that sing by day, confusing travelers, leading them from the true path with their clatter and their music.

To Barjazid he said, "What are those sounds?"

"Sounds?"

"You don't hear them? Voices, bells, footfalls, the humming of many travelers?"

Barjazid looked amused. "You mean the desert-songs."

"Ghost-songs?"

"That could be that. Or merely the sounds of wayfarers coming down the mountain, rattling chains, striking gongs. Which is more probable?"

"Neither is probable," said Dekkeret gloomily. "There are no ghosts in the world I inhabit. But there are no wayfarers on this road except ourselves."

"Are you sure, Initiate?"

"That there are no wayfarers, or no ghosts?"

"Either."

Dinitak Barjazid, who had been standing to one side taking in this interchange, approached Dekkeret and said, "Are you frightened?"

"The unknown is always disturbing. But at this point I feel more curiosity than fear."

"I will gratify your curiosity, then. As the heat of the day diminishes, the rocky cliffs and the sands give up their warmth, and in cooling they contract and release sounds. Those are the drums and bells you hear. There are no ghosts in this place," the boy said.

The elder Barjazid made a brusque gesture. Serenely the boy moved away.

"You didn't want him to tell me that, did you?" Dekkeret asked. "You prefer me to think that there are ghosts all about me."

Smiling, Barjazid said, "It makes no difference to me. Believe whichever explanation you find more cheering. You will meet a sufficiency of ghosts, I assure you, on the far side of the pass."

7

All Starday evening they climbed the winding road up the face of the mountain, and near midnight came to Khulag Pass. Here the air was cooler, for they were thousands of feet above sea level and warring winds brought some relief from the swelter. The pass was a broad notch in the mountain wall, surprisingly deep; it was early Sunday morning before they completed its traversal and began their descent into the greater desert of the interior.

Dekkeret was stunned by what lay before him. By bright moonlight he beheld a scene of unparalleled bleakness, that made the lands on the cityward side of the pass look like gardens. That other desert was a rocky one, but this was sandy, an ocean of dunes broken here and there by open patches of hard pebble-strewn ground. There was scarcely any vegetation, none at all in the duned places and the merest of sorry scraggles elsewhere. And the heat! Upward out of the dark bowl ahead there came currents of stupefying hot blasts, air that seemed stripped of all nourishment, air that had been baked to death. It astounded him that somewhere in that furnace there could be grazing lands. He tried to remember the map in the Archiregimand's office: the cattle country was a belt that flanked the continent's innermost zone of desert, but here below Khulag Pass an arm of the central wastes had somehow encroached—that was it. On the far side of this band of formidable sterility lay a green zone of grass and browsing beasts, or so he prayed.

Through the early morning hours they headed down the inner face of the mountains and onto the great central plateau. By first light Dekkeret noticed an odd feature far downslope, an oval patch of inky darkness sharply outlined against the buff breast of the desert, and as they drew nearer he saw that it was an oasis of sorts, the dark patch resolving itself into a grove of slender long-limbed trees with tiny violet-flushed leaves. This place was the second day's campsite. Tracks in the sand showed where other parties had camped; there was scattered debris under the trees; in a clearing at the heart of the grove were half a dozen crude shelters made of heaped-up rocks topped with old dried boughs. Just beyond, a brackish stream wound between the trees and terminated in a small stagnant pool, green with algae. And a little way beyond that was a second pool, apparently fed by a stream that ran wholly underground, the waters of which were pure. Between the two pools Dekkeret saw a curious construction, seven round-topped stone columns as high as his waist, arranged in a double arc. He inspected them.

"Shapeshifter work," Barjazid told him.

"A Meatmorph altar?"

"So we think. We know the Shapeshifters often visit this oasis. We find little Piurivar souvenirs here—prayer sticks, bits of feathers, small clever wickerwork cups."

Dekkeret stared about uneasily at the trees as if he expected them to transform themselves momentarily into a party of savage aborigines. He had had little contact with the native race of Majipoor, those defeated and displaced indigenes of the forests, and what he knew of them was mainly rumor and fantasy, born of fear, ignorance, and guilt. They once had had great cities, that much was certain—Alhanroel was strewn with the ruins of them, and in school Dekkeret had seen views of the most famous of all, vast stone Velalisier not far from the Labyrinth of the Pontifex; but those cities had died thousands of years ago, and with the coming of the human and other races to Majipoor the native Piurivars had been forced back into the darker places of the planet, mainly a great wooded reservation in Zimroel somewhere southeast of Khyntor. To this knowledge Dekkeret had seen actual Metamorphs only two or three times, frail greenish folk with strange blank-featured faces, but of course they slid from one form to another in mimicry of a marvelously easy kind and for all he knew this little Vroon here was a secret Shapeshifter, or Barjazid himself.

He said, "How can Shapeshifters or anyone else survive in this desert?"

"They're resourceful people. They adapt."

"Are there many of them here?"

"Who can know? I've encountered a few scattered bands, fifty, seventy-five all told. Probably there are others. Or perhaps I keep meeting the same ones over and over again in different guises, eh?"

"A strange people," Dekkeret said, rubbing his hand idly over the smooth stone dome atop the nearest of the altar-columns. With astonishing speed Barjazid grasped Dekkeret's wrist and pulled it back.

"Don't touch those!"

"Why not?" said Dekkeret, amazed.

"Those stones are holy."

"To you?"

"To those who erected them," said Barjazid dourly. "We respect them. We honor the magic that may be in them. And in this land one never casually invites the vengeance of one's neighbors."

Dekkeret stared in astonishment at the little man, at the columns, at the two pools, the graceful sharp-leaved trees that surrounded them. Even in the heat he shivered. He looked out, beyond the borders of the little oasis, to the swaybacked dunes all around, to the dusty ribbon of road that disappeared southward into the land of mysteries. The sun was climbing quickly now and its warmth was like a terrible flail pounding the sky, the land, the few vulnerable travelers wandering in this awful place. He glanced back, to the mountains he had just passed through, a huge and ominous wall cutting him off from what passed for civilization on this torrid continent. He felt frighteningly alone here, weak, lost.

Dinitak Barjazid appeared, tottering under a great load of flasks that he dropped almost at Dekkeret's feet. Dekkeret helped the boy fill them from the pure pool, a task that took an unexpectedly long while. He sampled the water himself:

cool, clear, with a strange metallic taste, not displeasing, that
Dinitak said came from dissolved minerals. It took a dozen
trips to carry all the flasks to the floater. There would be no
more sources of fresh water, Dinitak explained, for several
days.

They lunched on the usual rough provisions and afterward,
as the heat rose toward its overwhelming midday peak, they
settled on the straw mats to sleep. This was the third day that
Dekkeret had slept by day and by now his body was growing
attuned to the change; he closed his eyes, commended his
soul to the beloved Lady of the Isle, Lord Prestimion's holy
mother, and tumbled almost instantly into heavy slumber.

This time dreams came.

He had not dreamed properly for more days than he cared
to remember. To Dekkeret as to all other folk of Majipoor
dreams were a central part of existence, nightly providing
comfort, reassurance, instruction, clarification, guidance and
reprimands, and much else. From childhood one was trained
to make one's mind receptive to the messengers of sleep, to
observe and record one's dreams, to carry them with one
through the night and into the waking hours beyond. And always there was the benevolent omnipresent figure of the Lady
of the Isle of Sleep hovering over one, helping one explore
the workings of one's spirit and through her sendings offering
direct communication to each of the billions of souls that
dwelled on vast Majipoor.

Dekkeret now saw himself walking on a mountain ridge
that he perceived to be the crest of the range they had lately
crossed. He was by himself and the sun was impossibly great,
filling half the sky; yet the heat was not troublesome. So steep
was the slope that he could look straight down over the edge,
down and down and down for what seemed hundreds of
miles, and he beheld a roaring smoking cauldron beneath
him, a surging volcanic crater in which red magma bubbled
and churned. That immense vortex of subterranean power did
not frighten him; indeed it exerted a strange pull, a blatant
appeal, so that he yearned to plunge himself into it, to dive to
its depths and swim in its molten heart. He began to descend,
running and skipping, often leaving the ground and floating,
drifting, flying down the immense hillside, and as he drew
nearer he thought he saw faces in the throbbing lava, Lord
Prestimion, and the Pontifex, and Barjazid's face, and Golator Lasgia's—and were those Metamorphs, those strange sly

half-visible images near the periphery? The core of the volcano was a stew of potent figures. Dekkeret ran toward them
in love, thinking, Take me into you, here I am, here I come;
and when he perceived, behind all the others, a great white
disk that he understood to be the loving countenance of the
Lady of the Isle, a deep and powerful bliss invaded his soul,
for he knew this now to be a sending, and it was many
months since last the kind Lady had touched his sleeping
mind.

Sleeping but aware, watching the Dekkeret within the
dream, he awaited the consummation, the joining of dream-
Dekkeret to dream-Lady, the immolation in the volcano that
would bring some revelation of truth, some instant of
knowledge leading to joy. But then a strangeness crossed the
dream like some spreading veil. The colors faded; the faces
dimmed; he continued to run down the side of the mountain
wall, but now he stumbled often, he tripped and sprawled, he
abraded his hands and knees against hot desert rocks, and he
was losing the path entirely, moving sideways instead of
downward, unable to progress. He had been on the verge of a
moment of delight, and somehow it was out of reach now
and he felt only distress, uneasiness, shock. The ecstasy that
seemed to be the promise of the dream was draining from it.
The brilliant colors yielded to an all-encompassing gray, and
all motion ceased: he stood frozen on the mountain face,
staring rigidly down at a dead crater, and the sight of it made
him tremble and pull his knees to his chest, and he lay there
sobbing until he woke.

He blinked and sat up. His head pounded and his eyes felt
raw, and there was a dismal tension in his chest and shoulders. This was not what dreams, even the most terrifying of
dreams, were supposed to provide: such a gritty residue of
malaise, confusion, fear. It was early afternoon and the blinding sun hung high above the treetops. Nearby him lay Khaymak Gran and the Vroon, Serifain Reinaulion; a bit farther
away was Dinitak Barjazid. They seemed sound asleep. The
elder Barjazid was nowhere in view. Dekkeret rolled over and
pressed his cheeks into the warm sand beside his mat and attempted to let the tension ease from him. Something had
gone wrong in his sleep, he knew; some dark force had
meddled in his dream, had stolen the virtue from it and given
him pain in exchange. So this was what they meant by the
haunting of the desert? This was dream-stealing? He drew

himself together in a knotted ball. He felt soiled, used, invaded. He wondered if it would be like this every sleep-period now, as they penetrated deeper into this awful desert; he wondered whether it might get even worse.

After a time Dekkeret returned to sleep. More dreams came, stray blurred scraps without rhythm or design. He ignored them. When he woke, the day was ending and the desert-sounds, the ghost-sounds, were nibbling at his ears, tinklings and murmurings and far-off laughter. He felt more weary than if he had not slept at all.

8

The others showed no sign of having been disturbed as they slept. They greeted Dekkeret upon rising in their usual manners—the huge taciturn Skandar woman not at all, the little Vroon with amiable buzzing chirps and much coiling and interlacing of tentacles, the two Barjazids with curt nods—and if they were aware that one member of their party had been visited with torments in his dreams, they said nothing of it. After breakfast the elder Barjazid held a brief conference with Serifain Reinaulion concerning the roads they were to travel that night, and then they were off into the moonlit darkness once again.

I will pretend that nothing out of the ordinary happened, Dekkert resolved. I will not let them know that I am vulnerable to these phantoms.

But it was a short-lived resolution. As the floater was passing through a region of dry lakebeds out of which odd gray-green stony humps projected by the thousands, Barjazid turned to him suddenly and said, breaking a long silence, "Did you dream well?"

Dekkeret knew he could not conceal his fatigue. "I have had better rest," he muttered.

Barjazid's glossy eyes were fixed inexorably on his. "My son says you moaned in your sleep, that you rolled over many times and clutched your knees. Did you feel the touch of the dream-stealers, Initiate?"

"I felt the presence of a troubling power in my dreams. Whether this was the touch of the dream-stealers I have no way of knowing."

"Will you describe the sensations?"

"Are you a dream-speaker then, Barjazid?" Dekkeret snapped in sudden anger. "Why should I let you probe and poke in my mind? My dreams are my own!"

"Peace, peace, good knight. I meant no intrusion."

"Let me be, then."

"Your safety is my responsibility. If the demons of this wasteland have begun to reach your spirit, it is in your own interest to inform me."

"Demons, are they?"

"Demons, ghosts, phantoms, disaffected Shapeshifters, whatever they are," Barjazid said impatiently. "The beings that prey on sleeping travelers. Did they come to you or did they not?"

"My dreams were not pleasing."

"I ask you to tell me in what way."

Dekkeret let his breath out slowly. "I felt I was having a sending from the Lady, a dream of peace and joy. And gradually it changed its nature, do you see? It darkened and became chaotic, and all the joy was taken from it, and I ended the dream worse than when I entered it."

Nodding earnestly, Barjazid said, "Yes, yes, those are the symptoms. A touch on the mind, an invasion of the dream, a disturbing overlay, a taking of energy."

"A kind of vampirism?" Dekkeret suggested. "Creatures that lie in wait in this wasteland and tap the life-force from unwary travelers?"

Barjazid smiled. "You insist on speculations. I make no hypotheses of any kind, Initiate."

"Have you felt their touch in your own sleep?"

The small man stared at Dekkeret strangely. "No. No, never."

"Never? Are you immune?"

"Seemingly so."

"And your boy?"

"It has befallen him several times. It happens to him only rarely out here, one time out of fifty, perhaps. But the immunity is not hereditary, it appears."

"And the Skandar? And the Vroon?"

"They too have been touched," said Barjazid. "On infrequent occasions. They find it bothersome but not intolerable."

"Yet others have died from the dream-stealers' touch."

"More hypothesis," said Barjazid. "Most travelers passing this way in recent years have reported experiencing strange dreams. Some of them have lost their way and have failed to return. How can we know whether there is a connection between the disturbing dreams and the losing of the way?"

"You are a very cautious man," Dekkeret said. "You leap to no conclusions."

"And I have survived to a fair old age, while many who were more rash have returned to the Source."

"Is mere survival the highest achievement you think one can attain?"

Barjazid laughed. "Spoken like a true knight of the Castle! No, Initiate, I think there's more to living than mere avoidance of death. But survival helps, eh, Initiate? Survival's a good basic requirement for those who go on to do high deeds. The dead don't achieve a thing."

Dekkeret did not care to pursue that theme. The code of values of a knight-initiate and of such a one as Barjazid were hardly comparable; and, besides, there was something wily and mercurial about Barjazid's style of argument that made Dekkeret feel slow and stolid and hulking, and he disliked exposing himself to that feeling. He was silent a moment. Then he said, "Do the dreams get worse as one gets deeper into the desert?"

"So I am given to understand," said Barjazid.

Yet as the night waned and the time for making camp arrived, Dekkeret found himself ready and even eager to contend once more with the phantoms of sleep. They had camped this day far out on the bowl of the desert, in a low-lying area where much of the sand had been swept aside by scouring winds, and the underlying rock shield showed through. The dry air had a weird crackle to it, a kind of wind-borne buzz, as if the force of the sun were stripping the particles of matter bare in this place. It was only an hour before midday by the time they were ready for sleep. Dekkeret settled calmly on his mat of straw and, without fear, offered his soul on the verge of slumber to whatever might come. In his order of knighthood he had been trained in the customary notions of courage, naturally, and was expected to meet challenges without fear, but he had been little tested thus far. On placid Majipoor one must work hard to find such challenges, going into the untamed parts of the world, for in the settled regions life is orderly and courteous; therefore Dekkeret had gone abroad, but he had not done well by his first major trial, in the forests of the Khyntor Marches. Here he had another chance. These foul dreams held forth to him, in a way, the promise of redemption.

He gave himself up to sleep.

And quickly dreamed. He was back in Tolaghai, but a Tolaghai curiously transformed, a city of smooth-faced alabaster villas and dense green gardens, though the heat was still of tropical intensity. He wandered up one boulevard and down the next, admiring the elegance of the architecture and the splendor of the shrubbery. His clothing was the traditional green and gold of the Coronal's entourage, and as he encountered the citizens of Tolaghai making their twilight promenades he bowed gracefully to them, and exchanged with them the starburst finger-symbol that acknowledged the Coronal's authority. To him now came the slender figure of the lovely Archiregimand Golator Lasgia. She smiled, she took him by the hand, she led him to a place of cascading fountains where cool spray drifted through the air, and there they put their clothing aside and bathed, and rose naked from the sweet-scented pool, and strolled, feet barely touching the ground, into a garden of plants with arching stems and great glistening many-lobed leaves. Without words she encouraged him onward, along shadowy avenues bordered by rows of close-planted trees. Golator Lasgia moved just ahead of him, an elusive and tantalizing figure, floating only inches out of his reach and then gradually widening the distance to feet and yards. At first it seemed hardly a difficult task to overtake her, but he made no headway at it, and had to move faster and faster to keep within sight of her. Her rich olive-hued skin gleamed by early moonlight, and she glanced back often, smiling brilliantly, tossing her head to urge him to keep up. But he could not. She was nearly an entire length of the garden ahead of him now. With growing desperation he impelled himself toward her, but she was dwindling, disappearing, so far ahead of him now that he could barely see the play of muscles beneath her glowing bare skin, and as he rushed from one pathway of the garden to the next he became aware of an increase in the temperature, a sudden and steady change in the air, for somehow the sun was rising here in the night and its full force was striking his shoulders. The trees were wilting and drooping. Leaves were falling. He struggled to remain upright. Golator Lasgia was only a dot on the horizon now, still beckoning to him, still smiling, still tossing her head, but she grew smaller and smaller, and the sun was still climbing, growing stronger, searing, incinerating, withering everything within its reach. Now the garden was a place of gaunt bare branches and rough cracked arid soil. A dreadful thirst had come over him, but there was no water here, and when he saw figures lurking behind the blistered and blackened trees—Metamorphs, they were, subtle tricky creatures that would not hold their shapes still, but flickered and flowed in a maddening way—he called out to them for something to drink, and was given only light tinkling laughter to ease his dryness. He staggered on. The fierce pulsing light in the heavens was beginning to roast him; he felt his skin hardening, crackling, crisping, splitting. Another moment of this and he would be charred. What had become of Golator Lasgia? Where were the smiling, bowing, starburst-making townspeople? He saw no garden now. He was in the desert, lurching and stumbling through a torrid baking wasteland where even shadows burned. Now real terror rose in him, for even as he dreamed he felt the pain of the heat, and the part of his soul that was observing all this grew alarmed, thinking that the power of the dream might well be so great as to reach up to injure his physical self. There were tales of such things, people who had perished in their sleep of dreams that had overwhelming force. Although it went against his training to terminate a dream prematurely, although he knew he must ordinarily see even the worst of horrors through to its ultimate revelation, Dekkeret considered awakening himself for safety's sake, and nearly did; but then he saw that as a species of cowardice and vowed to remain in the dream even if it cost him his life. He was down on his knees now, groveling in the fiery sands, staring with strange clarity at mysterious tiny golden-bodied insects that were marching in single file across the rims of the dunes toward him: ants, they were, with ugly swollen jaws, and each in turn clambered up his body and took a tiny nip, the merest bite, and clung and held on, so that within moments thousands of the minute creatures were covering his skin. He brushed at them but could not dislodge them. Their pincers held and their heads came loose from their bodies: the sand about him was black now with headless ants, but they spread over his skin like a cloak, and he brushed and brushed with greater vigor while still more ants mounted him and dug their jaws in. He grew weary of brushing at them. It was actually cooler in this cloak of ants, he thought. They shielded him from the worst of the sun, although they too stung and burned him, but not as painfully as did the sun's rays. Would the dream never end? He attempted to take control of it himself, to turn the stream of onrushing ants into a rivulet of cool pure water, but that did not work, and he let himself slip back into the nightmare and went crawling wearily onward over the sands.

And gradually Dekkeret became aware that he was no longer dreaming.

There was no boundary between sleep and wakefulness that he could detect, except that eventually he realized that his eyes were open and that his two centers of consciousness, the dreamer who observed and the dream-Dekkeret who suffered, had merged into one. But he was still in the desert, under the terrible midday sun. He was naked. His skin felt raw and blistered. And there were ants crawling on him, up his legs as far as his knees, minute pale ants that indeed were nipping their tiny pincers into his flesh. Bewildered, he wondered if he had tumbled into some layer of dream beneath dream, but no, so far as he could tell this was the waking world, this was the authentic desert and he was out in the midst of it. He stood up, brushing the ants away—and as in the dream they gripped him even at the cost of their heads—and looked about for the campsite.

He could not see it. In his sleep he had wandered out onto the bare scorching anvil of the open desert and he was lost. Let this be a dream still, he thought fiercely, and let me awaken from it in the shade of Barjazid's floater. But there was no awakening. Dekkeret understood now how lives were lost in the Desert of Stolen Dreams.

"Barjazid?" he called. *"Barjazid!"*

9

Echoes came back to him from the distant hills. He called again, two, three times, and listened to the reverberations of his own voice, but heard no reply. How long could he survive out here? An hour? Two? He had no water, no shelter, not even a scrap of clothing. His head was bare to the sun's great blazing eye. It was the hottest part of the day. The landscape looked the same in all directions, flat, a shallow bowl swept by hot winds. He searched for his own footprints, but the trail gave out within yards, for the ground was hard and rocky here and he had left no imprint. The camp might lie anywhere about, hidden from him by the slightest of rises in the terrain. He called out again for help and again heard only echoes. Perhaps if he could find a dune he would bury himself to his neck, and wait out the heat that way, and by darkness he might locate the camp by its campfire; but he saw no dunes. If there were a high place here that would give him a sweeping view, he would mount it and search the horizon for the camp. But he saw no hillocks. What would Lord Stiamot do in such a situation, he wondered, or Lord Thimin, or one of the other great warriors of the past? What is Dekkeret going to do? This was a foolish way to die, he thought, a useless, nasty, ugly death. He turned and turned and turned again, scanning every way. No clues; no point in walking at all, not knowing where he was going. He shrugged and crouched in a place where there were no ants. There was no dazzlingly clever ploy that he could use to save himself. There was no inner resource that would bring him, against all the odds, to safety. He had lost himself in his sleep, and he would die just as Golator Lasgia had said he would, and that was all there was to it. Only one thing remained to him, and that was strength of character: he would die quietly and calmly, without tears or anger, without raging against the forces of fate. Perhaps it would take an hour. Perhaps less. The important thing was to die honorably, for when death is inevitable there's no sense making a botch of it.

He waited for it to come.

What came instead—ten minutes later, half an hour, an hour, he had no way of knowing—was Serifain Reinaulion. The Vroon appeared like a mirage out of the east, trudging slowly toward Dekkeret struggling under the weight of two flasks of water, and when he was within a hundred yards or so he waved two of his tentacles and called, "Are you alive?"

"More or less. Are you real?"

"Real enough. And we've been searching for you half the afternoon." In a flurry of rubbery limbs the small creature pushed one of the flasks upward into Dekkeret's hands. "Here. Sip it. Don't gulp. *Don't gulp.* You're so dehydrated you'll drown if you're too greedy."

Dekkeret fought the impulse to drain the flask in one long pull. The Vroon was right: sip, sip, be moderate, or harm will come. He let the water trickle into his mouth, swished it around, soaked his swollen tongue in it, finally let it down his throat. *Ah.* Another cautious sip. Another, then a fair swallow. He grew a little dizzy. Serifain Reinaulion beckoned for the flask. Dekkeret shook him off, drank again, rubbed a little of the water against his cheeks and lips.

"How far are we from the camp?" he asked finally.

"Ten minutes. Are you strong enough to walk, or shall I go back for the others?"

"I can walk."

"Let's get started, then."

Dekkeret nodded. "One more little sip—"

"Carry the flask. Drink whenever you like. If you get weak, tell me and we'll rest. Remember, I can't carry you."

The Vroon headed off slowly toward a low sandy ridge perhaps five hundred yards to the east. Feeling wobbly and lightheaded, Dekkeret followed, and was surprised to see the ground trending upward; the ridge was not all that low, he realized, but some trick of the glare had made him think otherwise. In fact it rose to two or three times his own height, high enough to conceal two lesser ridges on the far side. The floater was parked in the shadow of the farther one.

Barjazid was the only person at the camp. He glanced up at Dekkeret with what looked like contempt or annoyance in his eyes and said, "Went for a stroll, did you? At noontime?"

"Sleepwalking. The dream-stealers had me. It was like being under a spell." Dekkeret was shivering as the sunburn began to disrupt his body's heat-shedding systems. He dropped down alongside the floater and huddled under a light robe. "When I woke I couldn't see camp. I was sure that I would die."

"Half an hour more and you would have. You must be two-thirds fried as it is. Lucky for you my boy woke up and saw that you had disappeared."

Dekkeret pulled the robe tighter around him. "Is that how they die out here? By sleepwalking at midday?"

"One of the ways, yes."

"I owe you my life."

"You've owed me your life since we crossed Khulag Pass. Going on your own you'd have been dead fifty times already.

But thank the Vroon, if you have to thank anyone. He did the real work of finding you."

Dekkeret nodded. "Where's your son? And Khaymak Gran? Out looking for me also?"

"On their way back," said Barjazid. And indeed the Skandar and the boy appeared only moments later. Without a glance at him the Skandar flung herself down on her sleeping-mat; Dinitak Barjazid grinned slyly at Dekkeret and said, "Had a pleasant walk?"

"Not very. I regret the inconvenience I caused you."

"As do we."

"Perhaps I should sleep tied down from now on."

"Or with a heavy weight sitting on your chest," Dinitak suggested. He yawned. "Try to stay put until sundown, at least. Will you?"

"So I intend," said Dekkeret.

But it was impossible for him to fall asleep. His skin itched in a thousand places from the bites of the insects, and the sunburn, despite a cooling ointment that Serifain Reinaulion gave him, made him miserable. There was a dry, dusty feeling in his throat that no amount of water seemed to cure, and his eyes throbbed painfully. As though probing an irritating sore he ran through his memories of his desert ordeal again and again—the dream, the heat, the ants, the thirst, the awareness of imminent death. Rigorously he searched for moments of cowardice and found none. Dismay, yes, and anger, and discomfort, but he had no recollection of panic or fear. Good. Good. The worst part of the experience, he decided, had not been the heat and thirst and peril but the dream, the dark and disturbing dream, the dream that had once again begun in joy and midway had undergone a somber metamorphosis. To be denied the solace of healthy dreams is a kind of death-in-life, he thought, far worse than perishing in a desert, for dying occupies only a single moment but dreaming affects all of one's time to come. And what knowledge was it that these bleak Suvraelu dreams were imparting? Dekkeret knew that when dreams came from the Lady they must be studied intently, if necessary with the aid of one who practices the art of dream-speaking, for they contain information vital to the proper conduct of one's life; but these dreams were hardly of the Lady, seeming rather to emanate from some other dark Power, some sinister and oppressive force more adept at taking than giving. Shapeshifters? It could be. What if some tribe of them had, through deceit, obtained one of the devices by which the Lady of the Isle is able to reach the minds of her flock, and lurked here in the hot heartland of Suvrael preying on unwary travelers, stealing from their souls, draining their vitality, imposing an unknown and unfathomable revenge one by one upon those who had stolen their world?

As the afternoon shadows lengthened he found himself at last slipping back into sleep. He fought it, fearing the touch of the invisible intruders on his soul once again. Desperately he held his eyes open, staring across the darkening wasteland and listening to the eerie hum and buzz of the desert-sounds; but it was impossible to fend off exhaustion longer. He drifted into a light, uneasy slumber, broken from time to time by dreams that he sensed came neither from the Lady nor from any other external force, but merely floated randomly through the strata of his weary mind, bits of patternless incident and stray incomprehensible images. And then someone was shaking him awake—the Vroon, he realized. Dekkeret's mind was foggy and slow. He felt numbed. His lips were cracked, his back was sore. Night had fallen, and his companions were already at work closing down their camp. Serifain Reinaulion offered Dekkeret a cup of some sweet thick blue-green juice, and he drank it in a single draught.

"Come," the Vroon said. "Time to be going onward."

10

Now the desert changed again and the landscape grew violent and rough. Evidently there had been great earthquakes here, and more than one, for the land lay fractured and upheaved, with mighty blocks of the desert floor piled at unlikely angles against others, and huge sprawls of talus at the feet of the low shattered cliffs. Through this chaotic zone of turbulence and disruption there was only a single passable route—the wide, gently curving bed of a long-extinct river whose sandy floor swerved in long easy bends between the cracked and sundered rock-heaps. The large moon was full and there was almost a daylight brilliance to the grotesque scene. After some hours of passing through a terrain so much the same from one mile to the next that it seemed almost as though the floater were not moving at all, Dekkeret turned to

Barjazid and said, "And how long will it be before we reach Ghyzyn Kor?"

"This valley marks the boundary between desert and grazing lands." Barjazid pointed toward the southwest, where the riverbed vanished between two towering craggy peaks that rose like daggers from the desert floor. "Beyond that place—Munnerak Notch—the climate is altogether different. On the far side of the mountain wall sea-fogs enter by night from the west, and the land is green and fit for grazing. We will camp halfway to the Notch tomorrow, and pass through it the day after. By Seaday at the latest you'll be at your lodgings in Ghyzyn Kor."

"And you?" Dekkeret asked.

"My son and I have business elsewhere in the area. We'll return to Ghyzyn Kor for you after—three days? Five?"

"Five should be sufficient."

"Yes. And then the return journey."

"By the same route?"

"There is no other," said Barjaizd. "They explained to you in Tolaghai, did they not, that access to the rangelands was cut off, except by way of this desert? But why should you fear this route? The dreams aren't so awful, are they? And so long as you do no more roaming in your sleep, you'll not be in any danger here."

It sounded simple enough. Indeed he felt sure he could survive the trip; but yesterday's dream had been sufficient torment, and he looked without cheer upon what might yet come. When they made camp the next morning Dekkeret found himself again uneasy about entrusting himself to sleep at all. For the first hour of the rest-period he kept himself awake, listening to the metallic clangor of the bare tumbled rocks as they stretched and quivered in the midday heat, until at last sleep came up over his mind like a dense black cloud and took him unawares.

And in time a dream possessed him, and it was, he knew at its outset, going to be the most terrible of all.

Pain came first—an ache, a twinge, a pang, then without warning a racking explosion of dazzling light against the walls of his skull, making him grunt and clutch his head. The agonizing spasm passed swiftly, though, and he felt the soft sleep presence of Golator Lasgia about him, soothing him, cradling him against her breasts. She rocked him and murmured to him and eased him until he opened his eyes and sat up and looked around, and saw that he was out of the desert, free of Suvrael itself. He and Golator Lasgia were in some cool forest glade where giant trees with perfectly straight yellow-barked trunks rose to incomprehensible heights, and a swiftly flowing stream, studded with rocky outcroppings, tumbled and roared wildly past almost at their feet. Beyond the stream the land dropped sharply away, revealing a distant valley, and, on the far side of it, a great gray saw-toothed snow-capped mountain which Dekkeret recogniezd instantly as one of the nine vast peaks of the Khyntor Marches.

"No," he said. "This is not where I want to be."

Golator Lasgia laughed, and the pretty tinkling sound of it was somehow sinister in his ears, like the delicate sounds the desert made at twilight. "But this is a dream, good friend! You must take what comes, in dreams!"

"I will direct my dream. I have no wish to return to the Khyntor Marches. Look: the scene changes. We are on the Zimr, approaching the river's great bend. See? See? The city of Ni-moya sparkling there before us?"

Indeed he saw the huge city, white against the green backdrop of forested hills. But Golator Lasgia shook her head.

"There is no city here, my love. There is only the northern forest. Feel the wind? Listen to the song of the stream. Here—kneel, scoop up the fallen needles on the ground. Ni-moya is far away, and we are here to hunt."

"I beg you, let us be in Ni-moya."

"Another time," said Golator Lasgia.

He could not prevail. The magical towers of Ni-moya wavered and grew transparent and were gone, and there remained only the yellow-boled trees, the chilly breezes, the sounds of the forest. Dekkeret trembled. He was the prisoner of this dream and there was no escape.

And now five hunters in rough black haigus-hide robes appeared and made perfunctory gestures of deference and held forth weapons to him, the blunt dull tube of an energy-thrower and a short sparkling poniard and a blade of a longer kind with a hooked tip. He shook his head, and one of the hunters came close and grinned mockingly at him, a gap-toothed grin out of a wide mouth stinking from dried fish. Dekkeret recognized her face, and looked away in shame, for she was the hunter who had died on that other day in the Khyntor Marches a thousand thousand years ago. If only she were not here now, he thought, the dream might be bearable.

But this was diabolical torture, to force him to live through all this once again.

Golator Lasgia said, "Take the weapons from her. The steetmoy are running and we must be after them."

"I have no wish to——"

"What folly, to think that dreams respect wishes! The dream *is* your wish. Take the weapons."

Dekkeret understood. With chilled fingers he accepted the blades and the energy-thrower and stowed them in the proper places on his belt. The hunters smiled and grunted things at him in the thick harsh dialect of the north. Then they began to run along the bank of the stream, moving in easy loping bounds, touching the ground no more than one stride out of five; and willy-nilly Dekkeret ran with them, clumsily at first, then with much the same floating grace. Golator Lasgia, by his side, kept pace easily, her dark hair fluttering about her face, her eyes bright with excitement. They turned left, into the heart of the forest, and fanned out in a crescent formation that widened and curved inward to confront the prey.

The prey! Dekkeret could see three white-furred steetmoy gleaming like lanterns deep in the forest. The beasts prowled uneasily, growling, aware of intruders but still unwilling to abandon their territory—big creatures, possibly the most dangerous wild animals on Majipoor, quick and powerful and cunning, the terrors of the northlands. Dekkeret drew his poniard. Killing steetmoy with energy-throwers was no sport, and might damage too much of their valuable fur besides: one was supposed to get to close range and kill them with one's blade, preferably the poniard, if necessary the hooked machete.

The hunters looked to him. Pick one, they were saying, choose your quarry. Dekkeret nodded. The middle one, he indicated. They were smiling coldly. What did they know that they were not telling him? It had been like this that other time, too, the barely concealed scorn of the mountainfolk for the pampered lordlings who were seeking deadly amusements in their forests; and that outing had ended badly. Dekkeret hefted his poniard. The dream-steetmoy that moved nervously beyond those trees were implausibly enormous, great heavy-haunched immensities that clearly could not be slain by one man alone, wielding only hand-weapons, but here there was no turning back, for he knew himself to be bound upon whatever destiny the dream offered him. Now with hunting-

horns and hand-clapping the hired hunters commenced to
stampede the prey; the steetmoy, angered and baffled by the
sudden blaring strident sounds, rose high, whirled, raked trees
with their claws, swung around, and more in disgust than
fear began to run.

The chase was on.

Dekkeret knew that the hunters were separating the animals, driving the two rejected ones away to allow him a clear
chance at the one he had chosen. But he looked neither to
the right nor the left. Accompanied by Golator Lasgia and
one of the hunters, he rushed forward, giving pursuit as the
steetmoy in the center went rumbling and crashing through
the forest. This was the worst part, for although humans were
faster, steetmoy were better able to break through barriers of
underbrush, and he might well lose his quarry altogether in
the confusions of the run. The forest here was fairly open;
but the steetmoy was heading for cover, and soon Dekkeret
found himself struggling past saplings and vines and low
brush, barely able to keep the retreating white phantom in
view. With singleminded intensity he ran and hacked with the
machete and clambered through thickets. It was all so terribly
familiar, so much of an old story, especially when he realized
that the steetmoy was doubling back, was looping through the
trampled part of the forest as if planning a counterattack—

The moment would soon be at hand, the dreaming Dekkeret knew, when the maddened animal would blunder upon
the gap-toothed hunter, would seize the mountain woman and
hurl her against a tree, and Dekkeret, unwilling or unable to
halt, would go plunging onward, continuing the chase, leaving
the woman where she lay, so that when the squat thick-
snouted scavenging beast emerged from its hole and began to
rip her belly apart there would be no one to defend her, and
only later, when things were more quiet and there was time
to go back for the injured hunter, would he begin to regret
the callous uncaring focus of concentration that had allowed
him to ignore his fallen companion for the sake of keeping
sight of his prey. And afterward the shame, the guilt, the
unending self-accusations—yes, he would go through all that
again as he lay here asleep in the stifling heat of the Suvraelu
desert, would he not?

No.

No, it was not that simple at all, for the language of
dreams is complex, and in the thick mists that suddenly en-

folded the forest Dekkeret saw the steetmoy swing around and lash the gap-toothed woman and knock her flat, but the woman rose and spat out a few bloody teeth and laughed, and the chase continued, or rather it twisted back on itself to the same point, the steetmoy bursting forth unexpectedly from the darkest part of the woods and striking at Dekkeret himself, knocking his poniard and his machete from his hands, rearing high overhead for the death-blow, but not delivering it, for the image changed and it was Golator Lasgia who lay beneath the plunging claws while Dekkeret wandered aimlessly nearby, unable to move in any useful direction, and then it was the huntswoman who was the victim once more, and Dekkeret again, and suddenly and improbably old pinch-faced Barjazid, and then Golator Lasgia. As Dekkeret watched, a voice at his elbow said, "What does it matter? We each owe the Divine a death. Perhaps it was more important for you then to follow your prey." Dekkeret stared. The voice was the voice of the gap-toothed hunter. The sound of it left him dazed and shaking. The dream was becoming bewildering. He struggled to penetrate its mysteries.

Now he saw Barjazid standing at his side in the dark cool forest glade. The steetmoy once more was savaging the mountain woman.

"Is this the way it truly was?" Barjazid asked.

"I suppose so. I didn't see it."

"What did you do?"

"Kept on going. I didn't want to lose the animal."

"You killed it?"

"Yes."

"And then?"

"Came back. And found her. Like that—"

Dekkeret pointed. The snuffling scavenger was astride the woman. Golator Lasgia stood nearby, arms folded, smiling.

"And then?"

"The others came. They buried their companion. We skinned the steetmoy and rode back to camp."

"And then? And then? And then?"

"Who are you? Why are you asking me this?"

Dekkeret had a flashing view of himself beneath the scavenger's fanged snout.

Barjazid said, "You were ashamed?"

"Of course. I put the pleasures of my sport ahead of a human life."

"You had no way of knowing she was injured."

"I sensed it. I saw it, but I didn't *let* myself see it, do you understand? I knew she was hurt. I kept on going."

"Who cared?"

"I cared."

"Did her tribesmen seem to care?"

"I cared."

"And so? And so? And so?"

"It mattered to me. Other things matter to them."

"You felt guilty?"

"Of course."

"You *are* guilty. Of youth, of foolishness, of naïveté."

"And are you my judge?"

"Of course I am," said Barjazid. "See my face?" He tugged at his seamed weatherbeaten jowls, pulled and twisted until his leathery desert-tanned skin began to split, and the face ripped away like a mask, revealing another face beneath, a hideous ironic distorted face twisted with convulsive mocking laughter, and the other face was Dekkeret's own.

II

In that moment Dekkeret experienced a sensation as of a bright needle of piercing light driving downward through the roof of his skull. It was the most intense pain he had ever known, a sudden intolerable spike of racking anguish that burned through his brain with monstrous force. It lit a flare in his consciousness by whose baleful light he saw himself grimly illuminated, fool, romantic, boy, sole inventor of a drama about which no one else cared, inventing a tragedy that had an audience of one, seeking purgation for a sin without context, which was no sin at all except perhaps the sin of self-indulgence. In the midst of his agony Dekkeret heard a great gong tolling far away and the dry rasping sound of Barjazid's demonic laughter; then with a sudden wrenching twist he pulled free of sleep and rolled over, quivering, shaken, still afflicted by the lancing thrust of the pain, although it was beginning to fade as the last bonds of sleep dropped from him.

He struggled to rise and found himself enveloped in thick musky fur, as if the steetmoy had seized him and was crushing him against its breast. Powerful arms gripped him—*four* arms, he realized, and as Dekkeret completed the journey up out of dreams he understood that he was in the embrace of the giant Skandar woman, Khaymak Gran. Probably he had been crying out in his sleep, thrashing and flailing about, and as he scrambled to his feet she had decided he was off on another sleepwalking excursion and was determined to prevent him from going. She was hugging him with rib-cracking force.

"It's all right," he muttered, tight against her heavy gray pelt. "I'm awake! I'm not going anywhere!"

Still she clung to him.

"You're—hurting—me—"

He fought for breath. In her great awkward solicitousness she was apt to kill him with motherly kindness. Dekkeret pushed, even kicked, twisted, hammered at her with his head. Somehow as he wriggled in her grasp he threw her off balance, and they toppled together, she beneath him; at the last moment her arms opened, allowing Dekkeret to spin away. He landed on both knees and crouched where he fell, aching in a dozen places and befuddled by all that had happened in the last few moments. But not so befuddled that when he stood up he failed to see Barjaid, on the far side of the floater, hastily removing some sort of mechanism from his forehead, some slender crownlike circlet, and attempting to conceal it in a compartment of the floater.

"What was that?" Dekkeret demanded.

Barjaid looked uncharacteristically flustered. "Nothing. A toy, only."

"Let me see."

Barjaid seemed to signal. Out of the corner of his eye Dekkeret saw Khaymak Gran getting to her feet and beginning to reach for him again, but before the ponderous Skandar could manage it Dekkeret had skipped out of the way and darted around the floater to Barjaid's side. The little man was still busy with his intricate bit of machinery. Dekkeret, looming over him as the Skandar had loomed over Dekkeret, swiftly caught Barjaid's hand and yanked it up behind his back. Then he plucked the mechanism from its storage case and examined it.

Everyone was awake now. The Vroon stared goggle-eyed at what was going on; and young Dinitak, producing a knife that was not much unlike the one in Dekkeret's dream, glared up at him and said, "Let go of my father."

Dekkeret swung Barjaid around to serve as a shield.

"Tell your son to put that blade away," he said.

Barjazid was silent.

Dekkeret said, "He drops the blade or I smash this thing in my hand. Which?"

Barjazid gave the order in a low growling tone. Dinitak pitched the knife into the sand almost at Dekkeret's feet, and Dekkeret, taking one step forward, pulled it to him and kicked it behind him. He dangled the mechanism in Barjazid's face: a thing of gold and crystal and ivory, elaborately fashioned, with mysterious wires and connections.

"What is this?" Dekkeret said.

"I told you. A toy. Please—give it to me, before you break it."

"What is the function of this toy?"

"It amuses me while I sleep," said Barjazid hoarsely.

"In what way?"

"It enhances my dreams and makes them more interesting."

Dekkeret took a closer look at it. "If I put it on, will it enhance my dreams?"

"It will only harm you, Initiate."

"Tell me what it does for you."

"That is very hard to describe," Barjazid said.

"Work at it. Strive to find the words. How did you become a figure in my dream, Barjazid? You had no business being in that particular dream."

The little man shrugged. He said uncomfortably, "Was I in your dream? How would I know what was happening in your dream? Anyone can be in anybody's dream."

"I think this machine may have helped put you there. And may have helped you know what I was dreaming."

Barjazid responded only with glum silence.

Dekkeret said, "Describe the workings of this machine, or I'll grind it to scrap in my hand."

"Please—"

Dekkeret's thick strong fingers closed on one of the most fragile-looking parts of the device. Barjazid sucked in his breath; his body went taut in Dekkeret's grip.

"Well?" Dekkeret said.

"Your guess is right. It—it lets me enter sleeping minds."

"Truly? Where did you get such a thing?"

"My own invention. A notion that I have been perfecting over a number of years."

"Like the machines of the Lady of the Isle?"

"Different. More powerful. She can only speak to minds; I can read dreams, control the shape of them, take command of a person's sleeping mind to a great degree."

"And this device is entirely of your own making. Not stolen from the Isle."

"Mine alone," Barjazid murmured.

A torrent of rage surged through Dekkeret. For an instant he wanted to crush Barjazid's machine in one quick squeeze and then to grind Barjazid himself to pulp. Remembering all of Barjazid's half-truths and evasions and outright lies, thinking of the way Barjazid had meddled in his dreams, how he had wantonly distorted and transformed the healing rest Dekkeret so sorely needed, how he had interposed layers of fears and torments and uncertainties into that Lady-sent gift, his own true blissful rest, Dekkeret felt an almost murderous fury at having been invaded and manipulated in this fashion. His heart pounded, his throat went dry, his vision blurred. His hand tightened on Barjazid's bent arm until the small man whimpered and mewed. Harder—harder—break it off—

No.

Dekkeret reached some inner peak of anger and held himself there a moment, and then let himself descend the farther slope toward tranquillity. Gradually, he regained his steadiness, caught his breath, eased the drumming in his chest. He held tight to Barjazid until he felt altogether calm. Then he released the little man and shoved him forward against the floater. Barjazid staggered and clung to the vehicle's curving side. All color seemed to have drained from his face. Tenderly he rubbed his bruised arm, and glanced up at Dekkeret with an expression that seemed to be compounded equally of terror and pain and resentment.

With care Dekkeret studied the curious instrument, gently rubbing the tips of his fingers over its elegant and complicated parts. Then he moved as if to put it on his own forehead.

Barjazid gasped. "Don't!"

"What will happen? Will I damage it?"

"You will. And yourself as well."

Dekkeret nodded. He doubted that Barjazid was bluffing, but he did not care to find out.

After a moment he said, "There are no Shapeshifter dream-stealers hiding in this desert, is that right?"

"That is so," Barjazid whispered.

"Only you, secretly experimenting on the minds of other travelers. Yes?"

"Yes."

"And causing them to die."

"No," Barjazid said. "I intended no deaths. If they died, it was because they became alarmed, became confused, because they panicked and ran off into dangerous places—because they began to wander in their sleep, as you did—"

"But they died because you had meddled in their minds."

"Who can be sure of that? Some died, some did not. I had no desire to have anyone perish. Remember, when *you* wandered away, we searched diligently for you."

"I had hired you to guide and protect me," said Dekkeret. "The others were innocent strangers whom you preyed on from afar, is that not so?"

Barjazid was silent.

"You knew that people were dying as a result of your experiments, and you went on experimenting."

Barjazid shrugged.

"How long were you doing this?"

"Several years."

"And for what reason?"

Barjazid looked toward the side. "I told you once, I would never answer a question of that sort."

"And if I break your machine?"

"You will break it anyway."

"Not so," Dekkeret replied. "Here. Take it."

"*What?*"

Dekkeret extended his hand, with the dream-machine resting on his palm. "Go on. Take it. Put it away. I don't want the thing."

"You're not going to kill me?" Barjazid said in wonder.

"Am I your judge? If I catch you using that device on me again, I'll kill you sure enough. But otherwise, no. Killing is not my sport. I have one sin on my soul as it is. And I need you to get me back to Tolaghai, or have you forgotten that?"

"Of course. Of course." Barjazid looked astounded at Dekkeret's mercy.

Dekkeret said, "Why would I want to kill you?"

"For entering your mind—for interfering with your dreams—"

"Ah."

"For putting your life at risk on the desert."

"That too."

"And yet you aren't eager for vengeance?"

Dekkeret shook his head. "You took great liberties with my soul, and that angered me, but the anger is past and done with. I won't punish you. We've had a transaction, you and I, and I've had my money's worth from you, and this thing of yours has been of value to me." He leaned close and said in a low, earnest voice, "I came to Suvrael full of doubt and confusion and guilt, looking to purge myself through physical suffering. That was foolishness. Physical suffering makes the body uncomfortable and strengthens the will, but it does little for the wounded spirit. You gave me something else, you and your mind-meddling toy. You tormented me in dreams and held up a mirror to my soul, and I saw myself clearly. How much of that last dream were you really able to read, Barjazid?"

"You were in a forest—in the north—"

"Yes."

"Hunting. One of your companions was injured by an animal, yes? Is that it?"

"Go on."

"And you ignored her. You continued the chase. And afterward, when you went back to see about her, it was too late, and you blamed yourself for her death. I sensed the great guilt in you. I felt the power of it radiating from you."

"Yes," Dekkeret said. "Guilt that I'll bear forever. But there's nothing that can be done for her now, is there?" An astonishing calmness had spread through him. He was not altogether sure what had happened, except that in his dream he had confronted the events of the Khyntor forest at last, and had faced the truth of what he had done there and what he had not done, had understood, in a way that he could not define in words, that it was folly to flagellate himself for all his lifetime over a single act of carelessness and unfeeling stupidity, that the moment had come to put aside all self-accusation and get on with the business of his life. The process of forgiving himself was under way. He had come to Suvrael to be purged and somehow he had accomplished that. And he owed Barjazid thanks for that favor. To Barjazid he said, "I might have saved her, or maybe not; but my mind was elsewhere, and in my foolishness I passed her by to make my kill. But wallowing in guilt is no useful means of atonement, eh, Barjazid? The dead are dead. My services must be offered to the living. Come: turn this floater and let's begin heading back toward Tolaghai."

"And what about your visit to the rangelands? What about Ghyzyn Kor?"

"A silly mission. It no longer matters, these questions of meat shortages and trade imbalances. Those problems are already solved. Take me to Tolaghai."

"And then?"

"You will come with me to Castle Mount. To demonstrate your toy before the Coronal."

"No!" Barjazid cried in horror. He looked genuinely frightened for the first time since Dekkeret had known him. "I beg you—"

"Father?" said Dinitak.

Under the midday sun the boy seemed ablaze with light. There was a wild and fiery look of pride on his face.

"Father, go with him to Castle Mount. Let him show his masters what we have here."

Barjazid moistened his lips. "I fear—"

"Fear nothing. Our time is now beginning."

Dekkeret looked from one to the other, from the suddenly timid and shrunken old man to the transfigured and glowing boy. He sensed that historic things were happening, that mighty forces were shifting out of balance and into a new configuration, and this he barely comprehended, except to know that his destinies and those of these desertfolk were tied in some way together; and the dream-reading machine that Barjazid had created was the thread that bound their lives.

Barjazid said huskily, "What will happen to me on Castle Mount, then?"

"I have no idea," said Dekkeret. "Perhaps they'll take your head and mount it atop Lord Siminave's Tower. Or perhaps you'll find yourself set up on high as a Power of Majipoor. Anything might happen. How would I know?" He realized that he did not care, that he was indifferent to Barjazid's fate, that he felt no anger at all toward this seedy little tinkerer with minds, but only a kind of perverse abstract gratitude for Barjazid's having helped rid him of his own demons. "These matters are in the Coronal's hands. But one thing is certain, that you will go with me to the Mount, and this machine of yours with us. Come, now, turn the floater, take me to Tolaghai."

"It is still daytime," Barjazid muttered. "The heart of the day rages at its highest."

"We'll manage. Come: get us moving, and fast! We have a ship to catch in Tolaghai, and there's a woman in that city I want to see again, before we set sail!"

12

These events happened in the young manhood of him who was to become the Coronal Lord Dekkeret in the Pontificate of Prestimion. And it was the boy Dinitak Barjazid who would be the first to rule in Suvrael over the minds of all the sleepers of Majipoor, with the title of King of Dreams.

SIX

The Soul-Painter and the Shapeshifter

It has become an addiction. Hissune's mind is opening now in all directions, and the Register of Souls is the key to an infinite world of new understanding. When one dwells in the Labyrinth one develops a peculiar sense of the world as vague and unreal, mere names rather than concrete places: only the dark and hermetic Labyrinth has substance, and all else is vapor. But Hissune has journeyed by proxy to every continent now, he has tasted strange foods and seen weird landscapes, he has experienced extremes of heat and cold, and in all that he has come to acquire a comprehension of the complexity of the world that, he suspects, very few others have had. Now he goes back again and again. No longer does he have to bother with forged credentials; he is so regular a user of the archives that a nod is sufficient to get him within, and then he has all the million yesterdays of Majipoor at his disposal. Often he stays with a capsule for only a moment or two, until he has determined that it contains nothing that will move him farther along the road to knowledge. Sometimes of a morning he will call up and dismiss eight, ten, a dozen records in rapid succession. True enough, he knows, that every being's soul contains a universe; but not all universes are equally interesting, and that which he might learn from the innermost depths of one who spent his life sweeping the streets of Piliplok or murmuring prayers in the entourage of

153

*the Lady of the Isle does not seem immediately useful to him,
when he considers other possibilities. So he summons capsules
and rejects them and summons again, dipping here and there
into Majipoor's past, and keeps at it until he finds himself in
contact with a mind that promises real revelation. Even
Coronals and Pontifexes can be bores, he has discovered. But
there are always wondrous unexpected finds—a man who fell
in love with a Metamorph, for example—*

It was a surfeit of perfection that drove the soul-painter
Therion Nismile from the crystalline cities of Castle Mount
to the dark forests of the western continent. All his life he had
lived amid the wonders of the Mount, traveling through the
Fifty Cities according to the demands of his career, exchang-
ing one sort of splendor for another every few years. Dundilmir was his native city—his first canvases were scenes of the
Fiery Valley, tempestuous and passionate with the ragged energies of youth—and then he dwelled some years in marvelous Canzilaine of the talking statues, and afterward in Stee
the awesome, whose outskirts were three days' journey across,
and in golden Halanx at the very fringes of the Castle, and
for five years at the Castle itself, where he painted at the
court of the Coronal Lord Thraym. His paintings were prized
for their calm elegance and their perfection of form, which
mirrored the flawlessness of the Fifty Cities to the ultimate
degree. But the beauty of such places numbs the soul, after a
time, and paralyzes the artistic instincts. When Nismile
reached his fortieth year he found himself beginning to identify perfection with stagnation; he loathed his own most famous works; his spirit began to cry out for upheaval,
unpredictability, transformation.

The moment of crisis overtook him in the gardens of
Tolingar Barrier, that miraculous park on the plain between
Dundilmir and Stipool. The Coronal had asked him for a
suite of paintings of the gardens, to decorate a pergola under
construction on the Castle's rim. Obligingly Nismile made the
long journey down the slopes of the enormous mountain,
toured the forty miles of park, chose the sites where he meant
to work, set up his first canvas at Kazkas Promontory, where
the contours of the garden swept outward in great green symmetrical pulsating scrolls. He had loved this place when he
was a boy. On all of Majipoor there was no site more serene,
more orderly, for the Tolingar gardens were composed of

plants bred to maintain themselves in transcendental tidiness. No gardener's shears touched these shrubs and trees; they grew of their own accord in graceful balance, regulated their own spacing and rate of replacement, suppressed all weeds in their environs, and controlled their proportions so that the original design remained forever unbreached. When they shed their leaves or found it needful to drop an entire dead bough, enzymes within dissolved the cast-off matter quickly into useful compost. Lord Havilbove, more than a hundred years ago, had been the founder of this garden; his successors Lord Kanaba and Lord Sirruth had continued and extended the program of genetic modification that governed it; and under the present Coronal Lord Thraym its plan was wholly fulfilled, so that now it would remain eternally perfect, eternally balanced. It was that perfection which Nismile had come to capture.

He faced his blank canvas, drew breath deep down into his lungs, and readied himself for entering the trance state. In a moment his soul, leaping from his dreaming mind, would in a single instant imprint the unique intensity of his vision of this scene on the psychosensitive fabric. He glanced one last time at the gentle hills, the artful shrubbery, the delicately angled leaves—and a wave of rebellious fury crashed against him, and he quivered and shook and nearly fell. This immobile landscape, this static, sterile beauty, this impeccable and matchless garden, had no need of him; it was itself as unchanging as a painting, and as lifeless, frozen in its own faultless rhythms to the end of time. How ghastly! How hateful! Nismile swayed and pressed his hands to his pounding skull. He heard the soft surprised grunts of his companions, and when he opened his eyes he saw them all staring in horror and embarrassment at the blackened and bubbling canvas. "Cover it!" he cried, and turned away. Everyone was in motion at once; and in the center of the group Nismile stood statue-still. When he could speak again he said quietly, "Tell Lord Thraym I will be unable to fulfill his commission."

And so that day in Dundilmir he purchased what he needed and began his long journey to the lowlands, and out into the broad hot flood-plain of the Iyann River, and by riverboat interminably along the sluggish Iyann to the western port of Alaisor; and at Alaisor he boarded, after a wait of weeks, a ship bound for Numinor on the Isle of Sleep, where he tarried a month. Then he found passage on a pilgrim-ship sailing to Piliplok on the wild continent of Zimroel. Zimroel, he was sure, would not oppress him with elegance and perfection. It had only eight or nine cities, which in fact were probably little more than frontier towns. The entire interior of the continent was wilderness, into which Lord Stiamot had driven the aboriginal Metamorphs after their final defeat four thousand years ago. A man wearied of civilization might be able to restore his soul in such surroundings.

Nismile expected Piliplok to be a mudhole, but to his surprise it turned out to be an ancient and enormous city, laid out according to a maddeningly rigid mathematical plan. It was ugly but not in any refreshing way, and he moved on by riverboat up the Zimr. He journeyed past great Ni-moya, which was famous even to inhabitants of the other continent, and did not stop there; but at a town called Verf he impulsively left the boat and set forth in a hired wagon into the forests to the south. When he had traveled so deep into the wilderness that he could see no trace of civilization, he halted and built a cabin beside a swift dark stream. It was three years since he had left Castle Mount. Through all his journey he had been alone and had spoken to others only when necessary, and he had not painted at all.

Here Nismile felt himself beginning to heal. Everything in this place was unfamiliar and wonderful. On Castle Mount, where the climate was artificially controlled, an endless sweet springtime reigned, the unreal air was clear and pure, and rainfall came at predictable intervals. But now he was in a moist and humid rain-forest, where the soil was spongy and yielding, clouds and tongues of fog drifted by often, showers were frequent, and the vegetation was a chaotic, tangled anarchy, as far removed as he could imagine from the symmetries of Tolingar Barrier. He wore little clothing, learned by trial and error what roots and berries and shoots were safe to eat, and devised a wickerwork weir to help him catch the slender crimson fish that flashed like skyrockets through the stream. He walked for hours through the dense jungle, savoring not only its strange beauty but also the tense pleasure of wondering if he could find his way back to his cabin. Often he sang, in a loud erratic voice; he had never sung on Castle Mount. Occasionally he started to prepare a canvas, but always he put it away unused. He composed nonsensical poems, voluptuous strings of syllables, and chanted them to an audience of slender towering trees and incomprehensibly intertwined vines. Sometimes he wondered how it was going at the court of Lord Thraym, whether the Coronal had hired a new artist yet to paint the decorations for the pergola, and if the halatingas were blooming now along the road to High Morpin. But such thoughts came rarely to him.

He lost track of time. Four or five or perhaps six weeks—how could he tell?—went by before he saw his first Metamorph.

The encounter took place in a marshy meadow two miles upstream from his cabin. Nismile had gone there to gather the succulent scarlet bulbs of mud-lilies, which he had learned to mash and roast into a sort of bread. They grew deep, and he dug them by working his arm into the muck to the shoulder and groping about with his cheek pressed to the ground. He came up muddy-faced and slippery, clutching a dripping handful, and was startled to find a figure calmly watching him from a distance of a dozen yards.

He had never seen a Metamorph. The native beings of Majipoor were perpetually exiled from the capital continent, Alhanroel, where Nismile had spent all his years. But he had an idea of how they looked, and he felt sure this must be one: an enormously tall, fragile, sallow-skinned being, sharp-faced, with inward-sloping eyes and barely perceptible nose and stringy, rubbery hair of a pale greenish hue. It wore only a leather loin-harness and a short sharp dirk of some polished black wood was strapped to its hip. In eerie dignity the Metamorph stood balanced with one frail long leg twisted around the shin of the other. It seemed both sinister and gentle, menacing and comic. Nismile chose not to be alarmed.

"Hello," he said. "Do you mind if I gather bulbs here?"

The Metamorph was silent.

"I have the cabin down the stream. I'm Therion Nismile. I used to be a soul-painter, when I lived on Castle Mount."

The Metamorph regarded him solemnly. A flicker of unreadable expression crossed its face. Then it turned and slipped gracefully into the jungle, vanishing almost at once.

Nismile shrugged. He dug down for more mud-lily bulbs.

A week or two later he met another Metamorph, or perhaps the same one, this time while he was stripping bark from a vine to make rope for a bilantoon-trap. Once more the aborigine was wordless, materializing quietly like an ap-

parition in front of Nismile and contemplating him from the
same unsettling one-legged stance. A second time Nismile
tried to draw the creature into conversation, but at his first
words it drifted off, ghostlike. "Wait!" Nismile called. "I'd
like to talk with you. I—" But he was alone.

A few days afterward he was collecting firewood when he
became aware yet again that he was being studied. At once
he said to the Metamorph, "I've caught a bilantoon and I'm
about to roast it. There's more meat than I need. Will you
share my dinner?" The Metamorph smiled—he took that
enigmatic flicker for a smile, though it could have been anything—and as if by way of replying underwent a sudden astonishing shift, turning itself into a mirror image of Nismile,
stocky and muscular, with dark penetrating eyes and shoul-
der-length black hair. Nismile blinked wildly and trembled;
then, recovering, he smiled, deciding to take the mimicry as
some form of communication, and said, "Marvelous! I can't
begin to see how you people do it!" He beckoned. "Come.
It'll take an hour and a half to cook the bilantoon, and we can
talk until then. You understand our language, don't you?" It
was bizarre beyond measure, this speaking to a duplicate of
himself. "Say something, eh? Tell me: is there a Metamorph
village somewhere nearby? *Piurivar*," he corrected, remembering the Metamorphs' name for themselves. "Eh? A lot of
Piurivars hereabouts, in the jungle?" Nismile gestured again.
"Walk with me to my cabin and we'll get the fire going. You
don't have any wine, do you? That's the only thing I miss, I
think, some good strong wine, the heavy stuff they make in
Muldemar. Won't taste that ever again, I guess, but there's
wine in Zimroel, isn't there? Eh? Will you say something?"
But the Metamorph responded only with a grimace, perhaps
intended as a grin, that twisted the Nismile-face into something harsh and strange; then it resumed its own form between
one instant and the next and with calm floating strides went
walking away.

Nismile hoped for a time that it would return with a flask
of wine, but he did not see it again. Curious creatures, he
thought. Were they angry that he was camped in their territory? Were they keeping him under surveillance out of fear
that he was the vanguard of a wave of human settlers?
Oddly, he felt himself in no danger. Metamorphs were generally considered to be malevolent; certainly they were disquiet-

ing beings, alien and unfathomable. Plenty of tales were told
of Metamorph raids on outlying human settlements, and no
doubt the Shapeshifter folk harbored bitter hatred for those
who had come to their world and dispossessed them and
driven them into these jungles; but yet Nismile knew himself
to be a man of good will, who had never done harm to others
and wanted only to be left to live his life, and he fancied that
some subtle sense would lead the Metamorphs to realize that
he was not their enemy. He wished he could become their
friend. He was growing hungry for conversation after all this
time of solitude, and it might be challenging and rewarding
to exchange ideas with these strange folk; he might even
paint one. He had been thinking again lately of returning to
his art, of experiencing once more that moment of creative
ecstasy as his soul leaped the gap to the psychosensitive canvas and inscribed on it those images that he alone could fashion. Surely he was different now from the increasingly
unhappy man he had been on Castle Mount, and that difference must show itself in his work. During the next few days
he rehearsed speeches designed to win the confidence of the
Metamorphs, to overcome that strange shyness of theirs, that
delicacy of bearing which blocked any sort of contact. In
time, he thought, they would grow used to him, they would
begin to speak, to accept his invitation to eat with him, and
then perhaps they would pose—

But in the days that followed he saw no more Metamorphs. He roamed the forest, peering hopefully into thickets
and down mistswept lanes of trees, and found no one. He decided that he had been too forward with them and had
frightened them away—so much for the malevolence of the
monstrous Metamorphs!—and after a while he ceased to expect further contact with them. That was disturbing. He had
not missed companionship when none seemed likely, but the
knowledge that there were intelligent beings somewhere in the
area kindled an awareness of loneliness in him that was not
easy to bear.

One damp and warm day several weeks after his last Metamorph encounter Nismile was swimming in the cool deep
pond formed by a natural dam of boulders half a mile below
his cabin when he saw a pale slim figure moving quickly
through a dense bower of blue-leaved bushes by the shore.
He scrambled out of the water, barking his knees on the

rocks. "Wait!" he shouted. "Please—don't be afraid—don't go—" The figure disappeared, but Nismile, thrashing frantically through the underbrush, caught sight of it again in a few minutes, leaning casually now against an enormous tree with vivid red bark.

Nismile stopped short, amazed, for the other was no Metamorph but a human woman.

She was slender and young and naked, with thick auburn hair, narrow shoulders, small high breasts, bright playful eyes. She seemed altogether unafraid of him, a forest-sprite who had obviously enjoyed leading him on this little chase. As he stood gaping at her she looked him over unhurriedly, and with an outburst of clear tinkling laughter said, "You're all scratched and torn! Can't you run in the forest any better than that?"

"I didn't want you to get away."

"Oh, I wasn't going to go far. You know, I was watching you for a long time before you noticed me. You're the man from the cabin, right?"

"Yes. And you—where do you live?"

"Here and there," she said airily.

He stared at her in wonder. Her beauty delighted him, her shamelessness astounded him. She might almost be an hallucination, he thought. Where had she come from? What was a human being, naked and alone, doing in this primordial jungle?

Human?

Of course not, Nismile realized, with the sudden sharp grief of a child who has been given some coveted treasure in a dream, only to awaken aglow and perceive the sad reality. Remembering how effortlessly the Metamorph had mimicked him, Nismile comprehended the dismal probability: this was some prank, some masquerade. He studied her intently, seeking a sign of Metamorph identity, a flickering of the projection, a trace of knife-sharp cheekbones and sloping eyes behind the cheerfully impudent face. She was convincingly human in every degree. But yet—how implausible to meet one of his own kind here, how much more likely that she was a Shapeshifter, a deceiver—

He did not want to believe that. He resolved to meet the possibility of deception with a conscious act of faith, in the hope that that would make her be what she seemed to be.

"What's your name?" he asked.

"Sarise. And yours?"

"Nismile. Where *do* you live?"

"In the forest."

"Then there's a human settlement not far from here?"

She shrugged. "I live by myself." She came toward him—he felt his muscles growing taut as she moved closer, and something churning in his stomach, and his skin seemed to be blazing—and touched her fingers lightly to the cuts the vines had made on his arms and chest. "Don't those scratches bother you?"

"They're beginning to. I should wash them."

"Yes. Let's go back to the pool. I know a better way than the one you took. Follow me!"

She parted the fronds of a thick clump of ferns and revealed a narrow, well-worn trail. Gracefully she sprinted off, and he ran behind her, delighted by the ease of her movements, the play of muscles in her back and buttocks. He plunged into the pool a moment after her and they splashed about. The chilly water soothed the stinging of the cuts. When they climbed out, he yearned to draw her to him and enclose her in his arms, but he did not dare. They sprawled on the mossy bank. There was mischief in her eyes.

He said, "My cabin isn't far."

"I know."

"Would you like to go there?"

"Some other time, Nismile."

"All right. Some other time."

"Where do you come from?" she asked.

"I was born on Castle Mount. Do you know where that is? I was a soul-painter at the Coronal's court. Do you know what soul-painting is? It's done with the mind and a sensitive canvas, and—I could show you. I could paint you, Sarise. I take a close look at something, I seize its essence with my deepest consciousness, and then I go into a kind of trance, almost a waking dream, and I transform what I've seen into something of my own and hurl it on the canvas, I capture the truth of it in one quick blaze of transference—" He paused. "I could show you best by making a painting of you."

She scarcely seemed to have heard him.

"Would you like to touch me, Nismile?"

"Yes. Very much."

The thick turquoise moss was like a carpet. She rolled toward him and his hand hovered above her body, and then he hesitated, for he was certain still that she was a Metamorph playing some perverse Shapeshifter game with him, and a heritage of thousands of years of dread and loathing surfaced in him, and he was terrified of touching her and discovering that her skin had the clammy repugnant texture that he imagined Metamorph skin to have, or that she would shift and turn into a creature of alien form the moment she was in his arms. Her eyes were closed, her lips were parted, her tongue flickered between them like a serpent's: she was waiting. In terror he forced his hand down to her breast. But her flesh was warm and yielding and it felt very much the way the flesh of a young human woman should feel, as well as he could recall after these years of solitude. With a soft little cry she pressed herself into his embrace. For a dismaying instant the grotesque image of a Metamorph rose in his mind, angular and long-limbed and noseless, but he shoved the thought away fiercely and gave himself up entirely to her lithe and vigorous body.

For a long time afterward they lay still, side by side, hands clasped, saying nothing. Even when a light rainshower came they did not move, but simply allowed the quick sharp sprinkle to wash the sweat from their skins. He opened his eyes eventually and found her watching him with keen curiosity.

"I want to paint you," he said.

"No."

"Not now. Tomorrow. You'll come to my cabin, and—"

"No."

"I haven't tried to paint in years. It's important to me to begin again. And I want very much to paint you."

"I want very much not to be painted," she said.

"Please."

"No," she said gently. She rolled away and stood up. "Paint the jungle. Paint the pool. Don't paint me, all right, Nismile? All right?"

He made an unhappy gesture of acceptance.

She said, "I have to leave now."

"Will you tell me where you live?"

"I already have. Here and there. In the forest. Why do you ask these questions?"

"I want to be able to find you again. If you disappear, how will I know where to look?"

"I know where to find you," she said. "That's enough."

"Will you come to me tomorrow? To my cabin?"

"I think I will."

He took her hand and drew her toward him. But now she was hesitant, remote. The mysteries of her throbbed in his mind. She had told him nothing, really, but her name. He found it too difficult to believe that she, like he, was a solitary of the jungle, wandering as the whim came; but he doubted that he could have failed to detect, in all these weeks, the existence of a human village nearby. The most likely explanation still was that she was a Shapeshifter, embarked for who knew what reason on an adventure with a human. Much as he resisted that idea, he was too rational to reject it completely. But she *looked* human, she *felt* human, she *acted* human. How good were these Metamorphs at their transformations? He was tempted to ask her outright whether his suspicions were correct, but that was foolishness; she had answered nothing else, and surely she would not answer that. He kept his questions to himself. She pulled her hand gently free of his grasp and smiled and made the shape of a kiss with her lips, and stepped toward the fern-bordered trail and was gone.

Nismile waited at his cabin all the next day. She did not come. It scarcely surprised him. Their meeting had been a dream, a fantasy, an interlude beyond time and space. He did not expect ever to see her again. Toward evening he drew a canvas from the pack he had brought with him and set it up, thinking he might paint the view from his cabin as twilight purpled the forest air; he studied the landscape a long while, testing the verticals of the slender trees against the heavy horizontal of a thick sprawling yellow-berried bush, and eventually shook his head and put his canvas away. Nothing about this landscape needed to be captured by art. In the morning, he thought, he would hike upstream past the meadow to a place where fleshy red succulents sprouted like rubbery spikes from a deep cleft in a great rock: a more promising scene, perhaps.

But in the morning he found excuses for delaying his departure, and by noon it seemed too late to go. He worked in his little garden plot instead—he had begun transplanting some of the shrubs whose fruits or greens he ate—and that occupied him for hours. In late afternoon a milky fog settled over the forest. He went in; and a few minutes later there was a knock at the door.

"I had given up hope," he told her.

Sarise's forehead and brows were beaded with moisture. The fog, he thought, or maybe she had been dancing along the path. "I promised I'd come," she said softly.

"Yesterday."

"This is yesterday," she said, laughing, and drew a flask from her robe. "You like wine? I found some of this. I had to go a long distance to get it. Yesterday."

It was a young gray wine, the kind that tickles the tongue with its sparkle. The flask had no label, but he supposed it to be some Zimroel wine, unknown on Castle Mount. They drank it all, he more than she—she filled his cup again and again—and when it was gone they lurched outside to make love on the cool damp ground beside the stream, and fell into a doze afterward, she waking him in some small hour of the night and leading him to his bed. They spent the rest of the night pressed close to one another, and in the morning she showed no desire to leave. They went to the pool to begin the day with a swim; they embraced again on the turquoise moss; then she guided him to the gigantic red-barked tree where he had first seen her, and pointed out to him a colossal yellow fruit, three or four yards across, that had fallen from one of its enormous branches. Nismile looked at it doubtfully. It had split open, and its interior was a scarlet custardy stuff, studded with huge gleaming black seeds. "Dwikka," she said. "It will make us drunk." She stripped off her robe and used it to wrap great chunks of the dwikka-fruit, which they carried back to his cabin and spent all morning eating. They sang and laughed most of the afternoon. For dinner they grilled some fish from Nismile's weir, and later, as they lay arm in arm watching the night descend, she asked him a thousand questions about his past life, his painting, his boyhood, his travels, about Castle Mount, the Fifty Cities, the Six Rivers, the royal court of Lord Thraym, the royal Castle of uncountable rooms. The questions came from her in a torrent, the newest one rushing forth almost before he had dealt with the last. Her curiosity was inexhaustible. It served, also, to stifle his; for although there was much he yearned to know about her—everything—he had no chance to ask it, and just as well, for he doubted she would give him answers.

"What will we do tomorrow?" she asked, finally.

So they became lovers. For the first few days they did little but eat and swim and embrace and devour the intoxicating fruit of the dwikka-tree. He ceased to fear, as he had at the beginning, that she would disappear as suddenly as she had come to him. Her flood of questions subsided, after a time, but even so he chose not to take his turn, preferring to leave her mysteries unpierced.

He could not shake his obsession with the idea that she was a Metamorph. The thought chilled him—that her beauty was a lie, that behind it she was alien and grotesque—especially when he ran his hands over the cool sweet smoothness of her thighs or breasts. He had constantly to fight away his suspicions. But they would not leave him. There were no human outposts in this part of Zimroel and it was too implausible that this girl—for that was all she was, a girl—had elected, as he had, to take up a hermit's life here. Far more likely, Nismile thought, that she was native to this place, one of the unknown number of Shapeshifters who slipped like phantoms through these humid groves. When she slept he sometimes watched her by faint starlight to see if she began to lose human form. Always she remained as she was; and even so, he suspected her.

And yet, and yet, it was not in the nature of Metamorphs to seek human company or to show warmth toward them. To most people of Majipoor the Metamorphs were ghosts of a former era, revenants, unreal, legendary. Why would one seek him out in his seclusion, offer itself to him in so convincing a counterfeit of love, strive with such zeal to brighten his days and enliven his nights? In a moment of paranoia he imagined Sarise reverting in the darkness to her true shape and rising above him as he slept to plunge a gleaming dirk into his throat: revenge for the crimes of his ancestors. But what folly such fantasies were! If the Metamorphs here wanted to murder him, they had no need of such elaborate charades.

It was almost as absurd to believe that she was a Metamorph as to believe that she was not.

To put these matters from his mind he resolved to take up his art again. On an unusually clear and sunny day he set out with Sarise for the rock of the red succulents, carrying a raw canvas. She watched, fascinated, as he prepared everything.

"You do the painting entirely with your mind?" she asked.

"Entirely. I fix the scene in my soul, I transform and rearrange and heighten, and then—you'll see."

"It's all right if I watch? I won't spoil it?"

"Of course not."

"But if someone else's mind gets into the painting—"

"It can't happen. The canvases are tuned to me." He squinted, made frames with his fingers, moved a few feet this way and that. His throat was dry and his hands were quivering. So many years since last he had done this: would he still have the gift? And the technique? He aligned the canvas and touched it in a preliminary way with his mind. The scene was a good one, vivid, bizarre, the color contrasts powerful ones, the compositional aspects challenging, that massive rock, those weird meaty red plants, the tiny yellow floral bracts at their tips, the forest-dappled sunlight—yes, yes, it would work, it would amply serve as the vehicle through which he could convey the texture of this dense tangled jungle, this place of shapeshifting—

He closed his eyes. He entered trance. He hurled the picture to the canvas.

Sarise uttered a small surprised cry.

Nismile felt sweat break out all over; he staggered and fought for breath; after a moment he regained control and looked toward the canvas.

"How beautiful!" Sarise murmured.

But he was shaken by what he saw. Those dizzying diagonals—the blurred and streaked colors—the heavy greasy sky, hanging in sullen loops from the horizon—it looked nothing like the scene he had tried to capture, and, far more troublesome, nothing like the work of Therion Nismile. It was a dark and anguished painting, corrupted by unintended discords.

"You don't like it?" she asked.

"It isn't what I had in mind."

"Even so—how wonderful, to make the picture come out of the canvas like that—and such a lovely thing—"

"You think it's lovely?"

"Yes, of course! Don't you?"

He stared at her. This? Lovely? Was she flattering him, or

merely ignorant of prevailing tastes, or did she genuinely admire what he had done? This strange tormented painting, this somber and alien work—

Alien.

"You don't like it," she said, not a question this time.

"I haven't painted in almost four years. Maybe I need to go about it slowly, to get the way of it right again—"

"I spoiled your painting," Sarise said.

"You? Don't be silly."

"My mind got into it. My way of seeing things."

"I told you that the canvases are tuned to me alone. I could be in the midst of a thousand people and nothing of them would affect the painting."

"But perhaps I distracted you, I swerved your mind somehow."

"Nonsense."

"I'll go for a walk. Paint another one while I'm gone."

"No, Sarise. This one is splendid. The more I look at it, the more pleased I am. Come: let's go home, let's swim and eat some dwikka and make love. Yes?"

He took the canvas from its mount and rolled it. But what she had said affected him more than he would admit. Some kind of strangeness *had* entered the painting, no doubt of it. What if she had managed somehow to taint it, her hidden Metamorph soul radiating its essence into his spirit, coloring the impulses of his mind with an alien hue—

They walked downstream in silence. When they reached the meadow of the mud-lilies where Nismile had seen his first Metamorph, he heard himself blurt, "Sarise, I have to ask you something."

"Yes?"

He could not halt himself. "You aren't human, are you? You're really a Metamorph, right?"

She stared at him wide-eyed, color rising in her cheeks.

"Are you serious?"

He nodded.

"Me a Metamorph?" She laughed, not very convincingly. "What a wild idea!"

"Answer me, Sarise. Look into my eyes and answer me."

"It's too foolish, Therion."

"Please. Answer me."

"You want me to prove I'm human? How could I?"

"I want you to tell me that you're human. Or that you're something else."

"I'm human," she said.

"Can I believe that?"

"I don't know. Can you? I've given you your answer." Her eyes flashed with mirth. "Don't I feel human? Don't I act human? Do I seem like an imitation?"

"Perhaps I'm unable to tell the difference."

"Why do you think I'm a Metamorph?"

"Because only Metamorphs live in this jungle," he said. "It seems—logical. Even though—despite—" He faltered. "Look, I've had my answer. It was a stupid question and I'd like to drop the subject. All right?"

"How strange you are! You must be angry with me. You do think I spoiled your painting."

"That's not so."

"You're a very poor liar, Therion."

"All right. *Something* spoiled my painting. I don't know what. It wasn't the painting I intended."

"Paint another one, then."

"I will. Let me paint you, Sarise."

"I told you I didn't want to be painted."

"I need to. I need to see what's in my own soul, and the only way I can know—"

"Paint the dwikka-tree, Therion. Paint the cabin."

"Why not paint you?"

"The idea makes me uncomfortable."

"You aren't giving me a real answer. What is there about being painted that—"

"Please, Therion."

"Are you afraid I'll see you on the canvas in a way that you won't like? Is that it? That I'll get a different answer to my questions when I paint you?"

"Please."

"Let me paint you."

"No."

"Give me a reason, then."

"I can't," she said.

"Then you can't refuse." He drew a canvas from his pack. "Here, in the meadow, now. Go on, Sarise. Stand beside the stream. It'll take only a moment—"

"No, Therion."

"If you love me, Sarise, you'll let me paint you."

It was a clumsy bit of blackmail, and it shamed him to have attempted it; and angered her, for he saw a harsh glitter in her eyes that he had never seen before. They confronted each other for a long tense moment.

Then she said in a cold flat voice, "Not here, Therion. At the cabin. I'll let you paint me there, if you insist."

Neither of them spoke the rest of the way home.

He was tempted to forget the whole thing. It seemed to him that he had imposed his will by force, that he had committed a sort of rape, and he almost wished he could retreat from the position he had won. But there would never now be any going back to the old easy harmony between them; and he had to have the answers he needed. Uneasily he set about preparing a canvas.

"Where shall I stand?" she asked.

"Anywhere. By the stream. By the cabin."

In a slouching slack-limbed way she moved toward the cabin. He nodded and dispiritedly began the final steps before entering trance. Sarise glowered at him. Tears were welling in her eyes.

"I love you," he cried abruptly, and went down into trance, and the last thing he saw before he closed his eyes was Sarise altering her pose, coming out of her moody slouch, squaring her shoulders, eyes suddenly bright, smile flashing.

When he opened his eyes the painting was done and Sarise was staring timidly at him from the cabin door.

"How is it?" she asked.

"Come. See for yourself."

She walked to his side. They examined the picture together, and after a moment Nismile slipped his arm around her shoulder. She shivered and moved closer to him.

The painting showed a woman with human eyes and Metamorph mouth and nose, against a jagged and chaotic background of clashing reds and oranges and pinks.

She said quietly, "Now do you know what you wanted to know?"

"Was it you in the meadow? And the other two times?"

"Yes."

"Why?"

"You interested me, Therion. I wanted to know all about you. I had never seen anything like you."

"I still don't believe it," he whispered.

She pointed toward the painting. "Believe it, Therion."

"No. No."

"You have your answer now."

"I *know* you're human. The painting lies."

"No, Therion."

"Prove it for me. Change for me. Change now." He released her and stepped a short way back. "Do it. Change for me."

She looked at him sadly. Then, without perceptible transition, she turned herself into a replica of him, as she had done once before: the final proof, the unanswerable answer. A muscle quivered wildly in his cheek. He watched her unblinkingly and she changed again, this time into something terrifying and monstrous, a nightmarish gray pock-marked balloon of a thing with flabby skin and eyes like saucers and a hooked black beak; and from that she went to the Metamorph form, taller than he, hollow-chested and featureless, and then she was Sarise once more, cascades of auburn hair, delicate hands, firm strong thighs.

"No," he said. "Not that one. No more counterfeits."

She became the Metamorph again.

He nodded. "Yes. That's better. Stay that way. It's more beautiful."

"Beautiful, Therion?"

"I find you beautiful. Like this. As you really are. Deception is always ugly."

He reached for her hand. It had six fingers, very long and narrow, without fingernails or visible joints. Her skin was silky and faintly glossy, and it felt not at all as he had expected. He ran his hands lightly over her slim, practically fleshless body. She was altogether motionless.

"I should go now," she said at last.

"Stay with me. Live here with me."

"Even now?"

"Even now. In your true form."

"You still want me?"

"Very much," he said. "Will you stay?"

She said, "When I first came to you, it was to watch you, to study you, to play with you, perhaps even to mock and hurt you. You are the enemy, Therion. Your kind must always be the enemy. But as we began to live together I saw there was no reason to hate you. Not *you*, you as a special individual, do you understand?"

It was the voice of Sarise coming from those alien lips. How strange, he thought, how much like a dream.

She said, "I began to want to be with you. To make the game go on forever, do you follow? But the game had to end. And yet I still want to be with you."

"Then stay, Sarise."

"Only if you truly want me."

"I've told you that."

"I don't horrify you?"

"No."

"Paint me again, Therion. Show me with a painting. Show me love on the canvas, Therion, and then I'll stay."

He painted her day after day, until he had used every canvas, and hung them all about the interior of the cabin, Sarise and the dwikka-tree, Sarise in the meadow, Sarise against the milky fog of evening, Sarise at twilight, green against purple. There was no way he could prepare more canvases, although he tried. It did not really matter. They began to go on long voyages of exploration together, down one stream and another, into distant parts of the forest, and she showed him new trees and flowers, and the creatures of the jungle, the toothy lizards and the burrowing golden worms and the sinister ponderous amorfibots sleeping away their days in muddy lakes. They said little to one another; the time for answering questions was over and words were no longer needed.

Day slipped into day, week into week, and in this land of no seasons it was difficult to measure the passing of time. Perhaps a month went by, perhaps six. They encountered nobody else. The jungle was full of Metamorphs, she told him, but they were keeping their distance, and she hoped they would leave them alone forever.

One afternoon of steady drizzle he went out to check his traps, and when he returned an hour later he knew at once something was wrong. As he approached the cabin four Metamorphs emerged. He felt sure that one was Sarise, but he could not tell which one. "Wait!" he cried, as they moved past him. He ran after them. "What do you want with her? Let her go! Sarise? Sarise? Who are they? What do they want?"

For just an instant one of the Metamorphs flickered and he
saw the girl with the auburn hair, but only for an instant;
then there were four Metamorphs again, gliding like ghosts
toward the depths of the jungle. The rain grew more intense,
and a heavy fog-bank drifted in, cutting off all visibility.
Nismile paused at the edge of the clearing, straining desperately for sounds over the patter of the rain and the loud
throb of the stream. He imagined he heard weeping; he
thought he heard a cry of pain, but it might have been any
other sort of forest-sound. There was no hope of following
the Metamorphs into that impenetrable zone of thick white
mist.

He never saw Sarise again, nor any other Metamorph. For
a while he hoped he would come upon Shapeshifters in the
forest and be slain by them with their little polished dirks, for
the loneliness was intolerable now. But that did not happen,
and when it became obvious that he was living in a sort of
quarantine, cut off not only from Sarise—if she was still
alive—but from the entire society of the Metamorph folk, he
found himself unable any longer to dwell in the clearing
beside the stream. He rolled up his paintings of Sarise and
carefully dismantled his cabin and began the long and perilous journey back to civilization. It was a week before his fifti-
eth birthday when he reached the borders of Castle Mount.
In his absence, he discovered, Lord Thraym had become Pontifex and the new Coronal was Lord Vildivar, a man of little
sympathy with the arts. Nismile rented a studio on the riverbank at Stee and began to paint again. He worked only from
memory: dark and disturbing scenes of jungle life, often
showing Metamorphs lurking in the middle distance. It was
not the sort of work likely to be popular on the cheerful and
airy world of Majipoor, and Nismile found few buyers at
first. But in time his paintings caught the fancy of the Duke
of Qurain, who had begun to weary of sunny serenity and
perfect proportion. Under the duke's patronage, Nismile's
work grew fashionable, and in the later years of his life there
was a ready market for everything he produced.

He was widely imitated, though never successfully, and he
was the subject of many critical essays and biographical
studies. "Your paintings are so turbulent and strange," one
scholar said to him. "Have you devised some method of
working from dreams?"

"I work only from memory," said Nismile.

"From painful memory, I would be so bold as to venture."

"Not at all," answered Nismile. "All my work is intended to help me recapture a time of joy, a time of love, the happiest and most precious moment of my life." He stared past the questioner into distant mists, thick and soft as wool, that swirled through clumps of tall slender trees bound by a tangled network of vines.

...nt was amazingly easy to commit. Little Gleim was
the open window of the little upstairs room of
the inn — and where-be said Halfyme had agreed to

SEVEN

Crime and Punishment

That one takes him back to the beginning of his explorations of these archives. Thesme and the Ghayrog all over again, another forest romance, the love of human and non-human. Yet the similarities are all on the surface, for these were very different people in very different circumstances. Hissune comes away from the tale with what he thinks is a reasonably good understanding of the soul-painter Therion Nismile— some of whose works, he learns, are still on display in the galleries of Lord Valentine's Castle—but the Metamorph is a mystery to him still, as great a mystery perhaps as she had been to Nismile. He checks the index for recordings of Metamorph souls, but is unsurprised to find that there are none. Do the Shapeshifters refuse to record, or is the apparatus incapable of picking up the emanations of their minds, or are they merely banned from the archives? Hissune does not know and he is unable to find out. In time, he tells himself, all things will be answered. Meanwhile there is much more to discover. The operations of the King of Dreams, for instance—he needs to learn much more about those. For a thousand years the descendants of the Barjazids have had the task of lashing the sleeping minds of criminals; Hissune wonders how it is done. He prowls the archives, and before long fortune delivers up to him the soul of an outlaw, disguised drearily as a tradesman of the city of Stee—

174

The murder was amazingly easy to commit. Little Gleim was standing by the open window of the little upstairs room of the tavern in Vugel where he and Haligome had agreed to meet. Haligome was near the couch. The discussion was not going well. Haligome asked Gleim once more to reconsider.

Gleim shrugged and said, "You're wasting your time and mine. I don't see where you have any case at all."

At that moment it seemed to Haligome that Gleim and Gleim alone stood between him and the tranquillity of life that he felt he deserved, that Gleim was his enemy, his nemesis, his persecutor. Calmly Haligome walked toward him, so calmly that Gleim evidently was not in the least alarmed, and with a sudden smooth motion he pushed Gleim over the windowsill.

Gleim looked amazed. He hung as if suspended in mid-air for a surprisingly long moment; then he dropped toward the swiftly flowing river just outside the tavern, hit the water with scarcely a splash, and was carried away rapidly toward the distant foothills of Castle Mount. In an instant he was lost to view.

Haligome looked at his hands as though they had just sprouted on his wrists. He could not believe they had done what they had done. Again he saw himself walking toward Gleim; again he saw Gleim standing bewildered on air; again he saw Gleim vanish into the dark river. Probably Gleim was already dead. If not, then within another minute or two. They would find him sooner or later, Haligome knew, washed up on some rocky shore down by Canzilaine or Perimor, and somehow they would identify him as a merchant of Gimkandale, missing the past week or ten days. But would there be any reason for them to suspect he had been murdered? Murder was an uncommon crime. He could have fallen. He could have jumped. Even if they managed to prove—the Divine only knew how—that Gleim had gone unwillingly to his death, how could they demonstrate that he had been pushed from the window of a tavern in Vugel by Sigmar Haligome of the city of Stee? They could not, Haligome told himself. But that did not change the essential truth of the situation, which was that Gleim had been murdered and Haligome was his murderer.

His murderer? That new label astonished Haligome. He had not come here to kill Gleim, only to negotiate with him. But the negotiations had been sour from the start. Gleim, a small, fastidious man, refused entirely to admit liability over a matter of defective equipment, and said that it must have been Haligome's inspectors who were at fault. He refused to pay a thing, or even to show much sympathy for Haligome's awkward financial plight. At that final bland refusal Gleim appeared to swell until he filled all the horizon, and all of him was loathsome, and Haligome wished only to be rid of him, whatever the cost. If he had stopped to think about his act and its consequences he would not, of course, have pushed Gleim out the window, for Haligome was not in any way a murderous man. But he had not stopped to think, and now Gleim was dead and Haligome's life had undergone a grotesque redefinition: he had transformed himself in a moment from Haligome the jobber of precision instruments to Haligome the murderer. How sudden! How strange! How terrifying!

And now?

Trembling, sweating, dry-throated, Haligome closed the window and dropped down on the couch. He had no idea of what he was supposed to do next. Reoprt himself to the imperial proctors? Confess, surrender, and enter prison, or wherever it was that criminals were sent? He had no preparation for any of this. He had read old stories of crimes and punishments, ancient myths and fables, but so far as he knew murder was an extinct crime and the mechanisms for its detection and expiation had long ago rusted away. He felt prehistoric; he felt primeval. There was that famous story of a sea-captain of the remote past who had pushed a crazed crewman overboard during an ill-fated expedition across the Great Sea, after that crewman had killed someone else. Such tales had always seemed wild and implausible to Haligome. But now, effortlessly, unthinkingly, he had made himself a legendary figure, a monster, a taker of human life. He knew that nothing would ever again be the same for him.

One thing to do was to get away from the tavern. If someone had seen Gleim fall—not likely, for the tavern stood flush against the riverbank; Gleim had gone out a back window and had been swallowed up at once by the rushing flow—there was no point in standing around here waiting for investigators to arrive. Quickly he packed his one small suitcase, checked to see that nothing of Gleim's was in the room, and went downstairs. There was a Hjort at the desk.

Haligome produced a few crowns and said, "I'd like to settle my account."

He resisted the impulse to chatter. This was not the moment to make clever remarks that might imprint him on the Hjort's memory. Pay your bill and clear out fast, he thought. Was the Hjort aware that the visitor from Stee had entertained a guest in his room? Well, the Hjort would quickly enough forget that, and the visitor from Stee as well, if Haligome gave him no reason to remember. The clerk totalled the figures; Haligome handed over some coins; to the Hjort's mechanical "Please come again" Haligome made an equally mechanical reply, and then he was out on the street, walking briskly away from the river. A strong sweet breeze was blowing downslope. The sunlight was bright and warm. It was years since Haligome had last been in Vugel, and at another time he might well have taken a few hours to tour its famous jeweled plaza, its celebrated soul-painting murals, and the other local wonders, but this was not the moment for tourism. He hurried to the transit terminal and bought a one-way ticket back to Stee.

Fear, uncertainty, guilt, and shame rode with him on the journey around the flank of Castle Mount from city to city.

The familiar sprawling outskirts of gigantic Stee brought him some repose. To be home meant to be safe. With each new day of his entry into Stee he felt more comfort. There was the mighty river for which the city was named, tumbling in astonishing velocity down the Mount. There were the smooth shining facades of the Riverwall Buildings, forty stories high and miles in length. There was Kinniken Bridge; there was Thimin Tower; there was the Field of Great Bones. Home! The enormous vitality and power of Stee, throbbing all about him as he made his way from the central terminal to his suburban district, comforted him greatly. Surely here in what had become the greatest city of Majipoor—vastly expanded, thanks to the beneficence of its native son who was now the Coronal Lord Kinniken—Haligome was safe from the dark consequences, whatever they might be, of the lunatic deed he had committed in Vugel.

He embraced his wife, his two young daughters, his sturdy son. They could readily see his fatigue and tension, it appeared, for they treated him with a kind of exaggerated delicacy, as though he had become newly fragile on his journey. They brought him wine, a pipe, slippers; they bustled round, radiating love and good will; they asked him nothing about how his trip had gone, but regaled him instead with local gossip. Not until dinner did he say at last, "I think Gleim and I worked everything out. There's reason to be hopeful."

He nearly believed it himself.

Was there any way the murder could be laid to him, if he simply kept quiet about it? He doubted that there could have been witnesses. It would not be hard for the authorities to discover that he and Gleim had agreed to meet in Vugel—neutral ground—to discuss their business disagreements, but what did that prove? "Yes, I saw him in some tavern near the river," Haligome could say. "We had lunch and drank a lot of wine and came to an understanding, and then I went away. He looked pretty wobbly when I left, I must say." And poor Gleim, flushed and staggering with a bellyful of the strong wine of Muldemar, must have leaned too far out the window afterward, perhaps for a view of some elegant lord and lady sailing past on the river—no, no, no, let *them* do all the speculating, Haligome told himself. "We met for lunch and reached a settlement, and then I went away," and nothing more than that. And who could prove it had been otherwise?

He returned to his office the next day and went about his business as though nothing unusual had happened in Vugel. He could not allow himself the luxury of brooding over his crime. Things were precarious: he was close to bankrupt, his credit overextended, his plausibility with his prime accounts sadly diminished. All that was Gleim's doing. Once you ship shoddy goods, though, you go on suffering for it for a long time, no matter how blameless you may be. Having had no satisfaction from Gleim—and not likely to get any, now—Haligome's only recourse was to strive with intense dedication to rebuild the confidence of those whom he supplied with precision instruments, while at the same time struggling to hold off his creditors until matters returned to equilibrium.

Keeping Gleim out of his mind was difficult. Over the next few days his name kept coming up, and Haligome had to work hard to conceal his reactions. Everyone in the trade seemed to understand that Gleim had taken Haligome for a fool, and everyone was trying to seem sympathetic. That in itself was encouraging. But to have every conversation somehow wander around to Gleim—Gleim's iniquities, Gleim's vindictiveness, Gleim's tightfistedness—threw Haligome constantly off balance. The name was like a trigger. *"Gleim!"* and he would go rigid. *"Gleim!"* and muscles would throb in his cheeks. *"Gleim!"* and he would thrust his hands out of sight behind him, as if they bore the imprint of the dead man's aura. He imagined himself saying to some client, in a moment of sheer weariness, "I killed him, you know. I pushed him out a window when I was in Vugel." How easily the words would flow from his lips, if only he relaxed his control!

He thought of making a pilgrimage to the Isle to cleanse his soul. Later, perhaps: not now, for now he had to devote every waking moment to his business affairs, or his firm would collapse and his family would fall into poverty. He thought also of confessing and coming quickly to some understanding with the authorities that would allow him to atone for the crime without disrupting his commercial activities. A fine, maybe—though how could he afford a fine now? And would they let him off so lightly? In the end he did nothing at all except to try to shove the murder out of his consciousness, and for a week or ten days that actually seemed to work. And then the dreams began.

The first one came on Starday night in the second week of summer, and Haligome knew instantly that it was a sending of a dark and painful kind. He was in his third sleep, the deepest of the night just before the mind's ascent into dawn, and he found himself crossing a field of gleaming and slippery yellow teeth that churned and writhed beneath his feet. The air was foul, swamp air of a discouraging grayish hue, and ropy strands of some raw meaty substance dangled from the sky, brushing against his cheeks and arms and leaving sticky tracks that burned and throbbed. There was a ringing in his ears: the harsh tense silence of a malign sending, that makes it seem as though the world has been drawn far too tight on its drawstrings, and beyond that a distant jeering laughter. An intolerably bright light seared the sky. He was traversing a mouthplant, he realized—one of those hideous carnivorous floral monsters of far-off Zimroel, that he once had seen exhibited in a show of curios at the Kinniken Pavilion. But those were only three or four yards in diameter, and this was the size of a goodly suburb, and he was trapped in its diabolical core, running as fast as he could to keep from slipping down into those mercilessly grinding teeth.

So this is how it will be, he thought, floating above his

dream and bleakly surveying it. This is the first sending, and the King of Dreams will torment me hereafter.

There was no hiding from it. The teeth had eyes, and the eyes were the eyes of Gleim, and Haligome was scrambling and sliding and sweating, and now he pitched forward and tumbled against a bank of the remorseless teeth and they nipped his hand, and when he was able to get to his feet again he saw that the bloody hand was no longer his own familiar one, but had been transformed into the small pale hand of Gleim, fitting badly on his wrist. Again Haligome fell, and again the teeth nipped at him, and again came an unwelcome metamorphosis, and again, and again, and he ran onward, sobbing and moaning, half Gleim, half Haligome, until he broke from his sleep and discovered himself sitting up, trembling, sweatsoaked, clutching his astounded wife's thigh as though it were a liefline.

"Don't," she murmured. "You're hurting me. What is it? What is it?"

"Dream—very bad—"

"A sending?" she asked. "Yes, it must have been. I can smell the odor of it in your sweat. Oh, Sigmar, what was it?"

He shuddered. "Something I ate. The sea-dragon meat—it was too dry, too old—"

He left the bed unsteadily and poured a little wine, which calmed him. His wife stroked him and bathed his feverish forehead and held him until he relaxed a little, but he feared going back to sleep, and lay awake until dawn, staring into the gray darkness. The King of Dreams! So this was to be his punishment. Bleakly he considered things. He had always believed that the King of Dreams was only a fable to keep children in line. Yes, yes, they said that he lived in Suvrael, that the title was the hereditary holding of the Barjazid family, that the King and his minions scanned the night air for the guilts of sleepers, and found the souls of the unworthy and tormented them, but was it so? Haligome had never known anyone to have a sending from the King of Dreams. He thought he might once have had one from the Lady, but he was not sure of that, and in any case that was different. The Lady offered only the most general kind of visions. The King of Dreams was said to inflict real pain; but could the King of Dreams really monitor the entire teeming planet, with its billions of citizens, not all of them virtuous?

Possibly it was only indigestion, Haligome told himself.

When the next night and the next passed calmly, he allowed himself to believe that the dream had been no more than a random anomaly. The King might only be a fable after all. But on Twoday came another unmistakable sending.

The same silent ringing sound. The same fierce glaring light illuminating the landscape of sleep. Images of Gleim; laughter; echoes; swellings and contractions of the fabric of the cosmos; a wrenching giddiness blasting his spirit with terrible vertigo. Haligome whimpered. He buried his face against the pillow and fought for breath. He dared not awaken, for if he surfaced he would inevitably reveal his distress to his wife, and she would suggest that he take his dreams to a speaker, and he could not do that. Any speaker worth her fee would know at once that she was joining her soul with the soul of a criminal, and what would happen to him then? So he suffered his nightmare until the force of it was spent, and only then he awakened, to lie limp and quivering until the coming of the day.

That was Twoday's nightmare. Fourday's was worse: Haligome soared and dropped and was impaled on the ultimate summit of Castle Mount, spear-sharp and cold as ice, and lay there for hours while gihorna-birds with the face of Gleim ripped at his belly and bombarded his dripping wounds with blazing droppings. Fiveday he slept reasonably well, though he was tense, on guard for dreams; Starday too brought no sendings; Sunday found him swimming through oceans of clotted blood while his teeth loosened and his fingers turned to strips of ragged dough; Moonday and Twoday brought milder horrors, but horrors all the same; on Seaday morning his wife said, "These dreams of yours will not relent. Sigmar, what have you done?"

"Done? I've done nothing!"

"I feel the sendings surging through you night after night."

He shrugged. "Some mistake has been made by the Powers that govern us. It must happen occasionally: dreams meant for some child-molester of Pendiwane are delivered to a jobber of precision instruments in Stee. Sooner or later they'll see the error and leave me alone."

"And if they don't?" She gave him a penetrating glance. "And if the dreams are meant for you?"

He wondered if she knew the truth. She was aware that he had gone to Vugel to confer with Gleim; possibly, though it was hard to imagine how, she had learned that Gleim had never returned to his home in Gimkandale; her husband now was receiving sendings of the King of Dreams; she could draw her own conclusions all too readily. Could it be? And if so, what would she do? Denounce her own husband? Though she loved him, she might well do that, for if she let herself harbor a murderer she might bring the vengeance of the King upon her own sleep as well.

He said, "If the dreams continue, I will ask the officials of the Pontifex to intercede on my behalf."

Of course he could not do that. He tried instead to grapple with the dreams and repress them, so that he would arouse no suspicion in the woman who slept by his side. In his pre-sleep meditations he instructed himself to be calm, to accept what images might come, to regard them only as fantasies of a disordered soul, and not as realities with which he needed to cope. And yet when he found himself floating over a red sea of fire, dipping now and then ankle-deep, he could not keep from screaming; and when needles grew outward from his flesh and burst through his skin so that he looked like a manculain, that untouchable spiny beast of the torrid south-lands, he whimpered and begged for mercy in his sleep, and when he strolled through the immaculate gardens of Lord Havilbove by Tolingar Barrier and the flawless shrubs became mocking toothy hairy things of sinister ugliness, he wept and broke into torrents of sweat that made the mattress reek. His wife asked no more questions, but she eyed him uneasily and seemed constantly on the verge of demanding how long he intended to tolerate these intrusions on his spirit.

He could scarcely operate his business. Creditors hovered; manufacturers balked at extending further credit; customer complaints swirled about him like dead and withered autumn leaves. Secretly he burrowed in the libraries for information about the King of Dreams and his powers, as though this were some strange new disease that he had contracted and about which he needed to learn everything. But the information was scanty and obvious: the King was an agency of the government, a Power equal in authority to the Pontifex and the Coronal and the Lady of the Isle, and for hundreds of years it had been his role to impose punishment on the guilty.

There has been no trial, Haligome protested silently—

But he knew none was needed, and plainly the King knew that too. And as the dread dreams continued, grinding down Haligome's soul and fraying his nerves to threads, he saw that there was no hope of withstanding these sendings. His life in Stee was ended. One moment of rashness and he had made himself an outcast, doomed to wander across the vast face of the planet, searching for some place to hide.

"I need a rest," he told his wife. "I will travel abroad a month or two, and regain my inner peace." He called his son to his side—the boy was almost a man; he could handle the responsibilities now—and turned the business over to him, giving him in an hour a list of maxims that had taken him half a lifetime to learn. Then, with such little cash as he could squeeze from his greatly diminished assets, he set forth out of his splendid native city, aboard the third-class floater bound for—at random—Normork, in the ring of Slope Cities near the foot of Castle Mount. An hour into his journey he resolved never to call himself Sigmar Haligome again, and renamed himself Miklan Forb. Would that be sufficient to divert the force of the King of Dreams?

Perhaps so. The floater drifted across the face of Castle Mount, lazily descending from Stee to Normork by way of Lower Sunbreak, Bibiroon Sweep, and Tolingar Barrier, and at each night's hostelry he went to bed clutching his pillow with terror, but the only dreams that came were the ordinary ones of a tired and fretful man, without that peculiar ghastly intensity that typified sendings of the King. It was pleasant to observe that the gardens of Tolingar Barrier were symmetrical and perfectly tidy, nothing at all like the hideous wastelands of his dream. Haligome began to relax a bit. He compared the gardens with the dream-images, and was surprised to see that the King had provided him with a rich and detailed and accurate view of those gardens just before transforming them into horror, complete to the most minute degree; but he had never before seen them, which meant that the sending had transmitted into his mind an entire cluster of data new to him, whereas ordinary dreams merely called upon that which already was recorded there.

That answered a question that had troubled him. He had not known whether the King was simply liberating the detritus of his unconscious, stirring the murky depths from afar, or was actually beaming imagery into it. Evidently the latter was the case. But that begged another query: were the nightmares specifically designed for Sigmar Haligome, crafted by specialists to stir his particular terrors? Surely there could not be personnel enough in Suvrael to handle that job. But if

there were, it meant that they were monitoring him closely,
and it was folly to think he could hide from them. He preferred to believe that the King and his minions had a roster
of standard nightmares—send him the teeth, send him the
gray greasy blobs, now send him the sea of fire—that were
brought forth in succession for each malefactor, an imper-
sonal and mechanical operation. Possibly even now they were
aiming some grisly phantasms at his empty pillow in Stee.

He came up past Dundilmir and Stipool to Normork, that
somber and hermetic walled city perched atop the formidable
fangs of Normork Crest. It had not consciously occurred to
him before that Normork, with its huge circumvallation of cy-
clopean blocks of black stone, had the appropriate qualities
for a hiding-place: protected, secure, impregnable. But of
course not even the walls of Normork could keep out the
vengeful shafts of the King of Dreams, he realized.

The Dekkeret Gate, an eye in the wall fifty feet high, stood
open as always, the one breach in the fortification, polished
black wood bound with a Coronal's ransom of iron bands.
Haligome would have preferred that it be closed and triple-
locked as well, but of course the great gate was open, for
Lord Dekkeret, constructing it in the thirtieth year of his aus-
picious reign, had decreed that it be closed only at a time
when the world was in peril, and these days under the happy
guidance of Lord Kinniken and the Pontifex Thimin everything flourished on Majipoor, save only the troubled soul of
the former Sigmar Haligome, who called himself Miklan
Forb. As Forb he found cheap lodgings on the slopeside
quarter of the city, where Castle Mount reared up behind like
a second wall of immeasurable height. As Forb he took a job
with the maintenance crew that patrolled the city wall day after day, digging the tenacious wireweed out from between the
unmortared masonry. As Forb he sank down into sleep each
night fearful of what would come, but what came, week after
week, was only the blurred and meaningless dreamery of ordinary slumber. For nine months he lived submerged in Normork, wondering if he had escaped the hand of Suvrael; and
then one night after a pleasant meal and a flask of fine crimson wine of Bannikannikole he tumbled into bed feeling entirely happy for the first time since long before his baleful
meeting with Gleim, and dropped unwarily to sleep, and a
sending of the King came to him and seized his soul by the
throat and flailed him with monstrous images of melting flesh

and rivers of slime. When the dream was done with him he awoke weeping, for he knew that there was no hiding for long from the avenging Power that pursued him.

Yet life as Miklan Forb had been good for nine months of peace. With his small savings he bought a ticket downslope to Amblemorn, where he became Degrail Gilalin, and earned ten crowns a week as a bird-limer on the estate of a local prince. He had five months of freedom from torment, until the night when sleep brought him the crackle of silence and the fury of limitless light and the vision of an arch of disembodied eyes strung like a bridge across the universe, all those eyes watching only him. He journeyed along the River Glayge to Makroprosopos, where he lived a month unscathed as Ogvorn Brill before the coming of a dream of crystals of fiery metal multiplying like hair in his throat. Overland through the arid inlands he went as part of a caravan to the market city of Sisivondal, which was a journey of eleven weeks. The King of Dreams found him in the seventh of those and sent him out screaming at night to roll about in a thicket of whipstaff plants, and that was no dream, for he was bleeding and swollen when he finally broke free from the plants, and had to be carried to the next village for medicines. Those with whom he traveled knew that he was one who had sendings of the King, and they left him behind; but eventually he found his way to Sisivondal, a drab and monochromatic place so different from the splendid cities of Castle Mount that he wept each morning at the sight of it. But all the same he stayed there six months without incident. Then the dreams came back and drove him westward, a month here and six weeks there, through nine cities and as many identities, until at last to Alaisor on the coast, where he had a year of tranquillity under the name of Badril Maganorn, gutting fish in a dockside market. Despite his forebodings he allowed himself to begin believing that the King was at last done with him, and he speculated on the possibility of returning to his old life in Stee, from which he had now been absent almost four years. Was four years of punishment not enough for an unpremeditated, almost accidental, crime?

Evidently not. Early in his second year at Alaisor he felt the familiar ominous buzz of a sending throbbing behind the wall of his skull, and there came upon him a dream that made all the previous ones seem like children's holiday theatricals. It began in the bleak wastelands of Suvrael, where he stood on a jagged peak looking across a dry and blasted valley at a forest of sigupa trees, that gave off an emanation fatal to all life that came within ten miles, even unwary birds and insects that flew above the thick drooping branches. His wife and children could be seen in the valley, marching steadily toward the deadly trees; he ran toward them, in sand that clung like molasses, and the trees stirred and beckoned, and his loved ones were swallowed up in their dark radiance and fell and vanished entirely. But he continued onward until he was within the grim perimeter. He prayed for death, but he alone was immune to the trees. He came among them, each isolated and remote from the others, and nothing growing about them, no shrubs nor vines nor ground-covers, merely a long array of ugly leafless trees standing like palisades in the midst of nowhere. That was all there was to the dream, but it carried a burden of frightfulness far beyond all the grotesqueries of image that he had endured before, and it went on and on, Haligome wandering forlorn and solitary among those barren trees as though in an airless void, and when he awakened his face was withered and his eyes were quivering as if he had aged a dozen years between night and dawn.

He was defeated utterly. Running was useless; hiding was futile. He belonged to the King of Dreams forever.

No longer did he have the strength to keep creating new lives and identities for himself in these temporary refuges. When daybreak cleared the terror of the forest dream from his spirit he staggered to the temple of the Lady on Alaisor Heights, and asked to be allowed to make the pilgrimage to the Isle of Sleep. He gave his name as Sigmar Haligome. What had he left to conceal?

He was accepted, as everyone is, and in time he boarded a pilgrim-ship bound for Numinor on the northeastern flank of the Isle. Occasional sendings harassed him during the sea-crossing, some of them merely irritating, a few of terrible impact, but when he woke and trembled and wept there were other pilgrims to comfort him, and somehow now that he had surrendered his life to the Lady the dreams, even the worst of them, mattered little. The chief pain of the sendings, he knew, is the disruption they bring to one's daily life: the haunting, the strangeness. But now he had no life of his own to be disrupted, so what did it matter that he opened his eyes to a morning of trembling? He was no longer a jobber of precision instruments or a digger of wireweed sprouts or a limer of birds; he was nothing, he was no one, he had no self to defend against the incursions of his foe. In the midst of a flurry of sendings a strange kind of peace came over him.

In Numinor he was received into the Terrace of Assessment, the outer rim of the Isle, where for all he knew he would spend the rest of his life. The Lady called her pilgrims inward step by step, according to the pace of their invisible inner progress, and one whose soul was stained by murder might remain forever in some menial role on the edge of the holy domain. That was all right. He wanted only to escape the sendings of the King, and he hoped that sooner or later he would come under the protection of the Lady and be forgotten by Suvrael.

In soft pilgrim-robes he toiled as a gardener in the outermost terrace for six years. His hair was white, his back was stooped; he learned to tell weed-seedlings from blossom-seedlings; he suffered from sendings every month or two at first, and then less frequently, and though they never left him entirely he found them increasingly unimportant, like the twinges of some ancient wound. Occasionally he thought of his family, who doubtless thought him dead. He thought also of Gleim, eternally frozen in astonishment, hanging in mid-air before he fell to his death. Had there ever been such a person, and had Haligome truly killed him? It seemed unreal now; it was so terribly long ago. Haligome felt no guilt for a crime whose very existence he was coming to doubt. But he remembered a business quarrel, and an arrogant refusal by the other merchants to see his frightening dilemma, and a moment of blind rage in which he had struck out at his enemy. Yes, yes, it had all happened; and, thought Haligome, Gleim and I both lost our lives in that moment of fury.

Haligome performed his tasks faithfully, did his meditation, visited dream-speakers—it was required here, but they never offered comments or interpretations—and took holy instruction. In the spring of his seventh year he was summoned inward to the next stage on the pilgrimage, the Terrace of Inception, and there he remained month after month, while other pilgrims moved through and past to the Terrace of Mirrors beyond. He said little to anyone, made no friends, and accepted in resignation the sendings that still came to him at widely spaced intervals.

In his third year at the Terrace of Inception he noticed a man of middle years staring at him in the dining-hall, a short and frail man with an oddly familiar look. For two weeks this newcomer kept Haligome under close surveillance, until at last Haligome's curiosity was too strong to control; he made inquiries and was told that the man's name was Goviran Gleim.

Of course. Haligome went to him during an hour of free time and said, "Will you answer a question?"

"If I can."

"Are you a native of the city of Gimkandale on Castle Mount?"

"I am," said Goviran Gleim. "And you, are you a man of Stee?"

"Yes," said Haligome.

They were silent for some time. Then at last Haligome said, "So you have been pursuing me all these years?"

"Why no. Not at all."

"It is only coincidence that we are both here?"

Goviran Gleim said, "I think there is no such thing as coincidence, in fact. But it was not by my conscious design that I came to the place where you were."

"You know who I am, and what I have done?"

"Yes."

"And what do you want of me?" asked Haligome.

"Want? Want?" Gleim's eyes, small and dark and gleaming like those of his long-dead father, looked close into Haligome's. "What do I want? Tell me what happened in the city of Vugel."

"Come. Walk with me," said Haligome.

They passed through a close-clipped blue-green hedge and into the garden of alabandains that Haligome tended, thinning the buds to make for larger blooms. In these fragrant surroundings Haligome described, speaking flatly and quietly, the events that he had never described to anyone and that had become nearly unreal to him: the quarrel, the meeting, the window, the river. No emotion was apparent on the face of Goviran Gleim during the recitation, although Haligome searched the other man's features intently, trying to read his purpose.

When he was done describing the murder Haligome waited for response. There was none.

Ultimately Gleim said, "And what happened to you afterward? Why did you disappear?"

"The King of Dreams whipped my soul with evil sendings,

and put me in such torment that I took up hiding in Normork; and when he found me there I went on, fleeing from
place to place, and eventually in my flight I came to the Isle
as a pilgrim."

"And the King still follows you?"

"From time to time I have sendings," said Haligome. He
shook his head. "But they are useless. I have suffered, I have
done penance, and it has been meaningless, for I feel no guilt
for my crime. It was a moment of madness, and I have
wished a thousand thousand times that it had never occurred,
but I can find in myself no responsibility for your father's
death: he goaded me to frenzy, and I pushed, and he fell, but
it was not an act that bears any connection to the way I conducted the other aspects of my life, and it was therefore not
mine."

"You feel that, do you?"

"Indeed. And these years of tormented dreams—what good
did they do? If I had refrained from killing out of fear of the
King the whole system of punishment would be justified; but
I gave no thought to anything, least of all the King of
Dreams, and I therefore see the code under which I have
been punished as a futile one. So too with my pilgrimage: I
came here not so much to atone as to hide from the King
and his sendings, and I suppose I have essentially achieved
that. But neither my atonement nor my sufferings will bring
your father back to life, so all this charade has been without
purpose. Come: kill me and get it over with."

"Kill you?" said Gleim.

"Isn't that what you intend?"

"I was a boy when my father vanished. I am no longer
young now, and you are older still, and all this is ancient history. I wanted only to know the truth of his death, and I
know it now. Why kill you? If it would bring my father back
to life, perhaps I would, but, as you yourself point out, nothing can do that. I feel no anger toward you and I have no
wish to experience torment at the hands of the King. For me,
at least, the system is a worthy deterrent."

"You have no wish to kill me," said Haligome, amazed.
"None."

"No. No. I see. Why should you kill me? That would free
me from a life that has become one long punishment."

Gleim again looked astounded. "Is that how you see it?"

"You condemn me to life, yes."

"But your punishment ended long ago! The grace of the Lady is on you now. Through my father's death you have found your way to her!"

Haligome could not tell whether the other man was mocking him or truly meant his words.

"You see grace in me?" he asked.

"I do."

Haligome shook his head. "The Isle and all it stands for are nothing to me. I came here only to escape the onslaughts of the King. I have at last found a place to hide, and no more than that."

Gleim's gaze was steady. "You deceive yourself," he said, and walked away, leaving Haligome stunned and dazed.

Could it be? Was he purged of his crime, and had not understood that? He resolved that if that night a sending of the King came to him—and he was due, for it had been nearly a year since the last one—he would walk to the outer edge of the Terrace of Assessment and throw himself into the sea. But what came that night was a sending of the Lady, a warm and gentle dream summoning him inward to the Terrace of Mirrors. He still did not understand fully, and doubted that he ever would. But his dream-speaker told him in the morning to go on at once to that shining terrace that lay beyond, for the next stage of his pilgrimage had commenced.

EIGHT

Among the Dream-Speakers

Often now Hissune finds that one adventure demands immediate explantion by another; and when he has done with the somber but instructive tale of the murderer Sigmar Haligome he understands a great deal of the workings of the agencies of the King of Dreams, but of the dream-speakers themselves, those intermediaries between the sleeping and waking worlds, he knows very little at all. He has never consulted one; he regards his own dreams more as theatrical events than as messages of guidance. This is counter to the central spiritual tradition of the world, he knows, but much that he does and thinks runs counter to those traditions. He is what he is, a child of the streets of the Labyrinth, a close observer of his world but not a wholehearted subscriber to all of its ways.

There is in Zimroel, or was, a famous dream-speaker named Tisana, whom Hissune had met while attending the second enthronement of Lord Valentine. She was a fat old woman of the city of Falkynkip, and evidently she had played some part in Lord Valentine's rediscovery of his lost identity; Hissune knows nothing about that, but he recalls with some discomfort the old woman's penetrating eyes, her powerful and vigorous personality. For some reason she had taken a fancy to the boy Hissune: he remembers standing beside her, dwarfed by her, hoping that she would not get the

*notion of embracing him, for she would surely crush him in
her vast bosom. She said then, "And here's another little lost
princeling!" What did that mean? A dream-speaker might tell
him, Hissune occasionally thinks, but he does not go to
dream-speakers. He wonders if Tisana has left a recording in
the Register of Souls. He checks the archives. Yes, yes, there
is one. He summons it and discovers quickly that it was made
early in her life, some fifty years ago, when she was only
learning her craft, and there are no others of hers on file.
Nearly he sends it back. But something of Tisana's flavor lin-
gers in his mind after only a moment of her recording. He
might yet learn from her, he decides, and dons the helmet
once more, and lets the vehement soul of the young Tisana
enter his consciousness.*

On the morning of the day before Tisana's Testing it suddenly began to rain, and everyone came running out of the
chapter-house to see it, the novices and the pledgeds and the
consummates and the tutors, and even the old Speaker-Su-
perior Inuelda herself. Rain was a rare event here in the
desert of Velalisier Plain. Tisana emerged with all the others,
and stood watching the large clear drops descending on a
slanting course from the single black-edged cloud that
hovered high above the chapter-house's great spire, as though
tethered to it. The drops hit the parched sandy ground with
an audible impact: dark spreading stains, oddly far apart,
were forming on the pale reddish soil. Novices and pledgeds
and consummates and tutors flung aside their cloaks and frol-
icked in the downpour. "The first in well over a year," someone said.

"A omen," murmured Freylis, the pledged who was
Tisana's closest friend in the chapter-house. "You will have
an easy Testing."

"Do you really believe such things?"

"It costs no more to see good omens than bad," Freylis
said.

"A useful motto for a dream-speaker to adopt," said
Tisana, and they both laughed.

Freylis tugged at Tisana's hand. "Come dance with me out
there!" she urged.

Tisana shook her head. She remained in the shelter of the
overhang, and all Freylis' tugging was to no avail. Tisana was

a tall woman, sturdy, big-boned and powerful; Freylis, fragile and slight, was like a bird beside her. Dancing in the rain hardly suited Tisana's mood just now. Tomorrow would bring the climax to seven years of training; she still had no idea whatever of what was going to be required of her at the ritual, but she was perversely certain that she would be found unworthy and sent back to her distant provincial town in disgrace; her fears and dark forebodings were a ballast of lead in her spirit, and dancing at such a time seemed an impossible frivolity.

"Look there," Freylis cried. "The Superior!"

Yes, even the venerable Inuelda was out in the rain, dancing with stately abandon, the guant leathery white-haired old woman moving in wobbly but ceremonious circles, skinny arms outspread, face upturned ecstatically. Tisana smiled at the sight. The Superior spied Tisana lurking on the portico and grinned and beckoned to her, the way one would beckon to a sulky child who will not join the game. But the Superior had taken her own Testing so long ago she must have forgotten how awesome it loomed; no doubt she was unable to understand Tisana's somber preoccupation with tomorrow's ordeal. With an apologetic little gesture Tisana turned and went within. From behind her came the abrupt drumming of a heavy downpour, and then sharp silence. The strange little storm was over.

Tisana entered her cell, stooping to pass under the low arch of blue stone blocks, and leaned for a moment against the rough wall, letting the tension drain from her. The cell was tiny, barely big enough for a mattress, a washbasin, a cabinet, a workbench, and a little bookcase, and Tisana, solid and fleshy, with the robust healthy body of the farm-girl she once had been, nearly filled the little room. But she had grown accustomed to its crampedness and found it oddly comforting. Comforting, too, were the routines of the chapter-house, the daily round of study and manual labor and instruction and—since she had attained the rank of a consummate—the tutoring of novices. At the time the rainfall began Tisana had been brewing the dream-wine, a chore that had occupied an hour of every morning for her for the past two years, and now, grateful for the difficulties of the task, she returned to it. On this uneasy day it was a welcome distraction.

All the dream-wine used on Majipoor was produced right

here, by the pledgeds and consummates of the chapter-house of Velalisier. Making it called for fingers quicker and more delicate than Tisana's, but she had become adept all the same. Laid out before her were the little vials of herbs, the minuscule gray muorna-leaves and the succulent vejloo-roots and the dried berries of the sithereel and the rest of the nine-and-twenty ingredients that produced the trance out of which came the understanding of dreams. Tisana busied herself with the grinding and the mixing of them—it had to be done in a precise order, or the chemical reactions would go awry—and then the kindling of the flame, the charring, the reduction to powder, the dissolving into the brandy and the stirring of the brandy into the wine. After a while the intensity of her concentration helped her grow relaxed and even cheerful again.

As she worked she became aware of soft breathing behind her.

"Freylis?"

"Is it all right to come in?"

"Of course. I'm almost finished. Are they still dancing?"

"No, no, everything's back to normal. The sun is shining again."

Tisana swirled the dark heavy wine in the flask. "In Falkynkip, where I grew up, the weather is also hot and dry. Nevertheless, we don't drop everything and go cavorting the moment the rain comes."

"In Falkynkip," Freylis said, "people take everything for granted. A Skandar with eleven arms wouldn't excite them. If the Pontifex came to town and did handstands in the plaza it wouldn't draw a crowd."

"Oh? You've been there?"

"Once, when I was a girl. My father was thinking of going into ranching. But he didn't have the temperament for it, and after a year or so we went back to Til-omon. He never stopped talking about the Falkynkip people, though, how slow and stolid and deliberate they are."

"And am I like that too?" Tisana asked, a little mischievously.

"You're—well—extremely stable."

"Then why am I so worried about tomorrow?"

The smaller woman knelt before Tisana and took both her hands in hers. "You have nothing to worry about," she said gently.

"The unknown is always frightening."

"It's only a test, Tisana!"

"The last test. What if I bungle it? What if I reveal some terrible flaw of character that shows me absolutely unfit to be a speaker?"

"What if you do?" Freylis asked.

"Why, then I've wasted seven years. Then I creep back to Falkynkip like a fool, without a trade, without skills, and I spend the rest of my life pushing slops on somebody's farm."

Freylis said, "If the Testing shows that you're not fit to be a speaker, you have to be philosophical about it. We can't let incompetents loose in people's mind, you know. Besides, you're *not* unfit to be a speaker, and the Testing isn't going to be any problem for you, and I don't understand why you're so worked up about it."

"Because I have no clue to what it will be like."

"Why, they'll probably do a speaking with you. They'll give you the wine and they'll look in your mind and they'll see that you're strong and wise and good, and they'll bring you out of it and the Superior will give you a hug and tell you you've passed, and that'll be all."

"Are you sure? Do you know?"

"It's a reasonable guess, isn't it?"

Tisana shrugged. "I've heard other guesses. That they do something to you that brings you face to face with the worst thing you've ever done. Or the thing that most frightens you in all the world. Or the thing that you most fear other people will find out about you. Haven't you heard those stories?"

"Yes."

"If this were the day before *your* Testing, wouldn't you be a little edgy, then?"

"They're only stories, Tisana. Nobody knows what the Testing is really like, except those who've passed it."

"And those who've failed?"

"Do you know that anyone has failed?"

"Why—I assume—"

Freylis smiled. "I suspect they weed out the failures long before they get to be consummates. Long before they get to be pledgeds, even." She arose and began to toy with the vials of herbs on Tisana's workbench. "Once you're a speaker, will you go back to Falkynkip?"

"I think so."

"You like it there that much?"

"It's my home."

"It's such a big world, Tisana. You could go to Ni-moya, or Piliplok, or stay over here in Alhanroel, live on Castle Mount, even—"

"Falkynkip will suit me," said Tisana. "I like the dusty roads. I like the dry brown hills. I haven't seen them in seven years. And they need speakers in Falkynkip. They don't in the great cities. Everybody wants to be a speaker in Ni-moya or Stee, right? I'd rather have Falkynkip."

Slyly Freylis asked, "Do you have a lover waiting there?"

Tisana snorted. "Not likely! After seven years?"

"I had one in Til-omon. We were going to marry and build a boat and sail all the way around Zimroel, take three or four years doing it, and then maybe go up the river to Ni-moya and settle there and open a shop in the Gossamer Galleria."

That startled Tisana. In all the time she had known Freylis, they had never spoken of these things.

"What happened?"

Quietly Freylis said, "I had a sending that told me I should become a dream-speaker. I asked him how he felt about that. I wasn't even sure I would do it, you know, but I wanted to hear what he thought, and the moment I told him I saw the answer, because he looked stunned and amazed and a little angry, as if my becoming a dream-speaker would interfere with his plans. Which of course it would. He said I should give him a day to two to mull it over. That was the last I saw of him. A friend of his told me that that very night he had a sending telling him to go to Pidruid, and he went in the morning, and later on he married an old sweetheart he ran into up there, and I suppose they're still talking about building a boat and sailing it around Zimroel. And I obeyed my sending and did my pilgrimage and came here, and here I am, and next month I'll be a consummate and if all goes well next year I'll be a full-fledged speaker. And I'll go to Ni-moya and set up my speaking in the Grand Bazaar."

"Poor Freylis!"

"You don't have to feel sorry for me, Tisana. I'm better off for what happened. It only hurt for a little while. He was worthless, and I'd have found it out sooner or later, and either way I'd have ended up apart from him, except this way I'll be a dream-speaker and render service to the Divine, and the other way I'd have been nobody useful at all. Do you see?"

"I see."

"And I didn't really need to be anybody's wife."

"Nor I," said Tisana. She sniffed her batch of new wine and approved it and began to clean off her workbench, fussily capping the vials and arranging them in a precise order. Freylis was so kind, she thought, so gentle, so tender, so understanding. The womanly virtues. Tisana could find none of those traits in herself. If anything, her soul was more like what she imagined a man's to be, thick, rough, heavy, strong, capable of withstanding all sorts of stress but not very pliant and certainly insensitive to nuance and matters of delicacy. Men were not really like that, Tisana knew, any more than women were invariably models of subtlety and perception, but yet there was a certain crude truth to the notion, and Tisana had always believed herself to be too big, too robust, too foursquare, to be truly feminine. Whereas Freylis, small and delicate and volatile, quicksilver soul and hummingbird mind, seemed to her to be almost of a different species. And Freylis, Tisana thought, would be a superb dream-speaker, intuitively penetrating the minds of those who came to her for interpretations and telling them, in the way most useful to them, what they most needed to know. The Lady of the Isle and the King of Dreams, when in their various ways they visited the minds of sleepers, often spoke cryptically and mystifyingly; it was the speaker's task to serve as interlocutor between those awesome Powers and the billions of people of the world, deciphering and interpreting and guiding. There was terrifying responsibility in that. A speaker could shape or reshape a person's life. Freylis would do well at it: she knew exactly where to be stern and where to be flippant and where consolation and warmth were needed. How had she learned those things? Through engagement with life, no doubt of it, through experience with sorrow and disappointment and failure and defeat. Even without knowing many details of Freylis' past, Tisana could see in the slender woman's cool gray eyes the look of costly knowledge, and it was that knowledge, more than any tricks and techniques she would learn in the chapter-house, that would equip her for her chosen profession. Tisana had grave doubts of her own vocation for dream-speaking, for she had managed to miss all the passionate turmoil that shaped the Freylises of the world. Her life had been too placid, too easy, too—what had Freylis said?—*stable.* A Falkynkip sort of life, up with the sun, out to the chores, eat and work and play and go to sleep well fed and well tired out. No tempests, no upheavals, no high ambitions that led to great downfalls. No real pain, and so how could she truly understand the sufferings of those who suffered? Tisana thought of Freylis and her treacherous lover, betraying her on an instant's notice because her half-formed plans did not align neatly with his; and then she thought of her own little barnyard romances, so light, so casual, mere companionship, two people mindlessly coming together for a while and just as mindlessly parting, no anguish, no torment. Even when she made love, which was supposed to be the ultimate communion, it was a simple trivial business, a grappling of healthy strapping bodies, an easy joining, a little thrashing and pumping, gasps and moans, a quick shudder of pleasure, then release and parting. Nothing more. Somehow Tisana had slid through life unscarred, untouched, undeflected. How, then, could she be of value to others? Their confusions and conflicts would be meaningless to her. And, she saw, maybe that was what she feared about the Testing: that they would finally look into her soul and see how unfit she was to be a speaker because she was so uncomplicated and innocent, that they would uncover her deception at last. How ironic that she was worried now because she had lived a worry-free life! Her hands began to tremble. She held them up and stared at them: peasant hands, big stupid coarse thick-fingered hands, quivering as though on drawstrings. Freylis, seeing the gesture, pulled Tisana's hands down and gripped them with her own, barely able to span them with her frail and tiny fingers. "Relax," she whispered fiercely. "There's nothing to fret about!"

Tisana nodded. "What time is it?"

"Time for you to be with your novices and me to be making my observances."

"Yes. Yes. All right, let's be about it."

"I'll see you later. At dinner. And I'll keep dream-vigil with you tonight, all right?"

"Yes," Tisana said. "I'd like that very much."

They left the cell. Tisana hastened outside, across the courtyard to the assembly-room where a dozen novices waited for her. There was no trace now of the rain: the harsh desert sun had boiled away every drop. At midday even the lizards were hiding. As she approached the far side of the cloister, a senior tutor emerged, Vandune, a Piliplokki woman nearly as old as the Superior. Tisana smiled at her and went on; but the tutor halted and called back to her, "Is tomorrow your day?"

"I'm afraid so."

"Have they told you who'll be giving you your Testing?"

"They've told me nothing," said Tisana. "They've left me guessing about the whole thing."

"As it should be," Vandune said. "Uncertainty is good for the soul."

"Easy enough for you to say," Tisana muttered, as Vandune trudged away. She wondered if she herself would ever be so cheerily heartless to candidates for the Testing, assuming she passed and went on to be a tutor. Probably. Probably. One's perspective changes when one is on the other side of the wall, she thought, remembering that when she was a child she had vowed always to understand the special problems of children when she became an adult, and never to treat the young with the sort of blithe cruelty that all children receive at the hands of their unthinking elders; she had not forgotten the vow, but, fifteen or twenty years later, she had forgotten just what it was that was so special about the condition of childhood, and she doubted that she showed any great sensitivity to them despite everything. So, too, most likely, with this.

She entered the assembly-room. Teaching at the chapter-house was done mainly by the tutors, who were fully qualified dream-speakers voluntarily taking a few years from their practices to give instruction; but the consummates, the final-year students who were speakers in all but the last degree, were required also to work with the novices by way of gaining experience in dealing with people. Tisana taught the brewing of dream-wine, theory of sendings, and social harmonics. The novices looked up at her with awe and respect as she took her place at the desk. What could they know of her fears and doubts? To them she was a high initiate of their rite, barely a notch or two below the Superior Inuelda. She had mastered all the skills they were struggling so hard to comprehend. And if they were aware of the Testing at all, it was merely as a vague dark cloud on the distant horizon, no more relevant to their immediate concerns than old age and death.

"Yesterday," Tisana began, taking a deep breath and trying to make herself seem cool and self-possessed, an oracle, a fount of wisdom, "we spoke of the role of the King of Dreams in regulating the behavior of society on Majipoor. You, Meliara, raised the issue of the frequent malevolence of the imagery in sendings of the King, and questioned the underlying morality of a social system based on chastisement through dreams. I'd like us to address that issue today in more detail. Let us consider a hypothetical person—say, a sea-dragon hunter from Piliplok—who in a moment of extreme inner stress commits an act of unpremeditated but severe violence against a fellow member of her crew, and—"

The words came rolling from her in skeins. The novices scribbled notes, frowned, shook their heads, scribbled notes even more frantically. Tisana remembered from her own novitiate that desperate feeling of being confronted with an infinity of things to learn, not merely techniques of the speaking itself but all kinds of subsidiary nuances and concepts. She hadn't anticipated any of that, and probably neither had the novices before her. But of course Tisana had given little thought to the difficulties that becoming a dream-speaker might pose for her. Anticipatory worrying, until this business of the Testing had arisen, had never been her style. One day seven years ago a sending had come upon her from the Lady, telling her to leave her farm and bend herself toward dream-speaking, and without questioning it she had obeyed, borrowing money and going off on the long pilgrimage to the Isle of Sleep for the preparatory instruction, and then, receiving permission there to enroll at the Velalisier chapter-house, journeying onward across the interminable sea to this remote and forlorn desert where she had lived the past four years. Never doubting, never hesitating.

But there was so much to learn! The myriad details of the speaker's relationship with her clients, the professional etiquette, the responsibilities, the pitfalls. The method of mixing the wine and merging minds. The ways of couching interpretations in usefully ambiguous words. And the dreams themselves! The types, the significances, the cloaked meanings! The seven self-deceptive dreams and the nine instructive dreams, the dreams of summoning, the dreams of dismissal, the three dreams of transcendence of self, the dreams of postponement of delight, the dreams of diminished awareness, the eleven dreams of torment, the five dreams of bliss, the dreams of interrupted voyage, the dreams of striving, the dreams of good illusions, the dreams of harmful illusions, the dreams of mistaken ambition, the thirteen dreams of grace— Tisana had learned them all, had made the whole list part of her nervous system the way the multiplication table and the alphabet were, had rigorously experienced each of the many types through month upon month of programmed sleep, and so in truth she was an adept, she was an initiate, she had attained all that these wide-eyed unformed youngsters here were striving to know, and yet all the same tomorrow the Testing might undo her completely, which none of them could possibly comprehend.

Or could they? The lesson came to its end and Tisana stood at her desk for a moment, numbly shuffling papers, as the novices filed out. One of them, a short plump fair-haired girl from one of the Guardian Cities of Castle Mount, paused before her a moment—dwarfed by her, as most people were—and looked up and touched her fingertips lightly to Tisana's forearm, a moth-wing caress, and whispered shyly, "It'll be easy for you tomorrow. I'm certain of it." And smiled and turned away, cheeks blazing, and was gone.

So they knew, then—some of them. That benediction remained with Tisana like a candle's glow through all the rest of the day. A long dreary day it was, too, full of chores that could not be shirked, though she would have preferred to go off by herself and walk in the desert instead of doing them. But there were rituals to perform and observances to make and some heavy digging at the site of the new chapel of the Lady, and in the afternoon another class of novices to face, and then a little solitude before dinner, and finally dinner itself, at sundown. By then it seemed to Tisana that this morning's little rainstorm had happened weeks ago, or perhaps in a dream.

Dinner was a tense business. She had almost no appetite, something unheard-of for her. All around her in the dining-hall surged the warmth and vitality of the chapter-house, laughter, gossip, raucous singing, and Tisana sat isolated in the midst of it as if surrounded by an invisible sphere of crystal. The older women were elaborately ignoring the fact that this was the eve of her Testing, while the younger ones, trying to do the same, could not help stealing little quick glances

at her, the way one covertly looks at someone who suddenly
has been called upon to bear some special burden. Tisana
was not sure which was worse, the bland pretense of the consummates and tutors or the edgy curiosity of the pledgeds
and novices. She toyed with her food. Freylis scolded her as
one would scold a child, telling her she would need strength
for tomorrow. At that Tisana managed a thin laugh, patting
her firm fleshy middle and saying, "I've stored up enough already to last me through a dozen Testings."

"All the same," Freylis replied. "Eat."

"I can't. I'm too nervous."

From the dais came the sound of a spoon tinkling against
a glass. Tisana looked up. The Superior was rising to make
an announcement.

In dismay Tisana muttered, "The Lady keep me! Is she going to say something in front of everybody about my Testing?"

"It's about the new Coronal," said Freylis. "The news arrived this afternoon."

"What new Coronal?"

"To take the place of Lord Tyeveras, now that he's Pontifex. Where have you been? For the past five weeks—"

" —and indeed this morning's rain was a sign of sweet ti-
dings and a new springtime," the Superior was saying.

Tisana forced herself to follow the old woman's words.

"A message has come to me today that will cheer you all.
We have a Coronal again! The Pontifex Tyeveras has selected
Malibor of Bombifale, who this night on Castle Mount will
take his place upon the Confalume Throne!"

There was cheering and table-pounding and making of starburst signs. Tisana, like one who walks in sleep, did as the
others were doing. A new Coronal? Yes, yes, she had forgotten, the old Pontifex had died some months back and the
wheel of state had turned once more; Lord Tyeveras was
Pontifex now and there was a new man this very day atop
Castle Mount. "Malibor! Lord Malibor! Long live the Coronal!" she shouted, along with the rest and yet it was unreal
and unimportant to her. A new Coronal? One name on the
long, long list. Good for Lord Malibor, whoever he may
be, and may the Divine treat him kindly: his troubles are
only now beginning. But Tisana hardly cared. One was
supposed to celebrate at the outset of a reign. She remem-

bered getting tipsy on fireshower wine when she was a little girl and the famous Kinniken had died, bringing Lord Ossier into the Labyrinth of the Pontifex and elevating Tyeveras to Castle Mount. And now Lord Tyeveras was Pontifex and somebody else was Coronal, and some day, no doubt, Tisana would hear that this Malibor had moved on to the Labyrinth and there was another eager young Coronal on the throne. Though these events were supposed to be terribly important, Tisana could not at the moment care at all what the king's name happened to be, whether Malibor or Tyeveras or Ossier or Kinniken. Castle Mount was far away, thousands of miles, for all she knew did not even exist. What loomed as high in her life as Castle Mount was the Testing. Her obsession with her Testing overshadowed everything, turning all other events into wraiths. She knew that was absurd. It was something like the bizarre intensifying of feeling that comes over one when one is ill, when the entire universe seems to center on the pain behind one's left eye or the hollowness in one's gut, and nothing else has any significance. Lord Malibor? She would celebrate his rising some other time.

"Come," Freylis said. "Let's got to your room."

Tisana nodded. The dining-hall was no place for her tonight. Conscious that all eyes were on her, she made her way unsteadily down the aisle and out into the darkness. A dry warm wind was blowing, a rasping wind, grating against her nerves. When they reached Tisana's cell, Freylis lit the candles and gently pushed Tisana down on the bed. From the cabinet she took two wine-bowls, and from under her robe she drew a small flask.

"What are you doing?" Tisana asked.

"Wine. To relax you."

"Dream-wine?"

"Why not?"

Frowning, Tisna said, "We aren't supposed to—"

"We aren't going to do a speaking. This is just to relax you, to bring us closer together so that I can share my strength with you. Yes? Here." She poured the thick, dark wine into the bowls and put one into Tisana's hand. "Drink. Drink it, Tisana." Numbly Tisana obeyed. Freylis drank her own, quickly, and began to remove her clothes. Tisana looked at her in surprise. She had never had a woman for a lover. Was that what Freylis wanted her to do now? Why? This is a

mistake, Tisana thought. On the eve of my Testing, to be
drinking dream-wine, to be sharing my bed with Freylis—
"Get undressed," Freylis whispered.

"What are you going to do?"

"Keep dream-vigil with you, silly. As we agreed. Nothing
more. Finish your wine and get your robe off!"

Freylis was naked now. Her body was almost like a child's,
straight-limbed, lean, with pale clear skin and small girlish
breasts. Tisana dropped her own clothes to the floor. The
heaviness of her flesh embarrassed her, the powerful arms,
the thick columns of her thighs and legs. One was always
naked when one did speakings, and one quickly came not to
care about baring one's body, but somehow this was different,
intimate, personal. Freylis poured a little more wine for each
of them. Tisana drank without protest. Then Freylis seized
Tisana's wrists and knelt before her and stared straight into
her eyes and said, in a tone both affectionate and scornful,
"You big fool, you've got to stop worrying about tomorrow!
The Testing is *nothing*. Nothing." She blew out the candles
and lay down alongside Tisana. "Sleep softly. Dream well."
Freylis curled herself up in Tisana's bosom and clasped herself close against her, but she lay still, and in moments she
was asleep.

So they were not to become lovers. Tisana felt relief. Another time, perhaps—why not?—but this was no moment for
such adventures. Tisana closed her eyes and held Freylis as
one might hold a sleeping child. The wine made a throbbing
in her, and a warmth. Dream-wine opened one mind to another, and Tisana was keenly sensitive now to Freylis' spirit
beside her, but this was no speaking and they had not done
the focusing exercises that created the full union; from Freylis came only broad undefined emanations of peace and love
and energy. She was strong, far stronger than her slight body
led one to think, and as the dream-wine took deeper hold of
Tisana's mind she drew increasing comfort from the nearness
of the other woman. Slowly drowsiness overtook her. Still she
fretted—about the Testing, about what the others would
think about their going off together so early in the evening,
about the technical violation of regulations that they had
committed by sharing the wine this way—and eddying currents of guilt and shame and fear swirled through her spirit
for a time. But gradually she grew calm. She slept. With a

speaker's trained eye she kept watch on her dreams, but they were without form or sequence, the images mysteriously imprecise, a blank horizon illuminated by a vague and distant glow, and now perhaps the face of the Lady, or of the Superior Inuelda, or of Freylis, but mainly just a band of warm consoling light. And then it was dawn and some bird was shrieking on the desert, announcing the new day.

Tisana blinked and sat up. She was alone. Freylis had put away the candles and washed the wine-bowls, and had left a note on the table—no, not a note, a drawing, the lightning-bolt symbol of the King of Dreams within the triangle-within-triangle symbol of the Lady of the Isle, and around that a heart, and around that a radiant sun: a message of love and good cheer.

"Tisana?"

She went to the door. The old tutor Vandune was there.

"Is it time?" Tisana asked.

"Time and then some. The sun's been up for twenty minutes. Are you ready?"

"Yes," Tisana said. She felt oddly calm—ironic, after this week of fears. But now that the moment was at hand there no longer was anything to fear. Whatever would be, would be: and if she were to be found lacking in her Testing, so be it, it would be for the best.

She followed Vandune across the courtyard and past the vegetable plot and out of the chapter-house grounds. A few people were already up and about, but did not speak to them. By the sea-green light of early day they marched in silence over the crusted desert sands, Tisana checking her pace to keep just to the rear of the older woman. They walked eastward and southward, without a word passing between them, for what felt like hours and hours, miles and miles. Out of the emptiness of the desert there began to appear now the outlying ruins of the ancient Metamorph city of Velalisier, that vast and haunted place of forbidding scope and majesty, thousands of years old and long since accursed and abandoned by its builders. Tisana thought she understood. For the Testing, they would turn her loose in the ruins and let her wander among the ghosts all day. But could that be it? So childish, so simpleminded? Ghosts held no terrors for her. And they should be doing this by night, besides, if they meant to frighten her. Velalisier by day was just a thing of humps and snags of stone, fallen temples, shattered columns, sand-buried pyramids.

They came at last to a kind of amphitheater, well preserved, ring upon ring of stone seats radiating outward in a broad arc. In the center stood a stone table and a few stone benches, and on the table sat a flask and a wine-bowl. So this was the place of the Testing! And now, Tisana guessed, she and old Vandune would share the wine and lie down together on the flat sandy ground, and do a speaking, and when they rose Vandune would know whether or not to enroll Tisana of Falkynkip in the roster of dream-speakers.

But that was not how it would be either. Vandune indicated the flask and said, "It holds dream-wine. I will leave you here. Pour as much of the wine as you like, drink, look into your soul. Administer the Testing to yourself."

"I?"

Vandune smiled. "Who else can test you? Go. Drink. In time I will return."

The old tutor bowed and walked away. Tisana's mind brimmed with questions, but she held them back, for she sensed that the Testing had already begun and that the first part of it was that no questions could be asked. In puzzlement she watched as Vandune passed through a niche in the amphitheater wall and disappeared into an alcove. There was no sound after that, not even a footfall. In the crushing silence of the empty city the sand seemed to be roaring, but silently. Tisana frowned, smiled, laughed—a booming laugh that stirred far-off echoes. The joke was on her! Devise your own Testing, that was the thing! Let them dread the day, then march them into the ruins and tell them to run the show themselves! So much for dread anticipation of fearsome ordeals, so much for the phantoms of the soul's own making.

But how—

Tisana shrugged. Poured the wine, drank. Very sweet, perhaps wine of another year. The flask was a big one. All right: I'm a big woman. She gave herself a second draught. Her stomach was empty; she felt the wine almost instantly churning her brains. Yet she drank a third.

The sun was climbing fast. The edge of its forelimb had reached the top of the amphitheater wall.

"Tisana!" she cried. And to her shout she replied, "Yes, Tisana?"

Laughed. Drank again.

She had never before had dream-wine in solitude. It was always taken in the presence of another—either while doing a speaking, or else with a tutor. Drinking it now alone was like asking questions of one's reflection. She felt the kind of confusion that comes from standing between two mirrors and seeing one's image shuttled back and forth to infinity.

"Tisana," she said, "this is your Testing. Are you fit to be a dream-speaker?"

And she answered, "I have studied four years, and before that I spent three more making the pilgrimage to the Isle. I know the seven self-deceptive dreams and the nine instructive dreams, the dreams of summoning, the dreams of—"

"All right. Skip all that. Are you fit to be a dream-speaker?"

"I know how to mix the wine and how to drink it."

"Answer the question. Are you fit to be a dream-speaker?"

"I am very stable. I am tranquil of soul."

"You are evading the question."

"I am strong and capable. I have little malice in me. I wish to serve the Divine."

"What about serving your fellow beings?"

"I serve the Divine by serving them."

"Very elegantly put. Who gave you that line, Tisana?"

"It just came to me. May I have some more wine?"

"All you like."

"Thank you," Tisana said. She drank. She felt dizzy but yet not drunk, and the mysterious mind-linking powers of the dream-wine were absent, she being alone and awake. She said, "What is the next question?"

"You still haven't answered the first one."

"Ask the next one."

"There is only one question, Tisana. Are you fit to be a dream-speaker? Can you soothe the souls of those who come to you?"

"I will try."

"Is that your answer?"

"Yes," Tisana said. "That is my answer. Turn me loose and let me try. I am a woman of good will. I have the skills and I have the desire to help others. And the Lady has commanded me to be a dream-speaker."

"Will you lie down with all who need you? With humans

and Ghayrogs and Skandars and Liimen and Vroons and all others of all the races of the world?"

"All," she said.

"Will you take their confusions from them?"

"If I can, I will."

"Are you fit to be a dream-speaker?"

"Let me try, and then we will know," said Tisana.

Tisana said, "That seems fair. I have no further questions."

She poured the last of the wine and drank it. Then she sat quietly as the sun climbed and the heat of the day grew. She was altogether calm, without impatience, without discomfort. She would sit this way all day and all night, if she had to. What seemed like an hour went by, or a little more, and then suddenly Vandune was before her, appearing without warning.

The old woman said softly, "Is your Testing finished?"

"Yes."

"How did it go?"

"I have passed it," said Tisana.

Vandune smiled. "Yes. I was sure that you would. Come, now. We must speak with the Superior, and make arrangements for your future, Speaker Tisana."

They returned to the chapter-house as silently as they had come, walking quickly in the mounting heat. It was nearly noon when they emerged from the zone of ruins. The novices and pledgeds who had been working in the fields were coming in for lunch. They looked uncertainly at Tisana, and Tisana smiled at them, a bright reassuring smile.

At the entrance to the main cloister Freylis appeared, crossing Tisana's path as though by chance, and gave her a quick worried look.

"Well?" Freylis asked tensely.

Tisana smiled. She wanted to say, It was nothing, it was a joke, a formality, a mere ritual, the real Testing took place long before this. But Freylis would have to discover those things for herself. A great gulf now separated them, for Tisana was a speaker now and Freylis still merely a pledged. So Tisana simply said, "All is well."

"Good. Oh, good, Tisana, good! I'm so happy for you!"

"I thank you for your help," said Tisana gravely.

A shadow suddenly crossed the courtyard. Tisana looked up. A small black cloud, like yesterday's, had wandered into the sky, some strayed fragment, no doubt, of a storm out by the far-off coast. It hung as if hooked to the chapter-house's spire, and, as though some latch had been pulled back, it began abruptly to release great heavy raindrops. "Look," Tisana said. "It's raining again! Come, Freylis! Come, let's dance!"

And Valentine's time as Coronal
Lord Valentine and

NINE

A Thief in Ni-moya

Toward the close of the seventh year of the restoration of Lord Valentine, word reaches the Labyrinth that the Coronal soon will be arriving on a visit—news that sends Hissune's pulse rate climbing and his heart to pounding. Will he see the Coronal? Will Lord Valentine remember him? The Coronal once took the trouble to summon him all the way to Castle Mount for his re-crowning; surely the Coronal still thinks of him, surely Lord Valentine has some recollection of the boy who—

Probably not, Hissune decides. His excitement subsides; his cool rational self regains control. If he catches sight of Lord Valentine at all during his visit, that will be extraordinary, and if Lord Valentine knows who he is, that will be miraculous. Most likely the Coronal will dip in and out of the Labyrinth without seeing anyone but the high ministers of the Pontifex. They say he is off on a grand processional toward Alaisor, and thence to the Isle to visit his mother, and a stop at the Labyrinth is obligatory on such an itinerary. But Hissune knows that Coronals tend not to enjoy visits to the Labyrinth, which remind them uncomfortably of the lodgings that await them when it is their time to be elevated to the senior kingship. And he knows, too, that the Pontifex Tyeveras is a ghost-creature, more dead than alive, lost in impenetrable dreams within the cocoon of his life-support systems,

210

incapable of rational human speech, a symbol rather than a man, who ought to have been buried years ago but who is kept in maintenance so that Lord Valentine's time as Coronal can be prolonged. That is fine for Lord Valentine and doubtless for Majipoor, Hissune thinks; not so good for old Tyeveras. But such matters are not his concern. He returns to the Register of Souls, still speculating idly about the coming visit of the Coronal, and idly he taps for a new capsule, and what comes forth is the recording of a citizen of Ni-moya, which begins so unpromisingly that Hissune would have rejected it, but that he desires a glimpse of that great city of the other continent. For Ni-moya's sake he allows himself to live the life of a little shopkeeper—and soon he has no regrets.

I

Inyanna's mother had been a shopkeeper in Velathys all her life, and so had Inyanna's mother's mother, and it was beginning to look as though that would be Inyanna's destiny too. Neither her mother nor her mother's mother had seemed particularly resentful of such a life, but Inyanna, now that she was nineteen and sole proprietor, felt the shop as a crushing burden on her back, a hump, an intolerable pressure. She thought often of selling out and seeking her real fate in some other city far away, Piliplok or Pidruid or even the mighty metropolis of Ni-moya, far to the north, that was said to be wondrous beyond the imagination of anyone who had not beheld it.

But times were dull and business was slow and Inyanna saw no purchasers for the shop on the horizon. Besides, the place had been the center of her family's life for generations, and simply to abandon it was not an easy thing to do, no matter how hateful it had become. So every morning she rose at dawn and stepped out on the little cobbled terrace to plunge herself into the stone vat of rainwater that she kept there for bathing, and then she dressed and breakfasted on dried fish and wine and went downstairs to open the shop. It was a place of general merchandise—bolts of cloth and clay pots from the south coast and barrels of spices and preserved fruits and jugs of wine and the keen cutlery of Narabal and slabs of costly sea-dragon meat and the glittering filigreed lanterns that they made in Til-omon, and many other such things. There were scores of shops just like hers in Velathys; none of them did particularly well. Since her mother's death, Inyanna had kept the books and managed the inventory and swept the floor and polished the counters and filled out the governmental forms and permits, and she was weary of all that. But what other prospects did life hold? She was an unimportant girl living in an unimportant rainswept mountain-girt city, and she had no real expectation that any of that would change over the next sixty or seventy years.

Few of her customers were humans. Over the decades, this district of Velathys had come to be occupied mainly by Hjorts and Liimen—and a good many Metamorphs, too, for the Metamorph province of Piurifayne lay just beyond the mountain range north of the city and a considerable number of the shapeshifting folk had filtered down into Velathys. She took them all for granted, even the Metamorphs, who made most humans uneasy. The only thing Inyanna regretted about her clientele was that she did not get to see many of her own kind, and so, although she was slender and attractive, tall, sleek, almost boyish-looking, with curling red hair and striking green eyes, she rarely found lovers and had never met anyone she might care to live with. Sharing the shop would ease much of the labor. On the other hand, it would cost her much of her freedom, too, including the freedom to dream of a time when she did not keep a shop in Velathys.

One day after the noon rains two strangers entered the shop, the first customers in hours. One was short and thick-bodied, a little round stub of a man, and the other, pale and gaunt and elongated, with a bony face all knobs and angles, looked like some predatory creature of the mountains. They wore heavy white tunics with bright orange sashes, a style of dress that was said to be common in the grand cities of the north, and they looked about the store with the quick scornful glances of those accustomed to a far finer level of merchandise.

The short one said, "Are you Inyanna Forlana?"

"I am."

He consulted a document. "Daughter of Forlana Hayorn, who was the daughter of Hayorn Inyanne?"

"You have the right person. May I ask—"

"At last!" cried the tall one. "What a long dreary trail this has been! If you knew how long we've searched for you! Up the river to Khyntor, and then around to Dulorn, and across these damnable mountains—does it ever stop raining down here?—and then from house to house, from shop to shop, all across Velathys, asking this one, asking that one—"

"And I am who you seek?"

"If you can prove your ancestry, yes."

Inyanna shrugged. "I have records. But what business do you have with me?"

"We should introduce ourselves," said the short one. "I am Vezan Ormus and my colleague is called Steyg, and we are officials of the staff of his majesty the Pontifex Tyeveras, Bureau of Probate, Ni-moya." From a richly tooled leather purse Vezan Ormus withdrew a sheaf of documents; he shuffled them purposefully and said, "You mother's mother's elder sister was a certain Saleen Inyanna, who in the twenty-third year of the Pontificate of Kinniken, Lord Ossier being then Coronal, settled in the city of Ni-moya and married one Helmyot Gavoon, third cousin to the duke."

Inyanna stared blankly. "I know nothing of these people."

"We are not surprised," said Steyg. "It was some generations ago. And doubtless there was little contact between the two branches of the family, considering the great gulf in distance and in wealth."

"My grandmother never mentioned rich relatives in Ni-moya," said Inyanna.

Vezan Ormus coughed and searched in the papers. "Be that as it may. Three children were born to Helmyot Gavoon and Saleen Inyanna, of whom the eldest, a daughter, inherited the family estates. She died young in a hunting mishap and the lands passed to her only son, Gavoon Dilamayne, who remained childless and died in the tenth year of the Pontificate of Tyeveras, that is to say, nine years ago. Since then the property has remained vacant while the search for legitimate heirs has been conducted. Three years ago it was determined—"

"That I am heir?"

"Indeed," said Steyg blandly, with a broad bony smile.

Inyanna, who had seen the trend of the conversation for quite some time, was nevertheless astounded. Her legs quivered, her lips and mouth went dry, and in her confusion she jerked her arm suddenly, knocking down and shattering an expensive vase of Alhanroel ware. Embarrassed by all that, she got herself under control and said, "What is it I'm supposed to have inherited, then?"

"The grand house known as Nissimorn Prospect, on the northern shore of the Zimr at Ni-moya, and estates at three places in the Steiche Valley, all leased and producing income," said Steyg.

"We congratulate you," said Vezan Ormus.

"And I congratulate you," replied Inyanna, "on the cleverness of your wit. Thank you for these moments of amusement; and now, unless you want to buy something, I beg you let me get on with my bookkeeping, for the taxes are due and—"

"You are skeptical," said Vezan Ormus. "Quite properly. We come with a fantastic story and you are unable to absorb the impact of our words. But look: we are men of Ni-moya. Would we have dragged ourselves thousands of miles down to Velathys for the sake of playing jokes on shopkeepers? See—here—" He fanned out his sheaf of papers and pushed them toward Inyanna. Hands trembling, she examined them. A view of the mansion—dazzling—and an array of documents of title, and a genealogy, and a paper bearing the Pontifical seal with her name inscribed on it—

She looked up, stunned, dazed.

In a faint furry voice she said, "What must I do now?"

"The procedures are purely routine," Steyg replied. "You must file affidavits that you are in fact Inyanna Forlana, you must sign papers agreeing that you will make good the accrued taxes on the properties out of accumulated revenues once you have taken possession, you will have to pay the filing fees for transfer of title, and so on. We can handle all of that for you."

"Filing fees?"

"A matter of a few royals."

Her eyes widened. "Which I can pay out of the estate's accumulated revenues?"

"Unfortunately, no," said Vezan Ormus. "The money must be paid *before* you have taken title, and, of course, you have no access to the revenues of the estate until you have taken title, so—"

"An annoying formality," Steyg said. "But a trifling one, if you take the long view."

2

All told the fees came to twenty royals. That was an enormous sum for Inyanna, nearly her whole savings; but a study of the documents told her that the revenues of the agricultural lands alone were nine hundred royals a year, and then there were the other assets of the estate, the mansion and its contents, the rents and royalties on certain riverfront properties—

Vezan Ormus and Steyg were extremely helpful in the filling out of the forms. She put the CLOSED FOR BUSINESS sign out, not that it mattered much in this slow season, and all afternoon they sat beside her at her little desk upstairs, passing things to her for her to sign, and stamping them with impressive-looking Pontifical seals. Afterward she celebrated by taking them down to the tavern at the foot of the hill for a few rounds of wine. Steyg insisted on buying the first, pushing her hand away and plunking down half a crown for a flask of choice palm-wine from Pidruid. Inyanna gasped at the extravagance—she ordinarily drank humbler stuff—but then she remembered that she had come into wealth, and when the flask was gone she ordered another herself. The tavern was crowded, mainly with Hjorts and a few Ghayrogs, and the bureaucrats from the northland looked uncomfortable amid all these non-humans, sometimes holding their fingers thoughtfully over their noses as if to filter out the scent of alien flesh. Inyanna, to put them at their ease, told them again and again how grateful she was that they had taken the trouble to seek her out in the obscurity of Velathys.

"But it is our job!" Vezan Ormus protested. "On this world we each must give service to the Divine by playing our parts in the intricacies of daily life. Land was sitting idle; a great house was unoccupied; a deserving heir lived drably in ignorance. Justice demands that such inequities be righted. To us falls the privilege of doing so."

"All the same," said Inyanna, flushed with wine and leaning almost coquettishly close now to one man, now to the other, "You have undergone great inconvenience for my sake, and I will always be in your debt. May I buy you another flask?"

It was well past dark when they finally left the tavern.

Several moons were out, and the mountains that ringed the city, outlying fangs of the great Gonghar range, looked like jagged pillars of black ice in the chilly glimmer. Inyanna saw her visitors to their hostelry, at the edge of Dekkeret Plaza, and in her winy wooziness came close to inviting herself in for the night. But seemingly they had no yearning for that, were perhaps made even a little wary at the possibility, and she found herself smoothly and expertly turned away at the door. Wobbling a little, she made the long steep climb to her house and stepped out on the terrace to take the night air. Her head was throbbing. Too much wine, too much talk, too much startling news! She looked about her at her city, row upon row of small stucco-walled tile-roofed buildings descending the sloping bowl of Velathys Basin, a few ragged strands of parkland, some plazas and mansions, the duke's ramshackle castle slung along the eastern ridge, the highway like a girdle encircling the town, then the lofty and oppressive mountains beginning just beyond, the marble quarries like raw wounds on their flanks—she could see it all from her hilltop nest. Farewell! Neither an ugly city nor a lovely one, she thought: just a place, quiet, damp, dull, chilly, ordinary, known for its fine marble and its skilled stonemasons and not much else, a provincial town on a provincial continent. She had been resigned to living out her days here. But now, now that miracles had invaded her life, it seemed intolerable to have to spend as much as another hour here, when shining Ni-moya was waiting, Ni-moya, Ni-moya, Ni-moya!

She slept only fitfully. In the morning she met with Vezan Ormus and Steyg in the notary's office behind the bank and turned over to them her little sack of well-worn royal pieces, most of them old, some very old, with the faces of Kinniken and Thimin and Ossier on them, and even one coin of the reign of great Confalume, a coin hundreds of years old. In return they gave her a single sheet of paper: a receipt, acknowledging payment of twenty royals that they were to expend on her behalf for filing fees. The other documents, they explained, must go back with them to be countersigned and validated. But they would ship everything to her once the transfer was complete, and then she could come to Ni-moya to take possession of her property.

"You will be my guests," she told them grandly, "for a month of hunting and feasting, when I am in my estates."

"Oh, no," said Vezan Ormus softly. "It would hardly be

appropriate for such as we to mingle socially with the mistress of Nissimorn Prospect. But we understand the sentiment, and we thank you for the gesture."

Inyanna asked them to lunch. But they had to move on, Steyg replied. They had other heirs to contact, probate work to carry out in Narabal and Til-omon and Pidruid; many months would pass before they saw their homes and wives in Ni-moya again. And did that mean, she asked, suddenly dismayed, that no action would be taken on the filing of her claim until they had finished their tour? "Not at all," said Steyg. "We will ship your documents to Ni-moya by direct courier tonight. The processing of the claim will begin as soon as possible. You should hear from our office in—oh, shall we say seven to nine weeks?"

She accompanied them to their hotel, and waited outside while they packed, and saw them into their floater, and stood waving in the street as they drove off toward the highway that led to the southwest coast. Then she reopened the shop. In the afternoon there were two customers, one buying eight weights' worth of nails and the other asking for false satin, three yards at sixty weights the yard, so the entire day's sales were less than two crowns, but no matter. Soon she would be rich.

A month went by and no news came from Ni-moya. A second month, and still there was silence.

The patience that had kept Inyanna in Velathys for nineteen years was the patience of hopelessness, of resignation. But now that gerat changes were before her, she had no patience left. She fidgeted, she paced, she made notations on the calendar. The summer, with its virtually daily rains, came to an end, and the dry crisp autumn began, when the leaves turned fiery in the foothills. No word. The heavy torrents of winter began, with masses of moist air drifting south out of the Zimr Valley across the Metamorph lands and colliding with the harsh mountain winds. There was snow in the highest rims of the Gonghars, and streams of mud ran through the streets of Velathys. No word out of Ni-moya, and Inyanna thought of her twenty royals, and terror began to mingle with annoyance in her soul. She celebrated her twentieth birthday alone, bitterly drinking soured wine and imagining what it would be like to command the revenues of Nissimorn Prospect. Why was it taking so long? No doubt Vezan Ormus and Steyg had properly forwarded the

documents to the offices of the Pontifex; but just as surely
her papers were sitting on some dusty desk, awaiting action,
while weeds grew in the gardens of her estate.

One Winterday Eve Inyanna rsolved to go to Ni-moya and
take charge of the case in person.

The journey would be expensive and she had parted with
her savings. To raise the money she mortgaged the shop to a
family of Hjorts. They gave her ten royals; they were to pay
themselves interest by selling off her inventory at their own
profit; if the entire debt should be repaid before she returned,
they would continue to manage the place on her behalf, paying her a royalty. The contract greatly favored the Hjorts, but
Inyanna did not care: she knew, but told no one, that she
would never again see the shop, nor these Hjorts, nor Velathys itself, and the only thing that mattered was having the
money to go to Ni-moya.

It was no small trip. The most direct route between Velathys and Ni-moya lay across the Shapeshifter province of Piurifayne, and to enter that was dangerous and rash. Instead
she had to make an enormous detour, westward through Stiamot Pass, then up the long broad valley that was the Dulorn
Rift, with the stupendous mile-high wall of Velathys Scarp
rising on the right for hundreds of miles; and once she
reached the city of Dulorn itself she would still have half the
vast continent of Zimroel to cross, by land and by riverboat,
before coming to Ni-moya. But Inyanna saw all that as a glorious gaudy adventure, however long it might take. She had
never been anywhere, except once when she was ten, and her
mother, enjoying unusual prosperity one winter, had sent her
to spend a month in the hotlands south of the Gonghars.
Other cities, although she had seen pictures of them, were as
remote and implausible to her as other worlds. Her mother
once had been to Til-omon on the coast, which she said was
a place of brilliant sunlight like golden wine, and soft never-
ending summer weather. Her mother's mother had been as
far as Narabal, where the tropical air was damp and heavy
and hung about you like a mantle. But the rest—Pidruid,
Piliplok, Dulorn, Ni-moya, and all the others—were only
names to her, and the idea of the ocean was almost beyond
her imagining, and it was utterly impossible for her really to
believe that there was another continent entirely beyond the
ocean, with ten great cities for every city of Zimroel, and
thousands of millions of people, and a baffling lair beneath

the desert called the Labyrinth, where the Pontifex lived, and a mountain thirty miles high, at the summit of which dwelled the Coronal and all his princely court. Thinking about such things gave her a pain in the throat and a ringing in the ears. Awesome and incomprehensible Majipoor was too gigantic a sweetmeat to swallow at a single gulp; but nibbling away at it, a mile at a time, was wholly wondrous to someone who had only once been beyond the boundaries of Velathys.

So Inyanna noted in fascination the change in the air as the big transport floater drifted through the pass and down into the flatlands west of the mountains. It was still winter down there—the days were short, the sunlight pale and greenish—but the breeze was mild and thick, lacking a wintry edge, and there was a sweet pungent fragrance on it. She saw in surprise that the soil here was dense and crumbly and spongy, much unlike the shallow rocky sparkling stuff around her home, and that in places it was an amazing bright red hue for miles and miles. The plants were different—fat-leaved, glistening—and the birds had unfamiliar plumage, and the towns that lined the highway were airy and open, farming villages nothing at all like dark ponderous gray Velathys, with audacious little wooden houses fancifully ornamented with scrollwork and painted in bright splashes of yellow and blue and scarlet. It was terribly unfamiliar, too, not to have the mountains on all sides, for Velathys nestled in the bosom of the Gonghars, but now she was in the wide depressed plateau that lay between the mountains and the far-off coastal strip, and when she looked to the west she could see so far that it was almost frightening, an unbounded vista dropping off into infinity. On her other side she had Velathys Scarp, the outer wall of the mountain chain, but even that was a strangeness, a single solid grim vertical barrier only occasionally divided into individual peaks, that ran endlessly north. But eventually the Scarp gave out, and the land changed profoundly once again as she continued northward into the upper end of the Dulorn Rift. Here the colossal sunken valley was rich in gypsum, and the low rolling hills were white as if with frost. The stone had an eerie texture, spiderweb stuff with a mysterious chilly sheen. In school she had learned that all of the city of Dulorn was built of this mineral, and they had shown pictures of it, spires and arches and crystalline facades blazing like cold fire in the light of day. That had seemed mere fable to her, like the tales of Old

Earth from which her people were said to have sprung. But one day in late winter Inyanna found herself staring at the outskirts of the actual city of Dulorn and she saw that the fable had been no work of fancy. Dulorn was far more beautiful and strange than she had been able to imagine. It seemed to shine with an inner light of its own, while the sunlight, refracted and shattered and deflected by the myriad angles and facets of the lofty baroque buildings, fell in gleaming showers to the streets.

So this was a city! Beside it, Inyanna thought, Velathys was a bog. She would have stayed here a month, a year, forever, going up one street and down the next, staring at the towers and bridges, peering into the mysterious shops so radiant with costly merchandise, so much unlike her own pitiful little place. These hordes of snaky-faced people—this was a Ghayrog city, millions of the quasi-reptilian aliens and just a scattering of the other races—moving with such purposefulness, pursuing professions unknown to simple mountain-folk—the luminous posters advertising Dulorn's famous Perpetual Circus—the elegant restaurants and hotels and parks—all of it left Inyanna numb with awe. Surely there was nothing on Majipoor to compare with this place! Yet they said Ni-moya was far greater, and Stee on Castle Mount superior to them both, and then also the famous Piliplok, and the port of Alaisor, and—so much, so much!

But half a day was all she had in Dulorn, while the floater was discharging its passengers and being readied for the next leg of its route. That was like no time at all. A day later, as she journeyed eastward through the forests between Dulorn and Mazadone, she found herself not sure whether she had truly seen Dulorn or only dreamed that she had been there.

New wonders presented themselves daily—places where the air was purple, trees the size of hills, thickets of ferns that sang. Then came long stretches of dull indistinguishable cities, Cynthion, Mazadone, Thagobar, and many more. Aboard the floater passengers came and went, drivers were changed every nine hundred miles of so, and only Inyanna went on and on and on, country girl off seeing the world, getting glassy-eyed now and foggy-brained from the endlessly unrolling vista. There were geysers to be seen shortly, and hot lakes, and other thermal wonders: Khyntor, this was, the big city of the midlands, where she was to board the riverboat for Ni-moya. Here the River Zimr came down out of the

northwest, a river as big as a sea, so that it strained the eyes
to look from bank to bank. In Velathys, Inyanna had known
only mountain streams, quick and narrow. They gave her no
preparation for the huge curving monster of dark water that
was the Zimr.

On the breast of that monster Inyanna now sailed for
weeks, past Verf and Stroyn and Lagomandino and fifty
other cities whose names were mere noises to her. The riverboat became the whole of her world. In the valley of the
Zimr seasons were gentle and it was easy to lose track of the
passing of time. It seemed to be springtime, though she knew
it must be summer, and later summer at that, for she had
been embarked on this journey more than half a year. Perhaps it would never end; perhaps it was her fate merely to
drift from place to place, experiencing nothing, coming to
ground nowhere. That was all right. She had begun to forget
herself. Somewhere there was a shop that had been hers,
somewhere there was a great estate that would be hers, somewhere there was a young woman named Inyanna Forlana
who came from Velathys, but all that had dissolved into mere
motion as she floated onward across unending Majipoor.

Then one day for the hundredth time some new city began
to come in view along the Zimr's shores, and there was sudden stirring aboard the boat, a rushing to the rails to stare
into the misty distance. Inyanna heard them muttering, "Ni-
moya! Ni-moya!" and knew that her voyage had reached its
end, that her wandering was over, that she was coming into
her true home and birthright.

3

She was wise enough to know that to try to fathom Ni-
moya on the first day made no more sense than trying to
count the stars. It was a metropolis twenty times the size of
Velathys, sprawling for hundreds of miles along both banks
of the immense Zimr, and she sensed that one could spend a
lifetime here and still need a map to find one's way around.
Very well. She refused to let herself be awed or overwhelmed
by the grotesque excessiveness of everything she saw about
her here. She would conquer this city step by single step. In
that calm decision was the beginning of her transformation
into a true Ni-moyan.

Nevertheless there was still the first step to be taken. The riverboat had docked at what seemed to be the southern bank of the Zimr. Clutching her one small satchel, Inyanna stared out over a vast body of water—the Zimr here was swollen by its meeting with several major tributaries—and saw cities on every shore. Which one was Ni-moya? Where would the Pontifical offices be? How would she find her lands and mansion? Glowing signs directed her to ferries, but their destinations were places called Gimbeluc and Istmoy and Strelain and Strand Vista: suburbs, she guessed. There was no sign for a ferry to Ni-moya because *all* these places were Ni-moya.

"Are you lost?" a thin sharp voice said.

Inyanna turned and saw a girl who had been on the riverboat, two or three years younger than herself, with a smudged face and stringy hair bizarrely dyed lavender. Too proud or perhaps too shy to accept help from her—she was not sure which—Inyanna shook her head brusquely and glanced away, feeling her cheeks go hot and red.

The girl said, "There's a public directory back of the ticket windows," and vanished into the ferry-bound hordes.

Inyanna joined the line outside the directory, came at last to the communion booth, and poked her head into the yielding contact hood. "Directory," a voice said.

Inyanna replied smoothly, "Office of the Pontifex. Bureau of Probate."

"There is no listing for such a bureau."

Inyanna frowned. "Office of the Pontifex, then."

"853 Rodamaunt Promenade, Strelain."

Vaguely troubled, she bought a ferry ticket to Strelain: one crown twenty weights. That left her with exactly two royals, perhaps enough for a few weeks' expenses in this costly place. After that? I am the inheritor of Nissimorn Prospect, she told herself airily, and boarded the ferry. But she wondered why the Bureau of Probate's address was unlisted.

It was mid-afternoon. The ferry, with a blast of its horn, glided serenely out from its slip. Inyanna clung to the rail, peering in wonder at the city on the far shore, every building a radiant white tower, flat-roofed, rising in level upon level toward the ridge of gentle green hills to the north. A map was mounted on a post near the stairway to the lower decks. Strelain, she saw, was the central district of the city, just opposite the ferry depot, which was named Nissimorn. The men from the Pontifex had told her that her estate was on the northern shore; therefore, since it was called Nissimorn Prospect and must face Nissimorn, it should be in Strelain itself, perhaps somewhere in that forested stretch of the shore to the northeast. Gimbeluc was a western suburb, separated from Strelain by a many-bridged subsidiary river; Istmoy was to the east; up from the south came the River Steiche, nearly as great as the Zimr itself, and the towns along its bank were named—

"Your first time?" It was the lavender-haired girl again.

Inyanna smiled nervously. "Yes. I'm from Velathys. Country girl, I guess."

"You seem afraid of me."

"Am I? Do I?"

"I won't bite you. I won't even swindle you. My name's Liloyve. I'm a thief in the Grand Bazaar."

"Did you say *thief?*"

"It's a recognized profession in Ni-moya. They don't license us yet, but they don't interfere much with us, either, and we have our own official registry, like a regular guild. I've been down in Lagomandino, selling stolen goods for my uncle. Are you too good for me, or just very timid?"

"Neither," said Inyanna. "But I've come a long way alone, and I'm out of the habit of talking to people, I think." She forced another smile. "You're really a thief?"

"Yes. But not a pickpocket. You look so worried! What's your name, anyway?"

"Inyanna Forlana."

"I like the sound of that. I've never met an Inyanna before. You've traveled all the way from Velathys to Ni-moya? What for?"

"To claim my inheritance," Inyanna answered. "The property of my grandmother's sister's grandson. An estate known as Nissimorn Prospect, on the north shore of—"

Liloyve giggled. She tried to smother it, and her cheeks belled out, and she coughed and clapped a hand over her mouth in what was almost a convulsion of mirth. But it passed swiftly and her expression changed to a softer one of pity. Gently she said, "Then you must be of the family of the duke, and I should beg your pardon for approaching you so rudely here."

"The family of the duke? No, of course not. Why do you—"

"Nissimorn Prospect is the estate of Calain, who is the duke's younger brother."

Inyanna shook her head. "No. My grandmother's sister's—"

"Poor thing, no need to pick your pocket. Someone's done it already!"

Inyanna clutched at her satchel.

"No," Liloyve said. "I mean, you've been taken, if you think you've inherited Nissimorn Prospect."

"There were papers with the Pontifical seal. Two men of Ni-moya brought them in person to Velathys. I may be a country girl, but I'm not so great a fool as to make this journey without proof. I had my suspicions, yes, but I saw the documents. I've filed for title! Twenty royals, it cost, but the papers were in order!"

Liloyve said, "Where will you stay, when we reach Strelain?"

"I've given that no thought. An inn, I suppose."

"Save your crowns. You'll need them. We'll put you up with us in the Bazaar. And in the morning you can take things up with the imperial proctors. Maybe they can help you recover some of what you've lost, eh?"

4

That she had been the victim of swindlers had been in Inyanna's mind from the start, like a low nagging buzz droning beneath lovely music, but she had chosen not to hear that buzz, and even now, with the buzz grown to a monstrous roar, she compelled herself to remain confident. This scruffy little bazaar-girl, this self-admitted professional thief, doubtless had the keenly honed mistrustfulness of one who lived by her wits in a hostile universe, and saw fraud and malevolence on all sides, possibly even where none existed. Inyanna was aware that she might have led herself through gullibility into a terrible error, but it was pointless to lament so soon. Perhaps she *was* somehow of the duke's family after all, or perhaps Liloyve was confused about the ownership of Nissimorn Prospect; or, if in fact she had come to Ni-moya on a fool's chase, consuming her last few crowns in the fruitless journey, at least now she was in Ni-moya rather than Velathys, and that in itself was cause for cheer.

As the ferry pulled into the Strelain slip Inyanna had her first view of central Ni-moya at close range. Towers of dazzling white came down almost to the water's edge, rising so steeply and suddenly that they seemed unstable, and it was hard to understand why they did not topple into the river. Night was beginning to fall. Lights glittered everywhere. Inyanna maintained the calmness of a sleepwalker in the face of the city's splendors. *I have come home,* she told herself over and over. *I am home, this city is my home, I feel quite at home here.* All the same she took care to stay close beside Liloyve as they made their way through swarming mobs of commuters, up the passageway to the street.

At the gate of the terminal stood three huge metallic birds with jeweled eyes—a gihorna with vast wings outspread, a great silly long-legged hazenmarl, and some third one that Inyanna did not know, with an enormous pouched beak curved like a sickle. The mechanical figures moved slowly, craning their heads, fluffing their wings. "Emblems of the city," Liloyve said. "You'll see them everywhere, the big silly boobies! A fortune in precious jewels in their eyes, too."

"And no one steals them?"

"I wish I had the nerve. I'd climb right up there and snatch them. But it's a thousand years' bad luck, so they say. The Metamorphs will rise again and cast us out, and the towers will fall, and a lot of other nonsense."

"But if you don't believe the legends, why don't you steal the gems?"

Liloyve laughed her snorting little laugh. "Who'd buy them? Any dealer would know what they were, and with a curse on them there'd be no takers, and a world of trouble for the thief, and the King of Dreams whining in your head until you wanted to scream. I'd rather have a pocketful of colored glass than the eyes of the birds of Ni-moya. Here, get in!" She opened the door of a small street-floater parked outside the terminal and shoved Inyanna to a seat. Settling in beside her, Liloyve briskly tapped out a code on the floater's pay-plate and the little vehicle took off. "We can thank your noble kinsman for this ride."

"What? Who?"

"Calain, the duke's brother. I used his pay-code. It was stolen last month and a lot of us are riding free, courtesy of Calain. Of course, when the bills come in his chancellor will get the number changed, but until then—you see?"

"I am very naïve," said Inyanna. "I still believe that the Lady and King see our sins while we sleep, and send dreams to discourage such things."

"So you are meant to believe," Liloyve replied. "Kill someone and you'll hear from the King of Dreams, no question of it. But there are how many people on Majipoor? Eighteen billion? Thirty? Fifty? And the King has time to foul the dreams of everyone who steals a ride in a street-floater? Do you think so?"

"Well—"

"Or even those who falsely sell title to other people's palaces?"

Inyanna's cheeks flamed and she turned away.

"Where are we going now?" she asked in a muffled voice.

"We're already there. The Grand Bazaar. Out!"

Inyanna followed Liloyve into a broad plaza bordered on three sides by lofty towers and on the fourth by a low, squat-looking building fronted by a multitude of shallow-rising stone steps. Hundreds of people in elegant white Nimoyan tunics, perhaps thousands, were rushing in and out of the building's wide mouth, over the arch of which the three emblematic birds were carved in high relief, with jewels again in their eyes.

Liloyve said, "This is Pidruid Gate, one of thirteen entrances. The Bazaar itself covers fifteen square miles, you know—a little like the Labyrinth, though it isn't as far underground, just at street level mainly, snaking all over the city, through the other buildings, under some of the streets, between buildings—a city within a city, you might say. My people have lived in it for hundreds of years. Hereditary thieves, we are. Without us the shopkeepers would be in bad trouble."

"I was a shopkeeper in Velathys. We have no thieves there, and I think we never felt the need for any," said Inyanna dryly as they allowed themselves to be swept along up the shallow steps and into the gate of the Grand Bazaar.

"It's different here," said Liloyve.

The Bazaar spread in every direction—a maze of narrow arcades and passages and tunnels and galleries, brightly lit, divided and subdivided into an infinity of tiny stalls. Overhead, a single continuous skein of yellow sparklecloth stretched into the distance, casting a brilliant glow from its own internal luminescence. That one sight astounded Inyanna more than anything else she had seen so far in Ni-moya, for she had sometimes carried sparklecloth in her shop, at three royals the roll, and such a roll was good for decorating no more than a small room; her soul quailed at the thought of fifteen square miles of sparklecloth, and her mind, canny as it was in such matters, could not at all calculate the cost. Ni-moya! Such excess could be met only with the defense of laughter.

They proceeded inward. One little streetlet seemed just like the next, every one bustling with shops for porcelains and fabrics and tableware and clothes, for fruits and meats and vegetables and delicacies, each with a wine-shop and a spice-shop and a gallery of precious stones, and a vendor selling grilled sausages and one selling fried fish, and the like. Yet Liloyve seemed to know precisely which fork and channel to take, which of the innumerable identical alleys led toward her destination, for she moved purposefully and swiftly, pausing only occasionally to acquire their dinner by deftly snatching a stick of fish from one counter or a goblet of wine from another. Several times the vendor saw her make the theft, and only smiled.

Mystified, Inyanna said, "They don't mind?"

"They know me. But I tell you, we thieves are highly regarded here. We are a necessity."

"I wish I understood that."

"We maintain order in the Bazaar, do you see? No one steals here but us, and we take only what we need, and we patrol the place against amateurs. How would it be, in these mobs, if one customer out of ten filled his purse with merchandise? But we move among them, filling our own purses, and also halting *them*. We are a known quantity. Do you see? Our own takings are a kind of tax on the merchants, a salary of sorts that they pay us, to regulate the others who throng the passages. *Here, now!*" Those last words were directed not to Inyanna but to a boy of about twelve, dark-haired and eel-slim, who had been rummaging through hunting knives in an open bin. With a swift swoop Liloyve caught the boy's hand and in the same motion seized hold of the writhing tentacles of a Vroon no taller than the boy, standing a few feet away in the shadows. Inyanna heard Liloyve speaking in low, fierce tones, but could not make out a single word; the encounter was over in moments, and the Vroon and the boy slunk miserably away.

"What happened then?" Inyanna asked.

"They were stealing knives, the boy passing them to the Vroon. I told them to get out of the Bazaar right away, or my brothers would cut the Vroon's wrigglers off and feed them to the boy roasted in stinnim-oil."

"Would such a thing be done?"

"Of course not. It would be worth a life of sour dreams to anyone who did it. But they got the point. Only authorized thieves steal in this place. You see? We are the proctors here, in a way of speaking. We are indispensable. And here—this is where I live. You are my guest."

5

Liloyve lived underground, in a room of whitewashed stone that was one of a chain of seven or eight such rooms beneath a section of the Grand Bazaar devoted to merchants of cheeses and oils. A trapdoor and a suspended ladder of rope led to the subterranean chambers; and the moment Inyanna began the downward climb, all the noise and frenzy of the Bazaar became impossible to perceive, and the only reminder of what lay above was the faint but unarguable odor of red Stoienzar cheese that penetrated even the stone walls.

"Our den," Liloyve said. She sang a quick lilting melody and people came trailing in from the far rooms—shabby, shifty people, mostly small and thin, with a look about them much the same as Liloyve's, as of having been manufactured from second-rate materials. "My brothers Sidoun and Hanoun," she said. "My sister Medill Faryun. My cousins Avayne, Amayne, and Athayne. And this is my uncle Agourmole, who heads our clan. Uncle, this is Inyanna Forlana, from Velathys, who was sold Nissimorn Prospect for twenty royals by two traveling rogues. I met her on the riverboat. She'll live with us and become a thief."

Inyanna gasped. "I—"

Agourmole, courtly and elaborately formal, made a gesture of the Lady, by way of blessing. "You are one of us. Can you wear a man's clothing?"

Bewildered, Inyanna said, "Yes, I imagine so, but I don't under—"

"I have a younger brother who is registered with our guild. He lives in Avendroyne among the Shapeshifters, and has not been seen in Ni-moya for years. You will take his name and place. It is simpler that way than gaining a new registration. Give me your hand." She let him take it. His palms were moist and soft. He looked up into her eyes and said in a low intense tone, "Your true life is just commencing. All that has gone before has been only a dream. Now you are a thief in Ni-moya and your name is Kulibhai." Winking, he added, "Twenty royals is an excellent price for Nissimorn Prospect."

"Those were only the filing fees," said Inyanna. "They told me I had inherited it, through my mother's mother's sister."

"If it is true, you must hold a grand feast for us there, once you are in possession, to repay our hospitality. Agreed?" Agourmole laughed. "Avayne! Wine for your Uncle Kulibhai! Sidoun, Hanoun, find clothes for him! Music, someone! Who's for a dance? Show some life! Medill, prepare the guest bed!" The little man pranced about irrepressibly, barking orders. Inyanna, swept along by his vehement energies, accepted a cup of wine, allowed herself to be measured for a tunic by one of Liloyve's brothers, struggled to commit to memory the flood of names that had swept across her mind. Others now were coming into the room, more humans, three pudgy-cheeked gray-faced Hjorts, and, to Inyanna's amazement, a pair of slender silent Metamorphs. Accustomed though she was to dealing with Shapeshifters in her shopkeeping days, she had not expected to find Liloyve and her family actually sharing their quarters with these mysterious aborigines. But perhaps thieves, like Metamorphs, deemed themselves a race apart on Majipoor, and the two were drawn readily to one another.

An impromptu party buzzed about her for hours. The thieves seemed to be vying for her favor, each in turn cozying up to her, offering some little trinket, some intimate tale, some bit of confidential gossip. To the child of a long line of shopkeepers, thieves were natural enemies; and yet these people, seedy outcasts though they might be, seemed warm and friendly and open, and they were her only allies against a vast and indifferent city. Inyanna had no wish to take up their profession, but she knew that fortune might have done worse by her than to throw her in with Liloyve's folk.

She slept fitfully, dreaming vaporous fragmentary dreams and several times waking in total confusion, with no idea where she was. Eventually exhaustion seized her and she dropped into deep slumber. Usually it was dawn that woke her, but dawn was a stranger in this cave of a place, and when she awakened it might have been any time of day or night.

Liloyve smiled at her. "You must have been terribly tired."

"Did I sleep too long?"

"You slept until you were finished sleeping. That must have been the right amount, eh?"

Inyanna looked around. She saw traces of the party—flasks, empty globelets, stray items of clothing—but the others were gone. Off on their morning rounds, Liloyve explained. She showed Inyanna where to wash and dress, and then they went up into the maelstrom of the Bazaar. By day it was as busy as it had been the night before, but somehow it looked less magical in ordinary light, its texture less dense, its atmosphere less charged with electricity: it was no more than a vast crowded emporium, where last night it had seemed to Inyanna an enigmatic self-contained universe. They paused only to steal their breakfasts at three or four counters, Liloyve brazenly helping herself and passing the take to an abashed and hesitant Inyanna, and then—making their way through the impossible intricacy of the maze, which Inynana was sure she would never master—they emerged abruptly into the clear fresh air of the surface world.

"We have come out at Piliplok Gate," said Liloyve. "From here it's only a short walk to the Pontificate."

A short walk but a stunning one, for around every corner lay new wonders. Up one splendid boulevard Inyanna caught sight of a brilliant stream of radiance, like a second sun sprouting from the pavement. This, said Liloyve, was the beginning of the Crystal Boulevard, that blazed by day and by night with the glint of revolving reflectors. Across another street and she had a view of what could only be the palace of the Duke of Ni-moya, far to the east down the great slope of the city, at the place where the Zimr made its sudden bend. It was a slender shaft of glassy stone atop a broad many-columned base, huge even at this enormous distance, and surrounded by a park that was like a carpet of green. One more turn and Inyanna beheld something that resembled the loosely woven chrysalis of some fabulous insect, but a mile in length, hanging suspended above an immensely wide avenue. "The Gossamer Galleria," said Liloyve, "where the rich ones buy their playthings. Perhaps some day you'll scatter your royals in its shops. But not today. Here we are: Rodamaunt Promenade. We'll see soon enough about your inheritance."

The street was a grand curving one lined on one side by flat-faced towers all the same height, and on the other by an alternation of great buildings and short ones. These, apparently, were government offices. Inyanna was daunted by the complexity of it all, and might have wandered outside in confusion for hours, not daring to enter; but Liloyve penetrated the mysteries of the place with a series of quick inquiries and led Inyanna within, through the corridors and windings of a maze hardly less intricate than the Grand Bazaar itself, until at length they found themselves sitting on a wooden bench in a large and brightly lit waiting room, watching names flick on and off on a bulletin board overhead. In half an hour Inyanna's appeared on the board.

"Is this the Bureau of Probate?" she asked, as they went in.

"Apparently there's no such thing," said Liloyve. "These are the proctors. If anyone can help you, they can."

A dour-faced Hjort, bloated and goggle-eyed like most of his kind, asked for her problem, and Inyanna, hesitant at first, then voluble, poured out the story: the strangers from Ni-moya, the astounding tale of the grand inheritance, the documents, the Pontifical seal, the twenty royals in filing fees. The Hjort, as the story unfolded, slumped behind his desk, kneaded his jowls, disconcertingly swiveled his great globular eyes one at a time. When she was done he took her receipt from her, ran his thick fingers throughtfully over the ridges of the imperial seal it bore, and said gloomily, "You are the nineteenth claimant to Nissimorn Prospect who has presented herself in Ni-moya this year. There will be more, I am afraid. There will be many more."

"Nineteenth?"

"To my knowledge. Others may not have bothered to report the fraud to the proctors."

"The fraud," Inyanna repeated. "Is that it? The documents they showed me, the genealogy, the papers with my name on it—they traveled all the way from Ni-moya to Velathys simply to swindle me of twenty royals?"

"Oh, not simply to swindle *you*," said the Hjort. "Probably there are three or four heirs to Nissimorn Prospect in Velathys, and five in Narabal, and seven in Til-omon, and a dozen in Pidruid—it's not hard to get genealogies, you know. And forge the documents, and fill in the blanks. Twenty royals from this one, thirty perhaps from that, a nice livelihood if you keep moving, you see?"

"But how is this possible? Such things are against the law!"

"Yes," the Hjort agreed wearily.

"And the King of Dreams—"

"Will punish them severely, you may be sure of it. Nor will we fail to apply civil penalties once we apprehend them. You will give us great assistance by describing them to us."

"And my twenty royals?"

The Hjort shrugged.

Inyanna said, "There's no hope that I can recover a thing?"

"None."

"But I've lost everything, then!"

"On behalf of his majesty I offer my most sincere regrets," said the Hjort, and that was that.

Outside, Inyanna said sharply to Liloyve, "Take me to Nissimorn Prospect!"

"But surely you don't believe—"

"That it is really mine? No, of course not. But I want to see it! I want to know what sort of place it was that was sold to me for my twenty royals!"

"Why torment yourself?"

"Please," Inyanna said.

"Come, then," said Liloyve.

She hailed a floater and gave it its instructions. Wide-eyed, Inyanna stared in wonder as the little vehicle bore them through the noble avenues of Ni-moya. In the warmth of the midday sun everything seemed bathed with light, and the city glowed, not with the frosty light of crystalline Dulorn but with a pulsing, throbbing, sensuous splendor that reverberated from every whitewashed wall and street. Liloyve described the most significant of the places they were passing. "This is the Museum of Worlds," she said, indicating a great structure crowned by a tiara of angular glass domes. "Treasures of a thousand planets, even some things of Old Earth. And this is the Chamber of Sorcery, also a museum of sorts, given over to magic and dreaming. I have never been in it. And there— see the three birds of the city out front?—is the City Palace, where the mayor lives." They turned downhill, toward the river. "The floating restaurants are in this part of the harbor," she said, with a grand wave of her hand. "Nine of them, like little islands. They say you can have dishes from every province of Majipoor there. Someday we'll eat at them, all nine, eh?"

Inyanna smiled sadly. "It would be nice to think so."

"Don't worry. We have all our lives before us, and a thief's life is a comfortable one. I mean to roam every street of Nimoya in my time, and you can come with me. There's a Park of Fabulous Beasts out in Gimbeluc, off in the hills, you know, with creatures that are extinct in the wilds everywhere, sigimoins and ghalvars and dimilions and everything, and there's the Opera House, where the municipal orchestra plays—you know about our orchestra? A thousand instruments, nothing like it in the universe—and then there's—oh. Here we are!"

They dismounted from the floater. Inyanna saw that they were nearly at the river's edge. Before her lay the Zimr, the great river so wide at this point that she could barely see across it, and only dimly could she make out the green line of Nissimorn on the horizon. Just to her left was a palisade of metal spikes twice the height of a man, set eight or ten feet apart and linked by a gauzy, almost invisible webbing that gave off a deep and sinister humming sound. Within that fence was a garden of striking beauty, low elegant shrubs abloom with gold and turquoise and scarlet blossoms, and a lawn so closely cropped it might well have been sprayed against the ground. Farther beyond, the land began to rise, and the house itself sat upon a rocky prominence overlooking the harbor: a mansion of wonderful size, white-walled in the Ni-moya manner, which made much use of the techniques of suspension and lightness typical of Ni-moyan architecture, with porticoes that seemed to float and balconies cantilevered out for wondrous distances. Short of the Ducal Palace itself— visible not far down the shore, rising magnificently on its pedestal—Nissimorn Prospect seemed to Inyanna to be the most beautiful single building she had seen in all of Ni-moya thus far. And it was this that she thought she had inherited! She began to laugh. She sprinted along the palisade, pausing now and again to contemplate the great house from various angles, and laughter poured from her as though someone had told her the deepest truth of the universe, the truth that holds the secrets of all other truths and so must necessarily evoke a torrent of laughter. Liloyve followed her, calling out for her to wait, but Inyanna ran as one possessed. Finally she came to the front gate, where two mammoth Skandars in immaculate white livery stood guard, all their arms folded in an emphatic possessive way. Inyanna continued to laugh; the Skandars scowled; Liloyve, coming up behind, plucked at Inyanna's sleeve and urged her to leave before there was trouble.

"Wait," she said, gasping. She went up to the Skandars. "Are you servants of Calain of Ni-moya?"

They looked at her without seeing her, and said nothing.

"Tell your master," she went on, undisturbed, "that Inyanna of Velathys was here, to see the house, and sends her regrets that she could not come to dine. Thank you."

"*Come!*" Liloyve whispered urgently.

Anger was beginning to replace indifference on the hairy faces of the huge guards. Inyanna saluted them graciously, and broke into laughter again, and gestured to Liloyve; and together they ran back to the floater, Liloyve too finally joining in the uncontrollable mirth.

6

It was a long time before Inyanna saw the sunlight of Ni-moya again, for now she took up her new life as a thief in the depths of the Grand Bazaar. At first she had no intent of adopting the profession of Liloyve and her family. But practical considerations soon overruled her niceties of morality. She had no way of returning to Velathys, nor, after these first few glimpses of Ni-moya, had she any real wish to do so. Nothing waited for her there except a life of peddling glue and nails and false satin and lanterns from Til-omon. To stay in Ni-moya, though, required a livelihood. She knew no trade except shopkeeping, and without capital she could hardly open a shop here. Quite soon all her money would be exhausted; she would not live off the charity of her new friends; she had no other prospects; they were offering her a niche in their society; and somehow it seemed acceptable to take up a life of thieving, alien though that was to her former nature, now that she had been robbed of all her savings by the fast-talking swindlers. So she let herself be garbed in a man's tunic—she was tall enough, and a little awkward of bearing, enough to carry the deception off plausibly—and under the name of Kulibhai, brother to the master thief Agourmole, entered the guild of thieves.

Liloyve was her mentor. For three days Inyanna followed her through the Bazaar, watching closely as the lavender-haired girl skimmed merchandise here and there. Some of it was done as crudely as donning a cloak in a shop and vanishing suddenly into the crowds; some involved quick sleight-of-hand in the bins and counters; and some required elaborate deceptions, bamboozling some delivery boy with a promise of kisses or better, while an accomplice made off with his barrow of goods. At the same time there was the obligation to prevent freelance theft. Twice in the three days, Inyanna saw Liloyve do that—the hand on the wrist, the cold angry glare, the sharp whispered words, resulting both times in the look of fear, the apologies, the hasty withdrawal. Inyanna wondered if she would ever have the courage to do that. It seemed harder than thieving itself; and she was not at all sure she could bring herself to steal, either.

On the fourth day Liloyve said, "Bring me a flask of dragon-milk and two of the golden wine of Piliplok."

Inyanna said, appalled, "But they must sell for a royal apiece!"

"Indeed."

"Let me begin by stealing sausages."

"It's no harder to steal rare wines," said Liloyve. "And considerably more profitable."

"I am not ready."

"You only think you aren't. You've seen how it's done. You can do it yourself. Your fears are needless. You have the soul of a thief, Inyanna."

Furiously Inyanna said, "How can you say such a—"

"Softly, softly, I meant it as a compliment!"

Inyanna nodded. "Even so. I think you are wrong."

"I think you underestimate yourself," said Liloyve. "There are aspects of your character more apparent to others than to yourself. I saw them displayed the day we visited Nissimorn Prospect. Go, now: steal me a flask of Piliplok golden, and one of dragon-milk, and no more chatter. If you are ever to be a thief of our guild, today is your beginning."

There was no avoiding it. But there was no reason to risk doing it alone. Inyanna asked Liloyve's cousin Athayne to accompany her, and together they went swaggering down to a wine-shop in Ossier Lane—two youngs bucks of Ni-moya off to buy themselves some jollity. A strange calmness came over Inyanna. She allowed herself to think of no irrelevancies, such as morality, property rights, or the fear of punishment; there was only the task at hand to consider, a routine job of thievery. Once her profession had been shopkeeping, and now it was shoplooting, and it was useless to complicate the situation with philosophical hesitations.

A Ghayrog was behind the wine-shop counter: icy eyes that never blinked, glossy scaly skin, writhing fleshy hair. Inyanna, making her voice as deep as she could, inquired after the price of dragon-milk in globelet, flask, and duple. Meanwhile Athayne busied himself among the cheap red mid-country wines. The Ghayrog quoted prices. Inyanna expressed shock. The Ghayrog shrugged. Inyanna held a flask aloft, studied the pale blue fluid, scowled, and said, "It is murkier than the usual quality."

"It varies from year to year. And from dragon to dragon."

"One would think these things would be made standard."

"The effect is standard," said the Ghayrog, with the chilly reptilian Ghayrog equivalent of a leer and a smirk. "A few sips of that, my fellow, and you'll be good for the whole night!"

"Let me think about it a moment," said Inyanna. "A royal's no little sum, no matter how wonderful the effects."

It was the signal to Athayne, who turned and said, "This Mazadone stuff, is it really three crown the duple? I'm certain that last week it sold for two."

"If you can find it at two, buy it at two," the Ghayrog answered.

Athayne scowled, moved as if to put the bottle back on the shelf, lurched and stumbled, and knocked half a row of globelets over. The Ghayrog hissed in anger. Athayne, bellowing his regrets, clumsily tried to set things to rights, knocking still more bottles down. The Ghayrog scurried to the display, yelling. He and Athayne bumbled into one another in their attempts to restore order, and in that moment Inyanna popped the flask of dragon-milk into her tunic, tucked one of Piliplok golden beside it, and, saying loudly, "I'll check the prices elsewhere, I think," walked out of the shop. That was all there was to it. She forced herself not to break into a run, although her cheeks were blazing and she was certain that the passersby all knew her for a thief, and that the other shopkeepers in the row would come storming out to seize her, and that the Ghayrog himself would be after her in a moment. But without difficulty she made her way to the corner, turned to her left, saw the street of facepaints and perfumes, went the length of it, and entered the place of oils and cheeses where Liloyve was waiting.

"Take these," Inyanna said. "They burn holes in my breast."

"Well done," Liloyve told her. "We'll drink the golden tonight, in your honor!"

"And the dragon-milk?"

"Keep it," said Liloyve. "Share it with Calain, the night you are invited to dine at Nissimorn Prospect."

That night Inyanna lay awake for hours, afraid to sleep, for sleep brought dreams and in dreams came punishments. The wine was gone, but the dragon-milk flask lay beneath her pillow, and she felt the urge to slip off in the night and return it to the Ghayrog. Centuries of shopkeeper ancestors weighed against her soul. A thief, she thought, a thief, a thief, I have become a thief in Ni-moya. By what right did I take those things? By what right, she answered herself, did those two steal my twenty royals? But what had that to do with the Ghayrog? If *they* steal from me, and I use that as license to steal from *him*, and he goes to another's goods, where does it end, how does society survive? The Lady forgive me, she thought. The King of Dreams will whip my spirit. But at last she slept; she could not keep from sleeping forever; and the dreams that came to her were dreams of wonder and majesty, and she glided disembodied through the grand avenues of the city, past the Crystal Boulevard, the Museum of Worlds, the Gossamer Galleria, to Nissimorn Prospect, where the duke's brother took her hand. The dream bewildered her, for she could not in any way see it as a dream of punishment. Where was morality? Where was proper conduct? This went counter to all she believed. Yet it was as though destiny had intended her to be a thief. Everything that had happened to her in the past year had aimed her toward that. So perhaps it was the will of the Divine that she become what she had become. Inyanna smiled at that. What cynicism! But so be it. She would not fight destiny.

7

She stole often and she stole well. That first tentative terrifying venture into thievery was followed by many more over the days that followed. She roved freely through the Grand Bazaar, sometimes with accomplices, sometimes alone, helping herself to this and that and this and that. It was so easy that it came to seem almost not like crime. The Bazaar was always crowded: Ni-moya's population, they said, was close to thirty million, and it seemed that all of them were in the Bazaar all the time. There was a constant crushing flow of people. The merchants were harried and careless, bedeviled always by questions, disputes, bargainers, inspectors. There was little challenge in moving through the river of beings, taking as she pleased.

Most of the booty was sold. A professional thief might keep the occasional item for her own use, and meals were always taken on the job, but nearly everything was stolen with an eye toward immediate resale. That was mainly the responsibility of the Hjorts who lived with Agourmole's family. There were three of them, Beyork, Hankh, and Mozinhunt, and they were part of a wide-ranging network of disposers of stolen goods, a chain of Hjorts that passed merchandise briskly out of the Bazaar and into wholesale channels that often eventually resold it to the merchants from whom it had been taken. Inyanna learned quickly what things were in demand by these people and what were not to be bothered with.

Because Inyanna was new to Ni-moya she had a particularly easy time of it. Not all the merchants of the Grand Bazaar were complacent about the guild of thieves, and some knew Liloyve and Athayne and Sidoun and the others of the family by sight, ordering them out of their shops the moment they appeared. But the young man who called himself Kulibhai was unknown in the Bazaar, and so long as Inyanna picked over a different section of the all but infinite place every day, it would be many years before her victims became familiar with her.

The dangers in her work came not so much from the shopkeepers, though, as from thieves of other families. They did not know her either, and their eyes were quicker than the merchants'—so that three times in her first ten days Inyanna was apprehended by some other thief. It was terrifying at first to feel a hand closing on her wrist; but she remained cool, and, confronting the other without panic, she said simply, "You are infringing. I am Kulibhai, brother to Agourmole." Word spread swiftly. After the third such event, she was not troubled again.

To make such arrests herself was troublesome. At first she had no way of telling the legitimate thieves from the improper ones, and she hesitated to seize the wrist of some who, for all she knew, had been pilfering in the Bazaar since Lord Kinniken's time. It became surprisingly easy for her to detect thievery in progress, but if she had no other thief of Agourmole's clan with her to consult, she took no action. Gradually she came to recognize many of the licensed thieves of other families, but yet nearly every day she saw some unfamiliar figure rummaging through a merchant's goods, and finally, after some weeks in the Bazaar, she felt moved to act. If she found herself apprehending a true thief, she could always beg pardon; but the essence of the system was that she not only stole but also policed, and she knew she was failing in that duty. Her first arrest was that a grimy girl taking vegetables; there was hardly time to say a word, for the girl dropped her take and fled in terror. The next one turned out to be a veteran thief distantly related to Agourmole, who amiably explained Inyanna's mistake; and the third, unauthorized but also frightened, responded to Inyanna's words with spitting curses and muttered threats, to which Inyanna replied calmly and untruthfully that seven other thieves of the guild were observing them and would take immediate action in the event of trouble. After that she felt no qualms, and acted freely and confidently whenever she believed it was appropriate.

Nor did the thieving itself trouble her conscience, after the beginning. She had been reared to expect the vengeance of the King of Dreams if she wandered into sin—nightmares, torments, a fever of the soul whenever she closed her eyes—but either the King did not regard this sort of pilferage and purloinment as sin, or else he and his minions were so busy with even greater criminals that they had no time to get around to her. Whatever the reason, the King sent her no sendings. Occasionally she dreamed of him, fierce old ogre beaming bad news out of the burning wastelands of Suvrael, but that was nothing unusual; the King entered everybody's dreams from time to time, and it meant very little. Sometimes, too, Inyanna dreamed of the blessed Lady of the Isle, the gentle mother of the Coronal Lord Malibor, and it seemed to her that that sweet woman was shaking her head sadly, as though to say she was woefully disappointed in her child Inyanna. But it was within the powers of the Lady to speak more strongly to those who had strayed from her path,

and that she did not seem to be doing. In the absence of
moral correction Inyanna quickly came to have a casual view
of her profession. It was not crime; it was merely redistribu-
tion of goods. No one seemed to be greatly injured by it, after all.

In time she took as her lover Sidoun, the older brother of
Liloyve. He was shorter than Inyanna, and so bony that it
was a sharp business to embrace him; but he was a gentle
and thoughtful man, who played prettily on the pocket-harp
and sang old ballads in a clear light tenor, and the more often she went out thieving with him the more agreeable she
found his company. Some rearrangements of the sleeping-
quarters in Agourmole's den were made, and they were able
to spend their nights together. Lilovye and the other thieves
seemed to find this development charming.

In Sidoun's company she roved farther and farther through
the great city. So efficient were they as a team that often they
had their day's quota of larceny done in an hour or two, and
that left them free for the rest of the day, for it would not do
to exceed one's quota: the social contract of the Grand Bazaar allowed the thieves to take only so much, and no more,
with impunity. So it was that Inyanna began to make excursions to the delightful outer reaches of Ni-moya. One of her
favorite places was the Park of Fabulous Beasts in the hilly
suburb of Gimbeluc, where she could roam among animals of
other eras, that had been crowded out of their domains by
the spread of civilization on Majipoor. Here she saw such
rarities as the wobbly-legged dimilions, fragile long-necked
leaf-chompers twice as high as a Skandar, and the dainty tip-
toeing sigimoins with a thickly furred tail at either end, and
the awkward big-beaked zampidoon birds that once had darkened the sky over Ni-moya with their great flocks, and now
existed only in the park and as one of the city's official emblems. Through some magic that must have been devised in
ancient times, voices came from the ground whenever one of
these creatures sauntered by, telling onlookers its name and
original habitat. Then too the park had lovely secluded
glades, where Inyanna and Sidoun could walk hand in hand,
saying little, for Sidoun was not a man of many words.

Some days they went on boat-rides out into the Zimr and
over to the Nissimorn side, and occasionally down the gullet
of the nearby River Steiche, which, if followed long enough,
would bring them to the forbidden Shapeshifter territory. But

that was many weeks' journey upriver, and they traveled only
as far as the little Liiman fishing villages a short way south of
Nissimorn, where they bought fresh-caught fish and held pic-
nic on the beach and swam and lay in the sun. Or on moon-
less evenings they went to the Crystal Boulevard, where the
revolving reflectors cast dazzling patterns of ever-changing
light, and peered in awe at the exhibit cases maintained by
the great companies of Majipoor, a streetside museum of
costly goods, so magnificent and so opulently displayed that
not even the boldest of thieves would dare to attempt an entry. And often they dined at one of the floating restaurants,
frequently taking Liloyve with them, for she loved those
places above all else in the city. Each island was a miniature
of some far territory of the planet, its characteristic plants
and animals thriving there, and its special foods and wines a
feature: one of windy Piliplok, where those who had the
price dined on sea-dragon meat, and one of humid Narabal
with its rich berries and succulent ferns, and one of great
Stee on Castle Mount, and a restaurant of Stoien and one of
Pidruid and one of Til-omon—but none of Velathys, Inyanna
learned without surprise, nor was the Shapeshifter capital of
Ilirivoyne favored with an island, nor harsh sun-blasted Tolaghai on Suvrael, for Tolaghai and Ilirivoyne were places that
most folk of Majipoor did not care to think about, and Velathys was simply beneath notice.

Of all the places that Inyanna visited with Sidoun on these
leisurely afternoons and evenings, though, her favorite was
the Gossamer Galleria. That mile-long arcade, hanging high
above street level, contained the finest shops of Ni-moya,
which is to say the finest in all the continent of Zimroel, the
finest outside the rich cities of Castle Mount. When they went
there, Inyanna and Sidoun put on their most elegant clothes,
that they had stolen from the best stalls in the Grand Bazaar—nothing at all to compare with what the aristocrats
wore, but superior by far to their daily garb. Inyanna enjoyed
getting out of the male costumes that she wore in her role as
Kulibhai the thief, and dressing in slinky and clinging robes
of purples and greens, and letting her long red hair tumble
free. With her fingertips lightly touching Sidoun's, she made
the grand promenade of the Galleria, indulging in pleasant
fantasies as they inspected the eye-jewels and feather-masks
and polished amulets and metal trinkets that were available,
for a double handful of shining royal-pieces, to the truly

wealthy. None of these things would ever be hers, she knew, for a thief who thieved well enough to afford such luxuries would be a danger to the stability of the Grand Bazaar; but it was joyous enough merely to see the treasures of the Gossamer Galleria, and to pretend.

It was on one of these outings to the Gossamer Galleria that Inyanna strayed into the orbit of Calain, brother to the duke.

8

She had no notion that that was what she was doing, of course. All she thought she was doing was conducting a little innocent flirtation, as part of the adventure into fantasy that a visit to the Galleria ought to be. It was a mild night in late summer and she was wearing one of her lightest gowns, a sheer fabric less substantial even than the webbing of which the Galleria was woven; and she and Sidoun were in the shop of dragon-bone carvings, examining the extraordinary thumb-nail-sized masterpieces of a Skandar boat-captain who produced intricacies of interwoven slivers of ivory of the highest implausibility, when four men in the robes of nobility came in. Sidoun at once faded into a dark corner, for he knew that his clothing and his bearing and the cut of his hair marked him as no equal to these; but Inyanna, conscious that the lines of her body and the cool gaze of her green eyes could compensate for all sorts of deficiencies of manner, boldly held her place at the counter. One of the men glanced at the carving in her hand and said, "If you buy that, you'll be doing well for yourself."

"I have not made up my mind," Inyanna replied.

"May I see it?"

She dropped it lightly into his palm, and at the same time let her eyes make contact brazenly with his. He smiled, but gave his attention mainly to the ivory piece, a map-globe of Majipoor fashioned from many sliding panels of bone. After a moment he said to the proprietor, "The price?"

"It is a gift," answered the other, a slender and austere Ghayrog.

"Indeed. And also from me to you," said the nobleman, spilling the bauble back into the hand of the amazed

Inyanna. Now his smile was more intimate. "You are of this city?" he asked quietly.

"I live in Strelain," she said.

"Do you dine often at the Narabal Island?"

"When the mood takes me."

"Good. Will you be there at sunset tomorrow? There will be someone there eager to make your acquaintance."

Hiding her bewilderment, Inyanna bowed. The nobleman bowed and turned away; he purchased three of the little carvings, dropping a purse of coins on the counter; then they departed. Inyanna stared in astonishment at the precious thing in her hand. Sidoun, emerging from the shadows, whispered, "It's worth a dozen royals! Sell it back to the keeper!"

"No," she said. To the proprietor she said, "Who was that man?"

"You are unfamiliar with him?"

"I would not have asked you his name if I knew it."

"Yes. Yes." The Ghayrog made little hissing sounds. "He is Durand Livolk, the duke's chamberlain."

"And the other three?"

"Two are in the duke's service, and the third is a companion to the duke's brother Calain."

"Ah," said Inyanna. She held forth the ivory globe. "Can you mount this on a chain?"

"It will take only a moment."

"And the price for a chain worthy of the object?"

The Ghayrog gave her a long calculating look. "The chain is only accessory to the carving; and since the carving was a gift, so too with the chain." He fitted delicate golden links to the ivory ball, and packed the trinket in a box of shining stickskin.

"At least twenty royals, with the chain!" Sidoun muttered, amazed, when they were outside. "Take it across to that shop and sell it, Inyanna!"

"It was a gift," she said coolly. "I will wear it tomorrow night, when I dine at the Narabal Island."

She could not go to dinner in the gown she had worn that evening, though; and finding another just as sheer and costly in the shops of the Grand Bazaar required two hours of diligent work the next day. But in the end she came upon one that was the next thing to nakedness, yet cloaked everything in mystery; and that was what she wore to the Narabal Island, with the ivory carving dangling between her breasts.

At the restaurant there was no need to give her name. As she stepped off the ferry she was met by a somber and dignified Vroon in ducal livery, who conducted her through the lush groves of vines and ferns to a shadowy bower, secluded and fragrant, in a part of the island cut off by dense plantings from the main restaurant area. Here three people awaited her at a gleaming table of polished nightflower wood beneath a vine whose thick hairy stems were weighed down by enormous globular blue flowers. One was Durand Livolk, who had given her the ivory carving. One was a woman, slender and dark-haired, as sleek and glossy as the tabletop itself. And the third was a man of about twice Inyanna's age, delicately built, with thin close-pursed lips and soft features. All three were dressed with such magnificence that Inyanna cringed at her own fancied shabbiness. Durand Livolk rose smoothly, went to Inyanna's side, and murmured, "You look even more lovely this evening. Come: meet some friends. This is my companion, the lady Tisiorne. And this——"

The frail-looking man got to his feet. "I am Calain of Ni-moya," he said simply, in a gentle and feathery voice.

Inyanna felt confused, but only for a moment. She had thought the duke's chamberlain had wanted her himself; now she understood that Durand Livolk had merely been procuring her for the duke's brother. That knowledge sparked an instant's indignation in her, but it died quickly away. Why take offense? How many young women of Ni-moya had the chance to dine on the Narabal Island with the brother of the duke? If to another it might seem that she was being used, so be it; she meant to do a little using herself, in this interchange.

A place was ready for her beside Calain. She took it and the Vroon instantly brought a tray of liqueurs, all unfamiliar ones, of colors that blended and swirled and phosphoresced. She chose one at random: it had the flavor of mountain mists, and caused an immediate tingling in her cheeks and ears. From overhead came the patter of light rainfall, landing on the broad glossy leaves of the trees and vines, but not on the diners. The rich tropical plantings of this island, Inyanna knew, were maintained by frequent artificial rainfall that duplicated the climate of Narabal.

Calain said, "Do you have favorite dishes here?"

"I would prefer that you order for me."

"If you wish. Your accent is not of Ni-moya."

"Velathys," she replied. "I came here only last year."

"A wise move," said Durand Livolk. "What prompted it?"

Inyanna laughed. "I think I will tell that story another time, if I may."

"Your accent is charming," said Calain. "We rarely meet Velathyntu folk here. Is it a beautiful city?"

"Hardly, my lord."

"Nestling in the Gonghars, though—surely it must be beautiful to see those great mountains all around you."

"That may be. One comes to take such things for granted when one spends all one's life among them. Perhaps even Ni-moya would begin to seem ordinary to one who had grown up here."

"Where do you live?" asked the woman Tisiorne.

"In Strelain," said Inyanna. And then, mischievously, for she had had another of the liqueurs and was feeling it, she added, "In the Grand Bazaar."

"*In* the Grand Bazaar?" said Durand Livolk.

"Yes. Beneath the street of the cheesemongers."

Tisiorne said, "And for what reason do you make your home there?"

"Oh," Inyanna answered lightly, "to be close to the place of my employment."

"In the street of the cheesemongers?" said Tisiorne, horror creeping into her tone.

"You misunderstand. I am employed in the Bazaar, but not by the merchants. I am a thief."

The word fell from her lips like a lightning-bolt crashing on the mountaintops. Inyanna saw the sudden startled look pass from Calain to Durand Livolk, and the color rising in Durand Livolk's face. But these people were aristocrats, and they had aristocratic poise. Calain was the first to recover from his amazement. Smiling coolly, he said, "A profession that calls for grace and deftness and quick-wittedness, I have always believed." He touched his glass to Inyanna's. "I salute you, thief who says she's a thief. There's an honesty in that which many others lack."

The Vroon returned, bearing a vast porcelain bowl filled with pale blue berries, waxen-looking, with white highlights. They were thokkas, Inyanna knew—the favorite fruit of Narabal, said to make the blood run hot and the passions to rise. She scooped a few from the bowl; Tisiorne carefully chose a single one; Durand Livolk took a handful, and Calain more than that. Inyanna noticed that the duke's brother ate the berries seeds and all, said to be the most effective way. Tisiorne discarded the seeds of hers, which brought a wry grin from Durand Livolk. Inyanna did not follow Tisiorne's fashion.

Then there were wines, and morsels of spiced fish, and oysters floating in their own fluids, and a plate of intricate little fungi of soft pastel hues, and eventually a haunch of aromatic meat—the leg of the giant bilantoon of the forests just east of Narabal, said Calain. Inyanna ate sparingly, a nip of this, a bit of that. It seemed the proper thing to do, and also the most sensible. Some Skandar jugglers came by after a while, and did wondrous things with torches and knives and hatchets, drawing hearty applause from the four diners. Calain tossed the rough four-armed fellows a gleaming coin—a five-royal piece, Inyanna saw, astounded. Later it rained again, though not on them, and still later, after another round of liqueurs, Durand Livolk and Tisiorne gracefully excused themselves and left Calain and Inyanna sitting alone in the misty darkness.

Calain said, "Are you truly a thief?"

"Truly. But it was not my original plan. I owned a shop of general wares in Velathys."

"And then?"

"I lost it through a swindle," she said. "And came penniless to Ni-moya, and needed a profession, and fell in with thieves, who seemed thoughtful and sympathetic people."

"And now you have fallen in with much greater thieves," said Calain. "Does that trouble you?"

"Do you regard yourself, then, as a thief?"

"I hold high rank through luck of birth alone. I do not work, except to assist my brother when he needs me. I live in splendor beyond most people's imaginings. None of this is deserved. Have you seen my home?"

"I know it quite well. From the outside, of course, only."

"Would you care to see the interior of it tonight?"

Inyanna thought briefly of Sidoun, waiting in the white-washed stone room below the street of the cheesemongers.

"Very much," she said. "And when I've seen it, I'll tell you a little story about myself and Nissimorn Prospect and how it happened that I first came to Ni-moya."

"It will be most amusing, I'm sure. Shall we go?"

"Yes," Inyanna said. "But would it cause difficulties if I stopped first at the Grand Bazaar?"

"We have all night," said Calain. "There is no hurry."

The liveried Vroon appeared, and lit the way for them through the jungled gardens to the island's dock, where a private ferry waited. It conveyed them to the mainland; a floater had been summoned meanwhile, and shortly Inyanna arrived at the plaza of Pidruid Gate. "I'll be only a moment," Inyanna whispered, and, wraithlike in her fragile and clinging gown, she drifted swiftly through the crowds that even at this hour still thronged the Bazaar. Down into the underground den she went. The thieves were gathered around a table, playing some game with glass counters and ebony dice. They cheered and applauded as she made her splendid entrance, but she responded only with a quick tense smile, and drew Sidoun aside. In a low voice she said, "I am going out again, and I will not be back this night. Will you forgive me?"

"It's not every woman who catches the fancy of the duke's chamberlain."

"Not the duke's chamberlain," she said. "The duke's brother." She brushed her lips lightly against Sidoun's. He was glassy-eyed with surprise at her words. "Tomorrow let's go to the Park of Fabulous Beasts, yes, Sidoun?" She kissed him again and moved on, to her bedroom, and drew the flask of dragon-milk out from under her pillow, where it had been hidden for months. In the central room she paused at the gaming-table, leaned close beside Liloyve, and opened her hand, showing her the flask. Liloyve's eyes widened. Inyanna winked and said, "Do you remember what I was saving this for? You said, to share it with Calain when I went to Nissimorn Prospect. And so—"

Liloyve gasped. Inyanna winked and kissed her and went out.

Much later that night, as she drew forth the flask and offered it to the duke's brother, she wondered in sudden panic whether it might be a vast breach of etiquette to be offering him an aphrodisiac this way, perhaps implying that its use might be advisable. But Calain showed no offense. He was, or else pretended to be, touched by her gift; he made a great show of pouring the blue milk into percelain bowls so dainty they were nearly transparent; with the highest of ceremony he put one bowl in her hand, lifted the other himself, and signaled a salute. The dragon-milk was strange and bitter, difficult for Inyanna to swallow; but she got it down, and almost at once felt its warmth throbbing in her thighs. Calain smiled. They were in the Hall of Windows of Nissimorn Prospect, where a single band of gold-bound glass gave a three-hundred-sixty-degree view of the harbor of Ni-moya and the distant southern shore of the river. Calain touched a switch. The great window became opaque. A circular bed rose silently from the floor. He took her by the hand and drew her toward it.

9

To be the concubine of the duke's brother seemed a high enough ambition for a thief out of the Grand Bazaar. Inyanna had no illusions about her relationship with Calain. Durand Livolk had chosen her for her looks alone, perhaps something about her eyes, her hair, the way she held herself. Calain, though he had expected her to be a woman somewhat closer to his own class, had evidently found something charming about being thrown together with someone from the bottom rung of society, and so she had had her evening at the Narabal Island and her night at Nissimorn Prospect; it had been a fine interlude of fantasy, and in the morning she would return to the Grand Bazaar with a memory to last her the rest of her life, and that would be that.

Only that was not that.

There as no sleep for them all that night—was it the effect of the dragon-milk, she wondered, or was he like that always?—and at dawn they strolled naked through the majestic house, so that he could show her its treasures, and as they breakfasted on a veranda overlooking the garden he suggested an outing that day to his private park in Istmoy. So it was not to be an adventure of a single night, then. She wondered if she should send word to Sidoun at the Bazaar, telling him she would not return that day, but then she realized that Sidoun would not need to be told. He would interpret her silence correctly. She meant to cause him no pain, but on the other hand she owed him nothing but common courtesy. She was embarked now on one of the great events of her life, and when she returned to the Grand Bazaar it would not be for Sidoun's sake, but merely because the adventure was over.

As it happened, she spent the next six days with Calain. By

day they sported on the river in his majestic yacht, or strolled hand in hand through the private game-park of the duke, a place stocked with surplus beasts from the Park of Fabulous Beasts, or simply lay on the veranda of Nissimorn Prospect, watching the sun's track across the continent from Piliplok to Pidruid. And by night it was all feasting and revelry, dinner now at one of the floating islands, now at some great house of Ni-moya, one night at the Ducal Palace itself. The duke was very little like Calain: a much bigger man, a good deal older, with a wearied and untender manner. Yet he managed to be charming to Inyanna, treating her with grace and gravity and never once making her feel like a street-girl his brother had scooped out of the Bazaar. Inyanna sailed through these events with the kind of cool acceptance one displays in dreams. To show awe, she knew, would be coarse. To pretend to an equal level of rank and sophistication would be even worse. But she arrived at a demeanor that was restrained without being humble, agreeable without being forward, and it seemed to be effective. In a few days it began to seem quite natural to her that she should be sitting at table with dignitaries who were lately returned from Castle Mount with bits of gossip about Lord Malibor the Coronal and his entourage, or who could tell stories of having hunted in the northern marches with the Pontifex Tyeveras when he was Coronal under Ossier, or who had newly come back from meetings at Inner Temple with the Lady of the Isle. She grew so self-assured in the company of these great ones that if anyone had turned to her and said, "And you, milady, how have you passed the recent months?" she would have replied easily, "As a thief in the Grand Bazaar," as she had done that first night on the Narabal Island. But the question did not arise: at this level of society, she realized, one never idly indulged one's curiosity with others, but left them to unveil their histories to whatever degree they preferred.

And therefore when on the seventh day Calain told her to prepare to return to the Bazaar, she neither asked him if he had enjoyed her company nor whether he had grown tired of her. He had chosen her to be his companion for a time; that time was now ended, and so be it. It had been a week she would never forget.

Going back to the den of the thieves was a jolt, though. A sumptuously outfitted floater took her from Nissimorn Prospect to the Grand Bazaar's Piliplok Gate, and a servant of

Calain's placed in her arms the little bundle of treasures Calain had given her during their week together. Then the floater was gone and Inyanna was descending into the sweaty chaos of the Bazaar, and it was like awakening from a rare and magical dream. As she passed through the crowded lanes no one called out to her, for those who knew her in the Bazaar knew her in her male guise of Kulibhai, and she was dressed now in women's clothes. She moved through the swirling mobs in silence, bathed still in the aura of the aristocracy and moment by moment giving way to an inrushing feeling of depression and loss as it became clear to her that the dream was over, that she had re-entered reality. Tonight Calain would dine with the visiting Duke of Mazadone, and tomorrow he and his guests would sail up the Steiche on a fishing expedition, and the day after that—well, she had no idea, but she knew that she, on that day, would be filching laces and flasks of perfume and bolts of fabric. For an instant, tears surged into her eyes. She forced them back, telling herself that this was foolishness, that she ought not lament her return from Nissimorn Prospect but rather rejoice that she had been granted a week there.

No one was in the thieves' rooms except the Hjort Beyork and one of the Metamorphs. They merely nodded as Inyanna came in. She went to her chamber and donned the Kulibhai costume. But she could not bring herself so soon to return to her thieving. She stowed her packet of jewels and trinkets, Calain's gifts, carefully under her bed. By selling them she could earn enough to exempt her from her profession for a year or two; but she did not plan to part with even the smallest of them. Tomorrow, she resolved, she would go back into the Bazaar. For now, though, she lay face down on the bed she again shared with Sidoun, and when tears came again she let them come, and after a while she rose, feeling more calm, and washed and waited for the others to appear.

Sidoun welcomed her with a nobleman's poise. No questions about her adventures, no hint of resentment, no sly innuendos: he smiled and took her hand and told her he was pleased she had come back, and offered her a sip of a wine of Alhanroel he had just stolen, and told her a couple of stories of things that had happened in the Bazaar while she was away. She wondered if he would feel inhibited in their lovemaking by the knowledge that the last man to touch her body had been a duke's brother, but no, he reached for her fondly and unhesitatingly when they were in bed, and his gaunt bony body pressed warmly and jubilantly against her. The next day, after their rounds in the Bazaar, they went together to the Park of Fabulous Beasts, and saw for the first time the gossimaule of Glayge, that was so slender it was nearly invisible from the side, and they followed it a little way until it vanished, and laughed as though they had never been separated.

The other thieves regarded Inyanna with some awe for a few days, for they knew where she had been and what she must have been doing, and that laid upon her the strangeness that came from moving in exalted circles. But only Liloyve dared to speak directly to her of it, and she only once, saying, "What did he see in you?"

"How would I know? It was all like a dream."

"I think it was justice."

"What do you mean?"

"That you were wrongfully promised Nissimorn Prospect, and this was by way of making atonement to you. The Divine balances the good and the evil, do you see?" Liloyve laughed. "You've had your twenty royals' worth out of those swindlers, haven't you?"

Indeed she had, Inyanna agreed. But the debt was not yet fully paid, she soon discovered. On Starday next, working her way through the booths of the moneychangers and skimming off the odd coin here and there, she was startled suddenly by a hand on her wrist, and wondered what fool of a thief, failing to recognize her, was trying to make arrest. But it was Liloyve. Her face was flushed and her eyes were wide. "Come home right away!" she cried.

"What is it?"

"Two Vroons waiting for you. You are summoned by Calain, and they say you are to pack all your belongings, for you will not be returning to the Grand Bazaar."

10

So it happened that Inyanna Forlana of Velathys, formerly a thief, took up residence in Nissimorn Prospect as companion to Calain of Ni-moya. Calain offered no explanation, nor did she seek one. He wanted her by his side, and that was explanation enough. For the first few weeks she still expected to be told each morning to make ready to go back to the Bazaar, but that did not occur, and after a while she ceased to consider the possibility. Wherever Calain went, she went: to the Zimr Marshes to hunt the gihorna, to glittering Dulorn for a week at the Perpetual Circus, to Khyntor for the Festival of Geysers, even into mysterious rainy Piurifayne to explore the shadowy homeland of the Shapeshifters. She who had spent all her first twenty years in shabby Velathys came to take it quite for granted that she should be traveling about like a Coronal making the grand processional, with the brother of a royal duke at her side; but yet she never quite lost her perspective, never failed to see the irony and incongruity of the strange transformations her life had undergone.

Nor was it surprising to her even when she found herself seated at table next to the Coronal himself. Lord Malibor had come to Ni-moya on a visit of state, for it behooved him to travel in the western continent every eight or ten years, by way of showing the people of Zimroel that they weighed equally in their monarch's thoughts with those of his home continent of Alhanroel. The duke provided the obligatory banquet, and Inyanna was placed at the high table, with the Coronal to her right and Calain at her left, and the duke and his lady at Lord Malibor's far side. Inyanna had been taught the names of the great Coronals in school, of course, Stiamot and Confalume and Prestimion and Dekkeret and all the rest, and her mother often had told her that it was on the very day of her birth when news came to Velathys that the old Pontifex Ossier was dead, that Lord Tyeveras had succeeded him and had chosen a man of the city of Bombifale, one Malibor, to be the new Coronal; and eventually the new coinage had trickled into her province, showing this Lord Malibor, a broad-faced man with wide-set eyes and heavy brows. But that such people as Coronals and Pontifexes actually existed had been a matter of some doubt to her through all those years, and yet here she was with her elbow an inch from Lord Malibor's, and the only thing she marveled at was how very much this burly and massive man in imperial green and gold resembled the man whose face was on the coins. She had expected the portraits to be less precise.

It seemed sensible to her that the conversations of Coronals would revolve wholly around matters of state. But in fact Lord Malibor seemed to talk mainly of the hunt. He had gone to this remote place to slay that rare beast, and to that inaccessible and uncongenial place to take the head of this difficult creature, and so on and so on; and he was constructing a new wing of the Castle to house all his trophies. "In a year or two," said the Coronal, "I trust you and Calain will visit me at the Castle. The trophy-room will be complete by then. It will please you, I know, to see such an array of creatures, all of them prepared by the finest taxidermists of Castle Mount." Inyanna did indeed look forward to visiting Lord Malibor's Castle, for the Coronal's enormous residence was a legendary place that entered into everyone's dreams, and she could imagine nothing more wonderful than to ascend to the summit of lofty Castle Mount and wander that great building, thousands of years old, exploring its thousands of rooms. But she was only repelled by Lord Malibor's obsession with slaughter. When he talked of killing amorfibots and ghalvars and sigimoins and steetmoy, and of the extreme effort he expended in those killings, Inyanna was reminded of Ni-moya's Park of Fabulous Beasts, where by order of some milder Coronal of long ago those same animals were protected and cherished; and that put her in mind of quiet gaunt Sidoun, who had gone with her so often to that park, and had played so sweetly on his pocket-harp. She did not want to think of Sidoun, to whom she owed nothing but for whom she felt a guilty affection, and she did not want to hear of the killing of rare creatures so that their heads might adorn Lord Malibor's trophy-room. Yet she managed to listen politely to the Coronal's tales of carnage and even to make an amiable comment or two.

Toward dawn, when they were finally back at Nissimorn Prospect and preparing for bed, Calain said to her, "The Coronal is planning to hunt next for sea-dragons. He seeks one known as Lord Kinniken's dragon, that was measured once at more than three hundred feet in length."

Inyanna, who was tired and not cheerful, shrugged. Sea-dragons, at least, were far from rare, and it would be no cause for grief if the Coronal harpooned a few. "Is there room in his trophy-house for a dragon that size?"

"For its head and wings, I imagine. Not that he stands much chance of getting it. The Kinniken's been seen only four times since Lord Kinniken's day, and not for seventy years. But if he doesn't find that one, he'll get another. Or drown in the attempt."

"Is there much chance of that?"

Calain nodded. "Dragon-hunting's dangerous business. He'd be wiser not to try. But he's killed just about everything that moves on land, and no Coronal's ever been out in a dragon-ship, and so he'll not be discouraged from it. We leave for Piliplok at the end of the week."

"We?"

"Lord Malibor has asked me to join him on the hunt." With a rueful smile he said, "In truth he wanted the duke, but my brother begged off, claiming duties of state. So he asked me. One does not easily refuse such things."

"Do I accompany you?" Inyanna asked.

"We have not planned it that way."

"Oh," she said quietly. After a moment she asked, "How long will you be gone?"

"The hunt lasts three months, usually. During the season of the southerly winds. And then the time to reach Piliplok, and outfit the vessel, and to return—it would be six or seven months all told. I'll be home by spring."

"Ah. I see."

Calain came to her side and drew her against him. "It will be the longest separation we will ever endure. I promise you that."

She wanted to say, Is there no way you can refuse to go? Or, Is there some way I can be allowed to go with you? But she knew how useless that was, and what a violation of the etiquette by which Calain lived. So Inyanna made no further protest. She took Calain into her arms, and they embraced until sunrise.

On the eve of his departure for the port of Piliplok, where the dragon-ships made harbor, Calain summoned her to his study on the highest level of Nissimorn Prospect and offered her a thick document to sign.

"What is this?" she asked, without picking it up.

"Articles of marriage between us."

"This is a cruel joke, milord."

"No joke, Inyanna. No joke at all."

"But—"

"I would have discussed the matter with you this winter, but then the damnable dragon-voyage arose, and left me no time. So I have rushed things a little. You are no mere concubine to me: this paper formalizes our love."

"Is our love something that needs formality?"

Calain's eyes narrowed. "I am going off on a risky and

foolhardy adventure, from which I expect to return, but while I am at sea my fate will not be in my own hands. As my companion you have no legal rights of inheritance. As my wife—"

Inyanna was stunned. "If the risk is so great, abandon the voyage, milord!"

"You know that's impossible. I must bear the risk. And so I would provide for you. Sign it, Inyanna."

She stared a long time at the document, a draft of many pages. Her eyes would not focus properly and she neither could nor would make out the words that some scribe had indited in the most elegant of calligraphy. Wife to Calain? It seemed almost monstrous to her, a shattering of all proprieties, a stepping beyond every boundary. And yet—and yet—

He waited. She could not refuse.

In the morning he departed in the Coronal's entourage for Piliplok, and all that day Inyanna roamed the corridors and chambers of Nissimorn Prospect in confusion and disarray. That night the duke thoughtfully invited her for dinner; the next, Durand Livolk and his lady escorted her to dine at the Pidruid Island, where a shipment of fireshower-palm wine had arrived. Other invitations followed, so that her life was a busy one, and the months passed. It was mid-winter now. And then came word that a great sea-dragon had fallen upon the ship of Lord Malibor and sent it to the bottom of the Inner Sea. Lord Malibor was dead, and all those who had sailed with him, and a certain Voriax had been named Coronal. And under the terms of Calain's will, his widow Inyanna Forlana had come into full ownership of the great estate known as Nissimorn Prospect.

II

When the period of mourning was over and she had an opportunity to make arrangements for such matters, Inyanna called for one of her stewards and ordered rich gifts of money to be delivered to the Grand Bazaar, for the thief Agourmole and all members of his family. It was Inyanna's way of saying that she had not forgotten them. "Tell me their exact words when you hand the purses to them," she ordered the steward, hoping they would send back some warm remembrances of the old times together, but the man reported that none of them had said anything of interest, that they had simply expressed surprise and gratitude toward the Lady Inyanna, except for the man named Sidoun, who had refused his gift and could not be urged to accept it. Inyanna smiled sadly and had Sidoun's twenty royals distributed to children in the streets, and after that she had no further contact with the thieves of the Grand Bazaar, nor did she ever go near the place.

Some years later, while visiting the shops of the Gossamer Galleria, the Lady Inyanna observed two suspicious-looking men in the shop of the dragon-bone carvings. From their movements and the way they exchanged glances, it seemed quite clear to her that they were thieves, maneuvering to create a diversion that would allow them to plunder the shop. Then she looked at them more closely and realized that she had encountered them before, for one was a short thick-framed man, and the other tall and knobby-faced and pale. She gestured to her escorts, who moved quietly into position about the two.

Inyanna said, "One of you is Steyg, and one is called Vezan Ormus, but I have forgotten which of you is which. On the other hand, I remember the other details of our meeting quite well."

The thieves looked at one another in alarm. The taller one said, "Milady, you are mistaken. My name is Elakon Mirj, and my friend is called Thanooz."

"These days, perhaps. But when you visited Velathys long ago you went by other names. I see that you've graduated from swindling to thievery, eh? Tell me this: how many heirs to Nissimorn Prospect did you discover, before the game grew dull?"

Now there was panic in their eyes. They seemed to be calculating the chances of making a break past Inyanna's men toward the door; but that would have been rash. The guards of the Gossamer Galleria had been notified and were gathered just outside.

The shorter thief, trembling, said, "We are honest merchants, milady, and nothing else."

"You are incorrigible scoundrels," said Inyanna, "and nothing else. Deny it again and I'll have you shipped to Suvrael for penal servitude!"

"Milady—"

"Speak the truth," Inyanna said.

Through chattering teeth the taller one replied, "We admit the charge. But it was long ago. If we have injured you, we will make full restitution."

"Injured me? Injured me?" Inyanna laughed. "Rather, you did me the greatest service anyone could have done. I feel only gratitude toward you; for know that I was Inyanna Forlana the shopkeeper of Velathys, whom you cheated out of twenty royals, and now I am the Lady Inyanna of Ni-moya, mistress of Nissimorn Prospect. And so the Divine protects the weak and brings good out of evil." She beckoned to the guards. "Convey these two to the imperial proctors, and say that I will give testimony against them later, but that I ask mercy for them, perhaps a sentence of three months of road-mending, or something similar. And afterward I think I'll take the two of you into my service. You are worthless rogues, but clever ones, and it's better to keep you close at hand, where you can be watched, than to let you go loose to prey on the unwary." She waved her hand. They were led away.

Inyanna turned to the keeper of the shop. "I regret the interruption," she said. "Now, these carvings of the emblems of the city, that you think are worth a dozen royals apiece— what would you say to thirty royals for the lot, and maybe a little carving of the bilantoon thrown in to round things off—"

TEN

Voriax and Valentine

Of all the vicarious lives Hissune has experienced in the Register of Souls, that of Inyanna Forlana seems perhaps the closest to his heart. In part it is because she is a woman of modern times and so the world in which she dwelled seems less alien to him than those of the soul-painter or the sea-captain or Thesme of Narabal. But the main reason Hissune feels kinship with the one-time shopkeeper of Velathys is that she began with practically nothing, and lost even that, and nevertheless came to achieve power and grandeur and, Hissune suspects, a measure of contentment. He understands that the Divine helps those who helped themselves, and Inyanna seems much like him in that respect. Of course, luck was with her—she caught the attention of the right people at the right moment, and they saw her nicely along her journey; but does one not also shape one's own luck? Hissune, who had been in the right place when Lord Valentine in his wanderings came to the Labyrinth years ago, believes that. He wonders what surprises and delights fortune has in store for him, and how he can better shape his own destinies to achieve something higher than the clerkship in the Labyrinth that has been his lot so long. He is eighteen, now, and that seems very old for commencing his rise to greatness. But he reminds himself that Inyanna, at his age, was peddling clay pots and bolts of cloth on the wrong side of Velathys, and she came to

*inherit Nissimorn Prospect. No telling what waits for him.
Why, at any moment Lord Valentine might send for him—
Lord Valentine, who arrived at the Labyrinth the week be-
fore, and is lodged now in those luxurious chambers reserved
for the Coronal when he is in residence at the capital of the
Pontificate—Lord Valentine might summon him and say,
"Hissune, you've served long enough in this grubby place.
From now on you live beside me on Castle Mount!"*

At any moment, yes. But Hissune has heard nothing from
the Coronal and expects to hear nothing. It is a pretty fantasy, but he will not torment himself with false hopes. He
goes about his dreary work and mulls all that he has learned
in the Register of Souls, and a day or two after sharing the
life of the thief of Ni-moya he returns to the Register and
with the greatest boldness he has ever displayed he inquires
of the archival index whether there is on file a recording of
the soul of Lord Valentine. It is impudence, he knows, and
dangerous tempting of fate; Hissune will not be surprised if
lights flash and bells rings and armed guards come to seize
the prying young upstart who without the slightest shred of
authority is attempting to penetrate the mind and spirit of the
Coronal himself. What does surprise him is the actual event:
the vast machine simply informs him that a single record of
Lord Valentine is available, made long ago, in his earliest
manhood. Hissune, shameless, does not hesitate. Quickly he
punches the activator keys.

They were two black-haired black-bearded men, tall and
strong, with dark flashing eyes and wide shoulders and an
easy look of authority about them, and anyone could see at a
single glance that they must be brothers. But there were differences. One was a man and one was still to some degree a
boy, and that was evident not only from the sparseness of the
younger one's beard and the smoothness of his face, but from
a certain warmth and playfulness and gaiety in his eyes. The
older one was more stern, more austere of expression, more
imperious, as though he bore terrible responsibilities that had
left their mark on him. In a way that was true; for he was
Voriax of Halanx, elder son of the High Counsellor Damiandane, and it had been commonly said of him on Castle
Mount since his childhood that he was sure to be Coronal
one day.

Of course there were those who said the same thing about

his younger brother Valentine—that he was a fine boy of great promise, that he had the making of a king about him. But Valentine had no illusions about such compliments. Voriax was the older by eight years, and, beyond any doubt, if either of them went to dwell in the Castle it would be Voriax. Not that Voriax had any guarantees of the succession, despite what everyone said. Their father Damiandane had been one of Lord Tyeveras' closest advisers, and he too had universally been expected to be the next Coronal. But when Lord Tyeveras became Pontifex, he had reached all the way down the Mount to the city of Bombifale to choose Malibor as his successor. No one had anticipated that, for Malibor was only a provincial governor, a coarse man more interested in hunting and games than in the burdens of administration. Valentine had not yet been born then, but Voriax had told him that their father had never uttered a word of disappointment or dismay at being passed over for the throne, which perhaps was the best indication that he had been qualified to be chosen.

Valentine wondered whether Voriax would behave so nobly if the starburst crown were denied him after all, and went instead to some other high prince of the Mount—Elidath of Morvole, say, or Tunigorn, or Stasilaine, or to Valentine himself. How odd that would be! Sometimes Valentine covertly said the names to hear their sound: Lord Stasilaine, Lord Elidath, Lord Tunigorn. Lord Valentine, even! But such fantasies were idle folly. Valentine had no wish to displace his brother, nor was it likely to happen. Barring some unimaginable prank of the Divine or some bizarre whim of Lord Malibor, it was Voriax who would reign when it became Lord Malibor's time to be Pontifex, and the knowledge of that destiny had imprinted itself on Voriax' spirit and showed in his conduct and bearing.

The complexities of the court were far from Valentine's mind now. He and his brother were on holiday in the lower ranges of Castle Mount—a trip long postponed, for Valentine had suffered a terrible fracture of the leg the year before last while riding with his friend Elidath in the pygmy forest below Amblemorn, and only lately had he been sufficiently recovered for another such strenuous journey. Down the vast mountain he and Voriax had gone, making a grand and wonderful tour, possibly the last long holiday Valentine was apt to have before he entered the world of adult obligations. He was seventeen, now, and because he belonged to that select group of princelings from whom Coronals were chosen, there was much he must learn of the techniques of government, so that he would be ready for whatever might be asked of him.

And so he had gone with Voriax—who was escaping his own duties, and glad of it, for the sake of helping his brother celebrate his return to health—from the family estate in Halanx to the nearby pleasure-city of High Morpin, to ride the juggernauts and career through the power-tunnels. Valentine insisted on doing the mirror-slides, too, by way of testing the strength of his shattered leg, and just the merest look of uncertainty crossed Voriax' face, as if he doubted that Valentine could handle such sports but was too tactful to say it. When they stepped out on the slides Voriax hovered close by Valentine's elbow, irritatingly protective, and when Valentine moved away a few steps Voriax moved with him, until Valentine turned and said, "Do you think I will fall, brother?"

"There is little chance of that."

"Then why stand so close? Is it you that fears falling?" Valentine laughed. "Be reassured, then. I'll reach you soon enough to catch you."

"You are ever thoughtful, brother," said Voriax. And then the slides began to turn and the mirrors glowed brightly, and there was no time for more banter. Indeed Valentine felt a moment's uneasiness, for the mirror-slide was not for invalids and his injury had left him with a slight but infuriating limp that disturbed his coordination; but quickly he caught the rhythm of it and he stayed upright easily, sustaining his balance even in the wildest gyrations, and when he went whirling past Voriax he saw the anxiety gone from his brother's face. Yet the essence of the episode gave Valentine much to think about, as he and Voriax traveled on down the Mount to Tentag for the tree-dancing festival, and then to Ertsud Grand and Minimool, and onward past Gimkandale to Furible to witness the mating flight of the stone birds. While they had been waiting for the mirror-slides to start moving Voriax had been a concerned and loving guardian, and yet at the same time a bit condescending, a bit smothering: his fraternal care for Valentine's safety seemed to Valentine yet another way for Voriax to be maintaining authority over him, and Valentine, at the threshold of full manhood, did not at all like that. But he understood that brotherhood was part love and part warfare, and he kept his annoyance to himself.

From Furible they passed through Bimbak East and Bimbak West, pausing in each city to stand before one of the twin mile-high towers that made even the haughtiest swaggerer feel like an ant, and beyond Bimbak East they took the path that led to Amblemorn, where a dozen wild streams came together to become the potent River Glayge. On the downslope side of Amblemorn was a place some miles across where the soil was hard-packed and chalky-white, and trees that elsewhere grew to pierce the sky were dwarfed eerie things here, no taller than a man and no thicker than a girl's wrist. It was in this pygmy forest that Valentine had come to grief, goading his mount too hard in a place where treacherous roots snaked over the ground. The mount had lost its footing, Valentine had been thrown, his leg had been horribly bent between two slender but unyielding trees whose trunks had the toughness of a thousand years, and months of anguish and frustration had followed while the bones slowly knit and an irreplaceable year of being young slipped away from him. Why had they come back here now? Voriax prowled the weird forest as if searching for hidden treasure. At last he turned to Valentine and said, "This place seems enchanted."

"The explanation is simple. The roots of the trees are unable to penetrate very deeply into this useless gray soil; they take the best grip they can, for this is Castle Mount where everything grows, but they are starved for nourishment, and so—"

"Yes, I understand," said Voriax coolly. "I didn't say the place *is* enchanted, only that it *seems* that way. A legion of Vroon wizards couldn't have created anything so ugly. Yet I'm glad to be seeing it at last. Shall we ride through it?"

"How subtle you are, Voriax."

"Subtle? I fail to see—"

"Suggesting that I take another try at crossing the place that nearly cost me my leg."

Voriax' ruddy face turned even more florid. "I hardly think you'd fall again."

"Surely not. But you think I may think so, and you've long believed that the way to conquer fear is to take the offensive against whatever it is you dread, and so you maneuver me into a second race here, to burn away any lingering timidity this forest may have instilled in me. It is the opposite of what you were doing when we went on the mirror-slides, but it amounts to the same thing, does it not?"

"I understand none of this," said Voriax. "Do you have some sort of fever today?"

"Not at all. Shall we race?"

"I think not."

Valentine, baffled, pounded one fist against another. "But you just suggested it!"

"I suggested a ride," Voriax answered. "But you seem full of mysterious angers and defiance, and you accuse me of maneuvering and manipulating you where no such things were intended. If we cross the forest while you're in such a mood, you'll certainly fall again, and probably smash your other leg. Come: we'll go on into Amblemorn."

"Voriax—"

"Come."

"I want to ride through the forest." Valentine's eyes were steady on his brother's. "Will you ride with me, or do you prefer to wait here?"

"With you, I suppose."

"Now tell me to be careful and watch out for hidden roots."

A muscle flickered in annoyance in Voriax' cheek, and he let out a long sigh of exasperation. "You are no child. I would not say such a thing to you. Besides, if I thought you needed such advice, I'd deny you as my brother and cast you forth."

He stirred his mount and rode off furiously down the narrow avenues between the pygmy trees.

Valentine followed after a moment, riding hard, striving to close the gap between them. The path was difficult and here and there he saw obstacles as menacing as the one that had brought him down when he rode here with Elidath; but his mount was sure-footed and there was no need to pull back on the reins. Though the memory of his fall was bright in him, Valentine felt no fear, only a sort of heightened alertness: if he fell again, he knew he would fall less disastrously. He wondered it he might not be overreacting to Voriax. Perhaps he was too touchy, too sensitive, too quick to defend himself against the imagined overprotectiveness of his older brother. Voriax was in training to be lord of the world, after all; he could not help but seem to assume responsibility for everyone and everything, especially his younger brother. Valentine resolved to be less zealous in his defense of his autonomy.

They passed through the forest and into Amblemorn, oldest of the cities of Castle Mount, an ancient place of tangled streets and vine-encrusted walls. It was here, twelve thousand years ago, that the conquest of the Mount had begun—the first bold and foolish ventures into the bleak, airless wastes of the thirty-mile-high excrescence that jutted from Majipoor's flank. For one who had lived all his life amid its Fifty Cities and their eternal fragrant springtime, it was hard now to imagine a time when the Mount was bare and unihabitable; but Valentine knew the story of the pioneers edging up the titanic slopes, carrying the machines that brought warmth and air to the great mountain, transforming it over centuries into a fairyland realm of beauty, crowned at last by the small rugged keep at the summit that Lord Stiamot had established eight thousand years ago, and that had grown by incredible metamorphosis into the vast, incomprehensible Castle where Lord Malibor dwelled today. He and Voriax paused in awe before the monument in Amblemorn marking the old timber-line:

ABOVE HERE ALL WAS BARREN ONCE

A garden of wondrous halatinga trees with crimson-and-gold flowers surrounded the shaft of polished black Velathyntu marble that bore the inscription.

A day and a night and a day and a night in Amblemorn, and then Voriax and Valentine descended through the valley of the Glayge to a place called Ghiseldorn, off the main roads. At the edge of a dark and dense forest a settlement had sprung up here of a few thousand people who had retreated from the great cities; they lived in tents of black felt, made from the fleece of the wild blaves that grazed in the meadows beside the river, and had little to do with their neighbors. Some said that they were witches and wizards; some that they were a stray tribe of Metamorphs that had escaped the ancient expulsion of their kind from Alhanroel, and perpetually wore human form; the truth, Valentine suspected, was that these folk were simply not at home in the world of commerce and striving that was Majipoor, and had come here to live their own way in their own community.

By late afternoon he and Voriax reached a hill from which

they could see the forest of Ghiseldorn and the village of black tents just beyond it. The forest seemed unwelcoming— pingla-trees, short and thick-trunked, with their plump branches emerging at sharp angles and interlacing to form a tight canopy, admitting no light. Nor did the village appear to beckon. The ten-sided tents, widely spaced, looked like giant insects of a peculiar geometry, pausing for the moment before continuing an inexorable migration across a landscape to which they were utterly indifferent. Valentine had felt a powerful curiosity about Ghiseldorn and its folk, but now that he was here he was less eager to penetrate its mysteries.

He glanced over at Voriax and saw the same doubts on his brother's face.

"What shall we do?" Valentine asked.

"Camp on this side of the forest, I think. In the morning we can approach the village and see what our reception is like."

"Would they attack us?"

"Attack? I doubt it very much. I think they're even more peaceful than the rest of us. But why intrude if we're not wanted? Why not respect their seclusion?" Voriax pointed to a half-moon of grassy ground at the edge of a stream. "What do you say to making our camp there?"

They halted, set the mounts to pasture, unrolled their packs, gathered succulent sprouts for dinner, While they foraged for firewood Valentine said suddenly, "If Lord Malibor were chasing some rare beast through the forest here, would he give any thought to the privacy of the Ghiseldorn folk?"

"Nothing prevents Lord Malibor from pursuing his prey."

"Exactly. The thought would never occur to him. I think you will be a far finer Coronal than Lord Malibor, Voriax."

"Don't talk foolishness."

"It isn't foolishness. It's a sensible opinion. Everyone agrees that Lord Malibor is crude and thoughtless. And when it's your turn—"

"Stop this, Valentine."

"You *will* be Coronal," Valentine said. "Why pretend otherwise? It's certain to happen, and soon. Tyeveras is very old; Lord Malibor will move on to the Labyrinth in two or three years; and when he does, he'll surely name you Coronal. He's not so stupid as to fly in the face of all his advisers. And then—"

Voriax caught Valentine by the wrist and leaned close.

There was anguish and annoyance in his eyes. "This kind of chatter brings only bad luck. I ask you to stop."

"May I say one more thing?"

"I want no more speculation about who is to be Coronal."

Valentine nodded. "This is not speculation, but a question from brother to brother, that has been on my mind for some time. I don't say you will become Coronal, but I would like to know if you *wish* to become Coronal. Have they consulted you at all? Are you eager for the burden? Just answer me that, Voriax."

After a long silence Voriax said, "It is a burden no one dares refuse."

"But do you want it?"

"If destiny brings it to me, should I say no?"

"You aren't answering me. Look at us now: young, healthy, happy, free. Aside from our responsibilities at court, which are hardly overwhelming, we can do as we please, go anywhere in the world we like, a voyage to Zimroel, a pilgrimage to the Isle, a holiday in the Khyntor Marches, anything, anywhere. To give all that up for the sake of wearing the starburst crown, and signing a million decrees, and making grand processionals with all those speeches, and someday to have to live at the bottom of the Labyrinth—why, Voriax? Why would anyone want to do that? Do *you* want to do that?"

"You are still a child," said Voriax.

Valentine pulled back as though slapped. Condescension again! But then he realized that this had been merited, that he was asking naïve, puerile questions. He forced his anger to subside and said, "I thought I had moved somewhat into manhood."

"Somewhat. But you still have much to learn."

"Doubtless." He paused. "All right, you accept the inevitability of the kingship, if the kingship should come to you. But do you *want* it, Voriax, do you truly crave it, or is it only your breeding and your sense of duty that lead you to prepare yourself for the throne?"

Voriax said slowly, "I am not preparing myself for the throne, but only for a role in the government of Majipoor, as you also are doing, and yes, it is a matter of breeding and a sense of duty, for I am a son of the High Counsellor Damiandane, as I believe you also to be. If the throne is offered to me I will accept it proudly and discharge its burdens as capably as I can. I spend no time craving the kingship and even less time speculating on whether it will come to me. And I find this conversation tiresome in the extreme and I would be grateful if you permitted me to gather firewood in silence."

He glared at Valentine and turned away.

Questions blossomed in Valentine like alabandinas in summer, but he suppressed them all, for he saw Voriax' lips quivering and knew that he had already gone beyond a boundary. Voriax was ripping angrily at the fallen branches, pulling twigs free with a vehemence not at all necessary, for the wood was dry and brittle. Valentine did not attempt again to breach his brother's defenses, though he had learned only a little of what he wanted to know. He suspected, from Voriax' defensiveness, that Voriax did indeed hunger for the kingship and devoted all his waking hours to training himself for it; and he had an inkling, but only an inkling, of why he should want it. For its own sake, for the power and the glory? Well, why not? And for fulfillment of a destiny that called certain people to high obligations? Yes, that too. And doubtless to atone for the slight that had been shown their father when *he* had been passed over for the crown. But still, but still, to give up one's freedom merely to rule the world—it was a mystery to Valentine, and in the end he decided that Voriax was right, that these were things he could not fully comprehend at the age of seventeen.

He carried his load of firewood back to the campsite and began kindling a blaze. Voriax joined him soon, but he said nothing, and a chill of estrangement lingered between the brothers that gave Valentine great distress. He wished he could apologize to Voriax for having probed so deeply, but that was impossible, for he had never been graceful at such things with Voriax, nor Voriax with him. He still felt that brother could talk to brother concerning the most intimate matters without giving offense. But on the other hand this frostiness was hard to bear, and if prolonged would poison their holiday together. Valentine searched for a way of regaining amity and after a moment chose one that had worked well enough when they were younger.

He went to Voriax, who was carving the meat for their meal in a gloomy, sullen way, and said, "While we wait for the water to boil, will you wrestle with me?"

Voriax glanced up, startled. "What?"

"I feel the need for exercise."

"Climb those pingla-trees, then, and dance on their branches."

"Come. Take a few falls with me, Voriax."

"It would not be right."

"Why? If I overthrew you, would that offend your dignity even further?"

"Careful, Valentine!"

"I spoke too sharply. Forgive me." Valentine went into a wrestler's crouch and held out his hands. "Please? Some quick holds, a bit of sweat before dinner—"

"Your leg is only newly healed."

"But healed it is. You can use your full strength on me, as I will on you, and never fear."

"And if the leg snaps again, and we a day's journey from any city worth the name?"

"Come, Voriax," Valentine said impatiently. "You fret too much! Come, show me you still can wrestle!" He laughed and slapped his palms together and beckoned, and slapped his hands again, and thrust his grinning face almost against the nose of Voriax, and pulled his brother to his feet, and then Voriax yielded and began to grapple with him.

Something was wrong. They had wrestled often enough, ever since Valentine had been big enough to fight his brother as an equal, and Valentine knew all of Voriax' moves, his little tricks of balance and timing. But the man he wrestled with now seemed a complete stranger. Was this some Metamorph sneaked upon him in the guise of Voriax? No, no, no; it was the leg, Valentine realized, Voriax was holding back his strength, was being deliberately gentle and awkward, was once again patronizing him. In surprising rage Valentine lunged and, although in this early moment of the bout etiquette called on them only to be testing and probing one another, he seized Voriax with the intent to throw him, and forced him to one knee. Voriax stared in amazement. As Valentine caught his breath and gathered his strength to drive his brother's shoulders against the ground, Voriax rallied and pressed upward, unleashing for the first time all his formidable strength: he nearly went down anyway before Valentine's onslaught, but at the last moment he rolled free and sprang to his feet.

They circled one another warily.

Voriax said, "I see I underestimated you. Your leg must be entirely healed."

"So it is, as I've told you many times. I merely limp a little, which makes no difference. Come here, Voriax: come within reach again."

He beckoned. They sprang for one another and locked chest against chest, neither able to budge the other, and stayed that way for what seemed to Valentine an hour or more, though probably it was only minutes. Then he drove Voriax back a few inches, and then Voriax dug in and resisted, and forced Valentine back the same distance. They grunted and sweated and strained, and grinned at one another in the midst of the struggle. Valentine took the keenest pleasure in that grin of Voriax, for it meant that they were brothers again, that the chill between then was thawed, that he was forgiven for his impertinence. In that moment he yearned to embrace Voriax instead of wrestling with him; and in that same moment of relaxed tension Voriax shoved at him, twisted, pivoted, drew him to the ground, pinned his midsection with his knee, and clamped his hands against Valentine's shoulders. Valentine held himself firm, but there was no withstanding Voriax for long at this stage: steadily Voriax pushed Valentine downward until his shoulder blades pressed against the cool moist ground.

"Your match," Valentine said, gasping, and Voriax rolled free, lying beside him as laughter overtook them both. "I'll whip you the next one!"

How good it felt, even in defeat, to have regained his brother's love!

Abruptly Valentine heard the sound of applause coming from not very far away. He sat up and stared about in the twilight, and saw the figure of a woman, sharp-featured and with extraordinarily long straight black hair, standing by the edge of the forest. Her eyes were bright and wicked, her lips were full, her clothes were of a strange style—mere strips of tanned leather crudely tacked together. She seemed quite old to Valentine, perhaps as much as thirty.

"I watched you," she said, coming toward them with no trace of fear. "At first I thought it was a real quarrel, but then I saw it was for sport."

"At first it was a real quarrel," said Voriax. "But also it was sport, always. I am Voriax of Halanx, and this is Valentine, my brother."

She looked from one to the other. "Yes, of course, brothers. Anyone could see that. I am called Tanunda, and I am of Ghiseldorn. Shall I tell you your fortunes?"

"Are you a witch, then?" Valentine asked.

There was merriment in her eyes. "Yes, yes, certainly, a witch. What else?"

"Come, then, foretell for us!" cried Valentine.

"Wait," said Voriax. "I have no liking for sorceries."

"You are too sober by half," Valentine said. "What harm can it do? We visit Ghiseldorn the city of wizards; should we not then have our destinies read? What are you afraid of? It's a game, Voriax, only a game!" He walked toward the witch and said, "Will you stay with us for dinner?"

"Valentine—"

Valentine glanced boldly at his brother and laughed. "I'll protect you against evil, Voriax! Have no fear!" And in a lower voice he said, "We've traveled alone long enough, brother. I'm hungry for company."

"So I see," murmured Voriax.

But the witch was attractive and Valentine was insistent and shortly Voriax appeared to grow less uneasy about her presence; he carved a third portion of meat for her, and she went into the forest and came back with fruits of the pingla and showed them how to roast them to make their juice run into the meat and give a pleasingly dark and smoky flavor to it. Valentine felt his head swimming somewhat after a time, and he doubted that the few sips of wine he had had could be responsible, so quite probably it was the juice of the pinglas; the thought crossed his mind that there might be some treachery here, but he rejected it, for the dizziness that was overtaking him was an amiable and even exciting one and he saw no peril in it. He looked across at Voriax, wondering if his brother's more suspicious nature would arise to darken their feast, but Voriax, if he was feeling the effects of the juice at all, appeared only to be made more congenial by it: he laughed loudly at everything, he swayed and clapped his thighs, he leaned close to the witch-woman and shouted raucous things into her face. Valentine helped himself to more meat. Night was falling, now, a sudden blackness settling over the camp, stars abruptly blazing out of a sky lit only by one small sliver of moon. Valentine imagined he could hear distant singing and discordant chanting, though it seemed to him that Ghiseldorn must be too far away for such sounds to carry through the dense woods: a fantasy, he decided, stirred by these intoxicating fruits.

The fire burned low. The air grew cool. They huddled close together, Valentine and Voriax and Tanunda, and body pressed against body in what was at first an innocent way and then not so innocent. As they entwined Valentine caught his brother's eye, and Voriax winked, as if he were saying, *We are men together tonight, and we will take our pleasure together, brother.* Now and then with Elidath or Stasilaine Valentine had shared a woman, three tumbling merrily in a bed built for two, but never with Voriax, Voriax who was so conscious of his dignity, his superiority, his high position, so there was special delight for Valentine in this game now. The Ghiseldorn witch had shed her leather garments and showed a lean and supple body by firelight. Valentine had feared that her flesh would be repellent, she being so much older than he, older even than Voriax by some years, but he saw now that that was the foolishness of inexperience, for she seemed altogether beautiful to him. He reached for her and encountered Voriax' hand against her flank; he slapped at it playfully, as he would at a buzzing insect, and both brothers laughed, and above their deep laughter came the silvery chuckling of Tanunda, and all three rolled about in the dewy grass.

Valentine had never known so wild a night. Whatever drug was in the pingla-juice worked on him to free him of all inhibition and to spur his energies, and with Voriax it must have been the same. To Valentine the night became a sequence of fragmentary images, of sequences of events unlinked to others. Now he lay sprawled with Tanunda's head in his lap, stroking her gleaming brow while Voriax embraced her, and he listened to their mingled gasps with a strange pleasure; and then it was he who held the witch tight, and Voriax was somewhere close at hand but he could not tell where; and then Tanunda lay sandwiched between the two men for some giddy grappling; and somehow they went from there to the stream, and bathed and splashed and laughed, and ran naked and shivering to the dying fire, and made love again, Valentine and Tanunda, Voriax and Tanunda, Valentine and Tanunda and Voriax, flesh calling to flesh until the first grayish strands of morning broke the darkness.

All three were awake as the sun burst into the sky. Great swathes of the night were gone from Valentine's memory, and he wondered if he had slept unknowing from time to time, but now his mind was weirdly clear, his eyes were wide, as though this were the middle of the day. Voriax was the same, and the grinning naked witch who sprawled between them.

"Now," she said, "the telling of fortunes!"

Voriax made an uneasy sound, a rasping of the throat, but Valentine said quickly, "Yes! Yes! Prophesy for us!"

"Gather the pingla-seeds," she said.

They were scattered all about, glossy black nuts with splashes of red on them. Valentine scooped up a dozen of them, and even Voriax collected a few; these they gave to Tanunda, who had found a handful also, and she began to roll them in her fists and scatter them like dice on the ground. Five times she cast them, and scooped them up and cast again; then she cupped her hands and allowed a line of seeds to fall in a circle, and threw the remaining ones within that circle, and peered close a long while, squatting with face to the ground to study the patterns. At length she looked up. The wanton deviltry was gone from her face; she looked strangely altered, very solemn and some years older.

"You are high-born men," she said. "But that could be seen from the way you carry yourselves. The seeds tell me much more. I see great perils ahead for both of you."

Voriax looked away, scowling, and spat.

"You are skeptical, yes," she said. "But you each face dangers. You—" she indicated Voriax—"must be wary of forests, and you—" a glance at Valentine—"of water, of oceans." She frowned. "And of much else, I think, for your destiny is a mysterious one and I am unable to read it clearly. Your line is broken—not by death, but by something stranger, some change, a great transformation—" She shook her head. "It is puzzling to me. I can be of no other help."

Voriax said, "Beware of forests, beware of oceans—beware of nonsense!"

"You will be king," said Tanunda.

Voriax caught his breath sharply. The anger fled his face and he gaped at her.

Valentine smiled and clapped his brother's back and said, "You see? You see?"

"And you also will be king," the witch said.

"*What?*" Valentine was bewildered. "What foolishness is this? Your seeds deceive you!"

"If they do, it is for the first time," said Tanunda. She gathered the fallen seeds and flung them quickly into the stream, and wrapped her strips of leather about her body. "A king and a king, and I have enjoyed my night's sport with you both, your majesties-to-be. Shall you go on to Ghiseldorn today?"

"I think not," said Voriax, without looking at her.

"Then we will not meet again. Farewell!"

She moved swiftly toward the forest. Valentine stretched out a hand toward her, but said nothing, only squeezed the air helplessly with his trembling fingers, and then she was gone. He turned toward Voriax, who was scuffing angrily at the embers of the fire. All the joy of the night's revelry had fled.

"You were right," Valentine said. "We should not have let her dabble in prophecy at our expense. Forests! Oceans! And this madness of our both being kings!"

"What does she mean?" asked Voriax. "That we will share the throne as we shared her body this night past?"

"It will not be," said Valentine.

"Never has there been joint rule in Majipoor. It makes no sense! It is unthinkable! If I am to be king, Valentine, how are you also to be king?"

"You are not listening to me. I tell you, pay no attention to it, brother. She was a wild woman who gave us a night of drunken pleasure. There's no truth in prophecy."

"She said I was to be king."

"And so you probably shall be. But it was only a lucky guess."

"And if not? And if she is a genuine seer?"

"Why, then, you will be king!"

"And you? If she spoke truly about me, then you too must be Coronal, and how—"

"No," Valentine said. "Prophets often speak in riddles and ambiguities. She means something other than the literal. You are to be Coronal, Voriax, it is the common knowledge—and there is some other meaning to the thing she predicted for me, or else there is no meaning at all."

"This frightens me, Valentine."

"If you are to be Coronal there is nothing to fear. Why do you grimace like that?"

"To share the throne with one's brother—" He worried at the idea as at a sore tooth, refusing to move away from it.

"It will not be," said Valentine. He scooped up a fallen garment, found it to belong to Voriax, and tossed it to him. "You heard me speak yesterday. It goes beyond my understanding why anyone would covet the throne. Certainly I am no threat to you in that regard." He seized his brother's wrist. "Voriax, Voriax, you look so dire! Can the words of a forest-witch affect you so? I swear this to you: when you are Coronal, I will be your servant, and never your rival. By our mother who is to be the Lady of the Isle do I swear it. And I tell you that what passed here this night is not to be taken seriously."

"Perhaps not," Voriax said.

"Certainly not," said Valentine. "Shall we leave this place now, brother?"

"I think so."

"She used her body well, do you not agree?"

Voriax laughed. "That she did. It saddens me a little to think I'll never embrace her again. But no, I would not care to hear more of her lunatic soothsaying, however wondrous the movements of her hips may be. I've had my fill of her, and of this place, I think. Shall we pass Ghiseldorn by?"

"I think so," Valentine said. "What cities lie along the Glayge near here?"

"Jerrik is next, where many Vroons are settled, and Mitripond, and a place called Gayles. I think we should take lodging in Jerrik, and amuse ourselves with some gambling for a few days."

"To Jerrik, then."

"Yes, to Jerrik. And say no more concerning the kingship to me, Valentine."

"Not a word, I promise." He laughed and threw his arms around Voriax. "Brother! I thought several times on this journey that I had lost you altogether, but I see that all is well, that I have found you again!"

"We were never lost to one another," said Voriax, "not for an instant. Come, now: pack your things, and onward to Jerrik!"

They never spoke again of their night with the witch and of the things she had foretold. Five years later, when Lord Malibor perished while hunting sea-dragons, Voriax was chosen as Coronal, to no one's surprise, and Valentine was the first to kneel in homage before his brother. By then Valentine had virtually forgotten the troublesome prophecy of Tanunda, though not the taste of her kisses and the feel of her flesh. Both of them kings? How, after all, could that be, since only one man could be Coronal at a time? Valentine rejoiced for his brother Lord Voriax and was content to be what he was. And by the time he understood the full meaning of the prophecy, which was not that he would rule jointly with Voriax but that he would succeed him on the throne, though never before on Majipoor had brother followed brother in such a way, it was impossible for him to embrace Voriax and reassure him of his love, for Voriax was lost to him forever, struck down by a hunter's stray bolt in the forest, and Valentine was brotherless and alone as in awe and amazement he mounted the steps of the Confalume Throne.

ELEVEN

Those final moments, that epilogue that some scribe had appended to the young Valentine's soul-record, leave Hissune dazed. He sits motionless a long while; then he rises as if in a dream and begins to leave the cubicle. Images out of that frenzied night in the forest revolve in his stunned mind: the rival brothers, the bright-eyed witch, the bare grappling bodies, the prophecy of kingship. Yes, two kings! And Hissune has spied on them in the most vulnerable moment of their lives! He feels abashed, a rare emotion for him. Perhaps the time has come for a holiday from the Register of Souls, he thinks: the power of these experiences sometimes is overwhelming, and he may well require some months of recuperation. His hands shake as he steps through the doorway.

One of the usual functionaries of the Register admitted him an hour earlier, a plump and wall-eyed man named Penagorn, and he is still at his desk; but another person stands beside him, a tall, straight-backed individual in the green-and-gold uniform of the Coronal's staff, who studies Hissune severely and says, "May I see your identification, please?"

So this is the moment he has dreaded. They have found him out—unauthorized use of the archives—and he is to be arrested. Hissune offers his card. Probably they have known of his illegal intrusions here for a long time, but have simply been waiting for him to commit the ultimate atrocity, the playing of the Coronal's own recording. Very likely that one

bears an alarm, Hissune thinks, that silently summons the minions of the Coronal, and now—

"You are the one we seek," says the man in green and
gold. "Please come with me."

Silently Hissune follows—out of the House of Records and
across the great plaza to the entrance to the lowest levels of
the Labyrinth, and past a checkpoint to a waiting floater-car,
and then downward, downward, into mysterious realms Hissune has never entered. He sits motionless, numb. All the
world presses down on this place; layer upon layer of the
Labyrinth spirals over his head. Where are they now? Is this
place the Court of Thrones, where the high ministers hold
sway? Hissune does not dare ask, and his escort says not a
word. Through gate after gate, passage upon passage; then the
floater-car halts; six more in the uniforms of Lord Valentine's
staff emerge; they conduct him into a brightly lit room and
stand flanking him.

A door opens, sliding into a recess, and a golden-haired
man, wide-shouldered and tall, clad in a simple white robe,
enters the room. Hissune gasps.

"Your lordship—"

"Please. Please. We can do without all that bowing, Hissune. You *are* Hissune, aren't you?"

"I am, my lord. Somewhat older."

"Eight years ago, was that it? Yes, eight. You were this
high. And now a man. Well, I suppose I'm foolish to be surprised, but I suspected a boy even now. You're eighteen?"

"Yes, my lord."

"How old were you when you started poking about in the
Register of Souls?"

"You know of that, then, my lord?" Hissune whispers,
turning crimson, staring at his feet.

"Fourteen, were you? I think that's what they told me. I've
had you watched, you know. It was three or four years ago
that they sent word to me that you had bluffed your way into
the Register. Fourteen, pretending to be a scholar. I imagine
you saw a great many things that boys of fourteen don't ordinarily see."

Hissune's cheeks blaze. Through his mind rolls the thought,
*An hour ago, my lord, I saw you and your brother coupling
with a long-haired witch of Ghiseldorn.* He would let himself
be swallowed in the depths of the world before he says such a

thing aloud. But he is certain that Lord Valentine knows it anyway, and that awareness is crushing to Hissune. He cannot look up. This golden-haired man is not the Valentine of the soul-record, for that had been the dark-haired Valentine, later magicked out of his body in the way that everyone now has heard, and these days the Coronal wears other flesh; but the person within is the same, and Hissune has spied on him, and there is no hiding the truth of that.

Hissune is silent.

Lord Valentine says, "Possibly I should take that back. You always were precocious. The Register probably didn't show you many things that you hadn't seen on your own."

"It showed me Ni-moya, my lord," Hissune says in a croaking, barely audible voice. "It showed me Suvrael, and the cities of Castle Mount, and the jungles outside Narabal—"

"Places, yes. Geography. It's useful to know all that. But the geography of the soul—you learned that your own way, eh? Look up at me. I'm not angry with you."

"No?"

"It was by my orders that you had free access to the Register. Not so you could gawk at Ni-moya, and not so you could spy on people making love, particularly. But so you could get a comprehension of what Majipoor really is, so you could experience a millionth millionth part of the totality of this world of ours. It was your education, Hissune. Am I right?"

"That was how I saw it, my lord. Yes. There was so much I wanted to know."

"Did you learn it all?"

"Not nearly. Not a millionth millionth part."

"Too bad. Because you'll no longer have access to the Register."

"My lord? Am I to be punished?"

Lord Valentine smiles oddly. "Punished? No, that's not the right word. But you'll be leaving the Labyrinth, and chances are you'll not be back here for a very long time, not even when I'm Pontifex, and may that day not come soon. I've named you to my staff, Hissune. Your training period's over. I want to put you to work. You're old enough now, I think. You have family here still?"

"My mother, two sisters—"

"Provided for. Whatever they need. Say goodbye to them and pack your things. Can you leave with me in three days?"

"Three—days—"

"For Alaisor. The grand processional is demanded of me again. And then the Isle. We skip Zimroel this time. Back to the Mount in seven or eight months, I hope. You'll have a suite at the Castle. Some formal instruction—that won't be unpleasant for you, will it? Fancier clothes to wear. You saw all this coming, didn't you? You know I marked you for great things, when you were only a ragged little boy fleecing tourists?" The Coronal laughs. "It's late. I'll send for you again in the morning. There's much for us to discuss."

He extends his fingertips toward Hissune, a courtly little gesture, Hissune bows, and when he dares to look up, Lord Valentine is gone. So. So. It has come to pass after all, his dream, his fantasy. Hissune does not allow any expression to enter his face. Rigid, somber, he turns to the green-and-gold escort, and follows them to the corridors, and they convey him up into the public levels of the Labyrinth. There they leave him. But he cannot go to his room now. His mind is racing, feverish, wild with amazement. From its depths come surging all those long-vanished folk he has come to know so well, Nismile and Sinnabor Lavon, Thesme, Dekkeret, Calintane, poor anguished Haligome, Eremoil, Inyanna Forlana, Vismaan, Sarise. Part of him now, embedded forever in his soul. He feels as though he has devoured the entire planet. What will become of him now? Aide to the Coronal? A glittering new life on Castle Mount? Holidays in High Morpin and Stee, and the great ones of the realm as his companions? Why, he might be Coronal himself some day! Lord Hissune! He laughs at his own monstrous presumption. And yet, and yet, and yet, why not? Had Calintane expected to be Coronal? Had Dekkeret? Had Valentine? But one must not think of such things, Hissune tells himself. One must work, and learn, and live one's life a moment at a time, and one's destiny will shape itself.

He realizes that he has somehow become lost—he, who at the age of ten was the most skillful guide the Layrinth had. He has wandered in his daze from level to level, and half the night is gone, and he has no idea now where he is. And then he sees that he is in the uppermost level of the Labyrinth, on the desert side, near the Mouth of Blades. In fifteen minutes

he can be outside the Labyrinth entirely. To go out there is
not something he normally yearns to do; but this night is
special, and he does not resist as his feet take him toward the
gateway of the underground city. He comes to the Mouth of
Blades and stares a long while at the rusted swords of some
antique era that were set across its front to mark the boundary; then he steps past them and out into the hot dry wasteland beyond. Like Dekkeret roaming that other and far more
terrible desert he strides into the emptiness, until he is a good
distance from the teeming hive that is the Labyrinth, and
stands alone under the cool brilliant stars. So many of them!
And one is Old Earth, from which all the billions and billions
of humankind had sprung so long ago. Hissune stands as if
entranced. Through him pours an overwhelming sense of all
the long history of the cosmos, rushing upon him like an irresistible river. The Register of Souls contains the records of
enough lives to keep him busy for half of eternity, he thinks,
and yet what is in it is just the merest fraction of everything
that has existed on all those worlds of all those stars. He
wants to seize and engulf it all and make it part of him as he
had made those other lives part of him, and of course that
cannot be done, and even the thought of it dizzies him. But
he must give up such notions now, and forswear the tempta-
tions of the Register. He holds himself still until his mind has
ceased its whirling. I will be quite calm now, he tells himself.
I will regain control over my feelings. He allows himself one
final look toward the stars, and searches among them, in
vain, for the sun of Old Earth. Then he shrugs and swings
about and slowly walks back toward the Mouth of Blades.
Lord Valentine will send for him again in the morning. It is
important to get some sleep before then. A new life is about
to begin for him. I will live on Castle Mount, he thinks, and I
will be an aide to the Coronal, and who knows what will happen to me after that? But whatever happens will be the right
thing, as it was for Dekkeret, for Thesme, for Sinnabor Lavon, even for Haligome, for all of those whose souls are part
of my soul now.

Hissune stands just outside the Mouth of Blades for a moment, only a moment, and the moment stretches, and the
stars begin to fade, and the first light of dawn comes, and
then a mighty sunrise takes possession of the sky, and all the
land is flooded with light. He does not move. The warmth of
the sun of Majipoor touches his face, as so rarely has it done

in his life until now. The sun . . . the sun . . . the glorious blazing fiery sun . . . the mother of the worlds. . . . He reaches out his arms to it. He embraces it. He smiles and drinks in its blessing. Then he turns and goes down into the Labyrinth for the last time.

ABOUT THE AUTHOR

ROBERT SILVERBERG was born in New York and makes his home in the San Francisco area. He has written several hundred science fiction stories and over seventy science fiction novels. He has won two Hugo awards and four Nebula awards. He is a past president of the Science Fiction Writers of America. Silverberg's other Bantam titles include *Lord Valentine's Castle, The Majipoor Chronicles, The Book of Skulls, Born with the Dead, The World Inside, Thorns, The Masks of Time, World of a Thousand Colors, Dying Inside, Downward to the Earth, Lord of Darkness* and *The Tower of Glass.*

FANTASY AND SCIENCE FICTION FAVORITES

Bantam Spectra brings you the recognized classics as well as the current favorites in fantasy and science fiction. Here you will find the most recent titles by the most respected authors in the genre.

FANTASY AND SCIENCE FICTION FAVORITES

Bantam brings you the recognized classics as well as the current favorites in fantasy and science fiction. Here you will find the most recent titles by the most respected authors in the genre.

☐ 25260	THE BOOK OF KELLS R. A. MacAvoy	$3.50
☐ 25122	THE CHRISTENING QUEST Elizabeth Scarborough	$2.95
☐ 24370	RAPHAEL R. A. MacAvoy	$2.75
☐ 23853	THE SHATTERED STARS Richard McEnroe	$2.95
☐ 23575	DAMIANO R. A. MacAvoy	$2.75
☐ 25403	TEA WITH THE BLACK DRAGON R. A. MacAvoy	$2.95
☐ 24441	THE HAREM OF AMAN AKBAR Elizabeth Scarborough	$2.95
☐ 20780	STARWORLD Harry Harrison	$2.50
☐ 22939	THE UNICORN CREED Elizabeth Scarborough	$3.50
☐ 23120	THE MACHINERIES OF JOY Ray Bradbury	$2.75
☐ 22666	THE GREY MANE OF MORNING Joy Chant	$3.50
☐ 25097	LORD VALENTINE'S CASTLE Robert Silverberg	$3.95
☐ 20870	JEM Frederik Pohl	$2.95
☐ 23460	DRAGONSONG Anne McCaffrey	$2.95

Prices and availability subject to change without notice.

Buy them at your local bookstore or use this handy coupon for ordering:

Bantam Books, Inc., Dept. SF2, 414 East Golf Road, Des Plaines, Ill. 60016

Please send me the books I have checked above. I am enclosing $_____
(please add $1.50 to cover postage and handling). Send check or money
—no cash or C.O.D.'s please.

Mr/Mrs/Miss_____

Address_____

City_____ State/Zip_____

SF2—3/86

Please allow four to six weeks for delivery. This offer expires 9/86